Ben Bova

LAUGH LINES

The Starcrossed — copyright © 1975 by Ben Bova.

Cyberbooks — copyright © 1989 by Ben Bova.

"Crisis of the Month" — originally published in *F&SF*, March 1988, copyright © by Ben Bova.

"The Great Moon Hoax, or, A Princess of Mars") — originally published in *F&SF*, September 1996, copyright © by Ben Bova.

"The Supersonic Zeppelin" (originally published as "The Great Supersonic Zeppelin Race") — published in *The Far Side of Time*, ed. Roger Elwood, 1974, copyright © by Ben Bova.

"Vince's Dragon" — originally published in *Dragons of Darkness*, ed. Orson Scott Card, 1981 copyright © by Ben Bova.

"The Angel's Gift" — published under the pseudonym of Oxford Williams. First published in *The Omni Book of Science Fiction #1*, ed. Ellen Datlow, 1983, copyright © by Ben Bova.

"A Slight Miscalculation" — originally published in *F&SF*, August 1981, copyright © by Ben Bova.

A Baen Book

Baen Publishing Enterprises
P.O. Box 1403
Riverdale, NY 10471
www.baen.com

ISBN 10: 1-4165-5560-9
ISBN 13: 978-1-4165-5560-5

Cover art by Bob Eggleton

First Baen printing, July 2008

Distributed by Simon & Schuster
1230 Avenue of the Americas
New York, NY 10020

Library of Congress Cataloging-in-Publication Data

Bova, Ben, 1932-
  Laugh lines / by Ben Bova.
    p. cm.
  ISBN 1-4165-5560-9 (hc)
  1. Science fiction. 2. Humorous stories. I. Title.

  PS3552.O84L38 2008
  813'.54--dc22

2008010835

Printed in the United States of America

10 9 8 7 6 5 4 3 2 1

Contents

Introduction

Science fiction is serious business. Usually.

After all, science fiction writers are almost always dealing with the fate of the universe, or at least the future of the human race. That's serious stuff. Exploring the unknown. Facing hostile aliens. Dealing with artificial intelligences. Handling nanomachines. Hell, I have my hands full trying to program my DVD recorder.

But science fiction doesn't have to be somber and serious all the time. There's a humorous side to the future, just as there's a humorous side to everything.

Even the saintly Albert Einstein wasn't above cracking a joke now and then. Right after Hiroshima, a reporter asked him, "If World War III is fought with atomic bombs, what weapons will be used in World War IV?" Without missing a beat, Einstein replied, "Spears."

One of science fiction's many wonderful attributes is its ability to make social commentary. In the old, dark days of the Soviet Union I asked a Russian writer if the government in Moscow tolerated science fiction. He told me that the Kremlin didn't mind stories in which the government of Mars, hundreds of years in the future, was composed of bumbling idiots. A similar story about the existing government of the USSR would earn the writer an extended stay in Siberia. Gene Roddenberry created *Star Trek* in large part because television network executives would allow him to present ideas in a science fiction context that they would never permit in a "realistic" drama.

There's no better way to make social commentary than through

1

humor. You can skewer stuffed shirts and show the ridiculous side of life. You can make your points by making people laugh.

So here's a hatful of stories that look at the funny side of the future: two full-length novels and six shorter works of science fiction. Most of these stories are based on people and situations that I have personally known, although the circumstances have obviously been altered.

If these stories make you laugh, all to the good. But remember, you may be laughing at yourself.

Have fun!

—Ben Bova

The
Starcrossed

To Cordwainer Bird . . .
may he fly high and strike terror
in the hearts of the unjust.

Introduction to the Stars

The Starcrossed is *roman á clef*, a novel in which real persons and events are depicted, thinly disguised. Usually, the disguise is to protect the innocent. In this case, it's to protect the guilty. And one innocent person: Harlan Ellison.

Anyone who has met Harlan or heard of his rather ferocious reputation might be surprised to see him categorized as an innocent. But he is really. Harlan is at heart a moralist who is infuriated by the stupidity and evil that most of us ignore.

He's also one of my closest friends, despite the fact that we live several thousand miles apart.

Harlan originated a television series: *The Starlost*. It was such a beautiful idea that Twentieth-Century Fox bought it. Harlan asked me to serve as the show's science advisor, and I quickly agreed.

Alas, a writers' strike hit Hollywood before *The Starlost* started filming. Fox moved the production to Toronto, a move that ultimately spelled disaster. Aside from the star, Kier Dullea, and a few other actors, none of the crew of the production had any experience with a dramatic TV show.

Harlan worked manfully as long as he could, then quit the show in disgust, abandoning his mutilated brainchild and fleeing back to his home in California.

As science advisor, my job was to read the scripts, note scientific errors, and suggest ways to fix those errors that didn't require throwing the entire script into the trash barrel. This I did. I was thanked graciously. I was paid a handsome consultant's fee. And my advice was totally ignored. Each script was shot as originally written, goofs and all.

And at the end of each episode there was a full screen credit for SCIENCE ADVISOR BEN BOVA.

The show didn't last long. It received a mercy killing before the first season was through.

And, back in my apartment in Manhattan, I found myself writing *The Starcrossed*. My wife tells me I cackled fiendishly as I typed the manuscript.

So here it is, *a roman á clef* about what it was actually like to be working on a TV show. It all really happened, folks. Only the names have changed to protect the guilty. And one innocent.

1: The Bankers

"American ingenuity licked the pollution problem," said Bernard Finger, glowingly. "And the energy crisis too, by damn."

Tanned and golden in his new Vitaform Process body, Finger was impeccably dressed in the latest neo-Victorian style Bengal Lancer business suit, complete with epaulets and an authentic brigadier's insignia. He stood at the floor-to-ceiling windows of his sumptuous, spacious office and gazed fondly out at the lovely pink clouds that blanketed the San Fernando Valley.

The late morning sun blazed out of a perfect blue sky. As far as the eye could see, the entire Greater Los Angeles area—from sparkling sea to the San Berdoo Mountains—was swathed in perfumed, tinted clouds. Except for a few hilltops poking up here and there, it all looked like one enormous dollop of pink cotton candy.

"American ingenuity," Bernard Finger repeated. "And American know-how! That's how we beat those A-rabs and those bleeding heart conservationists."

Bill Oxnard watched Finger with some astonishment from his utterly comfortable position, sunk deep into a warmly plush water-chair. Surrounded by pleasantly yielding artificial hides, his loafers all but invisible in the thick pile of the office's carpet, he still kept his attention on Finger.

It was uncanny. Oxnard had met the man eighteen months earlier, before he had gone in for the Vitaform Process. Then he had been a short, pudgy, bald, cigar-chewing loudmouth approaching sixty years of age. Now he looked like Cary Grant in costume for *Gunga Din*. But he still sounded like a short, pudgy, bald, cigar-chewing loudmouth.

The lovely pink clouds that Finger was admiring were smog, of course. Oxnard had driven from his lab in the Malibu Hills through thirty miles of the gunk to get to Finger's lofty office. Sure, the smog was tinted and even perfumed, but you still needed noseplugs to survive fifty yards of the stuff and the price of them had gone up to eighteen-fifty a set. They only lasted a couple of weeks, at most. *The cost of breathing keeps going up,* he told himself.

Oxnard's mind was wandering off into the equations that governed photochemical smog when Finger turned from the window and strode to his airport-sized desk.

"It makes me proud," he pronounced, "to think of all the hard work that American men and women have put out to conquer the problems we faced when I was a kid."

As Finger sat in the imposing chrome and black leather chair behind his desk, Oxnard glanced at the two others in the room: Finger's assistants. The man was lean and athletic looking, with a carefully trimmed red beard. The woman was also slim; she hid much of her face behind old-fashioned bombardier's glasses. Her longish hair was also red, the same shade as the man's. Red hair was *in* this week.

They both stared fixedly at their boss, eager for every word.

"A hundred and sixty-seven floors below us," Finger went on, "down in that perfumed pink environment we've created for them, ordinary American men and women are hard at work. You can't see them from up here, but they're working, believe me. I know. I can *feel* them working. They're the backbone of America . . . the spinal column of our nation."

They're working, all right, Oxnard thought. Every morning he stared with dismay at the black waves of the Pacific turgidly lapping the blacker beaches, while the oil rigs lining the ocean shore busily sucked up more black gold.

"Men and women hard at work," Finger went on, almost reverently. "And when they come home from their labors, they want to be entertained. They demand to be entertained. And they deserve the best we can give them."

The woman dabbed at her eyes. The man, Les Something-or-Other, nodded and muttered, "With it, B.F."

Finger smiled. He carefully placed his palms down on the immaculately glistening, bare desktop. Leaning forward ever so slightly he suddenly bellowed:

"So how come we don't have one single top-rated series on The Tube? *How come?*"

Les actually leaned back in his chair. The woman looked startled, but never wavered from staring straight at Finger. Oxnard almost thought he could feel a shock wave blow across the room.

With the touch of a button, Finger projected a column of names and numbers on a wall where a Schoenher had been hanging.

"Look at the top ten!" he roared. "Do you see a Titanic Productions series? No! Look at the top twenty. . . ." The list grew longer. "The top *fifty*. . . ." And longer.

Les Montpelier, that's his name, Oxnard remembered. He seemed to be trying to sink deeper into his waterchair. He slumped further and further into its luxurious folds, pulling in his chin until his beard scraped his chest. The woman was just the opposite: she perched on the edge of her chair, all nerves, fists knotted on knees. *Nice legs.*

Finger flashed more lists on the screen. And pictures. *All two-dimensional,* Oxnard noted. Everything about the room was two-dimensional. Flat paintings on the walls. Flat desktop dominating the decor. The waterchairs were sort of three-dimensional, but only to the tactile sense. They looked just as flat as everything else. All planes and angles. Nothing holographic. Even the woman wasn't as three-dimensional as she should be, despite her legs.

It was a pleasant enough office, though. Brightly colored carpeting and draperies. Everything soft looking, even the padded walls. Up here on the one hundred and sixty-seventh floor of the Titanic Tower they never had to worry about smog or noise or dust. The air was pristine, cool, urged smoothly through the sealed offices by gently whispering machinery hidden behind the walls. Very much the same way that people were moved through Titanic's offices: quietly, efficiently, politely, relentlessly.

Oxnard remembered how nice everyone had been to him the first time he had visited Titanic, eighteen months earlier. They had all been very polite, very enthusiastic, had even pronounced *laser* and *holographic* correctly, although they never quite seemed to grasp the difference between a hologram and a holograph. He had first met Les Montpelier then, and had been ushered into Finger's lofty sanctuary, right here in this same room. Finger wasn't looking like Cary Grant in those days and his comment on Oxnard's invention was:

"Stop wasting my time with dumb gadgets! What we need is a show with growth potential. Spinoffs, repeats, byproducts. This thing's a pipedream!"

That was eighteen months ago. Now Finger was saying:

"Every major network has three-dee shows on the air! All top ten series are three-dees! People are standing in line all over the country to buy three-dee sets. And what have you and the other flunkies and drones working for me produced? *Nothing!* No-thing. Not a goddamned thing."

Finger was perspiring now. The sculptured planes of his face were glistening and somehow looked as if they might be beginning to melt. He touched another button on his desk and the faint whir of an extra air blower sounded from somewhere in the padded ceiling.

"I had to go out *myself* and find the *inventor* of the three-dee process and *personally* coax him to come here and consult with us," Finger said, his voice sounding at once hurt and outraged.

It was almost true. The woman, whose name Oxnard still couldn't recall, had called him and said Mr. Finger would like to meet with him. When Oxnard reminded her that they had met eighteen months earlier, the woman had merely smiled on the phone screen and suggested that the future of her career depended on getting him into Finger's office. Oxnard reluctantly agreed to a date and time.

"All right, then," Finger went on. "A less *loyal* man would make some heads roll in a situation like this. I haven't fired anybody. I haven't panicked. You still have your jobs. I hope you appreciate that."

They both bobbed their heads.

"After lunch, the New York people will want to see what we've got. Take him," Finger barely glanced in Oxnard's direction, "back to the studio and make sure all this fancy gadgetry is working when I arrive there."

"With it, B.F.," Montpelier said as he struggled up out of his waterchair.

The woman got to her feet and Oxnard did the same. Finger swivelled his chair slightly and started talking into the phone screen. They were dismissed.

It took exactly twenty-eight paces through the foot-smothering carpet to get to the office door. Les Montpelier swung it open gingerly and they stepped into the receptionist's area.

"One good thing about flightweight doors," Montpelier muttered. "You can't slam them."

The Titanic Tower was built to earthquake specifications, of course. Which meant that it was constructed like an oversized rocket booster, all aluminum or lighter metals, with a good deal of plastics. If the sensors in the subbasement detected an earth movement beyond the designed tolerances, rocket engines built into the pods along the building's sides roared to life and hurtled the entire tower, along with its occupants, safely out to a splashdown in the Pacific, beyond the line of oil rigs.

The whole system had been thoroughly tested by NASA; even though a few diehard conservative engineers thought that the tests weren't extensive enough, the City of Los Angeles decided that it couldn't grow laterally any more—all the land had been used up. So skyscrapers were the next step. Earthquake-proof skyscrapers.

There hadn't been an earthquake severe enough to really test the rocket towers, although the Tishman Tower had been blasted off by a gang of pranksters who tinkered with the seismographic equipment in its basement. The building arched beautifully out to sea, with no injuries to its occupants beyond the sorts of bruises and broken bones you'd expect from bouncing off the foam plastic walls, floors and ceilings. A few heart attacks, of course, but that was to be expected. The pedestrians who happened to be strolling on the walkways around the Tower were, unfortunately, rather badly singed by the rocket exhaust A few of them eventually died, including eighty-four in a sightseeing bus that was illegally parked in front of the Tower. Most of them were foreign visitors, though, and Korean missionaries at that.

As they walked down the corridor toward the studio, Oxnard noted how the foam plastic flooring absorbed the sounds of their footfalls, even without carpeting. It was a great building for sneaking up behind people.

"Why did you let Finger yell at you like that?" Oxnard wondered aloud. "Les, you brought me up here to see him a year and a half ago."

Montpelier glanced at the woman, who answered: "We've learned that it's best to let B.F. have his little tantrums, Dr. Oxnard. It's a survival technique."

Her voice was low, throaty, the kind that would be unbearably exotic if it had just the faintest trace of a foreign accent. But her pronunciation was flat Southern California uninspired. Over the phone she had managed to sound warm and inviting. But not now.

"I don't have a Doctorate, Miz . . . uh. . . ." Oxnard grimaced inwardly. He could remember equations, but not names.

"Impanema." She flashed a meaningless smile, like a reflex that went along with stating her name. "Brenda Impanema."

"Oh." For the first time, Oxnard consciously overrode his inherent shyness and really looked at her. Something about her name reminded him of an old song and a girl in an old-fashioned covered-top swimsuit. But Brenda didn't look like that at all. She seemed to be that indeterminate age between twenty and forty, when women used style and cosmetics before resorting to surgery and Vitaform Processing. She had the slight, slim body of the standard corporate executive female who spent most of her money on whatever style of clothing was fashionable that week and got most of her nutrition on dates with over-eager young stallions. Good legs, though. Flat chested, probably: it was difficult to tell through all the ribbons and flouncy stuff on her blouse. But she had good legs and the good sense to wear a miniskirt, even though it wasn't in style this week.

Behind those overlarge green glasses, her face was knotted into a frown of concentrated worry.

"Don't get upset," Oxnard said generously. "The laser system works like a charm. Finger and his New York bankers will be completely impressed. You won't lose your jobs."

Montpelier laughed nasally. "Oh, B.F. could never fire us. We've been too close for too many years."

"What he means," Brenda said, "is that we know too much about him."

Pointing a lean finger at her, Montpelier added, "And *he* knows too much about *us*. We're married to him—for better or for worse."

Oxnard wondered how far the marriage went. But he kept silent as they reached the elevator, stepped in and dropped downward.

"It must make for a nerve-wracking life," Oxnard said.

"Oh, no . . . the elevator's completely safe," Montpelier said over the whistling of the slipstream outside their shuddering, plummeting compartment.

"I didn't mean that," Oxnard said. "I mean . . . well, working for a man like Finger. He treats you like dirt."

Brenda shrugged. "It only hurts if you let him get to you."

Montpelier scratched at his beard. "Listen. I'll tell you about B.F. There's a lot more to him than you think, like that time he kicked me down the elevator shaft. . . ."

"He *what*?"

"It was an accident," Brenda said quickly.

"Sure," Montpelier agreed. "We were discussing something in the hallway; my memory's a little hazy. . . ."

"The chess show," said Brenda.

"Oh, yes." Montpelier's eyes gleamed with the memory of his idea. "I had this *terrific* idea for a chess show. With real people—contestants, you know, from the audience—on each square. We'd dress them in armor and all and let them fight it out when they got moved onto the same square. . . ."

"And the final survivor gets a million dollars," Brenda said.

"And the Hospital Trust gets the losers . . . which we would then use on our 'Medical Miracles' show!"

Oxnard felt a little dizzy. "But chess isn't . . ." Brenda touched him with the fingertips of one hand. "It doesn't matter. Listen to what happened." She was smiling. Oxnard felt himself grin back at her.

Montpelier went on, "Well, B.F. and I went round and round on this idea. He didn't like it, for some reason. The more I argued for it, the madder he got. Finally we were at the end of the hallway, waiting for the elevator and he got so mad he *kicked* me! He actually kicked me. He was taking Aikido lessons in those days and he kicked me right through the goddamned elevator door!"

"You know how flimsy the doors around here are," Brenda quipped.

Before Oxnard could say anything, Montpelier resumed: "I went bum-over-teakettle right down the elevator shaft!"

"Geez. . . ."

"Luckily, the elevator was on its way *up* the shaft, so I only fell twenty or thirty floors. They had me fixed up in less than a year."

"Les was the star of 'Medical Miracles' for a whole week . . . although he didn't know it at the time."

"And Bernard Finger," said Montpelier, his voice almost trembling, "personally paid every quarter of my expenses, over and above the company insurance. When I finally regained consciousness, he was right there, crying over me like he was my father."

Oxnard thought he saw the glint of a tear in Montpelier's right eye.

"*That's* the kind of man B.F. is," Montpelier concluded.

"Cruel but fair," Brenda said, trying to keep a straight face.

Just then the elevator stopped with a sickening lurch and the flimsy doors opened with a sound like aluminum foil crinkling.

Everything here happens on cue, Oxnard thought as they stepped out into the studio.

The laser system was indeed working quite well. Montpelier clapped his hands in childish glee and pronounced it "Perfect!" as they ran through the demonstration tapes, although Oxnard noted, from his perch alongside the chief engineer's seat in the control booth, that the output voltage on the secondary demodulator was down a fraction. Nothing to worry about, but he tapped the dial with a fingernail and the engineer nodded knowingly.

No sense scaring them, Oxnard thought. He went down the hall to the cafeteria and munched a sandwich with Brenda and Montpelier. There wasn't much conversation. Oxnard put on the abstracted air of a preoccupied scientist: his protective camouflage, whenever he didn't know what to say and was afraid of making a fool of himself.

Finger and his New York bankers glowed with the aura of *haute cuisine* and fine brandy when they entered the studio. Despite the NO SMOKING signs everywhere, they all had long black Havanas clamped in their teeth. Finger had changed his costume; now he wore a somber, stylish Pickwick business suit, just as the bankers wore. *Protective coloration,* Oxnard thought. *I'm not the only one who uses camouflage.*

The men from New York were old; no Vitaform Processing for

them. Their faces were lined, their mouths tight, their eyes suspicious. Three of them were lean and flinty. The fourth outweighed his three partners and Finger combined. He looked hard, not fat, like an overaged football lineman. Oxnard had seen his type in Las Vegas, watching over their casinos through dark glasses.

"And this is the *inventor* of the three-dee system," Finger said, smiling and waving Oxnard over to him. "Dr. William Oxnard. Come on over, Bill. Don't be shy. I want you to meet my friends here . . . they can be *very* helpful to a brilliant young scientist looking for capital."

Oxnard shook hands with each of them in turn. Their hands were cold and dry, but their grips were tight, as if they seldom let go easily.

Then Finger led them to the plush chairs that had been lined up for them around the receiver console. Ashstands were hurriedly set up at each elbow, while Finger stood in front of the bankers, scowling and shouting orders to his aides with a great flourish of armwaving. Montpelier and Brenda sat off to one side in plain folding chairs. Oxnard went back to the control consoles, got a fully confident nod from the chief engineer and then walked toward the cameras.

The lights in the studio went down, slowly at first, almost imperceptibly—then very suddenly dwindled to total darkness, except for a single overhead spot on Finger, who was still standing in front of the bankers.

"Everything seems to be in readiness," Finger said at last. "Gentlemen . . . once again may I present to you Dr. William Oxnard, the genius who invented the holographic home entertainment system."

Bill Oxnard stepped into the spotlight. Finger scuttled to the seat beside the beefy New Yorker, who had—sure enough—put on dark eyeglasses.

"Thank you, Mr. Finger. Gentlemen . . . as you very well know, three-dimensional holographic entertainment systems are the biggest thing to sweep the industry since the original inception of the old black-and-white television broadcasting, about a half-century ago.

"For the first time, fully three-dimensional projections can be shown in the home, using receiving equipment that is cheap enough for the average householder to buy, while low enough in manufacturing cost to provide an equitable profit to the manufacturers and distributors. . . ."

"We are neither manufacturers nor distributors, young man," rasped one of the frail-looking bankers. "We are here to see if Titanic has anything worth investing in. Spare us the preliminaries."

Bill nodded and suppressed a grin. "Yessir. What Titanic has, in brief, is a new and improved holographic photography system; as you know, the three-dimensional images now received over home sets are spotty, grainy, and streaked with quantum scintillations. . . ."

"Looks like the actors're always standin' in a pile of sequins," said the beefy one, with a voice like a cement truck shifting gears.

"You mean confetti," one of the flinty ones corrected.

Beefy turned slowly, making his chair creak under his bulk. "Naw. I mean sequins."

"I call it snow!" Finger broke in brightly. "But whatever you call it, the effect's the same. Watching three-dee gives you a headache after a while."

Beefy muttered something about headaches and Flinty returned his attention to Oxnard.

"Very well, young man," he said. "What are you leading up to?"

"Simply this," Oxnard replied, smiling to himself. "My laboratory. . . ."

"*Your* laboratory?" one of the bankers snapped. "I thought you worked for the RHB-General Combine?"

"I was Director of Research for their Western Labs, sir," Oxnard said, feeling the old acid seething in his guts. "I resigned when we had a difference of opinion about the royalties from my original holographic system inventions."

"Ahh," wheezed the oldest of the quartet of bankers. "They squeezed you out, eh?" He cackled to himself without waiting for Oxnard's answer.

"At any rate," Oxnard went on, feeling his face burn, "I now own my own modest laboratory and we've developed a much improved holographic projection system. The patents have come through on the new system and Titanic Productions has taken an option on the exclusive use of the new system for home entertainment purposes."

"What difference does the new system make?" Beefy asked. "Three-dee is three-dee."

"Not quite correct, sir," Oxnard replied. "The old system *is* very grainy. It does give viewers headaches after an hour or so. You see, the impedance matching of the primary. . . ."

"Skip the technical details," Finger called out. "Show us the results."

Oxnard blinked. For a moment he was terribly conscious of where he was, of the cold light streaming down over him, of the people he was speaking to. He longed for the safety of his familiar laboratory.

But he pressed onward. "All right. Basically, my new system gives an absolutely perfect image. No distortions, no scintillations, no visible graininess or snow. Unless you're an engineer and you know precisely what to look for, you can't tell a projected image apart from someone actually standing in front of you."

"And that's what you're going to demonstrate to us?" Flinty asked.

"Yes, sir. With the help of one of you gentlemen. Would one of you care to step up here in the spotlight with me?"

They all looked at each other questioningly, but no one moved from his chair. After a few seconds, Bernard Finger said, "Well I'll do it, if nobody else. . . ."

Beefy pushed him back down into his seat. Finger landed on the padding with an audible *thwunk*!

"I'll do it," Beefy said, with a grin that was almost boyish "Always wanted t'be in show business . . . like my *cumpar'* Frankie. . . ."

He lumbered into the spotlight, glanced around, suddenly self-conscious.

Oxnard stretched out his right hand. "Thank you for volunteering," he said. His palms were suddenly sweaty.

Beefy reached for Oxnard's hand. His own heavy paw went *through* Oxnard's.

The other bankers gasped. Beefy stared at his own hand, then grabbed at Oxnard's image. He got nothing but air.

"Actually I'm 'way over here," Oxnard said, as a couple of technicians pushed aside the screen that had hidden him from their view. He looked up from the tiny monitor he had been watching and saw the bankers, more than fifty yards across the huge empty studio. Beefy was standing under the spotlight, gaping at Oxnard's three-dimensional image; the others were half out of their chairs, craning for a view of where Oxnard *really* was standing.

"How about that?" Finger crowed and started pounding his palms together. The bankers took up the applause. Even Beefy clapped, grudgingly.

Turning back to the camera, Oxnard said, "If you gentlemen will forgive my little deception, we can proceed with the show. I think you'll find it entertaining.

It was.

For twenty minutes, the bankers saw strange and wonderful worlds taking shape not more than ten feet before their eyes. Birds flew, mermaids swam, elephants charged at them, all with flawless three-dimensional solidity. They visited the top of Mt. Everest (a faked set from the old MCA-Universal studios), watched a cobra fight a mongoose, then went on a whirlwind tour of all the continents and major seas of the world. A beautiful chanteuse sang to them in French, a Minnesota sexual athletics class competed for originality and style. The windup was a glider flight through the Grand Canyon, while the Mormon Tabernacle Choir sang "America the Beautiful."

"Breathtaking!"

"Perfect!"

"Awe-inspiring!"

"Terrific!"

As the lights came back up, Bernard Finger took the floor again, beaming at the four bedazzled bankers.

"Well," he asked, "what do you think? Do we have something here, or do we have something?"

"I liked the Balinese broad," said Beefy. "*She* had something, all right."

"She's right here. We flew her in from Ft. Worth, where she was working. Also a few members of the Minnesota team. I was planning to introduce you gentlemen to them all at a little cocktail party this evening."

Oxnard, walking across the studio toward them, could see that they were impressed with Finger's foresight and generosity.

All except Flinty. "That's well and good," he said, steepling his bony fingers as he sat back in his chair. He cocked an eye at Finger, standing poised before him. "But we haven't come to Titanic for technical products; your business, Bernie, is show business. What have you got that will get Titanic to the top of the ratings?"

Finger's teeth clicked shut. It was the only sign of distress he showed. Immediately they parted again in a cheery smile.

"Listen," he said, "shows are a dime a dozen. We're planning a whole raft of 'em . . . every kind of show, from quizzes to really deep drama—Simon and Allen, stuff like that. It's the *technical* side that we wanted to show you today."

Oxnard stopped a few feet behind their chairs. He could see the sort of desperate look on Finger's face. Beefy and the other two bankers seemed anxious to move on to the cocktail party. Montpelier and Brenda both had disappeared. Glancing over his shoulder, Oxnard saw that the engineers and technicians had cleared out, too. There was no one in the studio except Finger, the four bankers and himself.

The studio looked like a gaunt framework: big, mostly empty, skeletal girders showing where other rooms have walls and ceiling panels. It reminded Oxnard of an astronomical observatory, although it wasn't domed. *An unfinished chamber,* he thought. *Full of sound and fury; signifying nothing.* He felt a little surprised at his sudden burst of literary pretension.

"I'll admit the technical side is impressive," Flinty was saying adamantly. "But nobody's going to watch travelogues very long, no matter how perfectly they're broadcast You need *shows*, Bernie. Come up with good shows and we'll come up with money for you."

"But. . . ." Finger's composure broke down for the first time. "I need the money *now.*"

Flinty got slowly to his feet. Oxnard could see a crooked little grin forming on his granite-tight face. "Now? Really? You need the money now?"

He put a bony arm around Finger's shoulder and, trailed by the other bankers, they walked toward the red-glowing EXIT sign.

Oxnard stood there alone in the vast, empty studio, with nothing but the echo of Flinty's cackling laughter to keep him company. Just as he realized that he didn't know what to do, he heard a movement behind him.

Turning, he saw Brenda. She looked very serious.

"It's been a long day," she said.

"Yeah." He suddenly realized he was very tired.

"Come on; I'll buy you a drink."

"Thanks. But I suppose I should get along home." *Idiot!* he raged at himself. *Why'd you say that?*

Brenda pointed casually toward the exit and they started walking toward it.

"Wife and kids?" she asked.

Oxnard shook his head. "Worse. A fifty-person lab that needs me to make decisions and sign paychecks."

"You're there every day?"

"Bright and early."

"But you do eat and sleep, don't you?"

Why am I trying to run away? "Sure," he said. "Now and then."

They were at the exit door. She let him push it open for her.

"Well then," Brenda said as they stepped into the hallway, "why don't we have dinner together? I know B.F. will want to have a debriefing later tonight."

The debriefing came in the middle of dinner. Oxnard let Brenda drive him through the swirling pink smog—scented like rancid orchids, even through the noseplugs—to a small restaurant in the Valley. They had just finished the wine and asked for a second bottle when the owner trudged up to their table with a portable phone. He placed it on the edge of the table, so they could both see the screen.

Finger looked ominously unwell.

"They didn't put up the money?" Brenda asked.

Glowering from inside a rumpled Roman toga, Finger said, "They *wanted* the option on our new holosystem."

Oxnard was about to ask where the *our* came from, but Brenda preempted him. "What did you give them?"

"Sweet talk. Four solid hours of sweet talk and a horde of teeny-boppers from every part of the world."

"And?"

"They'll put up the money for one show. One series, that is. We can use the new system and see if the audience likes the series well enough to put us in the Top Ten. If not, they foreclose and take everything."

"Not my new system!" Oxnard blurted.

"The option," Finger answered tiredly. "They'll get the option. And sooner or later they'll get you too, if they really want you. Don't think you could fight 'em."

"But. . . ."

Again Brenda was quicker. "They'll put up the money for one new series? We've got that much?"

"Yeah."

"Then we'll have to make it a Top Ten series. We'll have to get the best writers and producers and. . . ."

Finger shook his head wearily. "They're not putting up *that* much money."

Oxnard was struck by the contrast in their two expressions. Finger looked utterly tired, on the verge of defeat and surrender. Brenda was bright, alive, thinking furiously.

"What we need first is an idea," she said.

"For the series?" Oxnard asked, almost under his breath.

"And I know just who to go to!" Brenda's eyes flashed with excitement. "Ron Gabriel!"

Finger's eyes flashed back. "No! I will not work with that punk! Never! I told you before, nobody calls me a lying sonofabitch and gets away with it. And he did it to my face! To my goddamned *face*! He'll never work for Titanic or anybody else in this town again. I swore it!"

"B.F.," Brenda cooed into the phone screen, "do you remember the first lesson you taught me about how to get along in this business?"

"No," he snapped.

"Well I do," she said. "It's an old Hollywood motto: 'Never let that sonofabitch back into this studio . . . unless we need him.'"

"I will *not*. . . ."

"B.F., we need him."

"No!"

"He's a great idea man."

"Never!"

"He works cheap."

"I'd sooner see Titanic sink! And the whole holographic project go down with it! Not Gabriel! Never!"

The image clicked off the screen.

Brenda looked up at Oxnard. "Better cancel the wine," she said.

"Why?"

"Because we're driving out to Ron Gabriel's place. Come on, it's not far."

2: The Writer

Oxnard and Brenda ran through cold, heavy sheets of rain to her car. Although it was only a few yards from the restaurant door, they were both gasping and drenched as they slid onto the plastic seats and slammed the car doors.

Brenda rubbed at her eyes. "At least it'll clear away the smog for a while."

Sucking in air through his mouth, Oxnard realized that for the first time in weeks there was no perfume smell pervading the environs. And he could breathe without noseplugs.

"Every cloud has a platinum catalytic filter for a lining," he said.

Brenda laughed as she gunned the car to life. In the dim light from the dashboard, Oxnard could see that her long red hair was glistening and plastered down around her face. It somehow looked incredibly sexy that way.

They roared off through the rain and soon were threading the torturous curves of Mulholland Drive, heading up into Sherman Oaks. The rain and sudden cold made the car's windshield steam up and it was impossible to see more than a few yards ahead. The headlights were drowned in gusting walls of rain.

Twice they found themselves on the shoulder of the road, with nothing between them and a sheer drop except a few inches of gravel. Once, on a hairpin curve, Brenda nearly steered into an oncoming set of headlights. Which car had drifted onto the wrong side of the road, it was impossible to tell.

Oxnard was just as drenched when the car finally glided to a stop as when he had first climbed in. But now he was soaked with clammy nervous sweat. Brenda seemed perfectly at ease, though.

"Here we are," she said cheerfully.

"Here" was a low-slung modernistic house perched on the shoulder of a hill, in the middle of a long winding street lined by similar houses. Brenda had pulled the car up on the driveway, so that by sliding out on the driver's side they could splash across one small puddle and dive directly under the protective overhang at the front door.

The door was more ornately carved than Queequeeg's sarcophagus, a really handsome piece of work. Hanging squarely in the middle of it, under the knocker, was a tiny hand-lettered sign that said:
TRY THE BELL

with a drawing of a hand pointing one finger toward an all-but-invisible button, hidden behind a flowering shrub.

Brenda touched the doorbell button and a speaker grill set above the door grated:

"Yeah?"

"Ron, it's Brenda."

"Brenda?"

"Brenda Impanema . . . from Bernard Finger's office."

"Oh, Brenda!"

"Can we come in?"

Oxnard was beginning to feel foolish, standing out there with the wind cutting through him, wet and chilled, all the rain in Southern California sluicing down around them, watching a girl he had just met talking to a door.

"Who's we?" the door asked.

Brenda seemed to be enjoying the fencing match; well, maybe not enjoying it, but at least neither surprised nor dismayed by it.

"Someone you'll enjoy meeting," she said. "He invented the. . . ."

"He?" The voice sounded disappointed.

For the first time, Brenda frowned. "Come on, Ron. It's cold and wet out here."

"Okay. Okay. Come on in."

The door clicked. Brenda pushed on it and it swung open. They stepped inside.

Oxnard blinked. It was like the first time he had tried sky-diving.

One minute you're safely strapped into the plane and the next you're out in the empty air, falling, disoriented, watching the blur of Earth spinning up to hit you.

The door slammed behind him. The entryway of the house was ablaze with lights. Oxnard and Brenda stood there dripping and disheveled, gaping at the cameras, people, props, chairs, lights.

"Smile!" a voice shouted. "You're on candid camera."

"*What?*"

Ron Gabriel pushed past a tripod-mounted camera directly in front of them, a huge grin on his face.

"Only kidding, *buhbula.* Don't panic."

He was wearing nothing but a bath towel draped around his middle. He was a smallish, compactly built man in his thirties, Oxnard guessed: dark straight hair cut in the latest neo-Victorian mode, blazing dark eyes, hairy chest, the beginnings of a pot belly.

He grabbed Brenda and kissed her mightily. Then turning casually to Oxnard, he asked, "You her husband or something?"

"Or something," Oxnard replied, feeling testy.

"Hey come on, I'm paying overtime already!"

A large, lumpy, bearded man stepped out from behind the cameras. He was swathed in a green and purple dashiki. Some sort of optical viewer hung from a silver cord around his neck.

Gabriel grabbed Brenda and Oxnard by the arms and walked them back behind the cameras.

"What's going on?" Brenda asked.

"I'm renting my foyer to Roscoe for filming his latest epic."

"Roscoe?" Oxnard was impressed. "The guy who did the underground film festival at Radio City Music Hall?"

"Who else?" Gabriel answered.

Now it all made sense to Oxnard. Two dozen girls of starlet dimensions stood around languidly, in various styles of undress. A couple of muscular, hairy guys were doing pushups over in a far corner of the foyer. Electricians, lighting women, camera persons of indeterminate gender, and a few other handymen were busily moving cameras and lights around the long, narrow foyer.

"All right already!" Roscoe bellowed in a voice four times too large for Grand Central Station. "Everybody take their places for the grope scene!"

Brenda said, "I'm awfully chilled. Could I borrow a hot shower?"

"Sure," Gabriel said. "Throw your clothes in the dryer and grab a couple of robes out of my closet. Brenda, you know where everything is. Show him around."

Oxnard stammered, "Uh . . . we're not . . . not together. I mean, not like that" *Dammit!* he raged to himself. *Why should I feel embarrassed?*

With a grin, Gabriel led him to the guest room and took a terry-plastic robe from a drawer.

"Gotta get back to work now," he said.

"You're in the movie?"

Gabriel's grin broadened. "I'm an assistant groper."

Brenda looked good with a rich brown robe pulled snugly around her, Oxnard decided. One glance in a mirror after his steamshower had convinced him that wearing a robe two sizes too small was better than prancing around nude. But not much. His hairy legs showed to midcalf. He had to be careful how he sat.

Brenda, Gabriel and Oxnard were sitting in the living room. It was furnished in old-fashioned Nineteen Sixties style, with authentic green berets and protest posters artfully arranged here and there. The walls were covered with paintings, drawings, sketches—all from stories that Gabriel had written.

The camera crew was in the process of stowing gear into the truck they had parked outside. Roscoe himself had borrowed Brenda's keys to move her car out of the driveway. Now, as the three of them sat in the comfortable living room, they could hear the wind-whipped rain and the sounds of grunting people moving heavy pieces of equipment out into the wet.

Oxnard and Brenda had brandy snifters in their hands. Gabriel, still clad in only his bath towel, had graciously poured them the drinks while making dates with three of Roscoe's starlets. He refrained from drinking, himself.

"When did you become a movie actor?" Brenda asked, a quizzical smile on her lips.

"Always been an actor, sweetie," he replied. "You think sitting through a story conference with some of those assholes you call executives doesn't take thespic talents?"

"I've seen histrionics from you. . . ."

One of the starlets walked barefoot into the living room as far as Gabriel's slingback chair. She was wearing a knit sweater that barely reached her thighs. Her cascading blonde hair was slightly longer. Her eyes didn't seem to focus well.

"Hey Ron, honey, can I use your shower?"

"Sure, sure," he said.

"Thanks." She bent over and kissed him on the cheek. The sweater rode up and Oxnard found himself tugging at the hem of his borrowed robe, trying to make certain that he was covered adequately. The blonde plodded sleepily out of the room without rearranging her sweater.

"But I don't understand why you're performing in Roscoe's movie," Brenda resumed.

Gabriel made a sour face. "Money, kid. Why else? You have any idea how much it takes to keep this house going? My gardener makes more than that cutesy-poo does." He jerked a thumb in the general direction of the partially sweatered starlet.

"But you've got so many books and filmscripts . . . you must make plenty on royalties."

With a wave of his hand that took in all the illustrations on the walls, Gabriel said, "What books? You know what you get from books? Nickels and dimes. Unless you write a book about a veterinarian's carnal lust for his customers. Nobody reads about *people* anymore. I write about people."

Oxnard felt puzzled. "Aren't you the Ron Gabriel who writes science fiction? I've read some of your stuff."

Gabriel's eyebrows went up a centimeter. "Yeah? like what?"

"Let's see now. . . ." Oxnard concentrated. "It was . . . oh yes, 'The Beast That Had No Mouth' and 'Repent . . . ' something about a watchmaker."

Nodding furiously, Gabriel said, "Yeah. And you know how much money I made from those two books? Peanuts! The goddam publishers give you peanuts for an advance, then they sell a zillion copies and claim that they haven't made enough money to start paying royalties yet!"

"I didn't know. . . ."

Gabriel leaped out of his chair. "Those humpers! You don't know the half of it!"

He stomped out of the room. Confused, Oxnard got up and watched Gabriel duck down the house's central atrium and into a doorway. He slammed the door behind him.

"That's his office," Brenda said.

"What's he. . . ."

The muffled sound of Gabriel's voice floated back to them. "Sue the bastards . . . I don't care what it costs . . . get them for every nickel they owe me. . . ."

Brenda stood up beside Oxnard. "He must be calling his lawyer."

"At this hour?" Oxnard glanced at his watch. It was after midnight.

"Ron's friends and associates are accustomed to his late hours. He starts working when the sun goes down."

"Must be part vampire."

"It's been suggested."

Abruptly, the office door opened and Gabriel came stamping back into the living room. "We'll get those mothers," he was muttering.

As they all sat down again, Brenda asked, "What about the TV series you were doing? I thought. . . ."

"Don't mention it!" Gabriel snapped. "The less said about that, the better."

For an instant the room was silent, except for the rain drumming on the roof.

Then Gabriel said, "We had the whole goddam series set up. Worked my tail off for six months; fights with the producers, fights with the network, the director, the actors. Finally they began to see the light It's all starting to go right. I could *feel* it! We had it all in the groove. . . ."

"What was the show about?" Oxnard asked.

"Huh? Oh, it was going to be a series based on a short story of mine, about a giant pterodactyl that attacks New York City."

"I heard about it," Brenda said. "And then it was cancelled, just before shooting began. What happened?"

"What happened?" Gabriel's voice went up several notches. "Those lumpheaded brain-damage cases that run the network decided they couldn't do the show because it wasn't in three-dee!"

"No!"

"Oh no? Those maggotheads are turning everything into three-dee shows. Everything! I thought, great. The series will be even more spectacular in three-dee. But we'd need a bigger budget and a couple weeks to work out some of the technical problems. *Wham!* Nothing doing. They cut us off. Done. Finished."

Oxnard felt vaguely guilty about it. He stirred uneasily in his chair, started to cross his legs, but remembered just in time and stopped himself.

"Know what they put into our timeslot?" Gabriel was still fuming. "A cops-and-robbers show. Some idiot thing about a robot and a Polack cop. Ever see an animated fireplug doing Polish jokes? Arrgghhh."

Roscoe suddenly called from the front doorway. "Hey superstar! We're leaving!"

Without moving from his chair, Gabriel bellowed, "So leave already! Just make sure you send the check tomorrow morning!"

"Will do," Roscoe hollered back. "Oh, Rita and Dee-Dee said they're too tired for the drive back to Glendale. They flaked out in your guest room. Okay by you?"

"Yah, sure. I'll unflake 'em later on."

"Good luck, buddy."

"Break a leg, C.B."

The door slammed.

Oxnard cleared his throat. "Do you mean that they really cancelled your show because it wasn't going to be shown in holographic projection?"

"That was their excuse," Gabriel answered. "They wanted to castrate me. I'm too honest for those Byzantine bronze nosers." He glowered at Brenda. "And I still say that Finger had something to do with it."

Brenda returned his gaze without flinching.

"But still," Gabriel grumbled, "I'd like to meet the jerk who started this three-dee crap and. . . ."

"What about that other project you were talking about?" Brenda broke in. "The historical thing. Was it going to be a musical?"

Gabriel scratched at his stubbly chin. "*That* thing! I got the shaft on that, too."

"What was it going to be?"

"I was going to do 'Romeo and Juliet' in modern terms. You know, instead of Italy in the old times, make it L.A., here, today. Make the two feuding families a pair of TV networks that are fighting it out for the ratings." He grew more animated, expressive. Getting to his feet, gesticulating: "Then the star from one show on the first network falls in love with a girl from a show on the other network. Their shows are on the air at the same time . . . they love each other, but their networks are enemies. Then when the executive producers find out about them. . . ."

It took nearly an hour before Gabriel calmed down enough to sit in his chair again. He ended his monologue with:

"Then some jerk says that it's just like some old opera called 'West Side Story.' I looked it up . . . wasn't anything like that at all."

"So that's fallen through, too?" Brenda asked.

"That's right," Gabriel said, slumping back in his soft chair, looking exhausted. "Every goddam thing I've touched for the past year has turned to shit. Every goddam thing." He sat bolt upright "It's gotta be Finger! He swore I'd never work for anybody in this town again. He's living up to his name, that no-good. . . ."

"That's not true, Ron," Brenda said. "He wants you to work for him. He needs you. He's desperate."

Gabriel stopped in midsentence and stared at her.

"He needs me?"

Brenda nodded gravely.

"Good! Tell him to go engage reflexively in sexual intercourse."

It took Oxnard a moment to interpret that one, although Brenda giggled immediately.

"No, Ron. I'm serious. B.F.'s really in a bind and you're the only one who can pull him out."

"Got any rocks? Heavy ones?"

"Wait a minute," Oxnard heard himself say. They both turned toward him. "Before we go any further, you ought to know . . . I invented the holographic projection system."

Half expecting Gabriel to leap for his throat, Oxnard sat tensed in his chair, ready to defend himself verbally or physically.

"You invented it?" asked Gabriel incredulously.

"I'm Bill Oxnard. The jerk who started this three-dee stuff."

They talked. They sat in the comfortably furnished living room, draped with towel and robes while the rain made background music for them, and talked for hours. One of the girls from further back in the house wandered sleepily into the room, naked, looking for the kitchen and murmuring about a midnight snack. The phone next to Gabriel's chair rang a couple of times and he snarled into it briefly. Oxnard told him about the exciting days when he was perfecting the first holographic system, how the corporate executives had beamed at him and given him bonuses. And then how they tossed him out of the corporation when he asked for a share of the royalties they were reaping.

"They screwed you out of your own invention," Gabriel said, with real pain in his voice. "Just like they've screwed me out of my royalties."

"It was my own stupid fault," Oxnard said. "I was so wrapped up in the technical work that I didn't pay any attention to the legal side."

"Why the hell should you have to?" Gabriel demanded. "If those pricks were honest men you wouldn't have to worry about them sticking it to you. They wear clean clothes, but their skins are slimy. The bastards."

Gabriel showed Oxnard his own three-dee set and they turned it on. The Keir Dullea simulacrum appeared in miniature, hovering in the far corner of the living room, riding a model spacecraft across a simulated Martian crater. The images looked solid, but they sparkled and shimmered.

"Most of that's in the transmission system," Oxnard said, squinting at the scintillations in the images. "But I think I can improve the picture quality a little, if you have a toolkit handy."

Gabriel produced a toolkit. Oxnard went happily to work on the mahogany-like plastic console that housed the three-dee receiver, tinkering with the controls in the back.

Brenda, meanwhile, outlined Titanic Productions' precarious fiscal situation. By the time Oxnard rejoined the conversation, she was saying:

"Of course, he's screaming that he'll never deal with you again. Repeat, never. But he knows that he needs a good show right away and you've got the imagination and talent to create it for him."

Gabriel was lying flat on the Rya carpet, stretched out in front of the sofa on which Brenda was sitting. She had her legs tucked demurely under her, Oxnard noticed. Keir Dullea had ridden off into the sunset, so Oxnard turned off the set.

"No, I won't work for Finger. That sonofabitch is just too slimy to deal with. He'd sell his own mother to the cannibals."

"But you wouldn't have to deal with Finger," Brenda urged. "You could work with Les. . . ."

"That turd!"

"And me."

Gabriel heaved a deep sigh, making the towel around his middle flutter slightly. "It would be nice, baby. I'd really like to work with you. You're one of the few honest people left in this town. . . ."

"I'd enjoy working with you, too, Ron. You know that."

Oxnard found himself frowning at both of them.

"But . . ." Gabriel said, his voice distant and small, "I've gotten so emotionally involved. . . ."

"You?"

"Yeah. With this 'Romeo and Juliet' project. I really wanted to tackle Shakespeare. Bring the Old Bard up to date. There's no greater challenge to a writer. I wanted to show them all that I could do it."

Brenda shook her head. "No, I don't think 'Romeo and Juliet' would be right for The Tube. Those New York bankers want something sound and safe . . . not Shakespeare. They need something much more conventional, like science fiction."

"Science fiction!" Gabriel complained. "Is that all those frog-brains can think of? I'm sick of science fiction; it's on every network, every show. Why can't we do something new, fresh, original?"

"Like 'Romeo and Juliet?'" Oxnard asked, sitting down beside Brenda.

"Yeah, why not?" Gabriel countered.

"Ron, Titanic won't go for a show that deals with the networks or the studios," Brenda said. "That's *realism*! You know how they steer clear of that. Why, even the news programs get permission before they put anything *real* on the air."

"Yeah, I know." Tiredly.

Oxnard said, "No starcrossed lovers, then."

Brenda started to reply, but Gabriel said, "What was that?"

"Huh? Oh, I said . . . no starcrossed lovers. You know, Romeo and Juliet."

Gabriel sat bolt upright. "Starcrossed lovers! Holy shit! That's *it*!" He leaped to his feet. "That's it! Wow, what an idea!"

The towel started sliding downward and Gabriel made an automatic grab for it as he pranced around the room. "That's it!" he said again. "That's it!"

Brenda was grinning but she looked just as befuddled as Oxnard felt. "What? Tell us."

Pouncing atop the three-dee console, Gabriel shouted: "They want science fiction and I want Shakespeare. We'll merge 'em. . . ." He stood on the console, stretched to his full height, flung his arms over his head and boomed:

"THE STARCROSSED!"

The towel fell to the floor.

Time lost its meaning. At some point the rain slackened, then died away altogether. The windows of the living room started to show the misty gray promise of a new day. Inside the room, Bill Oxnard felt himself being drawn into the chaotic vortex of creation. It was like being present at the creation of a new world.

"There're these two families, see," Gabriel was saying, oblivious of his nudity, "on two different spaceships. They're merchants . . . they go from planet to planet, trading goods. You know, spices, hardware. . . ."

"With a gambling casino in the back," Brenda suggested.

Gabriel eyed her. "Maybe . . . maybe it would work. Well, anyway. One family has this guy, the youngest son of the head of the family—"

"And the other family has a daughter."

"Right! The two families land on the same planet at the same time, see?"

Brenda nodded vigorously. "We could have a different planet every week . . . and the same major characters. That's just what a good series needs!"

"Sure," Gabriel agreed. "Good guest stars and the same regulars each week."

"So the boy and girl fall in love," Brenda said.

Gabriel was rubbing his hands together anxiously. "Right. But their families don't like it. They compete with each other, see, for the interstellar trade. They don't. . . ."

"Wait a minute," Oxnard said. "If these are interstellar ships there's going to be a time factor involved. You know, the twin paradox."

"The what?" Gabriel looked blank.

"If you travel at almost the speed of light, there's a time dilation. The two families wouldn't age at the same rate. The boy will get older than the girl or *vice versa.*"

"Oh that," Gabriel said. "Don't worry about it. We'll just make the ships go faster than light"

"But you can't do that. It's physically impos. . . ."

Gabriel flapped a hand at him. "We'll use a space warp. Been doing that for years."

"But it's not . . ."

"It's dramatic license," Brenda said.

Oxnard shook his head but kept silent.

"Okay," Gabriel said. "Every week the kids are trying to get together and every week the families try to keep 'em apart. We can have them stowing away on each other's ships, captured by the natives on the planets, lost in space . . . zowie, there's a *million* story-lines in this!"

"And we can have subplots every week," Brenda said eagerly. "With all sorts of different characters and cultures on each planet they visit. It's terrific!"

On and on they went, as the sky brightened outside and birds began to welcome the not-quite-risen sun. Gabriel pranced into his office and Brenda and Oxnard followed him into the cramped, cluttered little room. With an unlit pipe clamped between his teeth, Gabriel turned on his voicewriter; their free-for-all conversation began clattering out of the machine in black and white.

They sketched out the major characters while Gabriel ransacked the bookshelves lining the walls to find his *Asimov's Guide to Shakespeare.* The voicewriter dutifully typed up a summary of the series' basic theme and outline, plus outlines for the first three hour-long segments. Then they went into details of characterizations, the types of actors needed, the costuming. Oxnard found himself doing most of the talking when it came to describing the spaceships and their equipment.

Finally it got uproariously funny. They began giggling at every line coming out of the voicewriter. When the machine obediently began typing, "Ha-Ha-Ha," they broke up completely. Gabriel fell out of his desk chair onto the floor. Brenda had tears streaming down her cheeks. Oxnard felt as if his insides would burst. And they couldn't stop laughing. Not until the machine ran out of paper and shut itself off. Seventeen sheets of "Ha-Ha-Ha" littered the office floor.

They staggered into the kitchen, breathless and squinting at the morning light. As coffee perked and orange juice defrosted, the blonde in the knit sweater came along. She was wearing stretch slacks and jewelry now, as well as the sweater.

"You guys sure were having a good time," she said.

"Stay for breakfast," Gabriel told her.

She smiled sweetly and kissed him on the nose. "Can't, honey. Got to get back to the studio. I'm a working girl, you know. Not like you writers. 'Bye!"

And off she flounced.

Sobering, Oxnard mumbled, "I ought to get back to my lab, too."

"They can do without you for one day," Brenda said.

"They did. Yesterday."

"Grab a couple hours' sleep first," Gabriel said. "You can use the guest room."

"Might be a good idea at that," Oxnard let himself yawn. His eyes felt very heavy.

He was about to push himself up from the kitchen table when Gabriel put a steaming mug of coffee down in front of him and said:

"Listen, I appreciate all the advice you gave me about the spaceships and all. I want you to be my technical advisor for the series."

"The series?"

"Yeah. 'The Starcrossed.' Remember?"

"I'm no technical advisor. I run a laboratory. . . ."

Brenda was sitting across the table from him, with a curious expression on her sleepy face.

Gabriel said, "You know this science stuff. I'm going to need somebody I can trust, if we're going to do this series right. Right, Brenda?"

She nodded and murmured, "Aye-aye, master."

"But my responsibility's to the lab. That's. . . ."

Gabriel wagged a finger at him. "You don't have to leave the lab. All I'll need is some advice now and then. Probably handle most of it on the phone. Maybe read the scripts when they've gotten to second draft."

"My big chance in show biz," Oxnard said.

"It'll be a helluva help," Gabriel said. "To me personally."

Brenda nodded. "Finger will want you on the scene as a consultant anyway, on your new holographic process."

"I suppose so," Oxnard admitted.

Gabriel grasped him by the shoulder. "Go on, get some sleep. We can talk about it later."

Oxnard nodded and got up wearily from the table. Padding down the hall toward the guest room, he wondered what Gabriel and Brenda were going to do while he slept. *Hell, you know what they're going to do.* The thought irked him. Greatly.

The guest room was midnight dark. Oxnard was completely blind the instant he let the door snap shut behind him. He took two cautious steps forward, hoping to make a less-than-shincracking contact with the bed, and stumbled against something soft.

It squirmed and he fell on top of it.

"Hey, whatcha . . . oh, Ron, it's you," a sleepy voice murmured.

They were sprawled on a sea of pillows that the girl had evidently strewn across the guest room floor.

"No, it's not Ron." Oxnard whispered, feeling rather flustered. He wished he had pockets to put his hands into.

"Oh? Who're you?"

"Uh . . . Bill," he said into the darkness. He still couldn't see anything, but he felt her soft body and breathed in a tawny scent.

"What's goin' on?" another lissome voice whispered.

"It's Bill," said the first girl.

"Oh, gee, that's nice."

Oxnard felt another soft, warm body snuggle close to him. Four hands began fumbling with his robe. He thought furiously about the lab and his responsibilities. And about Brenda. He tried to remind himself that he was, after all, an adult who could take care of himself. He didn't need . . . didn't want . . . maybe they . . . but. . . .

Finally, he said to himself: *So this is show business.*

3: The Agent

Jerry Morgan had two hysterical unemployed actresses in his waiting room, one tightlipped producer who was trying to break into comedy writing, and a receptionist who had just given two days' notice. The actresses and producer were all formerly employed by Titanic Productions: a significant phenomenon, as Sherlock Holmes would have said if he'd been a theatrical and literary agent with an office off the Strip.

At the moment Morgan had a worse problem on his hands: a morose Ron Gabriel. It wasn't like Gabriel to be downcast: ebullient, brassy, argumentative, noisy, egregious, foolhardy, irreverent—all those yes. Morgan was accustomed to seeing Gabriel in those moods. But morose? And—fearful?

Morgan studied his client's face on the big view screen set into the wall of his private office. He had considered getting the phone company to put in a three-dee viewer, but so far hadn't gotten around to it.

"So it's been more than a week since Brenda brought the idea to Titanic," Gabriel was saying, his voice low, "and I haven't heard a word from her or anybody else."

"Neither have I, Ron," said Morgan as pleasantly as he could manage. "But, hell, you know Finger. He never moves all that quickly."

"Yeah, but Brenda would've gotten back to me if there'd been some good news. . . ."

Morgan glanced at the outline and fact sheet for "The Starcrossed" that rested on a corner of his desk.

"Did you give her the same poopsheet you gave me?" he asked.

Gabriel nodded. "We did it that morning, right on the voicewriter. Haven't seen her since. She just took off. . . ."

"She's probably waiting for Finger to finish reading it. You know he can't get through more than one page a day. His lips get tired."

Not even the joke stirred Gabriel. "They've torn it up," he said miserably. "I know they have. Finger took one look at my name on the cover and tore it into little pieces. Then he must've fired Brenda and she's too sore at me to even let me know about it."

"Nonsense, Ron. You know. . . ."

"Call him!" Gabriel said, his face suddenly intense, his voice urgent. "Call Finger and find out what he did with it! Make a personal pitch for the show. I'm broke, Jerry. Flat busted. I need *something*! That show. . . ."

With a sigh, Morgan said, "I'll call Les Montpelier. He'll know what's happened."

Morosely, Gabriel nodded and shut off the connection.

Three hours later, Morgan took off his sunglasses and peered into the dimly lit bar. Vague shapes of men and women were sitting on barstools; beyond them, the narrow room widened and brightened into a decent restaurant.

The hostess was dressed in the very latest Colonial high-necked, long-sleeved, floor-skirted outfit with the bosom cut out to show her bobbing breasts.

"Lookin' for somebody?" she said in her most cultured tones.

"Mr. Montpelier was supposed to meet me here," Morgan said, still trying to make out the faces of the men at the bar.

"Oh yeah, he was here, but he went on back into the restaurant. Said he couldn't wait and you could find him at his table. Big tipper."

Silently grumbling at the Freeway traffic jams that had made him late, Morgan worked past the executives and bar girls and quickly found Montpelier sitting alone at a booth near a window.

He waved and put on his heartiest smile at he approached the booth. The slim, redbearded Montpelier smiled back and Morgan saw a mirror image of his own phony graciousness.

"Hi, Les! How the hell are ya?" Morgan said as he slid into the booth.

"Just great, Jerry! And you? Geez, it's been a helluva long time since we've seen each other."

As Montpelier motioned for a waiter, Morgan said: "Well, you know how this town is. You can be in bed with the same guy for months and then never see him again for years."

"Yeah. Sure."

The waiter was professionally icy. "Cocktail, m'seur?"

"A Virgin Mary for me, please," Morgan said.

Montpelier grinned at him. "Off the toxics?"

Morgan grinned back. *The Game*, he sighed to himself. *The everlasting Game.* "I was never on it, Les. I drink a little wine with a meal, that's all. The hard stuff never appealed to me. I prefer smoking."

"Then why the camouflage?"

"The Virgin Mary? I like tomato juice . . . and besides, there are people in this town who don't trust an agent that doesn't drink."

"Hell," Montpelier said, "I've seen it just the opposite. I know an agent who drinks nothing but milk in public. Says, 'What kind of an agent would people think I am if I didn't have an ulcer?' One of the biggest juicers in town, in private."

You got that from an old TV show, Morgan replied silently.

The waiter brought Morgan's drink. Montpelier clinked his own half-finished rum sour with it and they began the serious business of inspecting the menus.

It wasn't until the salads had been served that the conversation got to the subject. Morgan deliberately avoided an opening gambit, which in itself was one of The Game's most frequently used opening gambits: let the other guy bring up the subject, makes him appear to be more anxious than you are.

"What's this brilliant new idea Gabriel's got? Brenda seems very impressed with it."

"I thought you knew about it," Morgan said.

"Yeah—in general. B.F.'s got it tucked under his arm, though. Hasn't let anybody see any details yet."

Morgan munched a lettuce leaf thoughtfully, then said, "It's the kind of idea that could save Titanic from the wolves."

"Wolves?" Montpelier looked startled. "There're no wolves at our doors."

With a shrug, Morgan said: "I must have heard wrong, then. Anyway, it's a powerful idea. It's got scope."

"What's it all about?"

Morgan leaned back and put his fork down. This was the part he liked best. It was like fishing. Only instead of standing hips-deep in an Alpine stream, he was sitting in a plush restaurant, wearing last year's zipsuit, trying to hook a wary young executive who was dressed like Buffalo Bill Cody. *Trout are fairer game,* Morgan told himself.

"It's got everything you could ever want in a successful series. Drama, action, love interest—a couple of attractive young central characters, lots of continuous characters and color. *Plus* exotic new settings every week, with plenty of scope for guest stars and in-depth characterizations. Plenty of spinoffs, too. And byproducts. . . ."

"What *is* it, for Chrissake?"

Morgan inwardly smiled. Montpelier had blown his cool: *Twenty points for our side.*

"It's called 'The Starcrossed.'"

Montpelier's anxious frown dissolved as he savored the title.

"The Starcrossed,'" he murmured.

"It draws its dramatic punch," Morgan quoted from Gabriel's poopsheet, tucked into his zipper pocket, "from the depths of the human heart in conflict with itself. The origins of this idea trace back through Shakespeare and the Renaissance, back into Medieval romance, and even. . . ."

Montpelier's face went sour. "It's not that damned 'Romeo and Juliet' thing he was trying to peddle at Mercury, is it?"

"Of course not," Morgan snapped and immediately wished he hadn't. *Too quick, he sees through it. Lose ten points.*

"Well, what is it then?"

"It draws on some of the same material as the 'Romeo and Juliet' idea . . ."

"Ah-hah!"

"But it's a completely new concept. Fully science fictional. No historical or contemporary parts to it at all."

"No realism?" Montpelier asked, with an expression that was close to a sneer.

"None."

"I know Gabriel. He's always trying to sneak some realism in."

With a grin, Morgan realized that Montpelier had suckered himself. He had set up a strawman; now all Morgan had to do was to knock it down.

"Let me tell you about this idea," Morgan said, hunching forward over the table conspiratorially. He hesitated just long enough to make Montpelier hold his breath, then started quoting again from the poopsheet:

"Picture a starship floating through space, just like any ordinary starship, like you see on all the shows, but this ship's been designed by the man who *invented* the three-dee process. Accurate. Technically detailed. A perfect jewel, shining in the black velvet of the infinite interstellar wilderness. Now, aboard that starship. . . ."

It was dark outside and people were starting to trickle in for dinner before Montpelier stopped asking questions about the show. Morgan was hoarse, as much from the nervous strain of improvising answers as from talking steadily for so many hours.

Montpelier was nodding. "It's got scope all right. I like the whole idea. It's got *depth*."

"Uh-huh," Morgan grunted. Then, as noncommittally as possible, he asked, "How's B.F. reacting to it?"

Montpelier shook his head. "If it was anybody else except Gabriel, B.F. would've snapped it up."

"Oh. I see."

"As it is," Montpelier went on, "he's stuck *me* with the job of getting along with Gabriel and not letting Ron get to the top."

"Oh?" Morgan felt his head go light.

"It's a pretty shitty job." Montpelier complained. "I'll have to handle Gabriel and keep him away from B.F. We'll have to settle on a damned executive producer; maybe Sheldon Fad. He's hot right now."

"Yes," Morgan agreed, with a genuine smile. "I think he'd be fine."

When Montpelier finally left the restaurant, there were stars in his eyes. *Or dollar signs*, Morgan reflected as he bade the executive goodbye and promised to be in touch with him the next day for some "hard-nosed, eyeball-to-eyeball, tough-assed money talk."

Morgan went to the men's room, threw up as he always did after one of these extended bull-flinging lunches, cleaned himself up, then found a phonebooth out near the bar. He sat down, closed the door firmly, and punched out Ron Gabriel's number.

It was busy. With a sigh, Morgan punched Gabriel's private number. Also busy. With a deeper sigh, he tried the writer's ultraprivate "hot line" number. *He can't be carrying on* three *conversations at once.* Morgan realized it was more a fond hope than a statement of fact.

A sultry brunette appeared on the tiny screen. "Mr. Gabriel's line," she moaned.

"Uh. . . ." With a distant part of his mind, Morgan was pleased that he could still be shaken up by apparitions such as this one. "Is, uh, Mr. Gabriel there? This is Jerry Morgan, his agent."

"I'll see, Mr. Morgan," she breathed.

The screen went gray for an instant, then Gabriel's hardbitten features came on the tiny screen.

"Well? How'd it go?"

Morgan said, "I just finished having lunch with Les Montpelier. . . ."

"God, you sound awful!" Gabriel said.

"I did a lot of talking."

Gabriel's face fell. "They don't want the show. They hated the idea."

"I talked it all out with Montpelier," Morgan said. "Finger's read the poopsheet and. . . ." He hesitated.

"And?"

It was criminal to tease Gabriel, but Morgan got the chance so seldom.

"And what?" Gabriel demanded, his voice rising.

"And . . . well, I don't know how to say it, Ron, so I might as well make it straight from the shoulder."

Gabriel gritted his teeth.

"They're buying it. We talk money tomorrow."

For an instant, nothing happened. No change in Gabriel's facing-the-firing-squad expression. Then his jaw dropped open and his eyes popped.

"What?" he squawked. "*They bought it?*" He leaped out of view of the phone's fixed camera, then reappeared some ten meters further away. He jumped up and down. "They bought it! They bought it! Ha-*ha!* They bought it! Those birdbrains bought it!"

The sultry brunette, another girl whom Morgan vaguely remembered as Gabriel's typist and a third woman rushed into the room.
Gabriel was still bounding all over the place, crowing with delight.

With the smile of a man who's put in a hard but successful day's
work, Morgan clicked off the phone and started on his way home.

4: The Producer

Sheldon Fad lay awake, staring at the ceiling as the sun rose over the Santa Monica Hills. Gloria snored lightly beside him, a growing mountain of flesh.

The baby was due in another month or so and Gloria had been no fun at all since she had found herself pregnant. No fun at all. Zero. Sheldon wondered, at quiet times like this, if it was really his baby that she was carrying. After all, she got pregnant suspiciously fast after moving in with him.

He frowned to himself. It all seemed so *macho* at first. An actress and dancer, lithe and exciting, Gloria had attached herself to Sheldon's arm when she could have gone with any guy in Los Angeles. They were all after her. He had ignored the stories about the vast numbers who had succeeded in their quest. That was all finished, she had told him tearfully, the night she moved in. All she wanted was him.

Yeah, Sheldon told himself. *Just me.* And a roof over her head. And not having to go to work. And a two-pound box of chocolates every day. And her underwear dripping in the bathtub every time he tried to take a shower. And her makeup littered all over the bathroom, the bedroom, even in the refrigerator.

A bolt, as the song says, of fear went through him as he realized that in a month—probably less—there'd be an infant sharing this one-bedroom apartment with them. What did Shakespeare say about infants? Mewling and puking. Yeah. And dirty diapers. A crib in the corner next to the bed; Gloria had already mentioned that.

Shit! Sheldon knew he had to get out of it. He turned his head on the pillow and gazed sternly at Gloria's face, serene and deeply asleep. *It's not my kid,* he told himself savagely. *It's not!*

And what if it is? another part of his mind asked. You didn't want it. She told you she was fixed. You believe her? And her line about hemophilia, so she can't have an abortion? Even if it is your kid, you didn't ask for this.

He sat up in bed, fuming to himself. Gloria didn't move a muscle, except to breathe. Her belly made a giant mound in the bedsheet.

No sense trying to go back to sleep. He swung his legs out of the bed and got to his feet. Stretching, he felt his vertebrae pop and heard himself grunt with the pain-pleasure that goes with it. He padded into the bathroom.

Twenty minutes later he was booming down the Freeway, heading for the Titanic Tower, listening to the early morning news:

". . . and smog levels will be at their usual moderate to heavy concentrations, depending on location, as the morning traffic builds up. Today's smog scent will be jasmine. . . ."

It was still clear enough to see where you were driving. The automatic Freeway guidance system hadn't turned on yet. Music came on the radio and began to soothe Sheldon slightly. Then he saw the Titanic Tower rising impressively from the Valley.

"I'll ask Murray what to do," Sheldon said to himself. "Murray will know."

It was still hours before most of the work force would stream into the Tower. Sheldon nodded grimly to the bored guards sitting at the surveillance station in the lobby. They were surrounded by an insect's eye of fifty TV screens showing every conceivable entryway into the building.

As Sheldon passed the guard, a solitary TV screen built into the wall alongside the main elevator bank flashed the words: GOOD MORNING MR. FAD. YOU'RE IN QUITE EARLY.

"Good morning, Murray," said Sheldon Fad. Then he punched the button for an elevator.

The *Multi-Unit Reactive Reasoning and Analysis Yoke* was rather more than just another business computer. In an industry where insecurity is a major driving force and more money has been spent on psychoanalyses than scripts, *Murray* was inevitable. One small segment of the huge computer's capacity was devoted to mundane chores such as handling accounts and sorting out bills and paychecks. Most of the giant computer complex was devoted to helping executives make business decisions. It was inevitable that the feedback loops in the computer's basic programming—the "Reactive Reasoning" function—would eventually come to be used as a surrogate psychotechnician, advisor and father confessor by Titanic's haggard executives.

Sheldon Fad didn't think of Murray as a machine. Murray was someone you could talk to, just like he talked to so many other people on the phone without ever meeting them in the flesh. Murray was kindly, sympathetic, and damned smart. He had helped Sheldon over more than one business-emotional crisis.

Well, there was *one* machine-like quality to Murray that Sheldon recognized. And appreciated. His memory could be erased. And was, often. It made for a certain amount of repetition when you talked to Murray, but that was better than running the risk of having someone else "accidentally" listen to your conversations. Someone like Bernard Finger, who wasn't above such things, despite the privacy laws.

In all, talking to Murray was like talking to a wise and friendly old uncle. A forgetful uncle, because of the erasures. But somehow that made Murray seem all the more human. He even adapted his speech patterns to fit comfortably with the user's style of speaking.

At precisely 7:32 Sheldon plopped tiredly into his desk chair. He felt as if he'd been working nonstop for forty days and nights. He took a deep breath, held it for twenty heartbeats, then exhaled through his mouth. He punched buttons on his desk-side console for orange juice and vitamin supplements. A small wall panel slid open, a soft chime sounded and the cold cup and pills were waiting for him.

Sheldon swallowed and gulped, then touched the sequence of buttons on the keyboard that summoned Murray.

GOOD MORNING SHELDON, the desktop viewing screen flashed, chartreuse letters against a gray background. WHAT CAN I DO FOR YOU THIS MORNING?

"This conversation is strictly private," Sheldon said. He noticed that his voice was trembling a little.

OF COURSE. PLEASE GIVE ME THE CORRECT ERASURE CODE.

"'Nobody knows the troubles I've seen,'" replied Sheldon.

THAT'S FINE, Murray printed. NOW WE CAN TALK IN PRIVATE AND THE TAPE WILL BE ERASED BETTER THAN THEY DO IN WASHINGTON.

Sheldon couldn't help grinning. He had told Murray all about Washington politics long ago.

"This is a personal problem," he began, "but I guess it affects my work, as well. . . ."

A PERSONAL PROBLEM IS A BUSINESS PROBLEM, Murray answered.

Sheldon outlined his feelings about Gloria, omitting nothing. Finally, feeling more exhausted than ever, he asked, "Well?"

Murray's screen stayed blank for a heartbeat—a long time for the computer to consider a problem. Then:

ABOUT THE SEX I DON'T KNOW. I'M BEYOND THAT SORT OF THING, YOU KNOW. BUT IF THE GIRL ISN'T MAKING YOU HAPPY AND YOU'RE NOT MARRIED TO HER, WHY DON'T YOU JUST TELL HER YOU WANT TO SPLIT.

"It's not that easy. She'd make a scene. It'd get into the news."

OH. SO. AND THAT WOULD BE BAD FOR BUSINESS.

"That's right. B.F. doesn't like to hear about rising young producers making messes of their personal lives."

BUT YOU'RE ONE OF HIS FAIR-HAIRED BOYS!

"That was last season. I had the only Titanic show to be renewed for this year."

FORTY-SIX SHOWS TITANIC PUTS ON LAST SEASON AND YOURS IS THE ONE RENEWED. GOOD WORK.

That came from Murray's general business memory bank, Sheldon realized. "That's about average for the industry," he said defensively. "Titanic didn't do any worse than Fox or Universal."

WE'RE GETTING SIDETRACKED, Murray pointed out.

"Right. Well . . . in addition to trying to figure out what to do with Gloria, I've got this new project on my hands . . . and it's a crucial one. The whole future of Titanic depends on it."

SEE? THEY'RE DEPENDING ON YOU!

"Yes, but . . ." Sheldon felt miserable. "Look at it from my point of view. If I don't get rid of Gloria somehow, I'm not going to be able to give my best to this new show. If I do get rid of her and she raises a stink, *and the new show flops,* B.F. will blame it all on me."

YOU'RE IN A DOUBLE BIND, ALL RIGHT.

"There's more," Sheldon said. "The show's creator, Ron Gabriel, doesn't get along with B.F. *at all.* I'm in the middle on that, too. And Gabriel wants to put on the most extravagant space opera you've ever seen, while I've got to stay within a budget that won't even buy peanut butter!"

AGAIN IN THE MIDDLE.

"Exactly."

SO? WHAT ELSE?

Sheldon pondered for several moments, while the sickly greenish letters glowed on the screen.

"I guess that's about all," he said at last. "I've got a meeting with Gabriel and his agent later this morning. I know Gabriel's going to make impossible demands . . . and he . . . he's so . . . *loud!* He shouts and screams. Sometimes he hits!"

SO SUE HIM.

"I don't *want* him to hit me!"

WHAT DO YOU WANT?

For the first time since he had become acquainted with Murray, Sheldon felt some slight impatience. "What do I want? I want to get rid of Gloria without a fight that'll ruin my career. I want to make a hit of this stupid idea of Gabriel's without driving the company broke. I want to get out of the middle!"

ALL RIGHT. ALL RIGHT, DON'T GET SO WORKED UP. HIGH BLOOD PRESSURE AND ULCERS NEVER SOLVED ANY PROBLEMS.

"But what can I *do?*"

I'M SEARCHING MY MEMORY BANKS FOR A CORRELA-TION. AND AT THE SAME TIME USING MY ANALYTICAL PROGRAMMING TO ATTACK THE PROBLEM. AHAH! THAT'S IT.

"What?" Sheldon leaned forward in his chair hopefully.

GET OUT OF THE COUNTRY.

"Get out. . . ." He sagged back.

IF YOU PRODUCE THIS SHOW OUTSIDE THE U.S., YOU

CAN TELL GLORIA THAT YOU'LL BE AWAY FOR SEVERAL MONTHS. CAN'T BE HELPED. BUSINESS. CAREER. ALL THAT SORT OF STUFF.

"But she'll see through. . . ."

CERTAINLY SHE WILL. SHE WILL UNDERSTAND WHAT YOU'RE REALLY TELLING HER. BUT SHE WON'T BE ABLE TO DO MUCH ABOUT IT. AND IF SHE'S THE SORT OF GIRL YOU TOLD ME SHE IS, SHE'LL SEE THE WISDOM IN PICKING UP SOME OTHER MAN TO SUPPORT HER.

Wearily, Sheldon asked, "But who in his right mind would let an eight-months-pregnant woman grab him. . . . ?"

YOU'D BE SURPRISED. THERE ARE LOTS OF MEN RIGHT HERE IN THIS COMPANY WITH ALL SORTS OF HANGUPS.

"You think she'd really find somebody else?"

CERTAINLY. IN THE MEANTIME, YOU CAN FIND A REAL-LY CHEAPO OUTFIT TO PRODUCE YOUR NEW SHOW AND GET OFF THE FISCAL HOOK THAT WAY. PRODUCTION COMPANIES OUTSIDE THE U.S. WORK MUCH MORE CHEAP-LY THAN OUR OWN UNIONIZED PEOPLE.

"Where?" Sheldon asked, suddenly eager to travel. "Yugoslavia? Argentina? New Zealand?"

NONE OF THE ABOVE. YOU'VE GOT TO BALANCE YOUR TRAVEL EXPENSES AGAINST THE EXPENSES OF PRODUC-TION. CALCULATIONS ARE THAT CANADA WILL BE THE CHEAPEST BET.

"Canada?" Sheldon felt his enthusiasm sinking.

CANADA. MEXICO LOOKS CHEAPER ON THE SURFACE, BUT MY SUBROUTINES TELL ME THAT YOU'VE GOT TO BRIBE EVERYBODY IN THE GOVERNMENT, FROM THE CUSTOMS INSPECTORS TO THE TRAFFIC COPS, IF YOU WANT TO DO BUSINESS DOWN THERE. RAISES THE COSTS BEYOND THOSE OF A CANADIAN OPERATION. THE CANADIANS ARE HONEST AS WELL AS PRETTY CHEAP.

"Canada?" Sheldon repeated. His mind filled with visions of snow, sled dogs, pine trees, Nelson Eddy in a red Mounties jacket.

"Canada," he said again.

Fad's office wasn't very large, considering he was an executive producer on the rise. Merely a couple of leatherite couches, a few deep chairs scattered here and there across the fakefur rug, his own desk and keyboard terminal and a few holographic pictures where windows would normally be. Sheldon preferred the holographic views of Mt. Shasta, San Francisco's Bay Bridge and Catalina Island to the view of a tinted smog that he could see through his window. He wasn't high enough in Titanic's hierarchy to be above the smog level.

When his secretary told him that Gabriel and Morgan had arrived, Sheldon carefully clicked on the *record* button on Murray's controls. A friendly blue light glowed steadily at him, from an angle that could be seen only from behind the desk. Sheldon felt as if he had a silent ally standing beside him.

His visitors were ushered into the office by his secretary, who discreetly went no further than the door. But Gabriel was already jotting down her phone number in the little book he always carried. She was giving him her most dazzling smile; he had apparently already turned the full force of his charisma on her.

Morgan was still wearing his same tired old red zipsuit; it had been out of style for a year or more. Gabriel, who was a style setter, wore tight black leather slacks and what looked like a genuine antique motorcycle jacket, complete with studs and chains.

Sheldon got up and came around the desk, arms outstretched. "Fellaaas . . . how *are* you?"

Morgan, who was tall enough to be a laughable contrast to the smaller, stockier Gabriel, backed away automatically. Gabriel aimed a mock punch at Sheldon's stomach. They ended up shaking hands.

"Isn't it great to be starting something new?" Sheldon enthused. "This is going to be the best series Titanic has ever done. I just know it!"

"Great. Great," said Gabriel, with something of a scowl on his face. "Where's Brenda? I thought she'd be here."

Retreating back to his desk chair, Sheldon answered, "Why no, she's not part of this project. She works directly for B.F., you know."

Morgan had taken the nearest deepchair and started to say, "We got all the financial arrangements ironed out with Les Montpelier last week. He says the legal department is drawing up the contracts."

Sheldon nodded. "That's entirely correct. Want some coffee? Juice? Anything?"

Gabriel was prowling around the room, still scowling. "I thought Brenda was going to be here. She was in on the beginning of this idea. . . ."

"Brenda," said Sheldon patiently, "is B.F.'s assistant She does *not* get involved in preproduction planning for a specific show."

"Lemme use your phone," Gabriel said, heading for the desk.

Sheldon quickly swivelled the phone around so that Gabriel could see the screen without coming around the desk and noticing Murray's recording eye. Gabriel sat on a corner of the desk and started punching numbers on the phone's keyboard.

Sheldon had to push his chair over a bit and lean sidewise to see Morgan.

"You and Les settled all the financial matters?" he asked, while Gabriel was saying:

"Brenda Impanema . . . whattaya mean she's not at this number? What number is she at? Screw information! *You* look it up, why dontcha?"

Morgan seemed to be taking it all in stride, the eye of Gabriel's hurricane. "There are a few minor matters that we're not happy with, but I'll straighten those out once the contracts are drawn up. Nothing to worry about. It's not as much money as we expected, though."

Sheldon shrugged. "Money's tight all over."

"Brenda! How the hell are you? Where've you been keeping yourself?"

"If money's so tight, how will this affect the production values on 'The Starcrossed?'" Morgan asked.

"That's what I wanted to discuss with you. I know Ron thinks big and I agree with him, I really do—but. . . ."

"Whattaya mean you think it's best if we don't see each other? Is this Finger's idea of getting even with me?"

"You know," Morgan said, "I've seen a lot of shows with great potential fold up because the producers didn't put enough backing into them."

"Yes, I know. But I think I've worked out a way to get the best production values and still keep the costs down. . . ."

"I don't care if Finger cancels the whole season!" Gabriel yelled at the phone. "I don't want you pussyfooting around because you think it'll make him sore if you see me. He can stick it. . . ."

"How are you going to do that, Sheldon?"

"Well, after an *exhaustive* computer analysis of the situation. . . ."

"I know you're doing it for me," Gabriel was shouting now, "but I'd rather see you than win an Emmy. Yah, that's exactly what I said."

"You were saying?"

"Our analysis shows that the optimum choice for producing the show. . . ."

"This is just a stall, isn't it? What you're really saying is that you can't stand the sight of me! Right?"

". . . would be outside the U.S., away from the high rates that all the unions here charge."

"Okay, kid. Maybe you're protecting me. But I think it's a Pearl Harbor job and I don't like it!"

"And where do you want to put it?"

"Goodbye!"

"In Canada."

"Canada?"

"Canada!" Gabriel leaped off the desk corner. "Who the hell's going to Canada?"

"We are."

"You are?"

"No, *you* are."

Morgan said calmly, "He wants to shoot the show in Canada."

Gabriel looked as if he was ready to lead a bayonet attack. "Canada! I can't go to Canada! What in hell is there that you don't have more of here? And better?"

Sheldon sank back in his chair. It was going to be just as rough as he had feared. Only the friendly stare of Uncle Murray's steady blue eye gave him the courage to go on.

Two hours later, Sheldon was still in his desk chair. His jacket was crumpled on the floor and had Gabriel's boot-prints all over it. His suppshirt was soaked with sweat. Morgan hadn't moved at all during that time, nor hardly spoken; he still looked calm, relaxed, almost asleep.

But the walls were still ringing with Gabriel's rhetoric. Two chairs were overturned. Both couches had been kicked out of shape. One of the holographic pictures was sputtering badly, for reasons unknown.

The Bay Bridge kept winking and shimmering . . . or maybe, thought Sheldon, it was merely cringing.

"This is the dumbest asshole trick I've ever heard of!" Gabriel was screaming. "I don't want to go to Canada! There's nothing and nobody in Canada! All the good Canadian directors and actors are *here*, in California, for Chrissakes! We've got everything we need right here. Going to Canada is crazy! With a capital K!"

He was heading for the phone again when Morgan lifted one hand a few centimeters off the armrest of his chair. "Ron," he said quietly.

Gabriel stopped in midstride.

"Ron, the decision's already been made. It's a money decision and there's nothing you can do about it."

Gabriel frowned furiously at his agent.

"That's the way it is," Morgan said blandly.

"Then I want out," Gabriel said.

"Don't be silly," Morgan countered.

"I'm walking."

"You can't *do* that!" Sheldon protested.

"No? Watch me!"

Gabriel started for the door. Halfway there, he stopped and turned back toward Sheldon. "Tell you what," he said. His face still looked like something that would stagger Attila the Hun. "If I have to go to Canada, I'm going first class."

Sheldon let his breath out a little. "Oh, of course. Top hotels. All the best."

"That's not what I mean."

"What then?"

"I'm not going to let this show get stuck out in the boondocks, with no pipeline back to the money and the decision makers."

"But *I'll* be there with you," Sheldon said.

Gabriel made as if to spit. "I want *personal* representation from top management, right there on the set every goddamned day. I want one of Finger's top assistants in Canada with us."

"Ohhh." The clouds began to dissipate and Sheldon could see a Canadian sunrise. "Maybe you're right. Maybe I could get Les Montpelier . . . or Brenda Impanema. . . ."

Gabriel pointed an index finger at him, pistol-like. "You've got the idea."

Nodding, Sheldon said, "I'll ask B.F. tonight, at the party. . . ."

"Party?"

That was a mistake! Sheldon knew. Backtracking, "Oh, nothing spectacular. B.F.'s just giving one of his little soirees . . . on the ship, you know . . . just a couple of hundred people. . . ." His voice trailed off weakly.

"Party, huh?" was all that Gabriel said.

After he and Morgan left the office, Sheldon went to his private John and took a quick needle shower. Toweling himself off, he yelled through the open door to Murray:

"Well, what do you think of our star writer and creator?"

The computer hummed to itself for a few moments, then the screen lit up:

SUCH A KVETCH!

5: The Decision Makers

Sheldon was dressing for the party. It had been a long, exhausting day. And it wasn't over yet. Bernard Finger's parties were always something of a cross between a longdistance marathon and being dropped out of an airplane.

After Gabriel and his agent had left, Sheldon spent the rest of the morning recuperating, popping tranquilizers and watching Murray run down lists of Canadian production companies. There weren't very many. Then the computer system started tracking down freelance Canadian directors, cameramen, electricians and other crew personnel. Distressingly, most of them lived in the States. Most of them, in fact, lived in *one* state: California, southern, Los Angeles County.

At a discreet lunch with Montpelier, Sheldon dropped the barest hint that he would have Titanic money to shoot the show in Canada. Montpelier scratched at his beard for a moment and then asked:

"What about Gabriel? What's he think of the idea?"

"Loves it," exaggerated Sheldon.

Montpelier's eyebrows went up. "He's willing to leave that sex palace he's got in Sherman Oaks to go to the Frozen North?"

"He wants the show to be a success," Sheldon explained, crossing his ankles underneath the table. "When I explained that we'd be able to make our limited budget go much farther in Canada, he agreed. He was reluctant at first, I admit. But he's got a huge emotional commitment to this show. I know how to lever him around."

With a shrug, Montpelier said, "Fine by me. If Gabriel won't screw up the works. . . ."

"He, eh . . . he wants one favor from us."

"Oh."

"It's not back breaking; don't get worried."

Tell me about it."

"He wants Brenda up there with him."

Grinning, Montpelier asked, "Does she know about it?"

"That Gabriel wants her?"

"No. The Canada part."

"Not yet."

"So if she doesn't go, Gabriel doesn't go."

Feeling somewhat annoyed at Montpelier's smirk, Sheldon replied, "Yes, I suppose that's so."

After a long silent moment, Montpelier finally said, "Well, I guess that means Brenda's going to Canada."

Sheldon let his breath out. It was going to work!

"I mean," Montpelier justified, "if it's vital to the company's interests, she'll just have to go to Canada."

"Right."

"Her relationship with Gabriel is her own business."

"Right," Sheldon said again.

"We're not responsible for her private life, after all. She's an adult. It's not like we're forcing her into Gabriel's clutches."

"Right." It was an important word to know.

Their lunch went on for several hours while they discussed serious matters over tasteful wines and a bit of anticaloric food. Sheldon tried to suppress the nagging memory of a recent magazine article about the carcinogenic properties of anticaloric foods. Muckraking journalism, of course. Who could work in an industry where more business was conducted in restaurants and bars than in offices, without the calorie-destroying active enzyme artificial foods? Besides, the news from the National Institutes of Health was that a cure for cancer was due within another few years. For sure, this time.

By the time lunch was over, Sheldon was too exhausted to go back to the office. So he drove home for a short nap, before getting ready for the party. Gloria was out when he got home and he gratefully jumped into the unoccupied bed and was asleep in seconds.

She woke him when she returned, but it didn't matter. She was already beginning to look slightly fuzzy at the edges, becoming transparent to Sheldon's eyes. Not that he could see through her, so much as the fact that now he could look *past* her. Beyond her swollen belly and sarcastic mouth he could see lovely, pristine Canada.

She whined about not going to the party, of course. Sheldon just stared at her bloated body and said, "Now really!" Instead of starting one of her scenes, she cried and retreated to the already rumpled bed.

Sheldon didn't tell her about Canada. He wanted to be barricaded in his office, with Murray at his side, when he popped that surprise. On the phone he could handle almost anything.

Now he stood at the costumer's, being cleverly made over into his Party Personality. While the two makeup men were building up his new plastic face, the viewscreen in front of Sheldon's chair played a long series of film clips showing his Personality in action. It was an old film star named Gary Cooper and it seemed to Sheldon that all he had to do was to say "Yep" and "Nope" at the appropriate times. He concentrated on remembering those lines while the makeup men altered his face.

As the sun sank into the sea—sank into the smog bank hovering over the line of drilling platforms out there, actually—Sheldon drove toward the harbor, where the party was already in progress.

Bernard Finger almost always gave his parties on shipboard. It wasn't that he could cruise outside the limits of U.S. and/or California law enforcement. After all, the nation claimed territorial rights out to the limits of the continental shelf and there were a few California legislators who claimed the whole ocean out as far as Hawaii.

It's just that a cruise ship relaxes people, Sheldon realized as he drove up to the pier. You forget your land-bound inhibitions once you pull away from the shore. And you can't walk home.

He parked his bubble-topped two seater in the lot on the pier and sprinted the fifty meters through smog to the air curtain that protected the main hatch of the ship. Out here, on the docks, the smog was neither perfumed nor tinted. It looked and smelled *dirty*.

The ship was called the *Adventurer*, a name that Bernard Finger apparently thought apt. Titanic had bought it as a mammoth set for an ocean liner series they made a few years back. They had gotten it cheaply after the old Cunard Line had collapsed in economic ruin. For a while, Finger wanted to rename the ship *Titanic*, but a team of PR people had finally dissuaded him.

Now Sheldon stepped through the curtain of blowing air that kept the shoreside smog out of the ship. He stood for a moment just inside the hatch, while the robot photographer—a stainless steel cylinder with optical lenses studding its knobby top—squeaked "Smile!" and clicked his picture.

Sheldon smiled at the camera. Gary Cooper smiled back at him, from the elaborate mirrors behind the photographer. Dressed in buckskins, with a pearl-handled sixgun on his hip, lean, tanned, full of woodsy lore, Sheldon actually felt that he could conquer the West single handedly.

John Wayne bumped into him from behind. "Well, move it, fella," he snarled. "This here wagon train's gotta get through!"

Feeling a little sheepish and more than a little awkward in his platform boots, Sheldon made room for John Wayne. The cowboy was taller than Sheldon. "Wait 'til I get my hands on the costumers," he muttered to himself. They had promised him that nobody would be taller than Gary Cooper.

Maneuvering carefully up the stairway in his boots, Sheldon made his way up to the Main Lounge, It was decorated in authentic midcentury desperation: gummy-looking velvet couches and genuine formica cocktail tables. The windowless walls glittered with metal and imitation crystal.

The party was already well under way. As he took the usual set of greenies from one live waiter and a tall drink from another to wash them down, Sheldon saw a sea of old movie stars: Welches, Hepburns, Gables, Monroes, Redfords, a pair of Siamese twins that looked like Newman and Woodward, Marx Brothers scuttling through the crowd, a few showoff Weismullers, one stunning Loren and the usual gaggle of Bogarts.

No other Coopers. Good.

Up on the stage, surrounded by Harlows and Wests, stood Bernard Finger. He was instantly recognizable because he wore practically no makeup at all. He looked like Cary Grant all the time and now he merely looked slightly more so. Sheldon didn't have to look around to know that there were no other Cary Grants at the party.

He drank and let the greenies put a pleasant buzz in his head. After a dance with a petite Debbie Reynolds, the ship's whistle sounded and everybody rushed up to the main deck to watch them cast off.

As the oil-slicked dock slid away and the ship throbbed with the power of its engines, everyone started back to the various bars sprinkled around the lower decks. Or to the staterooms.

Sheldon turned from the glassed-in rail to go back to the Main Lounge, but a tall smoldering Lauren Bacall was slouching insolently in his path.

She held a cigarette up in front of her face and asked casually, "Got a match?" Her voice was sultry enough to start a forest fire.

Trying to keep his hands from trembling, Sheldon said, "Yep." He rummaged through his buckskin outfit's pockets and finally found a lighter. Bacall watched him bemusedly. He finally got it out and touched the spot that started the lighter glowing.

"Good," said Bacall. She slowly drew on the cigarette, then puffed smoke in Sheldon's face. "Now stick it up your nose. And Canada too!"

"Brenda?" Sheldon gasped. "Is that you?"

She angled a hip, Bacall-like, and retorted, "It's not Peter Lorre, Sheldon."

"How'd you know who I was? I mean. . . ."

"Never mind," she said; her voice became less sultry, more like Brenda Impanema's normal throatiness. "What I want to know is what gives you the right to decide 'The Starcrossed' is going to Canada. And me with it."

"Oh," Sheldon said. There didn't seem to be any Cooper lines to cover this situation. "Les told you about it."

"No he didn't," Brenda-Bacall said. "Les is as big a snake as you are. Bigger. He kept his mouth shut."

Sheldon glanced around for a possible escape route. None. He and Brenda were alone on the sealed-in weather deck. The rest of the crowd had gone inside. Brenda stood between him and the nearest hatch leading to the party. If he tried to run for another hatch in these damned platform boots, he'd either fall flat on his face or she would catch him in a few long-legged strides. Either way it would be too humiliating to bear. So he stood there and tried to look brave and unshaken.

"If you must know how I found out," Brenda went on, "I asked Murray what you were up to."

"Murray told you?" Sheldon heard his voice go up an octave with shock. Uncle Murray was a fink!

"Murray's everybody's friend. Knows all and tells all."

"But he's not supposed to tell about private conversations! Only business matters!"

"That's all he told me," Brenda said. "Your business conversation with Ron Gabriel."

Sheldon felt a wave of relief wash over him. Or maybe it was a swaying of the ship. At any rate, Murray could be trusted. At least one central fixture in the universe stayed in place.

Lauren Bacall grinned at him and Brenda's voice answered, "I called Les's secretary for a lunch appointment and she told me he'd already gone to lunch with you. When he got back, he was kinda smashed. As usual. I dropped into his office before his sober-up pills could grab hold of him. He leered at me and asked how I like cold winters. Which means he approves of your plans."

Sheldon shook his head in reluctant admiration. "You ought to be a detective."

"I ought to be a lot of things," she said, "but I'm not a call girl. I'm not going to Canada."

"But I thought you liked Gabriel."

"Whatever's between Ron and me is between Ron and me. I'm not going to become part of his harem just to suit you."

"It's not me," Sheldon protested. "It's for Titanic."

"Nope," Brenda stole Cooper's line.

"It's for B.F."

She shook her head, but Sheldon thought he noticed the barest little hesitation in her action.

"B.F. wants you to do it," Sheldon pressed the slight opening.

"B.F. doesn't know anything about it yet," Brenda said, "and when he does find out. . . ."

The roar of a powerful motor drowned out her words. Looking around, Sheldon saw that a small boat was racing alongside the ship, not more than twenty meters from the *Adventurer*. The cruise ship had cleared the line of off shore oil rigs and was out of the smog area. The sky above was clear and awash with moonlight. A few very bright stars twinkled here and there.

"That damned fool's going to get himself killed," Sheldon said.

The motorboat was edging closer to the *Adventurer*, churning up a white wake as it cleaved through the ocean swells.

"He's going to sideswipe us!" Brenda shouted. "Do something, Sheldon."

But there was nothing he could do. No emergency phone or fire alarm box in sight along this stretch of plastic-domed deck.

The motorboat disappeared from their view, it was getting so close to the liner. Brenda and Sheldon pressed their noses against the plastic, but they'd have to be able to lean over the railing to see the motorboat now.

They heard a thump.

"Oh my god!" Brenda's voice was strangely high and shrill.

More bumps.

"They must be breaking up against our hull," Sheldon said. He still couldn't think of anything to do about it.

Then something hit against the plastic wall not five meters away from Sheldon's face. He shrieked and leaped backwards.

"Giant squid!" Sheldon shouted.

It did have suction cups on it. But after that first wild flash of panic, he saw that it was a mechanical arm, not a tentacle.

"It looks like a ladder," Brenda said.

His stomach churning, Sheldon said, "I think we'd better get back inside and tell somebody. . . ."

Brenda blocked his way and took hold of his buckskin sleeve. "No. Wait a minute. . . ."

As Sheldon watched, firmly clutched by Brenda, a man's hand appeared on one of the rungs that extended from either side of the mechanical tentacle. A small man in a dark suit came into view. He was wearing a 1920s Fedora pulled down low over his forehead.

"He'll never get through the dome. It's airtight," Sheldon said.

The man ran a hand along the outside of the transparent plastic, seemingly searching for something. Twice he made a sudden grab for his hat, which was flapping wildly in the twenty-knot breeze. His hand finally stopped below the line of the railing, so Sheldon couldn't see what he was doing. But from the action of his shoulder, it looked as if he pushed hard against something. The section of the plastic dome in front of him popped open with a tiny sigh and slid backward. The wind suddenly swirled along the deck.

"Must be an emergency hatch," Brenda murmured.

The man hesitated a moment; then, looking downward, he reached below the level where Sheldon could see. He hauled up a strange-looking object: long and slim at one end, thicker at the other, with a round drum in the middle.

"A Tommygun!" Sheldon realized, in a frightened whisper. "Like they used on the 'Prohibition Blues' show!"

The dark-suited man threw a leg over the rail and clambered onto the deck. He clutched the Tommygun with both hands now, his left arm stretched out almost as far as it could go to reach the front handgrip.

He turned slowly in the shadows along the deck and saw Brenda and Sheldon frozen near the rail.

"Don't make a move," he whispered. In a voice that Sheldon somehow knew.

Leaning over the rail, the dark-suited man called, "Come on up, you guys. It's okay."

Sheldon *knew* that voice. But he couldn't place it. And the hat was still pulled too low over the man's face to recognize him.

"They're going to hijack the ship." Brenda whispered. "Do something!"

Sheldon didn't answer. He was busy staring at the Tommygun.

Two more dark-suited men climbed up to the deck. Each of them carried huge, ugly-looking pistols. Colt .45s, Sheldon realized. Named after the beer commercial.

The first man stepped up to Sheldon and Brenda, shifting the Tommygun to the crook of his arm.

"You dirty rats," he said. "You didn't invite me to your party. So I'm crashing it."

He was close enough to Sheldon to see his face now. And recognize it They were being confronted by Jimmy Cagney.

Behind Cagney stood Allen Jenkins and Frank McHugh, both grinning rather foolishly.

Cagney hitched at his pants with his free hand. "Where's Finger?" he demanded. "I wanna find that rat. He's the guy that gave it to my brother and now I'm gonna give it to him."

The voice finally clicked in Sheldon's memory. It was Ron Gabriel doing his Cagney imitation.

"Ron?" Sheldon asked, a little timidly. "Is that you?"

Cagney's face fell. "You recognized me. Shit. I thought I had you fooled, Sheldon."

"You did. It's a *wonderful* costume."

Brenda said, "That's really you, Ron?"

"Reah . . . who're y . . . Brenda? Wow, you look terrific!"

"Thanks."

"How did you recognize me?" Sheldon wanted to know.

Cagney-Gabriel shrugged with one shoulder. "Gary Cooper. You always use the Cooper costume. Every party."

"Once or twice," said Sheldon, defensively.

"Often enough."

Sheldon started thinking. Not about his costume, but about Gabriel crashing the party. When he thought that Cagney and his henchmen were hijackers or thieves, he had been scared. But the thought of Gabriel coming face to face with B.F. terrified him. *I've got to keep them separated,* he realized.

"Let's go up to the Sky Bar and have a drink," Sheldon said, pointing forward and up.

"I wanna see Finger," Gabriel replied, switching back to his Cagney voice. "I wanna show him my violin." He hefted the Tommygun.

Brenda stepped closer to him and slipped an arm inside Gabriel's arm. "Come on, tough guy," she said, doing Bacall perfectly. "Buy a girl a drink."

Gabriel couldn't resist that. "Okay sweetheart. Umm . . . they got any grapefruit up in that bar?"

"Never mind," Brenda-Bacall said. "You don't need a grapefruit. All you've got to do is whistle."

As the five of them headed down the swaying, rolling deck toward the bar perched atop the ship's bridge, Sheldon thought, *And all I've got to do is keep Brenda with him.*

They took over a corner table in the Sky Bar, ordered drinks and watched the moonlight on the waves. Gabriel parked his Tommygun behind the sofa that they sat on. A blocky-looking computer over by the dancefloor was belting out the new atonal electronic music and flashing its lights in numbered sequence for the dancing couples slinking along: one, two, one-two-three; one, two, one-two three. Every once in a while the computer would throw in an extra beat, just to keep the humans off balance. Most of the dancing couples were heterosexual.

As the waiter brought their drinks, Brenda leaned close enough to Sheldon to whisper in his ear, "Thanks, hero."

He looked askance at her. "For what?"

"For sticking me with. . . ." She made a tiny nod in Gabriel's direction. He was busy watching the dancers and arching his eyebrows at the prettiest of the girls.

"You volunteered," Sheldon protested.

"Sure. When it looked like you were going to faint. You're hiding behind a woman's skirts!"

"You can handle him," Sheldon assured her. "Don't be afraid. . . ."

Brenda was suddenly yanked up from the sofa.

"Come on, kid," said Gabriel-Cagney. "Let's show them how to do it."

He pulled Brenda onto the dancefloor. Sheldon watched them gyrate as he sipped his drink and watched Gabriel's henchmen surreptitiously. They were paying no attention to him; instead, they were ogling a table full of Rita Hayworths, Jill St. Johns and Tina Russells.

Carefully putting his drink down on the table. Sheldon slowly got to his feet. Alan Jenkins gave him a sour look.

"Men's room," Sheldon said. Jenkins shrugged as if to say, *What do I care?*

He edged past the dancefloor, trying not to trip over anybody in his clumsy platform boots. Thankfully, Gabriel's back was to him. But that meant that Brenda was facing him and the look she shot at him was pure venom.

Sheldon mouthed at her, "Relax and enjoy it," and scuttled out of the bar.

He raced down three flights of stairs, clutching madly at the railing to keep from falling. The ship tossed and swayed and the stairs seemed to be trying to deliberately move out from under Sheldon.

But finally he made it to the Main Lounge. B.F. was sitting at a table near the bandstand, surrounded by blondes of all description, from a Pickford to a pair of Monroes. Lassie, believe it or not, was lying on the carpeting at his side.

A George Jessel was on the bandstand singing the Marine Corps Hymn, while George Burns and Jack Benny argued quietly but with great animation, off at the far end of the lounge, over who would go on next.

Sheldon made his way around the outer perimeter of the once-plush Lounge, squirmed through a phalanx of blondes and finally managed to get close enough to Bernard Finger to lean over his shoulder and whisper: "Trouble, B.F."

Finger raised his dimpled chin in Sheldon's direction. "So he sings off key. So did the original Jessel."

"That's not what I mean. Ron Gabriel's crashed the party."

"What?" Finger shouted loud enough to startle Jessel into almost a full bar on-key. "That little snot! Here? Uninvited?"

"What else?" Sheldon said.

"How'd he get here? Where is he? What's he want? Is he hitting anybody?"

If Sheldon weren't convinced that it was impossible, he'd have been tempted to speculate that B.F. was physically frightened of Ron Gabriel.

"He's in the Sky Bar. Brenda's got him in tow. . . ." And suddenly Sheldon realized that this was an opportunity straight out of the blue, a gift from Olympus. He had B.F.'s complete and undivided attention.

He took a quick breath, then suggested, "Maybe we'd better get you to a more protected location, B.F. You know how crazy Gabriel can be."

Finger pushed two blondes aside and stood up. He seemed almost dazed with fear. "Yeah . . . right. . . ."

"And there's a lot about this situation that I have to tell you about," Sheldon went on.

"Okay," Finger said. "Down in my stateroom."

Finger's stateroom was a suite, of course. And it was actually up one deck from the Main Lounge, not down. It wasn't until the steel doors of the luxurious suite were firmly locked behind them that Finger appeared to relax.

"That Gabriel," he muttered. "He's crazy. He hit Lucio Grinaldi once, just for adding two or three songs to one of his scripts."

"That was Gabriel's adaptation of *In Cold Blood,* wasn't it?"

"Yeah." Finger plopped down into an overstuffed chair. "Imagine punching a producer just for turning a show into a musical."

A butler appeared and took their order for drinks. Sheldon sat down. His chair accommodated itself to his body. The air was sweet and cool. The suite was dimly lit, quiet, tasteful, with the kind of silence and comfort that only a lot of money could buy.

"Who're you, anyway?" Finger said suddenly. "You work for me, don't you?"

"I'm Sheldon Fad."

"Oh?" No comprehension whatsoever dawned on Finger's Gary Grant face.

"I'm one of your producers. I did the 'Diet Quiz' show last year."

"Oh, *that* one!" Recognition beamed. "The one that got renewed."

The butler brought the drinks and Sheldon eased into a roundabout explanation of his problems with "The Starcrossed." How it was Gabriel's idea and the untrusting fink had immediately registered it with the Screen Writers Guild. How he, Sheldon, had hit on the money-saving idea of taking the show to Canada for production. (B.F. smiled again at that; Sheldon's heart did a flip-flop.) How Gabriel wanted Brenda as a hostage or harem girl.

"Probably both," Finger grunted.

Sheldon nodded and pressed on. He told Finger that only Brenda's body stood between him and a face-to-face confrontation with Gabriel.

"And he's carrying a Tommygun," Sheldon concluded.

"Now? Here?"

Sheldon nodded. "I think it's going to be very vital to us to have Brenda go with us to Canada."

"You're damned right," B.F. agreed.

"But she doesn't want to go."

"She'll go."

"I'm not sure. . . ."

"Don't worry about it. What I tell her to do, she does."

"She might quit."

B.F. shook his head, a knowing smile on his lips. Somehow, it didn't look pleasant. "She won't quit. She can't. She'll do what I tell her, no matter what it is."

b: The Confrontation

Ron Gabriel sipped a gingerale as he sat at one of the Sky Bar's tiny round tables. Brenda Impanema sat on the couch beside him, staring moodily out at the moonlit ocean. On his other side, Allen Jenkins and Frank McHugh were playing poker on a little table of their own.

The crowd in the bar had thinned considerably. Many couples had drifted outside, now that the ship was clear of the L.A. smog and the moon could be seen. Others had gone down to their staterooms for some serious sexual therapy.

"It's like a movie scene," Brenda said, reaching for her Hawaiian Punch. "Moonlight on the water, the ship plowing through the waves, romantic music. . . ."

Gabriel scowled at the computer, which was now issuing a late 1970s rotrock wail. "Call that romantic?"

Brenda, still in Lauren Bacall's looks, made a small shrug. "It could be romantic."

"If it was different music."

"Right."

"Then all you'd need would be Fred Astaire tapdancing out on the deck."

"And sweeping me off my feet."

Gabriel looked in the mirror across the room and saw Jimmy Cagney. But he no longer felt like Cagney. *I should have come as Astaire,* he told himself. But Cagney fitted his personality better, he knew.

"How come I can't sweep you off your feet?" he asked Brenda.

Bacall grinned back at him. "It's chemistry. We just don't react right."

"I'm crazy about you."

"You're crazy about every girl you meet. And I don't want to go to Canada with you."

Gabriel remembered why he had come aboard. He picked up his glass of gingerale. In the mirror, Cagney's face hardened.

"I don't want to go to Canada at all. Period."

"We can drink to that." Brenda touched her glass to Gabriel's.

Cagney scowled.

She tossed her head slightly, so that the long sweep of her hair flowed back over her bare shoulder. "Are you really after me or just my body? Or just a grip on B.F.?"

"That's a helluva question," he said.

"It's of more than passing interest to me."

Gabriel put his glass down firmly on the tabletop. Without looking up from it, he said, "I'm crazy about you. I don't know anything about your body. I've seen it clothed and it looks pretty good. But more than that I can't tell. And I don't go after girls for business reasons." He looked up at her. "What I have to settle with Finger I'll settle for myself. And it's time that I did."

Brenda put a hand on his arm. "If you confront B.F. you'll blow the whole series. He'll have you kicked off the ship and out of any connection with Titanic."

"So I'll take the idea someplace else. I don't need Titanic. He needs me."

"He'll make life miserable for you."

Gabriel pulled his arm free of her. With a light tap on her cheek, he went back to pure Cagney. "Don't you worry about me, kid. I know how to handle myself."

To his cronies, who looked up from their cardgame, Gabriel said, "Keep her out of trouble."

They nodded. Both unemployed, nonselling young writers, they were looking forward to script assignments on the series. If they could avoid starvation long enough to wait for the series to go into production. At the moment they were avoiding starvation—and work—by living in Gabriel's house.

The rest home for starveling writers, Gabriel thought as he made his way around the dancefloor and toward the Sky Bar's exit. But he remembered his own beginning years, the struggle and the hollow-gutted days of hunger. Somehow he seemed to have more fun in those days than he did now. *Shit! You'd think there'd be a time when a guy could relax and enjoy himself.*

He reached the exit and gave a final glance back. Jenkins and McHugh had resumed their cardgame. Bacall had moved closer to them and started kibbitzing.

Gabriel hitched up his pants and made a Cagney grimace. "Okay, Schemer," he whispered to himself. "Here's where you get yours."

It took a while for Gabriel to figure out where Finger had gone. He searched the Main Lounge, the pool area and all the bars before realizing that Finger must have retreated to his private suite.

Theoretically, the suite was impregnable. Only one entrance, through double-locked steel watertight doors. Nobody in or out without Finger's TV surveillance system scanning him. Gabriel considered knocking off one of the fire alarms, but rejected that idea. People might get hurt or even jump overboard and drown. Besides, Finger had his own motor launch just outside the emergency hatch of his suite. That much Gabriel knew from studying the ship's plans.

For a few moments he considered scrambling over the ship's rail and down the outer hull to get to the emergency hatch. But then he realized that there would still be no way for him to get inside.

With a frown of frustration, Gabriel paced down the ship's central staircase, thinking hard but coming up with no ideas.

He stopped on the deck where the ship's restaurant was. Looking inside the elaborately decorated cafeteria, where the walls and even the ceiling were plastered with photos from Titanic's myriad TV shows—all off the air now—Gabriel started on a chain of reasoning.

It was a short chain; the last link said that there must be some connection between the ship's galley, where the food was prepared, and Finger's suite on the deck above.

Gabriel made his way through the restaurant-turned-cafeteria, heading for the galley. A few couples and several singles were scroffing food hastily, as if they expected someone to tap them on the shoulder and put them off the ship. Gabriel noticed almost subliminally that they weren't the young hungry actors or writers or office workers; they were the older, middle-aged ones. The kind who dreaded the inevitable day when they were turned out to the *dolce vita* of forced retirement on fixed pensions and escalating cost of living.

Move up or move out, was the motto at Titanic and most other business establishments. The gold watch for a lifetime of service was a thing of ancient history. Nobody lasted that long unless they owned the company or were indispensable to it.

Gabriel walked like Cagney through the cafeteria: shoulders slightly forward, bouncing on the balls of his feet. He entered the galley, where a couple of cooks were loafing around a TV set.

"Hey, whatcha doin' back here?" one of them asked, a black tall enough for college basketball.

"City Health Inspector," Gabriel replied in his own voice.

The cook towered over Gabriel and waved a frozen dinner-sized fist at him. "What is this? We paid you guys off last week, on your regular collection day."

Gabriel shook his head. "Those guys are in jail. There's been a crackdown. Didn't anybody tell you?"

The cook's face fell.

"I ought to get your name and number," Gabriel bluffed, "so that you can be subpoenaed. . . ."

Hie other cooks had already backed away into the shadows. "Hey wait . . ." The black man's voice softened.

Gabriel put on a smile. "Look, I don't want to make trouble for you guys. I got a job to do, that's all. Now, how many exits are there from this area . . . for emergency purposes. . . ."

Within seconds, Gabriel was riding alone up the tiny service elevator to the kitchen of Finger's suite.

The door slid open silently and he stepped into the darkened kitchen. He stopped there, waiting for his eyes to adjust to the darkness so he could move without bumping into anything. He heard voices from another room.

". . . and according to the computer analysis, doing the show in Canada will save us a bundle of money." Sheldon Fad's singsong.

"Whadda' the Canadians know about making a dramatic series? All they do is documentaries about Eskimos." The dulcet tones of Bernard Finger, part foghorn and part fishmonger.

"They have commercial networks in Canada," Fad replied, dripping with honey.

"You seen any of their shows?"

"Well. . . ."

"They stink! They're even worse than ours."

Gabriel smiled in the darkness, uncertain whether Finger's "ours" referred to all of American commercial TV or merely to Titanic's steady string of fiascos.

"But we'll be using our own top staff to run things. The Canadians will be working under our supervision."

"And the writing? We're going to put up with Ron Gabriel? That loudmouth?"

"We'll handle him," Fad answered. "He'll be the top writer, but the scripts will actually be turned out by Canadians. They work cheaper and they listen to what you tell them."

Gabriel's smile faded. He started moving carefully toward the voices. As he got out of the kitchen and into what looked like a dining area, he could see a doorway framed in light; the door was closed, but light from the next room was seeping through the poor fit between the door and its jamb.

"I've even got a start on the theme music," Fad was saying, with more than the usual amount of oil in his voice. "It's from Tchaikovsky. . . ."

Fad must have worked the computer terminal, because the opening strains of the *Romeo and Juliet Overture* wafted into the suite. Finger must have reached the volume control, because the music was immediately turned down to a barely audible hum.

"Now about the production values. . . ." Fad began.

Gabriel kicked the door open and strode into the living room, chin tucked down in his collar, right fist balled in his jacket pocket as if he had a gun.

Fad was standing beside the computer terminal, at one end of a long sofa. Finger was sitting on the sofa. He was so startled that he dropped the glass he'd been holding. Fad jumped back two steps, a frightened Gary Cooper, so scared that the fringes of his buckskin jacket were twitching.

"Okay you guys," Gabriel said, in his Cagney voice.

"Who the hell are you?" Finger demanded.

"Never mind that." Gabriel walked slowly toward the sofa.

Backing away from him, Fad squeaked, "Is that a gun in your pocket?"

"Does a bear shit in the woods?"

"What're you doing here?" Finger asked. His voice cracked just the tiniest bit.

"You guys have been making life tough for Ron Gabriel. Now I'm going to give you what's coming to you."

Fad looked as if he was going to collapse. But Finger stared intently at Cagney's face.

"Gabriel," he said. "Is that you?"

"Who else, buhbula?" Ron took his hand from his pocket and scratched his nose. "Now what's all this shit about going to Canada?"

"The show's going to be shot in Canada," Finger said testily. "*If* I decide to do the show, that is. And how the hell did you get in here?"

"Whattaya mean, if you decide to do it?" Gabriel shot back. "It's the best damned idea you've seen in years."

"Ideas don't make successful shows. People do."

"Which explains why you've got a string of flops on your hands."

"Goddammit Gabriel!" Finger's voice rose. "I'm not going to take any of your crap!"

"Go stuff yourself with it, bigshot! I'm a creative artist. I don't need your greasy paws on my ideas!"

Fad edged around the sofa and tried to interpose himself between the two men. "Now wait, fellas. Let's not. . . ."

"Where the hell's the phone?" Finger turned as he sat, searching the room. "I'll get the security guards up here so fast. . . ."

"You reach for that phone and I'll break your arm," Gabriel warned. "You're going to listen to me for a change."

"I'm gonna get you thrown overboard, is what I'm gonna do!"

"The hell you are!"

"Fellaaas . . . be reasonable."

"Loudmouth creep."

"Moneygrubbing asshole!"

"Fellaaas. . . ."

It was a cosmic coincidence that at precisely that moment the love theme from *Romeo and Juliet* started on the computer-directed stereo. Such moments are rare, but they happen.

And precisely at that moment, the most exquisitely beautiful girl Gabriel had ever seen stepped sleepily into the living room, rubbing her eyes. She wore nothing but a whiff of a pink nightgown, barely long enough to reach to her thighs and utterly transparent. Her long golden hair was sleep tousled. Her face was all childish innocence, especially the sky-blue eyes, although her mouth was sensuous. Her body had everything the eternal woman possessed: the litheness of youth combined with the soft fullness of newly ripened maturity.

"What's all the shouting about?" she asked in a little girl voice. Petulantly: "You woke me up."

Finger scowled mightily and got up from the sofa. "See what you've done?" he grumbled at Gabriel. "You woke her up!" To the girl/woman he said soothingly, "It's all right, baby. We were just having a discussion. I'll be back with you in a few minutes. You just go back to sleep."

Gabriel remained rooted to the spot where he was standing. He couldn't move. He couldn't breathe. His blood seemed congealed in his veins. It was like being petrified, mummified, frozen into a cryogenic block of liquid helium. Yet his brain was whirling, feverish, spinning like a Fourth of July pinwheel shooting off sparks in every direction.

She made a little *moue* with her full, ripe lips and turned to head back to the bedroom.

"Wait!" Gabriel's voice sounded strained and desperate, even to himself.

She stopped and looked back at him, with those incredible blue eyes.

"Wha . . . I mean . . . who . . . what's your name? Who are you?"

"Never mind!" Finger urged the girl toward the bedroom with an impatient gesture.

"No, wait!" Gabriel shouted. He unfroze himself and moved toward her. "What's your name? I've got to know!"

"Rita," she said, almost shyly. "Rita Yearling. Why do you hafta know?"

"Because I'm in love with you," answered Gabriel, with absolute honesty.

7: The Agreement

Bernard Finger was not the kind of narrow-minded man to let his personal life interfere with business.

"Go on back to bed, Rita," he said in as fatherly a tone as he could produce.

She blinked once in Gabriel's direction. Finger could see the effect her long lashes had on the writer: the Cagney makeup seemed to be melting and Gabriel shuddered violently.

"Goodnight," she breathed.

Gabriel watched her go back into the bedroom. To Finger, he looked like a puppy watching its master take a train to Australia. Gabriel was no longer a free-swinging, independent, irreverent sonofabitch. He wanted something that Finger possessed. That was a basis for doing business.

"Ron," he said, as the bedroom door closed behind Rita Yearling.

Gabriel stared at the door. His eyes seemed to be unfocused.

"Ron!" Finger called more sharply.

The writer shook himself, as if suddenly awakening from an incredible dream.

"Who is she?" Gabriel asked. "Where did you find her?" Finger indicated the sofa with a gesture and Gabriel obediently sat down.

Pulling a chair close to him, Finger said to Fad, "Get us some brandy and cigars." The producer nodded once, briskly, and went to the phone.

"I've never seen anyone like her." Gabriel's voice was still awestruck. "Who is she?"

"Titanic's always searching for fresh talent," Finger said. "We have scouts everywhere. But we found Rita right here in L.A.; right under our noses." It was even the truth, Finger realized with an inward laugh. "She's fantastic!"

Fad sat at the end of the sofa, close enough to be included in the conversation if Finger so chose, yet far enough away so that he could continue a private-seeming talk with Gabriel. *Kid's got some good sense,* Finger noted. "What would you say," Finger asked Gabriel, "if I told you that Rita is one of the most accomplished actresses I've ever seen?"

"Who cares?" Gabriel said.

With a knowing grin, Finger added, "What would you say if I told you that I'm considering her for the female lead in 'The Starcrossed'?"

Gabriel actually gulped. Finger could see his Adam's Apple bob up and down. To a lesser man, what was about to happen would seem like taking milk away from an infant; but Bernard Finger was equal to the situation. False scruples had never interfered with his business acumen—nor true scruples, for that matter.

"I think she's a natural for the part," Finger went on, enjoying the perspiration that was breaking out on Gabriel's Cagneyish face. "She's got looks, talent, exper . . . eh, youth."

"The show couldn't miss with her in it," Fad chimed in.

"Yeah," said Gabriel.

Finger slapped his palms on his thighs, a sharp cracking sound that startled the other two men. "Listen," he said. "Let's let bygones be bygones. I know you and I have had our differences in the past, Ron. But let's work together to make 'The Starcrossed' a big hit. Titanic needs a hit and you need a hit. So let's work together, instead of against each other."

Gabriel nodded. He still seemed to be stunned. "Okay," he mumbled.

Looking over at Fad, Finger said: "Our producer's come up with the idea of doing the show in Canada. It'll let us stretch our money further. What we save in production costs we can add to production values: better sets, better scripts, better talent. . . ."

Gabriel was visibly trying to pull himself together, get his brain back in gear.

"This is going to be an expensive show to produce. Starships and exotic planets every week . . . expensive sets, expensive props, big-name guest stars every week . . . it's all very expensive."

"And costly," Fad echoed. Finger shot him down with a sharp glance.

Gabriel frowned. "Artistic control."

"What about it?"

"I want artistic control," Gabriel said. He was returning to the real world. "This show has got to have one strong conceptual vision, a consistent point of view . . . we can't have directors and assistant producers and script girls screwing things around from one week to the next."

Finger was too experienced to give in immediately, but after fifteen minutes of discussion, he had his arm around Gabriel's shoulders as they walked together toward the door.

"You've convinced me," Finger was saying expansively. "When you're right, you're right. Artistic control will be in your hands. One guy has got to keep the central vision of the show consistent from week to week. That's important."

"And it'll be written into my contract," Gabriel said warily.

"Of course! Everything down in black and white so there's no misunderstanding."

They shook hands at the door. Gabriel still looked uneasy, almost suspicious. Finger had his friendliest smile on.

"My agent will get in touch with you tomorrow," Gabriel said.

"Who you got . . . still Jerry Morgan?"

"Yeah."

"Good man, we'll work out the clauses with no trouble."

Gabriel left and Finger closed the door firmly. Fad was standing in the middle of the living room, shaking his head. He looked like Gary Cooper with an ulcer.

"What's the matter?"

"You let him have artistic control of the series! He'll want to do everything *his* way! The expense. . . ."

Finger raised a calming hand. "Listen. Right now he's on the other side of that door, going through his pockets to see what I stole

from him. And he won't find a thing missing. Tonight he'll have wet
dreams about Rita and tomorrow morning he'll phone Jerry Morgan
and tell him to be sure to get a clause about artistic control into his
contract."

"But we can't. . . ."

"Who gives a damn about artistic control?" Finger laughed at
the perplexed producer. "There's a million ways to get around
such a clause. We'll have clauses in there about financial limits and
decisions, clauses that tie him up six ways from Sunday. And even in
his artistic control clause we'll throw in the line about no holding up
production with unreasonable demands. Ever see anybody win a
lawsuit by proving his demands were not unreasonable? We got him
by the balls and he won't know it until we go into production."

"In Canada?"

"In Canada."

Sheldon's worried-hound face relaxed a little.

Someone tapped timidly at the door. Finger yanked it open. A
waiter stood there, bearing a tray with three snifters of brandy and
three cigars on it.

"S . . . sorry to take so long, Mr. Finger. Your special cigars were
in the vault and. . . ."

"Nah, don't worry about it." Finger ushered him in with a sweeping gesture of his arm. "It's good timing. I'd hate to waste a good
cigar on that little punk."

It was dawn.

Finger sat on the edge of his bed and gazed down at Rita Yearling.
Even under the bedclothes she looked incredibly beautiful.

Best money I ever spent, he told himself.

Her lovely eyelids fluttered and she awoke languorously. She
smiled at Finger, stretched like a cat, then turned and looked out the
porthole at the gray-white sky.

"Ain't it kinda early?"

"I want to go up to the bridge and see the sunrise over the mountains. We're almost back in port."

"Oh."

"How're you feeling?"

She stretched again. "Fine. Not an ache or pain anywhere."

He stroked her bare shoulder. "They did a beautiful job on you. When I had my Vitaform operations I was in agony for months."

"You didn't take good care of your original body," she chided, almost like Shirley Temple bawling out Wallace Beery. "I may have been older than you, but I took care of myself. The girls always said I had the best-kept body since Ann Corio."

"What about Mae West?" he joked.

"That hag!" Rita's luscious lips pulled back in a snarl, revealing slightly pointed teeth. "Her and her deepfreeze. As if anybody'd revive her in a hundred years."

Patting her in a fatherly way, Finger said, "I'm going to get dressed. I'll call you in an hour or so. We can have breakfast up on the bridge."

"Okay." She turned over and pulled up the covers.

"I want to talk to you about Ron Gabriel. He's going to be the head writer on the show, up in Canada."

"He's the Cagney that was in here last night?"

"Right. He can be troublesome. . . ."

She smiled at him; there was no innocent little girl in her face. "I can handle him and a dozen more like him, any time." Her tongue flicked across her sharp little teeth. "Any time," she repeated.

It was bracing up on the bridge. The sea breeze stirred Finger, invigorated him. Up ahead he could see the smog bank that marked the beginning of Los Angeles' territorial waters and the oil rigs that kept the city supplied with fuel.

He paced the open deck of the flying bridge, glancing inside now and then to see how the ship was being handled. A solitary officer slouched lazily in a soft chair, toking happily, while the automated radar, sonar, robot pilot and computer steered the *Adventurer* toward its smog-shrouded pier.

It always unnerved Finger just the slightest bit to realize that the ship's crew was more machine than human. And with the exception of the captain, who was a boozer, most of the crewmen were heads.

Finger turned his back on the lazing officer and stepped to the rail. Leaning over it slightly, he could see the white foam of the ship's wake cutting through the oily waters. He looked up at his last glimpse of blue sky. Gripping the rail with both hands, he was suddenly on the deck of a whaling vessel out of New Bedford, an iron captain running a wooden ship.

Thar she blows! he heard in his mind's inner ear. And with the eye of imagination he saw a wild and stormy ocean, with the spout of a gigantic whale off near the white-capped horizon.

After him, me hearties! Finger shouted silently. *A five-dollar gold piece to the boat that harpoons him!*

He grunted to himself. Maybe a whaling show would make a good series. The econuts would object to it, but they object to everything anyway. Special effects would be expensive: have to make a dummy whale. Nobody's seen a whale since the last Japanese expedition came back empty. Even the dolphins are getting scarce.

A frown of concentration settled on his face. The government would probably help with a series like that. They're always looking for outdoor stuff, so people will stay home and watch their three-dees instead of messing up the National Parks. And it could be a spectacular show—storms, shipwrecks, all that stuff. Got to be careful of the violence, though; get those parents and teachers on your neck and the sponsors disappear. Maybe a comedy show, with a crew that never catches a whale. A bunch of schmucks.

No. Finger shook his head. *A serious show. Iron men in wooden ships. Give the viewers some heroes to admire.* He squared his shoulders and faced straight into the wind. *Maybe I could do a sneak part in it, like Hitchcock used to do.*

He drew himself up to his full height. *Hell,* he told himself, *I could be the whaling ship's captain. Why not? I've got the look for it now.*

Why not do a whaling show instead of this science fiction thing with Gabriel?

Because, his business sense told him, it would be too realistic. Historicals are dead. Nobody watched them. The Hallmark Hall of Fame killed them years ago and nobody's had the guts to try them again. Too dull. And too realistic.

Still, he thought, it'll be good to have something like this in reserve. Doesn't have to be realistic or even historical. Maybe a science fiction whaler, on another planet. *Yeah!* With a different monster every week! He smiled; felt almost giddy. *Bernie,* he told himself, *you're a genius.* He made a mental note to look into the possibility of taking acting lessons. In secret. Like that football player for the Jets had done.

And then the *real* idea hit him. It came in a flash, the whole of it, so completely detailed that he saw the columns of figures adding up to a fortune, nine digits worth. It was blinding. Terrifying. He sagged against the rail.

"That's it," he whispered to himself. "That'll do it! But it's got to be done in secret." He squeezed his eyes shut and locked the secret deep within his convoluted brain.

"You looking for me?"

Finger whirled, startled, and saw Brenda Impanema standing at the hatch that led inside to the bridge. She was out of costume now, wearing a comfortable kaftan that billowed in the breeze against her lean figure.

"I got a phone message from the computer that said you wanted to see me," Brenda said.

Gathering himself together, Finger grumbled, "That was last night."

"Gabriel's two goons wouldn't let me out of the bar until you two had finished your business talk," she said. "By the time I got to my stateroom and saw the message, I figured you were asleep . . . or at least in bed."

From someone else, Finger would have taken that for insolence. But from Brenda—he smiled.

"You were right. Smart girl." Then he looked sharply at her. She seemed weary, red eyed. "You didn't sleep good?"

"Not very."

"Who were you with?"

"Nobody," she said.

Finger considered the pros and cons for a moment. His ultimate, secret new idea glowed within him like a warming beacon. "Gabriel and I came to an agreement last night. We're going to do the show up in Canada. Les will check on the available studios up there. The talent office will start looking for a suitable male lead this morning."

"What about the female lead?"

"Rita Yearling."

Brenda's mouth went tight.

"Nobody's going to find out about her previous life. That's why I've got a publicity department, to keep things quiet."

"Sure," Brenda said.

"So you don't like her," Finger said. "That's too bad."

Brenda looked away from him and let the salt wind blow at her hair. "No problem for me. I'm not going to have to work with her."

Taking a step closer to her, Finger said, "I still want you to go to Canada and keep an eye on things for me."

"You mean service Ron Gabriel."

"No. He's seen Rita and he's gone crazy over her. She'll keep him busy enough."

"You don't know Ron." Still looking away from Finger, she said, "I don't want to go."

"You're going!"

"I don't want to!"

"You'll do what I tell you. That's all there is to it."

"Thanks."

"I wouldn't send you up there if Gabriel was going to make things tough for you. You know that."

"Like hell."

She still wouldn't look at him. Feeling hurt, Finger said, "It's for the good of the show. There'll be a promotion in it for you."

"Wonderful," Brenda said. "But I'd rather jump over the rail."

He could feel his face getting red with anger. "So jump already!" he snapped and stamped off to the hatch.

8: The Team

It was spring in Southern California. The rains had finally stopped and for a few weeks everything was green and flowering. As long as it was domed over or otherwise protected from the smog.

Bill Oxnard's Holovision Laboratory was perched high enough on a Malibu hillside to be out of the usual smog banks, although when there was inversion the tinted clouds crept up and engulfed even the highest of the hills. But at the moment it was a beautiful spring day. Oxnard could lean back in his desk chair and see the surfers 'way down on the beach, in their colorful anticorrosion suits and motorized surfboards. In a few weeks—or perhaps days—he'd see the gardeners painting the lawns green and starting to worry about brush fires again. But for the moment, everything was beautiful.

His phone buzzed. He clicked it on and his secretary's grand-motherly face appeared on the screen.

"Ms. Impanema's here," she said.

Oxnard couldn't keep himself from grinning. "Send her right in."

Maybe she's the reason why I feel . . . he tried to identify exactly what it was that he did feel, and could only come up with a lame . . . *happy.*

Brenda strode into his office: tall, leggy, brightly dressed in a flowered slit-skirt sari that was becoming the hit of the new Oriental decorative style. Oxnard himself still wore his regular business clothes: an engineer's zipsuit of plain orange.

"Hope I'm not late," she said, smiling at him.

Oxnard came around the desk and took her hand. "No. Right on the tick. Here, have a seat. How's everything in Toronto? Have you eaten? Want some coffee or something?"

She took the chair and let the heavy-looking handbag she was carrying clunk to the floor. "A Bloody Mary, if you can produce one. I haven't had any breakfast. The damned airline didn't serve anything *again*. It's getting to be a regular scrooging with them."

Leaning over his desk to get at the phone, Oxnard called, "May . . . . can you dig up two Bloody Marys and some breakfast?"

His secretary's face showed that she clearly disapproved of drinking on company time. But after all, it *was* his company. She nodded and switched off.

"So what's happening in Toronto?" Oxnard asked as he went back around the desk and sat down. For some reason he felt that he needed the desk between them.

"Everything's in a whirl," Brenda replied. "Let's see . . . when's the last time we talked?"

"A week after you first went up there. Ron hadn't gone yet; he was still here."

She nodded. "Right . . . that was the flight where they didn't serve any dinner. 'Sorry to inconvenience you,' she whined nasally, 'but the food service on this flight has been rendered inoperative due to a malfunctioning of the ground-based portion of our logistical system.' Fancy way of saying they didn't stash any food aboard the plane."

They chatted easily for a while. May brought in a pair of drinks in plastic cups and a tray of real eggs and imitation bacon from the cafeteria. Brenda wolfed down everything hungrily. Oxnard answered a couple of routine phone calls while she ate, then told his secretary to hold all calls and visits.

"So what's happening in Toronto?" he asked again as she finished the last crumbs of her English muffin.

"Everything," Brenda said between dabs at her lips with a paper napkin. "It's wild."

"Ron's there? The scripts are being written?"

"Well. . . ." she cocked her head slightly to one side, as if waiting for the right words to come out of the air. "He's there . . . and there's a lot of writing being done. The production team is starting to put the sets together. . . ."

"But?"

Brenda's smile turned a little desperate. "Wasn't it you who told me about Murphy's Law?"

He grinned. "If anything can go wrong with an experiment, it will."

"Right. Well, that's what's happening in Toronto."

"That's too bad."

"It's worse than that. The show might never get on the air. All sorts of troubles have hit us."

Oxnard shook his head sympathetically. "Everything's going smoothly on this end. The new transmitters and cameras have tested out fine. We'll be ready to ship them up to Toronto right on schedule. And I've got some new ideas, too, about . . . well. . . ." Oxnard let his voice trail off. *She's got enough problems without listening to my untested brainstorms.*

"Will you be coming up to Toronto with the equipment?" Brenda asked.

"No need to," said Oxnard.

"But I thought. . . ."

"Oh, we'll send a couple of technicians along. I wouldn't dump the equipment on you without somebody to show your crew how to work it . . ."

"I know," she said. "But I thought you would come up yourself."

For some reason, Oxnard's insides went fluttery.

"I'd like to," he said quickly. "But I can't leave the lab here . . . I'm not just an executive, you know. I *work* here; the rest of the staff depends on me."

Brenda nodded and looked distressed. "Bill . . . I wouldn't want you to hurt your own company, of course. But we *need* you in Toronto. Ron needs you. He's being driven crazy up there, trying to whip the scripts into shape and handle the technical details of building the sets and working out the special effects and a million other things. I've tried to help him all I can, but you're the one he needs. You've got the scientific know-how. Nobody else up there knows *anything. . . .*"

He refused, of course. He explained to her, very carefully, how his laboratory operated and how much he was needed for day-by-day, hour-by-hour decisions. He took her down to the labs and shop, showed her what a small, tightly integrated group he had. He

explained to her over and over that these men and women didn't
work *for* him, they worked *with* him. And he worked with them.
Every day; ten, twelve hours per day.

He explained it all morning. He explained it over lunch. He took
the afternoon off and drove her down the coast so that they could be
alone and away from phones and business conferences while he
explained it thoroughly. He explained it over dinner at a candlelit
table looking out at the surf, not far from La Jolla.

He wanted to explain it to her in bed, in one of those plush La
Jolla hotels, but at the last minute he lost his nerve. Brenda nodded
and smiled and accepted everything he said without argument. But
she kept repeating that Ron Gabriel, and the whole show, was in dire
trouble and needed *him*. Now. In Toronto. And he kept getting the
unspoken message from her that she needed him. Not that she
promised anything or even hinted at it. But Oxnard realized that if
he helped the show, helped Gabriel and Finger and Montpelier, he
would be helping her.

And Bill Oxnard found that more than anything else in the world,
he wanted to help her.

So he drove her back to the airport and agreed that he would join
her in Toronto.

"Only for the weekend," he said. "I really can't stay away from the
lab during regular working days."

"I know," she answered, as they hurried down the terminal
corridor toward her flight's loading gate.

They made it to the gate with half a minute to spare. Brenda
turned to him, breathless from running, while the gate computer
examined her ticket and the overhead sensors scanned them both for
everything from contraband lemons to plastic explosives.

"I really appreciate it, Bill. I'll set you up with a hotel room and
try to make your weekend comfortable. Thanks for a fun day!"

He stood there tonguetied, trying to think of an appropriate
answer: something witty, maybe poetic.

The computer's scratchy voice upstaged him: "Final boarding for
Flight 68. Final boarding."

She reached up on tiptoes and kissed him lightly on the cheek.
Oxnard stood there grinning like a schoolboy as she scampered
through the doorway of the access tunnel that led to the plane.

Two nights later, on Friday, he followed her.

The studio was impressive.

It was huge, about the size of a modern jetliner hangar, Oxnard realized. But it looked even bigger because it was almost completely empty. The bare skeleton of its wall bracings and rows of rafter-mounted old-fashioned spotlights looked down on a bare wooden floor.

"You won't need all those lights," Oxnard said to his guide. "With laser holography, you can. . . ."

"We know all about it," said Gregory Earnest. He was small and wiry, with thickly curled dark hair and beard that hid most of his face, so that Oxnard couldn't see that he looked like one of Canada's most numerous residents—a weasel. "We're just as modern and up-to-date as you Yanks, you know."

Oxnard completely missed the edge to Earnest's voice. They continued their tour of Badger Studios, with Earnest proudly showing off his company's shops, equipment and personnel—most of them idle.

They ended in the model shop, where a half dozen intense young men and women were putting together a four-meter-long plastic model. It lay along a table that was too short for it, overlapping both ends. To Oxnard it looked something like a beached whale in an advanced stage of decomposition.

"The latest and most modern modeling techniques," Earnest told Oxnard. "Straight from Korea. No second-rate stuff around here."

"I see," Oxnard said.

"Americans always think that we Canadians are behind the times," Earnest said. "But we've learned to survive in spite of Yankee chauvinism. Like the flea and the elephant." His voice had an irritating nasal twang to it.

Oxnard replied with something like "Uh-huh."

His main interest was focused on the modeling team. They were buzzing around the long cylindrical model that rested on the chest-high worktable. They had a regular bucket brigade system going: two girls were taking tiny plastic pieces from their packing boxes and using whirring electrical buffers to erase the Korean symbols painted on them. Another woman and one of the men took the clean pieces and dabbed banana-smelling plastic glue on them.

Then the remaining two men took the pieces, walked around the model slowly and stuck pieces onto the main body.

At random, apparently, thought Oxnard.

"Hand craftsmanship," exuded Earnest. "The mark of true art."

Still watching the team at work, Oxnard asked, "What's it supposed to be?"

"The model? It's one of the starships! For the series, of course."

"Why does it have fins on it?"

"Huh? What do you mean?"

Ignoring the business-suited executive, Oxnard stepped between the two gluers and asked one of the stickers:

"What're you using for a blueprint?"

The youth blinked at him several times. "Blueprint? We don't have no blueprint."

One of the young women said with a slightly French sneer, "This is artistry, not engineering."

Oxnard scratched at his nose. The banana smell made him want to sneeze. "Yes," he said mildly. "But this model is supposed to be a starship, right? It never flies in a planet's atmosphere . . . it stays out in space all the time. It doesn't need aerodynamic fins."

"But it looks smash-o with the fins!" said one of the other young men.

"It looks like something out of the Nineteen Fifties," Oxnard replied, surprised at the sudden loudness of his own voice. "And out of Detroit, at that!"

"Now wait a moment," Earnest said, from well outside the ring of workers. "You can't tell these people how to do their jobs. . . ."

Oxnard asked, "Why? Union rules?"

"Union?"

"We don't have trade unions."

"Lord, that's *archaic*!"

Earnest smiled patiently. "Trade unions were disbanded in Canada years ago. That's one of the many areas where our society is far ahead of the States."

Shaking his head, Oxnard said, "All right. But a starship can't have wings and fins on it. What it does need is radiative surfaces. You can change those fins from an aerodynamic shape. . . ."

They listened to him with hostile, sullen countenances. Earnest folded his arms across his chest and smiled, like an indulgent uncle who would rather let his oddball nephew make an ass of himself than argue with him. Oxnard tried to explain some of the rationale of an interstellar vehicle and when he saw that it wasn't penetrating, he asked the crew if they'd ever seen photos of spacecraft or satellites. "They don't look like airplanes, do they?"

They agreed to that, reluctantly, and Oxnard had to settle for a moral victory.

For the time being, he thought.

When Earnest showed him the set they were constructing for the bridge of the starship, it was the same battle all over again. But this time it was with Earnest himself, since the carpenters and other contractors were nowhere in sight.

"But this looks like the bridge of a ship . . . an ocean liner!" Oxnard protested.

Earnest nodded. "It's been built to Mr. Finger's exact specifications. It's a replica of the bridge on his ship, the *Adventurer.*"

Oxnard puffed out an exasperated breath. "But a starship doesn't sail in the ocean! It wouldn't have a steering wheel and a compass for godsake!"

"It's what Mr. Finger wants."

"But it's *wrong!*"

Earnest smiled his patient, infuriating smile. "We're accustomed to you Yanks coming here and finding fault with everything we Canadians do."

And no matter what Oxnard said, the Badger Studios executive dismissed it as Yankee imperialism.

Brenda met him for lunch and drove out to one of the hotel restaurants, away from the studio cafeteria.

"I'm beginning to see what you're up against," Oxnard told her. "They're all going every which way with no direction, no idea of what the show needs."

"That's right," Brenda agreed.

"But where's Ron? Why isn't he straightening this out? He knows better. . . ."

"After lunch," Brenda said, "I'll take you to Ron's place . . . if the guards let us through, that is."

She wasn't kidding.

Two uniformed security police flanked the door of Gabriel's hotel suite. One of them recognized Brenda, asked her about Oxnard, then reluctantly let them both through.

The foyer of the suite looked normal enough, although there was an obviously broken typewriter on the floor next to the door. Its lid was open and it looked as if someone had stomped on its innards in a rage of frustration.

The sitting room was a mess. Wadded up sheets of paper were strewn everywhere, ankle deep. The sofas and chairs were covered with paper. The chandelier was piled high with it. The paper crackled and scrunched underfoot as they walked into the room. Invisible beneath the wads lay a luxurious carpet. Two more typewriters sat on two separate desks, near the windows. A huge pile of papers loomed over one of the typewriters.

"Ron?" called Brenda.

No answer.

She looked into the bedroom on the right, as Oxnard stood in the middle of the paper sea feeling rather stunned.

"Ron?" Brenda called again.

With a worried expression on her face, she waded through the litter and went into the other bedroom.

"Ron?" Her voice sounded panicky now.

Oxnard went into the bedroom after her. The double bed was rumpled. Drawers were hanging out of the dresser. The TV—a flat, two-dimensional set—was on and babbling some midday women's show.

The window was open.

"My god, he escaped!" Brenda shouted. "Or jumped!"

She ran to the window and peered down.

Oxnard pushed open the door to the bathroom. The floor was wet. Towels were hanging neatly beside the tub. The shower screen was closed.

Almost as if he were a detective in a mystery show, Oxnard gingerly slipped the shower screen back a few centimeters, wondering if he ought to be careful about fingerprints.

"Brenda," he said. "Here he is."

She hurried into the bathroom. "Is he. . . ."

Gabriel lay in the tub, up to his armpits in water. His eyes were closed, his mouth hung open. There was several days' stubble on his chin. His face looked awful.

Brenda gulped once and repeated, "Is he. . . ."

Without opening his eyes, Gabriel said, "He *was* asleep, until you two klutzes came barging in here."

Brenda sagged against Oxnard and let out a breath of relief.

Within a few minutes they were all sitting in the sitting room, Gabriel with the inevitable towel draped around his middle.

"They've had me going over these abortions they call story treatments for six days straight! They won't let me out of here. They even took out the goddamned phone! I'm a prisoner."

Brenda said, "They need the scripts, Ron. We're working against a deadline now. If we're not in production by. . . ."

"In production?" Gabriel's voice rose. "With what? Have you looked at these treatments? Have you tried to *read* any of them? The ones that are spelled halfway right, at least?"

"Are they that bad?" Oxnard asked.

"Bad?" Gabriel jumped to his feet. "Bad? They're abysmal! They're insufferable! They're rotten! Junk, nothing but junk. . . ."

He kicked at the paper on the floor and stomped over to the desk. "Listen to these treatments . . . these are the ideas they want to write about. . . ." Riffling through the pile of papers on the desk, he pulled out a single sheet.

Oxnard started to say, "Maybe we ought to. . . ."

"No, no . . . you listen. And you!" he jabbed a finger toward Brenda—"You better get back to Big Daddy in LA. and tell him what the hell's going on here. If we were in the States, I'd call the Civil Liberties Union. If I had a phone."

"What about the story ideas, Ron?" she asked.

"Hah! Story ideas. Okay, listen . . . here's one about two families working together to build a dam on a new planet that's described as, get this now . . . 'very much like upper Alberta Province, such as around Ft. Vermillion.'"

Oxnard looked at Brenda. She said, "Okay, so you don't care for the setting. What's the story idea?"

"That *is* the story idea! That's the whole treatment . . . about how to build a dam! Out of logs, yet!"

Brenda made a disapproving face. "You picked the worst one."

"Oh yeah? Lemme go down the list for you. . . ."

Gabriel spent an hour reading story treatments to them:

• A monster from space invades one of the starships, but it turns out to be a dream that the hero is having.

• The heroine (Rita Yearling) gets lost on an unexplored planet and the natives find her and think she's a goddess. She gets away by explaining astronomy to them.

• The heads of the two competing families of star traders engage in an Indian wrestling match in a frontier saloon "very much like those in upper Alberta Province, such as around Ft. Vermillion."

• The hero and heroine are stranded on an unpopulated planet and decide to call themselves Adam and Eve. Before they can bite the apple, they are rescued.

• A war between the two families is averted when the women of both families decide to stop cooking for their men if they fight.

By the end of the hour, Oxnard felt as if his head was stuffed with cotton wool. Brenda was stretched out on one of the sofas, looking equally dazed.

"And those are the best of them," Gabriel finished grimly.

"That's the best they can do?" Oxnard asked.

"Who's doing the writing?" Brenda wanted to know.

Gabriel glowered from his desk chair. "How the hell should I know? This Earnest Yazoo from Beaver Studios. . . ."

"Badger," Oxnard corrected.

"Same damned thing," Gabriel grumbled. "Earnest won't let me meet any of the writers. I have to write memos, suggestions, rewrites . . . which means I have to start from scratch and write everything! All thirteen goddamned scripts. I'm gonna have to do it all myself."

Brenda sat up and ran a hand through her hair. "But you can't! Our agreement with Badger and the Canadian government says that at least fifty percent of the scripts have to be written by Canadian citizens."

Gabriel threw a fistful of papers into the air.

"This is terrible," Oxnard said.

"I would've walked out a week ago," Gabriel told him, "if it wasn't for the goddamned guards. They've got me locked up in here!"

Brenda looked at him. "That's because you yelled so much

about walking out on them when they first gave you the story treatments."

Oxnard was shaking his head. "And I thought the modeling and sets were bad. . . ."

"What?" Gabriel was beside him instantaneously. "What about the models and the sets? What're they doing to *them*?"

Oxnard told him of his morning's tour of the studio Shops.

"That did it!" Gabriel screeched. "Get that sonofabitch in here! I'll kill him!"

Wearily, Brenda asked, "Which sonofabitch do you mean?"

"Any of them! All of them! I'll take them all on at once!"

Oxnard got up and stood beside the betoweled writer. "We'll both take 'em on," he said grimly. "I don't like what they're doing either."

Brenda grinned at the two of them. "Laurel and Hardy, ready to take on the whole Canadian army. Okay . . . I'll get you some action."

She returned twenty minutes later with an already flustered-looking Gregory Earnest.

In the interval, a maid had cleared up most of the mess, Oxnard had ordered a bottle of beer for himself and Gabriel had started packing. The two men were in the bedroom when they heard the front door of the suite open and Brenda call, "Ron? Bill?"

"In here," Gabriel yelled, as he tossed handfuls of socks into his open suitcase.

Oxnard saw that Earnest's face was red and he was a trifle sweaty. *Brenda must have filled his ears but good,* he thought.

"What're you doing?" Earnest asked as soon as he saw the half-filled suitcase on the bed.

"Leaving," replied Gabriel.

"You can't go."

"The hell I can't!"

Brenda walked over to the edge of the bed and sat down. "Ron," she said, her voice firm, "I brought him here to listen to your problems. The least you can do is talk to him."

"I'm talking," Gabriel said as he rummaged through a dresser drawer and pulled out a heap of underwear.

Oxnard sat back in the room's only chair and tried to keep himself from grinning.

"I, uh . . . understand," Earnest said to Gabriel's back, "that you're not, uh, happy with the story material so far."

Gabriel turned and draped a bathrobe over the bed, alongside the suitcase. He started folding it.

"You understand correctly," he said, concentrating on the folding. The robe was red and gold, with a barely discernible image of Bruce Lee on its back.

"Well," said Earnest, "you knew when you came here that fifty percent of the scripts would have to be written by Canadians."

"Canadian *writers*," Gabriel said, as he tenderly placed the folded robe in the suitcase. "What you've given me was produced by a team of Mongoloid idiots. It's hopeless. I'm leaving."

"You can't leave."

"Watch me."

"The guards won't let you out of here."

Oxnard raised his beer bottle. "Have you ever had your nose broken, Mr. Earnest?"

The Canadian backed away a short step. "Now listen," he said to Gabriel, "you know that Titanic hasn't given us the budget to take on big-name writers. . . ."

"These guys couldn't even *spell* a big name."

". . . and we're on a very tight production schedule. You can't walk out on us. It would ruin everything."

Gabriel looked up at him for the first time. "I can't make a script out of a turd. Nobody can. I can't write thirteen scripts, or even six and a half, in the next couple of weeks. We need writers!"

"We've got writers. . . ."

"We've got shit!" Gabriel yelled. "Excrement. Poop. Ka-ka. I've seen better-looking used toilet paper than the crap you've given me to work with!"

"It's the best available talent for the budget."

"Where'd you get these people?" Gabriel demanded. "The funny farm or the Baffin Island Old Folks' Home?"

He snapped the suitcase lid shut, but it bounced right up again.

"Too much in there," Oxnard said.

Gabriel gave him a look. "It'll close. I got it here and I'll get it out." He pushed the lid down firmly and leaned on it.

"Ron, those are the only writers we can *afford*," Earnest said, his voice taking on a faint hint of pleading. "We don't have the *money* for other writers."

Gabriel let go of the suitcase and the lid bounced up again. "As if that explains it all, huh? We go on the air with a public announcement: 'Folks, please excuse the cruddy quality of the scripts. We couldn't afford better writers.' That's what you want to do?"

"Maybe if you worked with the writers. . . ."

"You won't even let me meet them!"

Earnest shifted back and forth on his feet uneasily. "Well, maybe I was wrong there. . . ."

But Gabriel was peering at the suitcase again. "It won't work."

"I told you it wouldn't," Oxnard said.

Brenda added, "Try putting it on the floor and then leaning on it."

Earnest gaped at her, shocked.

Gabriel picked up the open suitcase and carefully placed it on the floor. "Where'd you get these so-called writers from?" he asked, squatting down to lean on the lid again.

Earnest had to step around the bed to keep him in sight. "Uh . . . from here in the city, mostly."

"What experience do they have?" What credits?"

"Well," Earnest squirmed, "not much, truthfully."

Holding down the lid, Gabriel said to Earnest, "Hey, you look like the heaviest one here. Stand on it."

Obediently, Earnest stepped up on the jiggling, slanting lid. Gabriel began to click the suitcase shut.

"Where'd you get these writers?" he asked again.

Earnest stood on the now-closed suitcase, looking foolish and miserable. "Uh, we had a contest. . . ."

"A contest?"

"In the local high schools. . . ."

Brenda gasped.

Oxnard began to laugh.

Gabriel got to his feet. His nose was about at the height of Earnest's solar plexus.

"You didn't say what I just heard," he said.

"What?"

Looking murderously up into Earnest's flustered face, Gabriel said, "You didn't tell me just now that the story treatments I've been beating out my brains over for the past two weeks were written by high school kids who sent them in as part of a writing contest."

"Uh . . . well. . . ."

"You didn't *imply*," Gabriel went on, his voice low, "that you haven't spent penny number one on any writers at all."

"We can use the money on. . . ."

Oxnard didn't think that Gabriel, with his short arms, could reach Earnest's head. But he did, with a punch so blurringly swift that Oxnard barely saw it. He heard the solid *crunch* of fist on bone, though, and Earnest toppled over backwards onto the bed, his face spurting blood.

"Sonofagun," Oxnard said, "you broke his nose after all."

Earnest bounced up from the bed and fled from the room, wailing and holding his bloody nose with both bands.

Brenda looked displeased. "You shouldn't have done that. It just complicates things."

Gabriel was rubbing his knuckles. "Yeah. I should've belted him in the gut a few times first. Would've been more satisfying."

"He's probably going straight to the lawyers. Or the police," she said.

Starting for the door, Oxnard said, "I'm going to the American consulate. They can't hold an American citizen prisoner like this."

"No. Wait," Brenda said. "Let me handle this."

"I don't care how you do it," Gabriel said, "but I want out."

Brenda faced him squarely. "Ron, that would be the end of everything. The show, the series, the whole Titanic company. . . ."

"What do I care? Those bastards have been screwing me. . . ."

"Ron, please!" Now it was Brenda who was pleading, and Oxnard wished he were in Gabriel's place.

"I'm walking," Gabriel insisted. "High school kids in a writing contest . . . making models and sets like tinker-toys. . . ."

"I'll straighten things out," Brenda said, as strongly as Gabriel. "That's why I'm here. That's why you wanted me here, wasn't it?"

"Well. . . ." He kicked lightly at the suitcase, still on the floor.

Brenda turned to Oxnard. *Her eyes are incredibly green,* he noticed for the first time. "Bill, if I get B.F. to straighten out Earnest and give you authority to act as science consultant, will you stay?"

"I've really got to get back. . . ."

She bit her lower lip, then said, "But you can come up here on weekends, can't you? To make sure that the crew's building things the right way?"

With a shrug, he agreed, "Sure, I suppose I could do that."

Turning to Gabriel again, Brenda went on, "And Ron, *if* I get you complete authority over the scripts and make Earnest bring in some real writers and a story editor, will you stay?"

"No."

"Why not?"

Gabriel scuffed at the suitcase again, like a kid punishing the floor for tripping him. "Because these flatworm-brained idiots are just going to screw things over, one way or the other. They're a bunch of pinheads. Working with them is hopeless."

"But we'll form a team, the three of us," Brenda said. "You head up the writing and creative side, Ron. Bill will handle the scientific side. And I'll make sure that Titanic does right by you."

Gabriel shook his head.

"Listen," Brenda said, with growing enthusiasm. "They haven't made a decision on the male lead for the series. Suppose I tell B.F. that if we don't get a major star the show will fold. He'll understand that kind of talk. We can go out and get a big name. That'll force everybody else to live up to the star's level."

Gabriel's eyebrows inched upward. "A big name star?"

"Right." Brenda smiled encouragingly.

Oxnard could see wheels within wheels at work inside Gabriel's head.

"Okay," the writer said at last. "You go talk to B.F. But first . . . get Rita Yearling over here. I want to talk with her. About who she thinks would make a good co-star."

Oxnard looked at Brenda. She understood perfectly what was going on in Gabriel's mind. And she didn't like it.

But she said, "All right, Ron. If that's what you want." Flat. Emotionless.

She started for the door. Gabriel stooped down and pushed the suitcase under the bed. Oxnard called out:

"Wait up, Brenda. I'm going with you."

9: The Star

The studio was alive at last. It rang with the sounds of busy workmen: carpenters hammering; electricians yelling to each other from atop giddy-tall ladders; painters and lighting men and gofers carrying the tools of their trades across the vast floor of the hangar-sized room.

Four different sets were being erected in the four corners of the studio, fleshing over its bare metal walls and reaching upward to the girders that supported row after row of lights which seemed to stare down at the beehive below in silent disbelief.

Ron Gabriel was standing in the middle of the big, clangorous whirl. He wore what had come to be known over the past few months as his "official working costume:" a pair of cutoff Levis and a tee shirt with *Starcrossed* lettered on front and back. Somewhere in the offices and workshops adjoining the studio, the art director was dreaming up a special symbol for the show. Gabriel would get Badger or Titanic to make tee shirts for the entire cast and crew with the symbol on them, no matter who protested about the cost.

Standing beside him, in a conservative one-piece business suit, was Sam Lipid. He was only slightly taller than Gabriel, roundish, with a prematurely balding pate. His face was soft and young look-ing. Lipid was Production Manager for the show and Gabriel's major point of contact with Badger Films. Gregory Earnest had given Gabriel a wide berth ever since bouncing off the bed in his hotel room, months earlier. There had been some talk of a lawsuit, but

Brenda got Titanic to pay for a nose job and Earnest wound up look-ing better than he ever had before Gabriel socked him.

". . . and here on the turntable," Lipid was saying, "will be the 'planet' set. We'll redress it every week to make it look like a different world."

Gabriel nodded. "Why the turntable?"

Lipid's babyface actually pinked sightly with enthusiasm, "Oh, we used to use this studio for filming a musical show, the Lawrence Welk Simulacrum, you know? It was very popular. They had audi-ence seats along all four walls of the studio and the orchestra rotated at a different speed for each song, in time with the music."

"You're kidding," Gabriel said.

"No, they really did it." His face went pinker. "That is, until the speed mechanism broke down and flung all those animated dummies into the audience. It was a terrible scene. That's when they cancelled the show."

Gabriel chuckled to himself as he and Lipid slowly walked across the noisy studio to inspect the "bridge" set. This would be used as the bridge of both starships, with slight redressings to change it from one ship to the other.

"What do you think of it?" Lipid asked, over the shouting and hammering.

Gabriel took it in. The two walls of the corner were now lined by desk-type consoles studded with elaborate keyboard buttons and viewing screens. About them were big observation screens, taller than a man and many times wider. They were blank, of course, nothing but sheets of painted plastic covering the studio's bare walls. But with electronic picture matting, they would appear to look out on the vast universe and reveal stars, strange new worlds, other spaceships of the series. The floor had been turned into a metallized deck, thanks to judicious spray painting, and there were very modernistic chairs and crew stations arranged in a semicircle facing the corner.

Nodding, Gabriel admitted, "It looks good. Real substantial. Needs some personalized touches, though."

Lipid quickly agreed. "Oh sure. Right. We've been talking with one of our Ontario vineyards . . . they might come in as a sponsor for part of the show. One of the captains can have a flask of wine set up at his command console."

Gabriel said, "Just make sure it's a futuristic flask. We're seven hundred years in the future, remember."

"Oh, sure."

Gabriel stood there and tried to visualize how the actors would look on the set. *Not bad,* he thought. *It's finally starting to shape up.*

"You like it?" Lipid asked. His voice went a little squeaky, like a kid who's desperately anxious for a word of approval.

"It'll do, I guess. At least we got rid of that damned steering wheel."

Lipid blushed. "Oh. That. I didn't understand what you needed. Dr. Oxnard straightened me out on that."

"He's been a help," Gabriel said.

Lipid stared down at his sneakers. "You don't like it, do you? What'd we do wrong?"

"I like it," Gabriel said. "It's okay. Nothing's wrong."

Looking up at him, the Production Manager said, "But you're . . . well, you're not excited by it. It doesn't really raise your metabolism."

With a weary smile, Gabriel said, "Listen kid. I've been going flat out for more than three months now. I've been trying to get the scripts in shape, working with high school kids and every amateur playwright north of Saskatoon. I haven't seen a single script or story treatment that I didn't have to rewrite from start to finish. I'm hoarse from talking to these bean-brains and going blind from reading and typing twenty-eight hours a day. My ass hurts from sitting and my feet hurt from running and my gut hurts from fighting. So don't expect me to flip handstands and start swinging from the rafters. Okay?"

Lipid's face glowed with awe. "Oh sure, Mr. Gabriel. I understand. There's been a lot of talk around the studio about how hard you've been working on the scripts."

"Okay," Gabriel said. Then, looking at Lipid's trembling lower lip, he added, "And call me Ron. I don't like this Mr. Gabriel shit."

"Oh . . . okay, Mr. Ga . . . uh, Ron."

Gabriel forced a smile and they started for the next set, in the next corner of the studio.

Lipid asked as they walked, "Uh, Ron . . . can I ask you a question?"

"Sure." They had to detour around a burly guy carrying a long plank on his shoulder. *Laurel and Hardy would have a field day in here,* Gabriel thought.

"Why do you do it?" the Production Manager asked, his voice filled with admiration and wonder.

"Do what?"

"Why do you put up with us? I mean, you could be working with the bigtime outfits down in Hollywood. Or writing books. I've been reading your sci-fi books since I was a kid. . . ."

Gabriel winced. Twice.

But Lipid didn't notice it. "You're a famous writer. You've won a lot of awards. Why are you putting up with this cheap outfit? I mean, this is the best job *I* can get right now. But you . . . you can do a lot better."

Gabriel looked at him. *The kid means it. He's not putting me on.*

Without breaking stride, he said gruffly, "This is *my* show. Comprend? Mine. I *created* this idea; it came out of my brain. I may have to deal with shitheads at Titanic and beaver-brains at Badger, but that doesn't matter. I want this show to be *good*, man. Not pretty good. Not good enough to get some sponsors. Not good enough to get renewed after the first thirteen weeks."

His voice was rising and the heat was building up inside him. Months of anger and frustration were bubbling close to the surface.

"I want it to be *good*! Good enough to satisfy me. Good enough for any one of us to point at with pride. I want you and me and every carpenter and electrician in this crazy cave to be proud to have worked on 'The Starcrossed.' I want even assholes like Earnest—and Finger back in his padded room in California—to feel proud of this show. They won't, because they haven't got the capacity. But we do, you and me. That's what I want. Pride of accomplishment."

"Wow," gasped Lipid. "What commitment."

And the money helps, Gabriel added silently. *And the fact that nobody else in town would touch my work because Mongoloid idiots like Finger convinced everybody I'm too tough to get along with. And I'm broke. And this is the only decent idea I've had in the past year. And if I don't make some money out of this I'll have to give up my house.*

As they stopped and looked over the next set, Gabriel realized that even those eminently practical reasons that didn't sound so good when you voiced them, even they didn't go deep enough.

I'm staying because she's here, he admitted to himself. *Rita's close enough to touch and so beautiful that she's driving me crazy. She smiles and says all the right words to me, but she never gets within arm's reach.*

He laughed silently, sardonically, at himself. *They do articles in magazines about me, one of the ten most available bachelors in Hollywood. I have all the women I want. I spend half my Blue Cross getting cleaned up from them. And this one goddamned girl just smiles at me and I'm all putty inside.*

His mind completely detached from his physical surroundings, Gabriel wondered where Rita Yearling was at that precise moment. *Getting her costumes fitted? Taking color tests with the new camera system? Talking on the three-dee phone Finger gave her? Talking to him? Planning to go back to L.A. for the weekend to be with him?*

Gabriel grimaced inwardly. *I haven't been writing fiction,* he realized. *I know exactly how Romeo felt.*

Rita Yearling did not go to Los Angeles that weekend. Bernard Finger came to Toronto.

Gabriel was standing on the balcony of his hotel room, looking out disconsolately at the park-like front grounds of the hotel and beyond to the towers of the city that blocked what had once been a decent view of Lake Ontario. There wasn't much smog in Toronto, since the Canadians used nuclear energy to a large extent. But the lake was still a fetid cesspool of industrial wastes.

Rita had smilingly accepted Gabriel's dinner invitation the night before; he had treated her to a quick jet flight to New York for authentic delicatessen fare. All through the evening she was warm, friendly, outgoing, obviously happy to be with Gabriel. And that's as far as it went. She eluded his grasp. Even in the plush passenger compartment of the rented jet (five thousand bucks, Canadian, for the night) she somehow managed to stay at arm's length.

Gabriel couldn't figure it out. Women didn't act that way. Or at least, he'd never had any patience with those who did. "You either do or you don't," he had told hundreds of girls. *But Rita's different.* Shy yet friendly. Innocent yet knowing. Desirable but distant. *She's driving me nuts,* Gabriel told himself for the thousandth time.

He burped pastrami. The morning air wasn't helping to settle his stomach. Just as he decided to go back inside and take some antacid, a long stream of cars came purring off the superhighway and onto the hotel's approach road.

Finger! Gabriel knew instantly. No one else would demand such commotion. The carefully landscaped grounds of the old hotel had never seen such a flurry of sycophants. Bellmen and doormen seemed to spring out of the front entrance. Yesmen by the dozens poured out of the cars and yeswomen, too. Finger was no sexist.

As Gabriel leaned over his balcony railing to watch, it seemed as if the hotel was disgorging whole phalanxes of flunkies. It was easy to tell the Californians from the Canadians. The L.A. contingent wore the latest mode: fur-trimmed robes and boots and hats that made them look like extras from an old Ivan the Terrible flick. *Or the minions of Ming the Merciless.* The locals wore conservatively zippered business suits, while the hotel staff was decked out in bluish uniforms faintly reminiscent of the old RAF.

The whole conglomeration swirled and eddied around the cars for nearly fifteen minutes. Then everyone seemed to fall into a pre-arranged pattern, and the rear door of the longest, blackest, shiniest limousine was opened by one of the RAF uniforms. Despite himself, Gabriel grinned. *He ought to have a line of trumpeters announcing his arrival.*

Bernard Finger's expensively booted foot appeared in the limousine's doorway, followed by the rest of his Cary Grant body. He looked gorgeous, resplendent in royal purple and ermine. And he bumped his head on the car's low doorway.

Gabriel hooted. "You're still a klutz, you klutz!" he hollered. But his balcony was too far above street level for anyone to hear him. Briefly he wondered if he'd have time enough to make a water bomb and drop it on Finger's ermine-trimmed hat. But he couldn't tear himself away from the barbaric splendor of the scene below, even for an instant.

Finger straightened his hat and sneaked a small rub on the bump he'd just received, then stood tall and beaming at the sea of servility surrounding him.

Rita's not there to greet him, Gabriel noticed, and felt good about it.

Then with an expansive gesture, Finger said something to the people nearest him. Several of them were holding recorders and minicameras, Gabriel noticed. *Media flaks.*

Finger turned back toward his limousine and ducked slightly, beckoning to someone inside. *New girlfriend?* Gabriel wondered.

It was a man who got out. A guy who wasn't terribly tall, but looked wide across the shoulders and narrow at the hips. Muscleman. He wasn't wearing Hollywood finery, either. He wore a simple turtleneck sweater and a very tight pair of pants. Athlete's striped sneakers. Dirty blond hair, cropped short and curly. Rugged looking face; nose must've been broken more than once. Good smile, dazzling teeth. Must be caps.

The newcomer grinned almost boyishly at the cameras, then turned and, grabbing Finger by the shoulders so strongly that he lifted the mogul off his feet, he kissed B.F. soundly on both cheeks.

As he let Finger's boots smack down on the pavement again, Gabriel howled to himself, *He's got a new girlfriend, all right! Wait'll Rita sees this!*

But Gabriel was completely wrong.

Les Montpelier phoned almost as soon as Gabriel stepped back inside his room, inviting him to a "command performance" dinner.

"The whole team's going to be here tonight," Les said gravely, "to meet the show's male lead."

Gabriel blinked at Montpelier's image on the tiny phone screen. "You mean that guy is going to be our big star?"

"That's right." Montpelier cut the connection before Gabriel could ask who the man was.

Briefly, Gabriel considered throwing himself off the balcony. But he decided to attend B.F.'s dinner instead.

Finger bought out the hotel's main restaurant for the evening and filled it with media people and the top-level crew of "The Starcrossed." *No working types allowed,* Gabriel grumbled to himself. No painters or electricians or carpenters. Just us white-collar folks. Not even Bill Oxnard had been invited, although Gabriel knew he was in Toronto for the weekend.

Finger sat at the head table, flanked by Rita Yearling on one side and the rugged-looking, erstwhile star of the show on the other. Gabriel had been placed halfway across the big dining room, as far removed from Gregory Earnest as possible, and seated at a table of what passed for writers. They were a grubby lot. The high schoolers weren't allowed to stay up late or drink alcoholic beverages (and marijuana was still illegal in Canada), so they hadn't been invited. Gabriel sat amid a motley crew of semi-retired engineers who had always wanted to write sci-fi, copyboys and reporters from the area news media who saw their futures in dramaturgy, and one transplanted Yank who had exiled himself to Canada millennia ago and could outwrite the entire staff, when he wasn't outdrinking them.

Something about Finger's male "discovery" was bothering Gabriel. His face looked vaguely familiar. Gabriel spent the entire dinner—of rubber chicken and plastic peas—trying to figure out where he had seen the man before. A bit player in some TV series? An announcer? One of the gay blades who're always hanging around the studios and offices? Maybe a dancer?

None of them seemed to click.

Then, as coffee and joints were passed around by the well-beyond-retirement-age waiters, Finger got to his feet.

"I suppose you're wondering why I asked you here this evening."

Everyone roared with laughter. Except Gabriel, who clutched his stomach and tried to keep from shrieking.

"Even though I've been staying in sunny Southern California. . . ." More canned laughter from the throats of Finger's lackeys. ". . . I've been keeping a close eye on your work up here. 'The Starcrossed' is an important property for Titanic and even though we're working with an extremely tight budget . . ." *Who's paying for this bash tonight?* Gabriel wondered. ". . . I can assure you that Titanic is doing everything possible to make this show a success."

Loud applause. Even the media people clapped. *Local flaks,* Gabriel knew. *They want the show to succeed, too.*

Finger cocked his head in Gabriel's direction, like Cary Grant sizing up Katharine Hepburn. "I know we've had some troubles in the script department, but I think that's all been ironed out satisfactorily." *Maybe,* Gabriel answered silently.

"And thanks to our foresight in hiring one of the world's foremost scientists as our technical consultant—Dr. William Oxnard, that is, who unfortunately couldn't be with us here tonight because he's literally spending night and day at the studio . . . let's hear it for Dr. Oxnard. . . ."

They all dutifully applauded while Finger tried to figure out where he was in his speech. "Um, well, as I was saying, we've got terrific scientific advice. And we're going to have the best show, from the technical standpoint, of anything in the industry." More applause.

"But when you get right down to it . . ." Finger went on, reaching for a napkin to dab at his brow. The lights were hot, especially under those fur-trimmed robes. "When you get right down to it, what the audience sees is mainly the performers. Sure, the scripts and the sets are important, but those millions of viewers out there, they react to *people* . . . the performers who perform for them, right there in their living rooms—or bedrooms, whichever the case may be."

I'll never make it all the way through this speech without throwing up, Gabriel told himself.

"It's crucially important to have a pair of brilliant costars," Finger said, gesturing with the white napkin, "especially for a show like 'The Starcrossed,' which is, after all, a show about two young people, lovers, who will captivate the millions of viewers out there."

Someone broke into enthusiastic applause, found that he was alone, quickly stopped, looked around and slid down in his chair halfway under the table.

Finger glanced in his direction, then resumed. "We are extremely fortunate in having one of the most exciting young new talents in the world to play our feminine lead, our Juliet: Rita Yearling."

Rita stood up amid a pleasant round of applause and took a cautious bow. Considering the gown she'd been poured into and her cleavage, caution was of utmost importance. She remained standing as Finger went on:

"Isn't she beautiful? And she can *act*!" Some laughter; Rita herself smiled tolerantly, while Gabriel squirmed in his chair with indignation for her.

"But although Rita Yearling will be a superstar by the end of the coming season, she's still relatively unknown to the TV audience. So what we needed, I knew, was a male costar who would be instantly recognizable to the whole world. . . ."

Gabriel found his puzzlement deepening. The guy sitting at Finger's right side looked vaguely familiar, but Gabriel *knew* he wasn't a well-known actor.

"So I went out and got a guy who *is* known the whole world over," Finger was at his self-congratulatory best, "and signed him up to play our Romeo, our male lead. And here he is! A superstar in his own right! Francois Dulaq!"

Everyone in the big dining room rose to their feet and roared approval. *"Du-laq! Du-laq!"* they began chanting. Even the crystal chandeliers started swaying in rhythm with their shouts.

And then it hit Gabriel. Francois Dulaq. The hockey star. The guy who broke Orr's old scoring record and made the Canadian Maple Stars world champions. They even beat the Russo-Chinese All-Stars, Gabriel remembered from last season's sportscasts.

A hockey player as the male lead? *It's Buster Crabbe all over again,* Gabriel moaned to himself.

He had to climb up on his chair to see what was going on. The crowd was still on its feet, roaring. Dulaq had gone around Finger to where Rita was standing. They put their arms around each other and bared the most expensive sets of teeth in television history for the media cameramen. Finger beamed approvingly.

The expatriate American tugged at Gabriel's sleeve and yelled over the crowd's hubbub, "Whaddaya think?"

Gabriel shrugged. "He might be okay. Looks good enough. Probably can't act worth shit, but he wouldn't be the first big star who couldn't act."

Frowning and shaking his head, the expatriate said, "Yeah, but he can't even speak English."

Gabriel almost fell off his chair. "What? What's he speak, French?"

"Nope. Neanderthal."

Not knowing whether it was a joke or not, Gabriel climbed off his perch and sat down. The crowd settled down, too, as Finger nudged Dulaq to the microphone.

"I wancha t'know," Dulaq said, "dat I'll t'row evert'ing I got into dis job . . . jus' like I t'rew dem body checks inta dem Chinks last May!"

They all roared again. Gabriel sank his head down onto his arms and tried to keep from crying.

At precisely two a.m. Gabriel's phone buzzed.

He wasn't sleeping. His trusty suitcase was open on the bed, half filled with his clothes. Since the end of the dinner, Gabriel had spent the night phoning Finger, Montpelier, Brenda, Sam Lipid and anyone else who would listen, telling them that if Dulaq was the male star of the show, they could get themselves another chief writer.

They all argued with him. They cited contracts and clauses. They spoke glowingly of Dulaq's magnetic personality and star quality and sex appeal. They promised voice coaching and speech therapy and soundtrack dubbing. Still, Gabriel packed his suitcase as he fought with them.

Then his phone buzzed.

Gabriel leaned across the bed and flipped the switch that turned it on. Rita Yearling's incredibly lovely face appeared on the phone's screen.

"Hi," she breathed.

Gabriel hung suspended, stretched across the bed with one foot in his suitcase, tangled in his dirty underwear.

"Hello yourself," he managed.

Her eyes seemed to widen as she noticed the open suitcase. "You're not leaving?"

Gabriel nodded. He couldn't talk.

"Don't you care about the show?" she asked.

He shook his head.

"Don't you care about me?"

With an effort, Gabriel said, "I care a lot. Too much to watch you ruin your career before it really starts. That hockey puck of a leading man is going to *destroy* this show."

She dimpled at him. "You're jealous!"

"No," he said. "Just fed up."

"Oh, Ron. . . ." Her face pulled together slightly in a small frown.

"I can't take it anymore," Gabriel said. "It's just one battle after another . . . like fighting with a Hydra. Every time I chop off one head, seven more pop up."

But she wasn't listening. "Ron . . . you poor sweet boy. Come out onto your balcony. I've got a surprise for you."

"On the balcony?"

"Go out and see," Rita cooed.

Untangling himself from the suitcase, Gabriel padded barefoot to the balcony. He was wearing nothing but his knee-length dashiki and the chill night air cut into him the instant he opened the sliding glass door.

"Surprise!" he heard from over his head.

Looking up, he saw Rita smiling lusciously down at him. She was on the balcony one floor up and one room over from his own. She stood there smiling down at him, clothed in a luminous wisp of a gown that billowed softly in the breeze.

"I took this room for the weekend. I wanted to get away from the suite where B.F. is," she said.

Ron's knees went weak. "It is the east," he murmured, "and Juliet is the sun."

"This is a lot more fun than talking over the phone, isn't it?" Rita gave a girlish wriggle. "Like, it's more romantic, huh?"

Without even thinking about it, Gabriel leaped up on the railing of his own balcony. He stretched and his fingertips barely grazed the bottom of Rita's balcony.

"Hey! Be careful!"

Gabriel glanced below. Ten floors down, the street lamps glowed softly in the cold night air. Wind whipped at his dashiki and his butt suddenly felt terribly exposed.

"What are you *doing*?" Rita called, delighted.

He jumped for her balcony. His fingers clutched at the cold cement, then he reached, straining, and grabbed a fistful of one of the metal posts supporting the railing.

His feet dangled in empty air and his dashiki billowed in the wind. Somewhere far back in his mind, Gabriel realized what a ridiculous picture this would present to anyone passing below. But that didn't matter.

Beads of cold sweat popped out all over his body as he strained, muscles agonized by the unaccustomed effort, hand over hand to the edge of the balcony's railing. His bare toes found a hold on the balcony's cement floor at last and he heaved himself, puffing and trembling with exertion, over the railing to collapse at Rita's feet.

She dropped to her knees beside him. "Ron, darling, are you all right?"

He smiled weakly up at her. "Hiya kid." It wasn't Shakespeare, he knew, but it was the best he could manage under the conditions.

They went arm in arm into her hotel room. Rita's gown was a see-through and Gabriel was busily looking into it.

She sat him down on the edge of the bed. "Ron," she said, very seriously, "you can't leave the show."

"There's no reason for me to stay," he said.

"Yes there is."

"What?"

She lowered her eyelids demurely. "There's me."

10: The Director

Mitch Westerly sat scowling to himself behind his archaic dark glasses. The other passengers on the jet airliner shuffled past him, down the narrow aisle, overcoats flopping in their arms and hand baggage banging against the seats and each other.

Westerly ignored them all, just as he had ignored the stewardesses who had recognized him and asked for his autograph. They were up forward now, smiling their mechanical "Have a good day" at the outgoing passengers and sneaking glances at him.

I should never have come back, he thought. *This is going to be a bad scene. I can feel it in my karma.*

He was neither tall nor particularly handsome, but since puberty he had somehow attracted women without even trying. His face was rugged, weatherbeaten, the face of an oldtime cowboy or mountaineer, even though he had spent most of his life in movie sound stages—and even in Nepal, where he had been for the past two years, he had seen the Himalayas only through very well-insulated windows. His body was broad shouldered, solid, stocky, the kind that goes to fat when you reach forty. But Westerly had always eaten very sparingly and hardly ever drank at all; there was no fat on him.

He wore his standard outfit, a trademark that never changed no matter what the current fashion might be: a pullover sweater, faded denims, boots, the dark shades and a pair of soft leather race driver's gloves. He had started wearing the gloves many years earlier, when he had been second-unit director on a racing car TV series. The

111

gloves kept him from biting his fingernails, and he rarely took them off. It ruined his image to be seen biting his fingernails.

Finally, all the passengers had left. The plane was empty except for the three stewardesses. The tallest one, who also seemed to be the boss stew, strode briskly toward him, her microskirt flouncing prettily and revealing her flowered underpants.

"End of the line, I'm sorry to say," she told him.

"Hate to leave," Westerly said. His voice was as soft as the leather of his gloves.

"I hope you enjoyed the flight."

"Yeah. Sure did." *And the offers of free booze, the names and numbers your two assistants scribbled on my lunch tray and the note you slipped under the washroom door.*

He slowly pulled himself out of the plush seat, while the stewardess reached up into the overhead rack and pulled out his sheepskin jacket.

"Will you be in Toronto for long?" she asked, as they started up the aisle together, with him in the lead.

"Directing a TV series here," Westerly said, over his shoulder.

"Oh really?" Her voice said *How exciting!* without using the words. "Will you be staying at the Disney Hilton? That's where we stay for our layovers."

That dump. Not even the fleas go there anymore. "Nope. They've got us at one of the older places—Inn on the Park."

"Ohhh. That's beautiful. A . . . friend, he took me to dinner there once."

They were at the hatch now. The other two stews were smiling glitteringly at him. With his Himalayan-honed senses he could almost hear them saying, *Put me in your TV series. Make me famous. I'll do anything for that. Glamour, glamour, romance and glamour.*

He hesitated at the hatch and made a smile for them. They shuddered visibly. "Y'all come out to the studio when you get a chance. Meet the TV people. Just ask for me at the gate. Anytime."

"Ohh. We will!"

His smile self-destructed as soon as he turned his back on them and trudged down the connecting tunnel that led into the airport terminal building.

They were at the gate area waiting for him. The photographers, the media newshounds, the newspaper reporters, the lank-haired droopy-mouthed emaciated young women who covered Special Events for the local TV stations and show business magazines, the public relations flaks for Titanic and Badger and Shiva knows who else. They all looked alike, from Bhutan to Brooklyn.

They might be the same people who were at the airport in Delhi . . . and in Rome . . . and in London, Westerly realized with a thrill of horror. *My own personal set of devils hounding me wherever I go. Eternally. Hell is an airport terminal!*

He kept his head down and refused even to listen to their shouting, pleading questions until the PR flaks—*Why are they always balding and desperate faced?*—steered him to one of those private rooms with unmarked doors that line the long impersonal corridors of every airport terminal in the world.

The room inside had been set up for a press conference. A table near the door was groaning with bottles of liquor and trays of hors d'oeuvres. A battery of microphones studded a small podium at the front of the room. Folding chairs were neatly arranged in rows.

Inside of three minutes, Westerly was standing at the podium (which bore the stylized trademark of Titanic Productions, a rakishly angled "T" in which the cross piece was a pair of wings), the hors d'oeuvres were totally demolished, half the booze was gone, the chairs were scattered as if by a tsunami and the PR men were smiling with self-satisfaction.

One of the lank-haired young women was asking, "When you left Hollywood two years ago, you vowed you'd never return. What changed your mind?"

Westerly fiddled with his glasses for a moment. "Haven't changed my mind," he said slowly, with just a trace of fashionable West Virginia accent. "Didn't go back to Hollywood. This is Toronto, isn't it?"

The news people laughed. But the scrawny girl refused to be embarrassed.

"You said you were finished with commercial films and you were going to seek inner peace; now you're back. Why?"

Because inner peace comes at eleven-fifty a week at the Katmandu-Sheraton, baby. "I spent two years absorbing the wisdom of the East in the Himalayas," Westerly replied aloud. "One of the most important things the lamas taught me is that a man should use his inborn talents and use them wisely. My talent is making movies and television shows. It's my karma . . . my destiny."

"Didn't you make a movie in Tibet last year?" asked an overweight, mustachioed reporter.

"Surely did," said Westerly. "But that was purely for self-expression . . . to help release my soul from its bondage. That film will never be released for commercial viewing." *Not that bomb. Never make that mistake again—hash and high altitudes just don't mix.*

One of the media interviewers, his videotape camera strapped securely to the side of his head, asked, "You left the States right after the Academy Awards dinner, with no explanations at all except that you had to—quote, find yourself, end quote. Why did you turn down the Oscar?"

"Didn't think I deserved it. A director shouldn't get an Oscar for his first feature film. There were many other directors who had amassed a substantial body of work who deserved to get an Oscar before Mitch Westerly did." *And the IRS and the Narcs were getting too close; it was no time to show up at a prearranged affair.*

"Do you still consider yourself the Boy Genius of Hollywood?"

"Never been a boy." *Pushing forty and running scared.*

"Why have you come here to Toronto, instead of going back to Hollywood?"

Taxes, pushers, alimony . . . take your pick. "Gregory Earnest convinced me that 'The Starcrossed' was a vehicle worthy of my Krishna-given talents."

"Have you met the people who'll be working for you on "The Starcrossed'?"

"Not yet."

"Have you read any of the scripts?"

I gagged over the first six pages. "Looked over some of the scripts and read the general concept of the show. Looks great."

"Do you think Shakespeare and science fiction can be mixed?"

"Why not? If Will were alive today, he'd be writing science fiction."

"What do you think is the best film you've ever directed?"

Without an instant's hesitation, Westerly replied, "The one I'm working on now. In this case, the entire series, 'The Starcrossed.'"

But in his mind, his life flashed before his consciousness like a videotape spun at dizzying, blurring speed. He knew the best film he had done; everyone in the room knew it; the one original piece of work he had been able to do, the first major job he had tackled, as a senior back at UCLA: *The Reawakening.* The hours, the weeks, the months he had spent. First as a volunteer worker at the mental hospital, then convincing them to let him bring his tiny pocket camera in. Following Virginia, sallow, pathetic, schizophrenic Virginia through the drug therapy, the primal sessions, the EEGs, the engram reversals. Doctors, skinny fidgety nurses who didn't trust him at first, Virginia's parents tight and suspicious, angry at her for the dream world they had thrust her into, the psychotechs and their weird machines that mapped the brain and put the *mind* on a viewscreen. Virginia's gradual awakening to the real world, her understanding that the parents who said they loved her actually wanted nothing to do with her, her acceptance of adulthood, of maturity, of her own individuality and the fact that she was a lovely, desirable woman. Mitch's wild hopeless love for her and that heart-stopping instant when she smiled and told him in a voice so low that he could barely hear it that she loved him too. That was his best film; his life and hers recorded in magnetic swirls on long reels of tape. Truth frozen into place so that people could see it and understand and cry and laugh over it.

He had never done anything so fine again. He became successful. He directed "True to Life" TV shows and made money and fame. He married Virginia while they were both still growing and changing. Unlike the magnetic patterns on video tape, they did not stay frozen in place forever. They split, slowly and sadly at first, then with the wild burning anger of betrayal and hate. By the time he directed his first major production and was nominated for an Oscar, his world had already crashed around him.

"Do you really think 'The Starcrossed' is award-winning material?"

The question snapped him back to this small stuffy overcrowded room, with the news people playing their part in the eternal charade. So he went back to playing his.

"'The Starcrossed' has the potential of an award-winning series. It won't be eligible for an Oscar because it's not a one-time production.

But it should be in contention for an Emmy as Best Dramatic Series."

Satisfied that they had put his neck in the noose, the news people murmured their thanks and headed on to their next assignments.

Westerly went straight to the studio, while two of the PR flaks took his luggage to the hotel. He almost asked why it took a pair of them to escort his one flight bag to the hotel, but thought better of it. If he raised a question about it, Westerly knew, they'd wind up assigning a third PR man to supervise the first two.

Gregory Earnest met him at the studio, looking somber in a dark gray jumpsuit. His face was as deeply hidden by bushy beard and tangled mane as ever, but since Westerly had seen him last—many months earlier, in Nepal—Earnest's face had subtly changed, improved. His nose seemed slightly different, somehow.

"I'm glad you're finally here," Earnest said, with great seriousness. "Now maybe we can start to bring some order out of this chaos."

He showed Westerly around the sets that had been built in the huge studio. The place was empty and quiet, except for a small group of people off to one side who were working on some kind of aerial rigging. Westerly ignored them and studied the sets.

"This is impossible," he said at last.

"What?" Earnest's eyebrows disappeared into his bushy forelocks. "What do you mean?"

"These sets." Westerly stood in the middle of the starship bridge, surrounded by complicated-looking cardboard consoles. "They're too deep. How're we going to move cameras in and out around all this junk? It'll take hours to make a single shot!"

Earnest sighed with relief. "Oh *that*. You've never directed a three-dee show before, have you?"

"No, but . . ."

"Well, one of the things audiences like is a lot of depth in each scene. We don't put all the props against the walls anymore . . . we scatter them around the floor. Makes a better three-dimensional effect"

"But the cameras. . . ."

"They're small enough to move through the standing props. We measured all the tolerances. . . ."

"But I thought three-dee cameras were big awkward mothers."

Earnest cast a rare smile at him. It was not a pleasant thing to see.

"That was two years ago. Time marches on. A lot of transistors have flown under the bridge. You're not in the Mystic East anymore."

Westerly pushed his glasses up against the bridge of his nose. "I see," he said.

"Hey! There you are!" A shout came echoing across the big, nearly empty room.

Earnest and Westerly turned to see a stubby little guy dashing toward them. He wore a *Starcrossed* tee shirt and a pair of old-fashioned sailor's bell-bottoms, complete with a thirteen-button trapdoor in front.

"Oh *God*," Earnest whined nasally. "It's Ron Gabriel."

Gabriel skidded to a halt in front of the director. They were almost equal in height, much to Earnest's surprise.

"You're Mitch Westerly," Gabriel panted.

"And you're Ron Gabriel." He grinned and took Gabriel's offered hand.

"I've been a fan of yours," Gabriel said, "ever since 'The Reawakening.' Best damned piece of tape I ever saw."

Westerly immediately liked the writer. "Well, thanks."

"Everything else you've made since then has been crap."

Westerly liked him even more. "You're damn right," he admitted.

"How the hell they ever gave you an Oscar for that abortion two years ago is beyond me."

Westerly shrugged, suddenly carefree because there were no pretenses to maintain. "Money and politics, man. You know the game. Same thing goes for writers' awards."

Gabriel made a face that was halfway between rue and embarrassment. Then he grinned. "Yeah. Guess so."

Earnest said, "I'm taking Mr. Westerly on a tour of the studio facilities. . . ."

"Go pound sand up your ass," Gabriel said. "I've gotta talk about the scripts." He grabbed at Westerly's arm. "Come on, I'll buy you a beer or something."

"I don't drink."

"Great. Neither do I." They started off together, leaving Earnest standing there. Behind his beard, his face was redder than a Mounties jacket at sunset.

((◦)) ((◦)) ((◦))

The studio cafeteria was murky with pot smoke, since smoking of all sorts was forbidden on the sets because of the fire hazard.

"Now let me get this straight," Westerly was saying. "The original scripts were written by high school kids as part of a contest?"

They were sitting at a corner table, near the air conditioning blowers, sipping ginger ales.

Gabriel nodded slowly. "I've been working since summer with Brenda and Bill Oxnard to make some sense out of them. I've also written two original scripts of my own."

"And that's all we've got to shoot with?"

"That's right."

"Krishna's left eyebrow!"

"Huh?"

Westerly waved at the encroaching smoke. "Nothing. But it's a helluva situation."

"They didn't tell you about the scripts?"

"Earnest said there were some problems with you . . . you're supposed to be tough to get along with."

"I am," Gabriel admitted, "when I'm being shat on."

"I don't blame you."

Gabriel hunched forward in his chair. "So what do we do?"

With a small shrug, Westerly said, "I'll have to talk to Fad about it . . . it's the Executive Producer's job. . . ."

Gabriel shook his head. "Sheldon split. Went back to L.A. as soon as his girl moved out of his apartment, and turned over the E.P. title to Earnest."

"Earnest?" Westerly felt his lip curling.

"The boll weevil of the north," said Gabriel.

"Well," with a deep sigh, "I guess I'll have to mention it to Finger. I'm supposed to have a conference with him tonight. . . ."

"I thought he was back in L.A."

"He is. We're talking by phone. Private link . . . satellite relay, they tell me."

"Oh."

"I'll just tell Finger we have to get better script material."

"You can read the scripts, if you want to."

"I already saw a couple. I thought they were rejects. I'd like to see yours. At least we'll have a couple to start with."

Gabriel looked pleased, but still uncertain.

"Is there anything else?" Westerly asked.

With a grimace, Gabriel said, "Well, I hate to bring it up."

"Go on."

For an instant, the writer hesitated. Then, like a man who's decided to step off the high board no matter what, "You've got a reputation for being an acid freak. Did they bring you in here just for the name or are you gonna stay straight and do the kind of work you're capable of doing?"

So there it is, right out in the open. Westerly almost felt relieved. "Both," he said.

"Huh?"

"Finger and Earnest called me back from the Roof of the World because I have a big name with the public and I need money so bad that I'm willing to work cheap. They know I've blown my head off; I doubt that they care."

Gabriel gritted his teeth but said nothing.

"But *I* care," Westerly went on. "I finally got off the stuff in Nepal and I want to stay off it. I want to do a good job on this series. I want to get back to work again."

"No shit?"

"No shit, buddy."

"You're not kidding me? Or yourself?"

"No kidding."

Gabriel broke into a grin. "Okay, *buhbie.* We'll show the whole world."

By the time Westerly got back to the studio, the quiet little knot of technicians who had been working on the aerial rigging had turned into a studio full of shouting, milling people. One of the men was hanging suspended in the rig, wires disappearing up into the shadows of the high ceiling, his feet dangling a good ten meters off the floor.

Gregory Earnest seemed to rise up out of the floorboards as Westerly stood near the studio's main door, watching.

"That's Francois Dulaq, our star," Earnest explained, pointing to the dangling man. "We're getting him accustomed to the zero-gravity simulator."

"Shouldn't we use a stuntman? It looks kind of dangerous. . . ."

Earnest shook his head. "We don't have any stuntmen on the budget. Besides, Dulaq's a trained athlete . . . strong as an ox."

Dulaq hung in midair, shouting at the men below him. To Westerly, there was a faint tinge of terror in the man's voice. Someone yelled from off in the distance, "Okay, try it!" Dulaq's body jerked into motion. The rig started moving him across the vast emptiness of the studio's open central area.

"Hold it!" the voice yelled; the rig halted so abruptly that Dulaq was almost thrown out of his skin. Westerly could feel his own eyeballs slam against his lids, in psychic communion with the man in the rig.

"Shouldn't we test the rig with a dummy first?" he asked Earnest.

For the second time that day the executive smiled. "What do you think we've got up there now?"

It was agonizing to watch. The technicians spent hours setting up the lights and whisking Dulaq backward and forward through the spacious studio on the aerial rig. They slammed him against walls, amidst frantic yells of "Slow it down!" or "Watch it!" Once the rig seemed to slip and Dulaq went hurtling to the floor, only to be snatched up again and yanked almost out of sight, into the shadows up near the ceiling. From the far corner where the technicians manipulated the controls came the sounds of multilingual swearing. And from the rigging itself came shrieks and groans.

Finally, the star of the show went gracefully swooping past Westerly, smiling manfully, as a trio of tiny unattended cameras automatically tracked him from the floor, like radar-directed antiaircraft guns getting a bead on an intruding attack plane. The technicians were clustered around the controls and watched their monitor screens. "Beautiful!" somebody shouted.

Meanwhile, Dulaq had traversed the length of the studio, still smiling, sailing like Superman through thin air and rode headfirst into the upper backwall of the starship bridge set.

Westerly heard a concussive *thunk*! The backwall tottered for a moment as Dulaq hung there, suddenly as stiff and wooden as a battering ram. Then the wall tumbled, taking most of the set apart with a series of splintering crashes. Amidst the flying dust and crashing two-by-threes, and all the rending, shrieking noises, Westerly clearly heard the same master technician shout out, "Hold it!"

They got Dulaq down from the rig, nearly dropping him from ten meters up in the process. He was still smiling and apparently conscious, although to Westerly his eyes definitely looked glassy. The technicians bundled him off to the infirmary, which fortunately was in the same building as the studio. By the time Westerly got there, a smiling medic was telling the assembled technicians:

"He's all right . . . didn't even get a splinter. I took an x-ray of his head and it showed nothing."

The technicians smiled and joked and went back to their work. As they dispersed, Westerly introduced himself to the medic and asked permission to see the star of the show.

The medic graciously ushered him into the infirmary's tiny emergency room. Dulaq was sitting up on the only cot, still smiling, with an icepack perched on his head.

"Hi," Westerly said. "How're you feeling?"

"Okay."

"That was one terrific shot you took out there."

"I got worst," Dulaq mumbled. "Onst, against de Redwings, I went right t'rough da glass."

They talked together for about a half hour, as Westerly's heart sank lower and lower. *This is the star of the show?* he kept asking himself.

"Do you think you'll be all right to start working on Monday?" he asked, feeling his head give a body-language *no*, despite his conscious efforts to keep it from shaking.

"Sure. I could go back now, if ya wanna."

"No! No . . . that's all right. You rest."

Westerly got up to leave, but Dulaq grasped his wrist in a grip of steel.

"Hey, one t'ing you do for me, huh?"

"Uh, sure. What?"

"Don't gimme no long speeches t'remember, huh? I don' want no long speeches. Too tough."

Krishna, Shiva and Vishnu, Westerly prayed. *Why have they done this to me?*

"Sure," he told Dulaq. "Don't worry about it."

"Okay. No long speeches."

"Right."

Dulaq let go of him and Westerly ducked through the accordion-fold door of the little sickroom, rubbing his wrist.

The doctor was at his cubbyhole desk.

"You examined him thoroughly?" Westerly asked.

"Yep," said the doctor.

"Did he talk that way before he hit his head?"

The doctor glowered at him.

Westerly had dinner with Rita Yearling, who seemed incredibly beautiful, utterly sure of herself and dismally cold toward him.

His hotel suite was sumptuously furnished, including a strange electronic console of shining metal and multicolored buttons that squatted bulkily in the far corner of the sitting room. Gregory Earnest had explained that the device was a three-dee phone station, which would link him instantaneously via satellite with Finger's private office in Los Angeles.

Somehow the phone loomed in his mind like an alien presence as he and Rita ate their dinner at the other end of the sitting room, near the windows.

Rita was polite, respectful and distant. The vibes coming from her were strictly professional, totally impersonal.

"Do you know Bernie Finger very well?"

"Of course."

"He discovered you?"

"Yes."

"Through an agent?"

"Oh, on his own."

"Where was that?"

"It doesn't really matter, does it?"

"No, I guess not. Um . . . what do you think of Ron Gabriel?"

"His brain's in his crotch."

"And your costar, Dulaq?"

"No brains at all."

And so it went, right through dinner, all the way through to the ice cream dessert that neither of them would do more than taste.

A part of Westerly's mind was almost amused. Here he was having dinner with the loveliest woman he had seen in years and he was bored silly by her. While she referred to other people as brainless, she came across as heartless, which in many ways was infinitely worse.

Finally he pushed aside his coffee cup and glanced at his wrist. "Finger will be calling in a few minutes, if he's on time."

"He's always on time," Rita said. She got up from her chair, a vision of Venus, Helen of Troy, Cleopatra, Harlow, Hayworth, Monroe—and equally cold, unalive.

"I'll let you two talk business together," Rita said.

Westerly got up and went to the door with her. She stopped just as he reached for the doorknob.

Without so much as a smile, Rita said, "B.F. won't mind if we ball, but we'll hafta keep it quiet from Gabriel. Ron thinks he's got me falling for him."

"Oh," was just about all that Westerly could manage.

"Just let me know where and when," she said.

He opened the door and she left the room.

For several minutes Westerly leaned against the closed door, his mind spinning. *It's not me,* he kept telling himself. *She really said it and that's the way it is with her. It means as much to her as filling out an application blank at the unemployment office.*

Still his hands trembled. He wished for the pleasant euphoria that a pinch of coke would bring. Or even the blankness of cat, the synthetic hypnotic drug that he started taking when Virginia was still in chemotherapy.

The phone chimed.

For an instant, Westerly didn't understand what the sound was. He had started the day in Rome, stopped in London and now—he remembered Earnest's instructions on operating the three-dee phone. He went to the desk near the rolling dinner table and picked up the handset. *The red button,* he mused. Turning toward the strange, squat apparatus across the room, he thumbed the red button.

The far half of the room seemed to disappear, dissolving into a section of Bernard Finger's Los Angeles office. The bright blue sky of early twilight was visible in the window behind Finger's imposing high-backed chair.

"H . . . hello," Westerly said shakily.

"Surprises you, eh?" Finger said back at him. "Just like being in the same room. That's how good Oxnard's new three-dee system is.

It's the system we're using on 'The Starcrossed" and *that's* what's gonna make it a great show."

"I'm glad we've got something going for us," said Westerly.

"Huh? Whaddaya mean by that?" Finger said.

Westerly pulled up his chair. This wasn't going to be a pleasant chat, he realized. "Well," he said, "I've only been here a few hours, but this is the way it looks to me. . . ."

He outlined what he had heard and seen, from his opening discussions with Earnest through his talk with Gabriel and the accident with Dulaq and its aftermath. He stopped short of telling about his dinner with Rita. Finger looked slightly upset at first, angry when he heard Gabriel's name, then ultimately bored of the whole litany of problems.

"You finished?" he asked when Westerly stopped.

"That seems like enough for the first day."

"H'mmp." Finger got up from his desk and the camera tracked him. To Westerly, it looked as if half his sitting room was shifting around, the walls and furnishings moving, as Finger paced slowly toward a sofa that appeared in one corner and then centered itself in his view.

Finger sat on the sofa and touched a button that was set into its arm. On the wall behind him, a professional football game suddenly appeared on a flat, two-dimensional wall-sized TV screen.

"You see that?"

"Pro football. That's our competition?"

Finger shook his head. "That's our salvation, if everything works out right."

"What do you mean?" asked Westerly.

Glancing furtively on either side of himself, Finger said, "This is a private, scrambled connection. If you try to tell anybody about this, I'll deny it and sue you. I'll make sure that you never work again *anywhere!*"

"What in hell. . . ."

"Shut up and listen. Part of the money that the bankers put up for 'The Starcrossed' is now invested in the Honolulu Pineapples."

"The what?"

"The football team! The Honolulu Pineapples! If they win the Superbowl, Titanic Productions is out of the red."

Westerly's mind was reeling again. For a moment he couldn't remember if he had brought the pills with him or not. *I was going to dump them in the Ganges, but I think I left them . . .*

"I'll give you the whole story," Finger was saying, "because you're the guy who's got to come through for me."

. . . in the zipper compartment of the flightbag.

"The bankers gave me enough money for one series. If it hits, Titanic gets more money to pull us out of debt. Got that? But we're up to our assholes in bills right now, baby! Now! Not the end of next season, but now!"

None of this is real, Westerly told himself.

"So I'm using some of the bankers' money to keep our heads above water, pay a few bills here and there. And the rest of it I'm betting on the Pineapples. As long as they keep winning, we can keep treading water. If they take the Superbowl, we're home free."

"What's this got to do with 'The Starcrossed'?" Westerly heard himself ask.

"Don't you understand? The money for the show is already spent!" Finger's voice was almost pleading. *For what? Understanding? Mercy? Appreciation?* "There isn't any more money for 'The Starcrossed.' It's spent. Bet on the Pineapples. The budget you've got is *all* you're going to get. There's not another nickel in the drawer."

"There's no money for writers?"

"No."

"No money for better actors?"

"No."

"No money for staff or technicians or art directors or. . . ."

"No money for nothing!" Finger bellowed. "Not another penny. Just what's on the budget now. Nothing more. You've got enough to do thirteen shows. That's it. If the series isn't a hit after the first couple weeks, it's over."

"I can't work like that," Westerly said. "I've got to have decent material, competent staff. . . ."

"You work with what you've got. That's *it*, baby!"

"No sir. Not me."

"That's all there is," Finger insisted.

"I can't work that way."

"Yes you can."

"I won't!"

"You've got to!"

Westerly got to his feet. For an instant he was tempted to walk over and grab Finger by the throat and *make* him understand. Then he realized that the man was a safe five thousand kilometers away.

"I won't do it," he said quietly. "I quit."

"You can't quit."

"Says who?"

"Says me." Finger's voice went low and ugly. "You try quitting and I'll send you some visitors. Guys you owe money to."

"Who? The IRS? My ex-wife's lawyers? They can't touch me in Canada."

"Not them. The guys you bought your goodies from, just before you took off for the far hills. *They* can touch you . . . oh, brother, can they touch you."

Westerly felt a river of flame run through his guts. "You told me you had squared that!" he shouted.

"I told *them* that I'd square it . . . after you'd done the first thirteen shows. They're waiting. Patiently."

"You lying sonofabitch. . . ."

"And you're a cathead, an acid freak. So what? You do your job and you'll be okay. You just make do with what you've got there. And no complaints."

With his eyes closed, Westerly echoed, "No complaints."

"Good," Finger said. "Maybe we can all get out of this in one piece. Even if the show flops, the Pineapples are winning pretty good."

"Wonderful."

"Damned right it's wonderful. Now you take good care of yourself and have fun. I'm already contacting the right people about the Emmies. They'll be watching you. Them . . . and others."

"Thanks."

"You're entirely welcome. Good night."

Finger and his office abruptly disappeared, replaced by the rest of the sitting room and the ugly three-dee console.

Westerly stood without moving for several minutes. Then he stirred himself and headed for the bedroom. The flightbag was on the bed. And inside the zipper compartment, he knew, were enough pills to make him forget about this phone conversation.

At least, for a little while.

11: The First Day's Shooting

Gregory Earnest sat in the control booth; high above the rebuilt starship bridge set.

Directly in front of him were the engineers and technicians who ran the complex three-dee holographic equipment. They sat along a row of desk consoles, earphones clamped to their heads, eyes fixed on the green, glowing dials and viewscreens that were the only illumination in the darkened control booth.

Beyond the soundproof window in front of them, the set was alive with crewmen and actors. Electricians were trailing cables across the floor; cameramen were jockeying their self-propelled units and nodding their laser snouts up and down, right and left, like trainers taking high-spirited horses for a morning trot. Mitch Westerly was deep in conversation with Dulaq, one arm around the burly hockey star's shoulders. Rita Yearling lounged languidly on her special liquafoam couch, glowing with the metallic sheen of her skintight costume. Ron Gabriel paced nervously around the set, orbiting closer and closer to Rita.

Earnest's nose throbbed whenever he saw Gabriel. And a special vein in his forehead, reserved exclusively for passions of hatred and revenge, pulsed visibly.

"The first take of the first scene," a voice whispered from behind Earnest.

He turned to scowl, but saw that the speaker was Les Montpelier, from Titanic. He let his scowl vanish. Montpelier was B.F.'s special

128

representative, here to lend an air of official enthusiasm to the first day's shooting. He was higher in the pecking order than the Executive Producer, entitled to scowl but not to be scowled at.

For a moment neither man said anything. They simply sat there looking at each other, Montpelier's trim little red beard nearly touching the Canadian's shaggier black one.

Then, over the loudspeaker, they heard Westerly's voice crackle: "Okay, let's get started."

A technician held out the clapboard and shouted, "Starcrossed. Episode One, Scene One. Take One."

"We're on our way!" Montpelier said with almost genuine enthusiasm, as the clapboard cracked and fell apart. The embarrassed technician picked up the pieces and scuttled out of camera range, shaking his head at the broken clapboard in his hands.

An omen? Earnest wondered.

Brenda Impanema stayed well back in the shadows, away from the bustling men and women on the blazingly lighted set.

"Would you like a chair?"

Startled, she looked around to see Bill Oxnard smiling at her. He was carrying a pair of folding chairs, one in each hand.

"I won't be able to see if I sit down," she whispered.

"Then stand on it," he said as he flicked the chairs open and set them down on the cement floor.

With a grin of thanks, Brenda clambered up on a chair. Oxnard climbed up beside her.

"I thought you were back at Malibu," she said, without taking her eyes from the two minor actors who were going through their lines under the lights.

"Couldn't stay there," he replied. "Kept fidgeting. Guess I wanted to see how the equipment works the first day. And I've got some new ideas to discuss with you, when you have some free time."

"Business ideas?"

He looked at her and Brenda saw a mixture of surprise, hurt and anticipation in his face.

With a slow nod, he replied, "Uh, yes . . . business ideas."

"Fine," said Brenda.

The actors were clomping across the bridge set, pronouncing their lines and fiddling with the props that were supposed to be the starship's controls. Out of the corner of her eye, Brenda could see Oxnard shaking his head and muttering to himself.

"What's the matter?" she whispered.

"The lights. I told them we don't need so much wattage with this holographic system. They're going to wash out everything . . . the tape will be overexposed."

"Can't they take care of that electronically, up in the control booth?"

"Up to a point. I just wish they'd listen to what I tell them. Once, at least."

His teeth were clenched and he looked very unhappy.

"It'll be all right," she said soothingly.

Oxnard grimaced and jabbed a finger toward the actors. "You don't use an astrolabe for navigating a starship! I *told* Earnest and the rest of them . . . why don't they *listen*?"

Mitch Westerly wasn't worried about the astrolabe or any other technical details. His head was still buzzing from last night's high. Faced with the first day's shooting, he hadn't been able to get to sleep without help. Which came in the form of pills that floated him up among the stars and then dumped him on the cement floor of the studio with a bad case of shakes.

Liven it up, you guys! he ordered the actors, mentally. *We don't have time or money for retakes. Put some life into it.*

"We haven't seen any signs of the Capulet starship since we left Rigel Six," said the first bit player, pronouncing "Wriggle" instead of "Rye-gel."

"Maybe they never got away from the planet," spoke the second, as if he were being forced to repeat the words at gunpoint. "They were having trouble with their engines, weren't they?"

With some feeling! Westerly pleaded silently.

"I'll check the radars," said Actor One.

"Cut!" Westerly yelled.

Both actors looked blankly toward him. "What's the matter?"

Westerly strode out onto the set. He felt the glare of the lights on his shoulders like a palpable force.

"The word in the script is 'scanners,' not 'radar,'" Westerly said, squinting in the light despite his shades.

The actor shrugged. "What's the difference?"

Ron Gabriel came trotting up. "What's the difference? You're supposed to be seven hundred years in the future, dim-dum! They don't use radar anymore!"

The actor was tall and lanky. When he shrugged, it looked like a construction crane stirring into motion. "Aww, who's gonna know the difference?"

Gabriel started hopping up and down. "*I'll* know the difference! And so will anybody with enough brains in his head to find the men's room without a seeing-eye dog!"

Westerly placed a calming hand on the writer's shoulder. "Don't get worked up, Ron."

"Don't get worked up?"

Turning back to the actor, Westerly said, "The word is *scanners.*"

"Scanners." Sullenly.

"Scanners," Westerly repeated. "And you two guys are supposed to be joking around, throwing quips at each other. Try to get some life into your lines."

"Scanners," the actor repeated.

Westerly went back to his position next to the Number One camera unit. The script girl—a nondescript niece of somebody's who spoke nothing but French—pointed to the place in the scene where they had stopped.

"Okay," Westerly said, with a deep breath. "Let's take it from . . . 'Maybe they never got away from that planet.' With life." *Cat,* he said to himself. *I've got to find some cat or I'll never sleep again.*

Ron Gabriel was trying not to listen. He prowled around the edges of the clustered crew, peeking between electricians and idle actors as they stood watching the scene being taped. *They're mangling my words,* he knew. *They're taking the words I wrote and grinding them up in a cement mixer. Whatever's left, they're putting into a blender and then beating it with a stick when it comes crawling out.*

He felt as if he himself were being treated the same way.

He paced doggedly, his back to the lighted set.

Farther back, away from the action, Brenda and Oxnard were standing on their chairs, watching. Off to one side, Rita Yearling reclined on her couch, the one Finger had flown up from Hollywood for her.

Gabriel stopped pacing and stared at her. *If it wasn't for her,* he thought, *I'd have walked out on this troop of baboons long ago. Maybe I ought to split anyway. She's a terrific lay, but. . . .*

Rita must have felt him watching her. She looked up and smiled beckoningly. Gabriel went over to her side and hunkered down on his heels.

"Nervous?" he asked her.

Her eyes were extraordinarily blue today and they widened with girlish surprise. "Nervous? Why should I be nervous? I know all my lines. I could say them backwards."

Gabriel frowned. "We've already got one clown who's going to be doing that."

"What do you mean?" Her voice was an innocent child's.

"Dulaq. He's going to get it all ass-backwards. I just know it."

"Oh, he'll be all right," Rita said soothingly. "Don't get yourself flustered."

"He's an idiot. He'll never get through one scene."

Rita smiled and patted Gabriel's cheek. "Francois will be all right. He can be very much in control. He's a take-charge kind of guy."

"How do you know?" Gabriel demanded.

She made her surprised little girl face again, and Gabriel somehow found it irritating this time. "Why, by watching him play hockey, of course. How else?"

Before Gabriel could answer, the assistant director's voice bellowed (assistant directors are hired for their lungpower): "Okay, set up for Scene Two, Dulaq and Yearling, front and center."

"I've got to go to work," Rita said, swinging her exquisite legs off the couch.

"Yeah," said Gabriel.

"Wish me luck."

"Break a fibia."

She blew him a kiss and slinked off toward the set. Gabriel watched her disappear among the technicians and actors, and suddenly realized that her walk, which used to be enough to engorge all his erectile tissue, didn't affect him that way anymore. The thrill was gone. With a rueful shake of his head, he walked toward the set like Jimmy Cagney heading bravely down the Last Mile toward the little green door.

Scene Two: Int., starship bridge. BEN is sitting at the control console, watching the viewscreens as the ship flies through the interstellar void at many times the speed of light. On the viewscreens we see nothing but scattered stars against the blackness of space.

BEN
(To himself.) Guess we've shaken off those Capulets. Haven't seen another ship within a hundred parsecs of us.

ROM enters. He is upset, despondent. (Tell Dulaq that the Redwings will win the Stanley Cup next year; that should work him up enough for this scene.) He glances at the viewscreens, then goes to BEN and stands beside him.

BEN
(Looking up at Rom.) Greetings, cousin. How are you this day?

ROM
Not as good. (Shakes his head)

BEN
What's the trouble, cousin?

ROM
I dunno. Must'a been somet'in I picked up back on Rigel Six. Maybe a bug. . . .

"*Cut!*"
"Francois . . . the script says 'virus,' not 'bug.'"
"Ahh. 'Bug' sounds better. I don't like all dose fancy words."

"Try to say 'virus,' will you? And watch your diction."
"My what?"
"Your pronunciation!"
"Hey, you want me to say all dose funny words and pernounce everyt'ing your way? At de same time? Come on!"
"Take it from, 'What's the trouble, cousin.'"

BEN
What's the trouble, cousin?

ROM
I dunno. Must'a been somet'in I picked up back on Rigel Six. Maybe a b . . . a virus or somet'ing.

BEN
(With a grin.) Or that Capulet girl you were eyeing, Julie.
ROM grabs BEN's lapels and lifts him out of his chair.

ROM
(With some heat.) Hey, I don't mess around with Capulets. Dey're our enemies!

BEN
(Frightened.) Okay . . . okay! I was only joking.

ROM
(Lets him go. He drops back into his seat.) Some t'ings you shouldn't kid about. . . . Go on back and grab somet'ing to eat. I'll take over.

BEN
(Glad to get away.) Sure. It's all yours, cousin.

BEN hurries off-camera. ROM sits at the command console, stares out at the stars.

ROM

(Pensively.) All dose stars . . . all dat emptiness. I wish she
was right here, instead of back on Rigel Six.
JULIE steps out from behind the electronic computer,
where she's been hiding since she stowed away on the
Montague starship.

JULIE
(Shyly.) I *am* here, ROM. I stowed away aboard your ship.

ROM
(Dumbfounded.) You . . . you . . . Hey, Mitch, what th'hell's
my next line?

"Cut!!!"

From up in the control booth, Les Montpelier kept telling himself, *It's not as bad as it looks. They'll fix up all the goofs in the editing
process. Maybe we can even get somebody to dub a voice over Dulaq's
lines. He looks pretty good, at least.*
At that moment, Dulaq was pointing to the blank side wall of the
set, where the Capulets' starship would be matted in on the final tape.
"How'd your ship catch up wit' us so soon?" he was asking Rita
Yearling. But he was looking neither at her nor the to-be-inserted
view of the other starship. He was peering, squint-eyed, toward
Mitch Westerly. The director had his face sunk in his hands, as if he
were crying.
"Rita looks stunning," said Gregory Earnest, with a hyena's leer
on his face.
"She sure does," Montpelier agreed. "But there's something
wrong about her . . . something. . . ."
Rita's face was all dewy-cheeked youth, her eyes wide and blue as
a new spring sky. But her body was adult seductress and she slinked
around the set with the practiced undulations of a bellydancer.
". . . something about her that doesn't seem quite right for the
character she's supposed to be playing," Montpelier finished.
"The audience will love her," Earnest said. "We've got to give
them a little pizazz."
Montpelier started to answer, but hesitated. *Maybe he's right.*

"And Dulaq looks magnificent," the Canadian went on. "Look at that costume. Shows plenty of muscles, doesn't it?" Earnest's voice was almost throbbing with delight.

"Too bad it doesn't cover his mouth," Montpelier said.

Earnest shot him an angry glance.

On the set, Dulaq was staring off into space. He thought he was looking at the red light of an active camera unit, as Westerly had instructed him to do. Actually, he was fixing his gaze on a red EXIT sign glowing in the darkness on the other end of the huge studio. Dulaq's eyes weren't all that good.

"I know it's wrong," he was saying, "But I love you, Julie. I'm mad about you."

Rita was entwining herself about his muscular frame, like a snake climbing a tree.

"And I love you, Rom darling," she breathed. The boom microphone, over her head, seemed to wilt in the heat of her torridly low-pitched voice.

"That's a shy, innocent young girl?" Montpelier asked rhetorically,

Dulaq finally focused his ruggedly handsome gaze on her, as their noses touched. Suddenly he gave a strangled growl and clutched at her. Rita shrieked and they both went tumbling to the floor.

"Cut!" Mitch Westerly yelled. "Cut!"

The cameramen were grinning and training their equipment on the squirming couple. Then, out of the crowd, came a blur of fury.

Ron Gabriel leaped on Dulaq's back and started pounding the hockey star's head. "Leggo of her, you goddamn ape!" he screamed.

It took Dulaq several moments to notice what was happening to him. Then, with a roar, he swung around and flipped Gabriel off his back. The writer staggered to his knees, got up quickly and launched himself at Dulaq.

With a surprised look on his face, Dulaq took Gabriel's charge. The writer's head rammed into his stomach, but produced nothing except a slight "Oof" which might have come from either one of them. Gabriel rebounded, looking a bit glassy eyed. He charged at Dulaq again and kicked him in the shins, hard.

It finally seemed to penetrate Dulaq's head that he was being attacked by someone who had no hockey stick in his hands. The athlete's face relaxed into a pleasant grin as he picked Gabriel up off his feet with one hand and socked him between the eyes so hard that the writer sailed completely off the set while his shirt remained in Dulaq's left fist.

Pandemonium raged. The only recognizable sound to come out of the roiling crowd on the set was Westerly, pathetically screaming "Cut! Cut!"

Montpelier and the technicians in the control booth bolted out the door and down the steps to the floor of the studio. Gregory Earnest sat in the darkened booth alone, watching the riot develop, and smiled to himself.

He knew at last how to get rid of Ron Gabriel. And how to cash in on what little money would be made by "The Starcrossed."

12: The Squeeze Play

Gregory Earnest's home was a modest ranch house in one of the new developments between Badger Studio and the busy Toronto International Jetport. Although nearly half the expense to the house had gone into insulation—thermal and acoustic—the entire place still rumbled and shivered with the infrasonic, barely audible vibrations of the big jets screaming by just over the roof.

The living quarters were actually underground, in what was originally the basement level. Earnest had spent many weekends digging, cementing, enlarging the underground portion of the house, until now—after five years' occupancy—he had a network of bunkers that would have made Adolf Hitler feel homesick. His wife made all her neighbors envious with tales of Gregory's single-minded handiness and devotion to home improvement. While she turned the neighborhood women green and they nagged their husbands, Earnest dug with the dedication of a prisoner of war, happily alone and free of his wife and their two milk-spilling, runny-nosed, grammar-school children.

Les Montpelier was a little puzzled when he first rang Earnest's doorbell. It was Sunday, the studio was still closed for repairs. Ron Gabriel had left the hospital with two black eyes and several painfully cracked ribs, but no broken bones. Francois Dulaq had a bruised hand and some interesting bite marks on his upper torso. Rita Yearling was doing television talk shows all weekend, back in the States. Mitch Westerly had disappeared under a cloud of marijuana smoke.

Montpelier was not in the jauntiest of moods. "The Starcrossed" was a dead duck, he knew, even before the second day of shooting in the studio. It was hopeless.

Yet Gregory Earnest obviously had something optimistic in mind when he had called Montpelier at the hotel.

So, puzzled and depressed, with a microfilm copy of the *L.A. Free Press-News-Times* Sunday help wanted ad section in the pocket of his severely styled mod Edgar Allan Poe business suit, he leaned on the bell button of Earnest's front door. A jumbo jet came screaming up from what seemed like a few meters away, making the very ground shake with the roar of its mighty engines, and spewing fumes and excess kerosene in its wake. Montpelier suddenly realized why the lawns looked so greasy. He was glad that his suit was dead black.

The door opened and he was greeted by a smiling Eskimo. At least, she looked like an Eskimo. Her round face was framed by a furry hood. Her coat was trimmed with antlered designs from the far north. She smiled and moved her mouth, but Montpelier couldn't hear a word over the rumbling whine of the dwindling jet.

"Can't hear you," he said and found that he couldn't even hear himself.

They stood in the doorway smiling awkwardly at each other for a few minutes as the jet flew off into the distance.

"You must be Mr. Montpelier," said the round-faced woman. Her accent was more Oxford than igloo and Montpelier realized that her face really had none of the oriental flatness of an Eskimo's.

"I'm Gwendoline Earnest, Gregory's wife. I was just taking Gulliver and Gertrude to the skating rink. . . ."

Two more Eskimos appeared. Little ones, round and furry in their plastiskin parkas. It wasn't that cold outside, Montpelier realized. *Maybe Eskimo is the next big style trend.*

Gwendoline Earnest shooed her two little ones out and down the driveway. "Greg's down in the study, waiting for you," she said, squeezing past Montpelier at the doorway. She started down the driveway toward the minibus parked at the curb. "And thank you," she called over her shoulder, "for taking him away from his eternal digging for one Sunday! It's such a pleasure not to hear the pounding and the swearing!"

She waved a cheery "Ta-ta!" and pushed the kids into the yawning side door of the minibus.

With a bewildered shake of his head, Montpelier stepped inside what he thought would be the house's living room. It looked more like an attic. There were bicycles, toys, crates, suitcases, piles of books and spools of videotape. Another jetliner roared overhead; even with the front door closed, the ear-splitting sound made Montpelier's teeth ache.

He threaded his way through the maze of junk, looking for a living area. The entire house seemed to be cluttered with storage materials.

It took ten minutes of shouting back and forth before Montpelier tumbled to the fact that Earnest—and the real living quarters—were downstairs in the erstwhile basement. Another few minutes to find the right door and the stairs leading down, then the usual meaningless words of greeting, and Montpelier found himself sitting in a comfortable panelled den, in a large overstuffed chair, with a beer in his hand.

Gregory Earnest sat across the corner from him, equally at ease with a beer mug in one hand. It had an old corporation logo on it: GE. *Gregory, Gwendoline, Gulliver and Gertrude Earnest,* Montpelier reflected. *He must've bought a case of those mugs when the antitrust boys broke up old GE.*

In the opposite corner of the den, the three-dee set was tuned to the National Football League's game of the week. Montpelier couldn't tell who was playing: all he saw was a miniature set of armored players tumbling and grunting across the other side of Earnest's den, like Lilliputian buffoons who'd been hired to entertain a sadistic king. Only the scintillations and shimmerings of the imperfect three-dee projection betrayed the fact that they were watching holographic images, rather than real, solid, miniature figures.

Earnest touched a button in the keyboard that was set into the arm of his recliner chair and the sound of pain and cheering disappeared. But the game went on.

"Imagine how terrific the games will look," Earnest said in his nasal, oily way of speaking, "when Oxnard's new system is used. Then you can buy giant-sized three-dee tubes. It'll look like you're right there on the field with them."

Montpelier nodded. There was something about Earnest that always disturbed him. The man was too sly, too roundabout. He'd fit in well at Titanic.

Earnest was wearing a pullover sweater and an ancient pair of patched jeans. He seemed utterly at ease, smiling. Montpelier was reminded of the cobra and the mongoose, but he didn't know who was supposed to be which.

"You look relaxed and happy," Montpelier said.

Earnest's smile showed more teeth. "Why shouldn't I be?"

After a sip of beer, Montpelier said, "If I were the producer of a show that started off as disastrously as 'The Starcrossed' did last week. . . ."

"Oh that." Earnest made a nonchalant gesture. "I wouldn't worry about that."

"No?"

"Why worry? Is B.F. worried?"

"He sure is," Montpelier said. "He almost went into shock when I told him what happened in the studio."

"Really?"

Earnest's voice got so arch that Montpelier found himself getting angry, something he never did with a potential ally. Or enemy. It was a luxury you couldn't afford in this business. Not if you wanted to survive.

"What are you driving at?" Montpelier asked, trying to keep his voice level.

Earnest nodded toward the three-dee game that still rolled and thudded across the far side of the den.

"The Pineapples," he said. "They're winning."

"So?"

"So long as they keep winning, B.F.'s money is safe. Right?"

Montpelier fought down a gnawing panic. Either Earnest had completely flipped, which was not too unlikely, and was now certifiably insane—or he knew something that he himself didn't know, which was a very dangerous position for Montpelier to be in.

"Are, ah . . . you betting on the Pineapples?" he fished.

"Sure I am. Especially since I found out that B.F. is sinking almost all his cash into them. When they win the title, we can forget about 'The Starcrossed.' Won't matter if the show never goes beyond the first seven weeks."

Slowly, without revealing how little he actually knew, Montpelier coaxed the story out of Earnest. It wasn't difficult. The Canadian was very proud of himself. He had some friends in the local phone company tap all the special three-dee phones that Finger had installed in the various hotel suites. Montpelier was suddenly grateful that he didn't rank high enough for such luxury. Only Westerly, Gabriel and Yearling had them. And Gabriel got one only because he screamed and threw tantrums until Brenda put through a call to Finger's office.

"You should hear the conversations between Rita and B.F.," Earnest said, licking his chops. "And *see* the display she puts on for him. In three-dee yet! I've got some of them taped, you know."

Montpelier guided him back to the main subject. "So as long as the Pineapples keep winning their football games, Titanic's cash is safe."

"Right," Earnest answered. "And 'The Starcrossed' is just a front operation to keep those New York bankers convinced that B.F. has invested their money in a show."

"So the show gets as little money as possible. . . ."

"Sure. Just enough to keep it going. Oh, I think B.F. really wants to make Rita into a star . . . but that doesn't mean he's going to spend more than he has to. Just enough to get her on The Tube for a few weeks and see how the public reacts to her."

"Yeah, that sounds like B.F.'s way of doing business," Montpelier agreed.

But Earnest had turned his attention to the football game. One of the miniature players was scampering like mad and other players were chasing after him while the background whizzed past. Yet none of them actually moved very far across Earnest's floor. It was like watching midgets struggling on a treadmill.

"The Pineapples just intercepted another pass!" Earnest was chortling. "I *knew* those Mexicans couldn't play our style of football!"

Montpelier leaned over and nudged his shoulder. "I didn't come here to watch a football game. You said you had something important to tell me."

Earnest's smile went nasty. "That's right. What do you think would happen if those New York bankers found out what B.F.'s doing with their money? Those banks are *Mafioso*, you know. The mob owns the banks and the WASPs are just front-men."

Montpelier didn't answer. But he had figured out which of them was the cobra.

"Now, I happen to be smart enough," Earnest went on, "to understand what's going on in B.F.'s mind. 'The Starcrossed' is *supposed* to flop. When it does, B.F. will tell his bankers that the show went broke and their investment is down the drain. Maybe they'll get Rita or some other goods as a booby prize." He grinned at his feeble pun.

"That's crazy. . . ."

"Is it?" Earnest shrugged, the scratched at his beard. "Maybe so. But it would make a fun story in *New York*, don't you think?"

"If anybody believed you. . . ."

"They would. But why should I cut off the hand that feeds me? Especially when it's going to feed me so well."

"You mean blackmail."

Earnest shook his head. "No, that's not nice. And it could be risky. No, you just tell B.F. that I understand what he wants and I'm willing to help him. It won't cost him an extra cent."

"What do you want?"

"Nothing very much. I'll bet on the Pineapples, too. Maybe he can put me in touch with his own brokers, so that I can get the same rates he does."

From the inflection in Earnest's voice, Montpelier knew that there was more.

"And what else?" he asked.

"Oh nothing much, really." Earnest spread his arms out, expansively. "Just control of the show. I *am* the Executive Producer, after all. All I want is complete authority. I want to do the hiring and firing. All of it. From here on. With no interference from you or Brenda or anybody at Titantic."

"Complete authority," Montpelier echoed.

"Right. I can handle Westerly. He's through as a director, but he still has a good name. I can keep him supplied with enough cat to make him docile. . . ."

"Cat?" Montpelier's insides winced, as if they'd been electroshocked.

"Oh, it's all completely legal," Earnest assured him. "I have a few friends at the hospital here who'll make out prescriptions for him. I get a cut of their fees and the pharmacy price, of course; cat's *very* expensive stuff, you know. But that'll keep Westerly happy and under control."

Montpelier found that his hands were shaking.

"And then there's Gabriel," Earnest said with relish. "He goes. I'm going to fire his ass right out of here so fast he won't know what hit him."

"Now wait . . . we need him for the scripts. Those high school kids can't turn out shootable scripts and you know it."

"I can find a dozen writers who'll work for *free*," Earnest crowed, "just for the glory of getting their names on The Tube. The local science fiction writers' chapter has plenty of people who'll gladly fill in."

"But Gabriel has talent! His scripts are the only decent thing we've got going for us!"

"Who cares? The show's not supposed to be a hit. Get that through your skull. Think of it as a tax writeoff."

Montpelier felt his jaw muscles clenching. "But Ron is. . . ."

"Ron Gabriel is out!" Earnest shouted, a vein on his forehead throbbing visibly. "His scripts are out, too. Wait until the network censors see them! There won't be enough left to wipe your backside with."

"But the censors have already. . . ."

"No they haven't," Earnest said, with the most malicious grin Montpelier had ever seen. "Gabriel was so late turning them in. . . ."

"That's because he had to work on all the other scripts."

". . . that I let the crew start up production *before* sending the scripts to the censors. I'll be meeting with them tomorrow. And with the sponsor's representatives, too. *That* will finish Mr. Gabriel and his high-and-mighty scripts!"

"But . . ."

"And what do you think B.F. is going to say about Gabriel when I tell him how he's been sacking with Rita all these weeks, behind his back?"

"It hasn't been exactly behind his back."

Earnest smiled another chilling smile. "I know that, and you know that, and B.F. knows that. But what will the gossip programs say about it? Eh? Can B.F. afford to have his image belittled in public?"

Calling this character a snake is insulting the snakes, Montpelier told himself. But he said nothing.

"Come on," Earnest said, suddenly very hearty and full of beery good cheer. "Don't look so glum. We're all going to make a good pile of money out of this. So what if the series folds early? We'll cry all the way to the bank."

For the first time in many years, Montpelier found himself contradicting one of his primary survival rules. Out of the depth of his guts, he spoke his feelings:

"I'd always heard that the rats were the first to leave a sinking ship. But I never realized that some of the rats are the sonsofbitches that scuttled the ship in the first place."

13: The Three Monkeys

The restaurant was poised atop Toronto's tallest office tower, balanced delicately on a well-oiled mechanism that smoothly turned the entire floor around in a full circle once every half hour. It was too slow to be called a merry-go-round, so the restaurant management (it was part of an American-owned chain) called it the Roundeley Room.

The building was very solidly constructed, since there were no earthquake fears so close to the Laurentian Shield. Since the worldwide impact of a theater movie a generation earlier, dealing with a fire in a glass tower, there were sprinklers everywhere—in the ceilings, under the tables of the restaurant, in the elevators and restrooms and even along the walls, cleverly camouflaged as wrought iron decorations.

The restaurant was up high enough so that on a clear day diners could see the gray-brown smudge across Lake Ontario that marked the slums of Buffalo. To the north, they could watch the city of Toronto peter out into muskeg and dreary housing developments.

The weather had turned cold, with an icy wind howling down from the tundra. But it was a clear, dry cold, the kind of air meteorologists call an Arctic High. Air crisp enough to shatter like crystal.

From his seat in a soundproofed booth, Les Montpelier watched the last rays of the sinking sun turn the city into a vermilion fantasyland. Lights were winking on; automobile traffic made a continuous ribbon of white light on one side of the highways, red on the other. Safely behind the insulated windows, Montpelier could hear the polar wind whispering past. But he felt warm and comfortable. Physically.

"It's a beautiful view," said the man across the booth from him.

"That it is," Montpelier agreed.

The man was Elton Good, who had flown up from New York. He was a tall, spare, almost cadaverous man in that indistinct age category between Saturday afternoon softball games and Saturday afternoon checkers games. His eyes were alive, deep brown, sparkling. He wore an almost perpetual smile, but it looked more like an apology than anything joyful. His clothes were straight Madison Avenue chic—neo-Jesuit, minus the religious icons, of course.

Elton Good worked for the Federal Inter-Network Combine (FINC), the quasipublic, quasigovernmental, quasicorporate overview group that interconnected the rulings of the Federal Communications Commission, the pressures of the Consumer Relations Board, the demands of the national networks, and the letters from various PTA and religious groups. Since network executives usually filled the posts of the FCC and CRB, the job wasn't as taxing as it might sound to an outsider.

Elton Good was a censor. His job was to make certain that nothing disturbing to the public, contrary to FCC regulations or harmful to network profits got onto The Tube.

"Is Mr. Gabriel always this late?" Good asked, with a slight edge to his reedy voice.

Montpelier couldn't reconcile the voice with the sweetly smiling face. "He had to stop at the hospital. They're taking the bandages off his face."

"Oh, yes . . . that . . . brawl he got himself into." Good edged back away from the table slightly, as if he might become contaminated by it all. "Very ugly business. Very ugly."

This is going to be some dinner, Montpelier knew.

In another soundproofed booth, across the restaurant, Brenda Impanema was smiling at Keith Connors, third assistant vice president for marketing of Texas New Technology, Inc.

Connors wore a Confederate-gray business suit, hand-tooled Mexican boots, and had an RAF mustache that curled up almost to the corners of his eyes.

"I knew I'd spot y'all in the middle of a crowded restaurant even though I'd never see y'all befoah," he was saying. "I jes' tole myself, Keith, ol' buddy, y'all jes' go lookin' for the purtiest gal in the place. These Canadian chicks don't have the class of California gals."

Brenda smiled demurely. "Actually, I was born in New Mexico."

"Hey! That's practically in Texas! No wonder yo're so purty."

Connors was beaming at her, the glow of his toothy smile outshining the candle on their table by several orders of magnitude. He had already shown Brenda holograms of his Mexican wife and their six children—all under seven years of age. "Guess I'm jes' a powerful ol' lover," he had smirked when she commented on the size of his family.

Brenda hadn't quite known what to expect of the executive from TNT. Bernard Finger had called her that afternoon and ordered her to have dinner with the man and show him some of Toronto's night life.

"TNT could take over sponsorship of the whole show, all by themselves," Finger had said. "They're big and they're not afraid to spend money."

Brenda glowered at Titanic's chief. "How nice do you want me to be to him?"

Finger glowered back at her. "You get paid for using your brains, not your pelvis. There's plenty action for a Texas cowboy in town. You just show him where the waterholes are."

So she had dressed in a demure, translucent knee-length gown and decorated it with plenty of the electronic jewelry that TNT manufactured. As she sat in the booth, silhouetted against the gathering twilight, she glittered like an airport runway.

"Yessir, you shore are purty," Connors said, with a puppydog wag in his voice.

"Do you think," Brenda asked coolly, "that your company will want to advertise your electronic jewelry on 'The Starcrossed'? Seems like a natural, to me."

The booths at the Roundeley Room were soundproofed so that private conversations could not be overheard, and also to protect the restaurant's patrons from the noisy entrances made by some customers.

Gloria Glory swept into the restaurant's foyer, flanked by Francois Dulaq, Rita Yearling and Gregory Earnest. The effect was stunning.

Once a regally tall, statuesque woman, Gloria Glory had allowed many years of success as a gossip columnist to freeze her self-image. While she still thought of herself as regal and statuesque, to the outside world she closely resembled an asthmatic dirigible swathed in neon-bright floor-length robes.

No one ever told her this, of course, because her power to make or destroy something as fragile as a "show-business personality" was enormous. In the delicate world of the entertainment arts, where talent and experience counted for about a tenth of what publicity and perseverance could get for you, Gloria Glory possessed a megatonnage unapproached by any other columnist. Her viewers were fanatically devoted to her: what Gloria said was "in" was *in*; who she said was "out" went hungry.

So words such as *fat, overweight* and *diet* had long since disappeared from Gloria's world. They were as unspoken near her as descriptions of nasal protuberances went unsaid near Cyrano de Bergerac.

The maître d', the hatcheck girl, two headwaiters who usually did nothing but stand near the entrance and look imperious, and a dozen other customers all clustered around Gloria and her entourage.

The hatcheck girl and most of the customers were asking Dulaq for his autograph. They recognized the hockey star's handsome face, his rugged physique, and his name spelled on the back of the All-Canadian All-Stars team jacket that he was wearing.

The headwaiters and most of the men in the growing crowd were panting around Rita Yearling, who wore a see-through clingtight dress with nothing under it except her own impressive physique. The traffic jam was beginning to cause a commotion and block the newcomers who were piling up at the head of the escalator.

The maître d', with the unerring instinct of the breed, gravitated toward Gloria Glory. He had never seen her before and never watched television. But he knew money when he sniffed it. Calmly ignoring the rising tide of shrieks and curses from the top of the escalator as body tumbled upon body, he gave Gloria the utmost compliment: he didn't ask if she had a reservation.

"Madam would you prefer a private room, perhaps?"

Gregory Earnest, roundly ignored by all present, started to say, "I made a reserva. . . ."

But Gloria's foghorn voice drowned him out. "Naah . . . I like to be right in the middle of all the hustle and bustle. How about something right in the center of everything?"

"Of course," said the maître d'.

Gloria swept regally across the crowded restaurant, like a Montgolfier Brothers hot-air balloon trailing pretty little pennants and fluttering ribbons of silk. Earnest and the two stars followed in her wake, while the maître d' preceded her with the haughty air of Grand Vizier. The jumbled, tumbled, grumbling crowd at the top of the escalator was left to sort itself out. After all, that's what insurance lawyers were for, was it not?

Montpelier couldn't hear the shouts and shrieks from the foyer, of course. But he watched Gloria and her entourage march to the table nearest the computer-directed jukebox. He breathed a silent thanksgiving that Gabriel hadn't arrived at the same time as Earnest.

"Um, would you like a drink, Mr. Good?" he asked.

Good held up a long-fingered hand. "Never touch alcohol, Mr. Montpelier. . . ."

"Les."

"Alcohol and business don't mix. Never have."

"Well, that's one thing you and Ron Gabriel have in common," Montpelier said.

"Oh? What's that?"

"He doesn't drink, either."

"Really?" Good's perpetual smile got wider and somehow tenser. "That's a surprise."

"What do you mean?"

"From all the depravity in his scripts, I assumed he was either an alcoholic or a drug fiend. Or both."

"Depravity?" Montpelier heard his voice squeak.

"Yer not married or nuthin', are yew?" asked Connors.

Brenda shook her head slowly. "No, I'm a rising young corporate executive."

He was working on his second bourbon and water. Their dinners remained on a corner of the table, untouched.

"Must be tough to get ahead. Lotsa competition."

"Quite a bit." Brenda sipped at her vodka sour.

"If TNT sponsored yer new show, it's be a real feather in yore cap, huh?"

"Yes it would. But I won't go to bed with you for it."

Connors' face fell. "Wh . . . who said anything about *that*? I'm a married man!"

Now Brenda permitted herself to smile again. "I'm sorry," she said with great sincerity. "I didn't mean to shock you. But, well . . . there are lots of men who try to take advantage of a woman in a situation like this. I'm glad you're not that kind of man."

"Hell, no," said Connors, looking puzzled, disappointed and slightly nettled.

Brenda sweetened her smile. *Have to introduce him to some of the professional ladies working at the hotel,* she knew, *before he decides to get angry.*

Earnest sat across the table from Dulaq. Between the two men sat Gloria Glory and Rita Yearling. Four appetizers had been served; two were still sitting untouched but Dulaq's and Gloria's were already demolished.

"And you, you great big hunk of muscle," Gloria turned to Dulaq, "how do you like acting?"

The hockey star shrugged. "It's okay. Ain't had a chance t'really do much . . . wit' the riot and all. . . ."

Earnest felt his blood pressure explode in his ears.

"Riot?" Gloria looked instantly alert. "What riot?"

"It wasn't a *riot*," Earnest said quickly. "It was just a bit of a misunderstanding. . . ."

"I'm afraid it was all my fault," Rita offered.

"Dis Gabriel guy gimme a hard time, so I punched him out."

"You *hit* Ron Gabriel?"

For an instant there was absolute silence at the table. Even Dulaq seemed to realize, in his dim way, that Gloria's reaction would have enormous implications for his future in show business.

"Uh . . . yeah. Once. Between de eyes."

Gloria's bloated face seemed to puff out even more and she suddenly let loose a loud guffaw. "Oh no! You punched that little creep between the eyes! Oh, it's *too* marvelous!" She roared with laughter.

Dulaq and Rita joined in. Earnest laughed too, but his mind was racing. Fearfully, he touched Gloria's bouffant sleeve. She wiped tears from her eyes as she turned to him.

"Um, Gloria," he begged. "You're not going to, uh . . . broadcast this, are you?"

"Broadcast it? Ron Gabriel getting what he's always asking for? It's too delicious!"

"Yes, but it could, well . . . it could reflect poorly on the show."

Gloria put her napkin to her lips and for a wild instant Earnest thought she was going to devour it. But instead she wiped her mouth and then flapped the napkin in Earnest's direction, saying:

"Greg . . . you don't mind me calling you Greg, do you?"

Earnest hated being called Greg, but he said, "No, of course not."

"All right, Greg, now listen. It has always been my policy to speak no evil of the people I like. I like Bernie Finger and I *love* this heavyweight champion you've got here. . . ." She nodded in Dulaq's direction. "And you've got a lovely new starlet. She's going to be a winner, I know. So, no matter how much I loathe Gabriel, I won't breathe a word about the fight over the air."

Earnest sighed. "Oh, thank you, Gloria."

"Nothing to it. You *are* getting rid of the little creep, though, aren't you?"

"Oh we certainly are," Earnest assured her. "He's on his way out. Never fear."

Ron Gabriel, meanwhile, had arrived and let himself be led quietly to Les Montpelier's booth. He didn't see Gloria, Earnest, *et. al.,* mainly because he was wearing dark glasses and the restaurant's twilight lighting level was quite dim. As it was, Gabriel had a little difficulty following the head waiter who showed him to the booth. He tripped over a step and bumped into a waitress on the way. He cursed at the step and made a date with the girl.

As he slid into the booth, he said, "I'm not eating anything. They just pumped me so full of antibiotics at the hospital that all I want to do is go home and sleep. Let's just talk business and skip the socializing."

Before Montpelier could respond, Elton Good pulled a thick wad of notes from his jacket pocket.

"Very well, Mr. Gabriel. I like a man who speaks his mind. There are eighty-seven changes that need to be made in your script before its acceptable to FINC."

"Eighty-seven?"

Good nodded smilingly. "Yes. And as you know, heh-heh, without FINC's mark of approval, your script cannot be shown on American television."

"Eighty-motherloving-seven," Gabriel moaned.

"Here's the first of them," said Good, peering at his notes in the dim lighting. His smile widened. "Ah, yes . . . when you have the character Rom standing behind the character Ben, who's sitting at the command console, I believe. . . ."

"That's in the second scene," Montpelier murmured.

"Yes. Rom puts his hand on Ben's shoulder . . . that's got to come out."

"Huh? Why?"

Good's smile turned sickening. "Can't you see? It's too suggestive. One man standing behind another man and then touching him on the shoulder! Children will be watching this show, after all!"

Gabriel looked across the table at Montpelier. Even though half the writer's face was covered by dark glasses, Montpelier could read anguish and despair in his expression.

"I shorely do love my wife," Connors was telling Brenda, between bites of steak. "But, well, hell, honey . . . I travel an awful lot. And I'm not exactly repulsive. When I see somethin' I like, I don't turn my back to it."

"That's understandable," Brenda said. She toyed with her salad for a moment, then asked, "And what does your wife do while you're away on all these business trips?"

He dropped his fork into his lap. "Whattaya mean?"

Brenda widened her eyes. "I mean, does she fill in the time with volunteer work or social clubs or at the golf course? She doesn't stay home with the children *all* the time, does she?"

Connors scowled at her. "No, I reckon she doesn't. We belong to the country club. And she's a voluntary librarian, over t'the school."

"I see."

He retrieved his fork and studied it for a moment, then changed the subject as he went back to the attack on his steak. "I wanted t'get yore opinion about how many TNT products we can use on the show? As props, I mean."

"Well," Brenda said, "the action's supposed to be taking place seven hundred years in the future. I don't think too many existing products will be in keeping with the scenario. . . ."

Connors' face brightened. "They'll still be usin' wristwatches, won't they? We make wristwatches. And pocket radios, calculators, all sorts of stuff."

"Yes, but if they're the same products that are being advertised during the commercial breaks, then the viewers will. . . ."

"Well, spit, why not? The viewers'll think that TNT's stuffs so good people'll still be usin' 'em seven hunnert years from now. That's terrific!"

"I don't know if that will work. . . ."

"Shore it will. And I'll tell yew somethin' else, honey. I don't want any shows about computers breakin' down or goin' crazy or any of that kinda stuff. We make computers that *don't* break down or go crazy and we ain't gonna sponsor any show that says otherwise."

Brenda nodded. "I can understand that."

"And where do you get your hair done?" Gloria Glory was asking Rita.

Earnest watched with growing concern as the two women chatted about clothes, hairdos, cosmetics, vitamins. *Is Gloria probing Rita to find out about her real age? Does she know about Rita's earlier life and her Vitaform Processing?*

Across the table from him, Dulaq was demolishing a haunch of venison, using both hands to get at the meat.

If he had thumbs on his feet he'd use those, too, Earnest told himself with an inward wince of distaste.

Then he felt something odd. Something soft and tickly was rubbing against his left ankle. *A cat? Not in a place like this. Don't be absurd.* There it was again, touching his ankle, just above his low-cut boots and below the cuff of his Fabulous Forties trousers.

He pulled his left foot back abruptly. It bumped into something. Glancing surreptitiously down to the floor, Earnest saw the heel of a woman's shoe peeking out from under the tablecloth. A pink shoe.

Gloria's shoe. And the tickling, rubbing sensation started on his right ankle.

She's playing toesies with me!

Earnest didn't know what to do. One doesn't rebuff the most powerful columnist in the business. Not if one wanted to remain in the business. Yet. . . .

He frankly stared at Gloria's face. She was still chatting with Rita, eyes focused—glowing, actually—on the beautiful starlet. But her toes were on Earnest's ankle.

Suddenly his stomach heaved. He fought it down, manfully, but the thought of getting any closer to that mountain of female flesh distressed him terribly. *She's fat and ugly and . . . old!* But what really churned his guts was the realization that whatever Gloria wanted, Gloria got. There were no exceptions to the rule; in her own powerful way, she was quite irresistible.

Maybe it's Dulaq she's after. How to let her know she had the wrong ankle? Earnest pondered the problem and decided that the best course of action was a cautious retreat.

Slowly he edged his right foot back toward the safety of his own chair, where his left foot cowered. He tried not to look directly at Gloria as he did so, but out of the corner of his eye he noticed a brief expression of disappointment cross her bloated face.

His feet tucked firmly under his chair, Earnest watched as Gloria squirmed slightly and seemed to sink a little lower in her seat. Dulaq chomped away on his venison, oblivious to everything else around him. *If she's made contact with him,* Earnest raged to himself, *he hasn't even noticed it. He'll ruin us all!*

Rita was saying, "And I take all the megavitamins. Have you tried the new multiple complexes? They're great for your complexion and they give you scads of energy. . . ."

Earnest squeezed his eyes shut with the fierceness of concentrated thought. *If she's after Dulaq and he doesn't pay attention to her, we're all sunk. I'll have to get into the act and* (his stomach lurched) *volunteer for duty with her. At least, she'll be flattered enough to forget about Dulaq.*

Trying not to think of what he'd have to do if Gloria liked him or was after him in the first place, Earnest quietly slipped off one boot and stuck his toes out cautiously toward Dulaq's side of the table.

His stockinged toes bumped into a leg. He quickly pulled back. Trying not to frown, he wished he could see what was going on under the table. Gloria's leg shouldn't be extended so far, she was missing Dulaq entirely, no doubt.

Very carefully, he sent his toes on a scouting mission *around* Gloria's extended foot, trying to find where Dulaq's massive hooves might be. And he bumped into another leg. Rita gave a stifled little yelp as he touched the second leg. It was hers.

Earnest froze. Only his eyes moved and they ping-ponged back and forth between Gloria and Rita. *They're playing toesies with each other!* he realized, horrified.

But from the smiles on both their faces, he saw that he was the only one startled by the idea.

Dulaq kept on eating.

". . . and here in Act Two, shot twenty-seven," Elton Good was saying, "you can't have the girl and the man holding each other and kissing that way. This is a family show."

Montpelier hadn't bothered to order dinner. He kept a steady flow of beer coming to the table. It was a helluva way to get drunk, but Good didn't seem to consider beer as sinful as hard liquor. Or wine, for some reason. So Montpelier sipped beer and watched the world get fuzzier and fuzzier.

As Ron Gabriel bled to death.

"They can't hug and kiss?" Gabriel was a very lively corpse. He was bouncing up and down as he sat in the booth. The seat cushions complained squawkingly under him. "They're *lovers*, for god's sake. . . ."

"Please!" Good closed his eyes as tightly as his mind. "Do not take the Deity's name in vain."

"What?" It was a noise like a goosed duck.

"You don't seem to understand," Good said with nearly infinite patience, "that children will be watching this show. Impressionable young children."

"So they can't see two adults kissing each other? They can't see an expression of love?"

"It could affect their psyches. It would be an inconsistency in their young lives, watching adults act lovingly toward each other."

Gabriel shot a glance at Montpelier. The executive merely leaned his head on his hand and propped his elbow on the table next to the beer. It was an age-old symbol of noninvolved surrender.

"But . . . but. . . ." Gabriel sputtered and flapped back through several pages of Good's notes, startling the gentleman. ". . . back here in shot seventeen, where the two Capulets beat up the Montague . . . you didn't say anything about that. I was worried about the violence. . . ."

"That's not 'violence,' Mr. Gabriel," Good said, with a knowing condescension in his voice. "That's what is called 'a fight scene.' It's perfectly permissible. Children fight all the time. It won't put unhealthy new ideas into their heads."

"Besides," Montpelier mumbled, "maybe we can get Band-Aids or somebody to sponsor that segment of the show."

Good smiled at him.

"What about the night life in this hyar town?" Connors was asking. "I hear they got bellydancers not far from here."

Brenda nodded. "Yes, that's right. They do."

"Y'all wanna come along with me?"

"I'd love to, but I really can't. We start shooting again tomorrow and I have to get up awfully early."

Connors' normally cheerful face turned sour. "Shee-it, I shore don't like the idea of prowlin' around a strange city all by myself."

Thinking about the Mexican wife and six children back home in Texas, Brenda found herself in a battle with her conscience. She won.

"I'll tell you what, Mr. Connors . . . there are a couple of girls here at the hotel—they're going to be used as extras in some of our later tapings. But they're not working tomorrow." *Not the day shift!* "Would you like me to call one of them for you?"

Connors' face lit up. "Starlets?" he gasped.

Hating herself, Brenda said, "Yes, they have been called that."

Earnest was still in a state of shock. Dulaq had polished off two desserts and was sitting back in his chair, mouth slack and eyes drooping, obviously falling asleep. Gloria and Rita had joined hands over the table now, as well as feet underneath. They spoke to each other as if no one else was in the restaurant.

But Earnest reconciled himself with the thought, *at least we ought to get some good publicity out of the old gasbag.*

Gabriel was actually pulling at his hair.

"But why?" His voice was rising dangerously, like the steam pressure in a volcano vent just before the eruption. "Why can't they fight with laser guns? That's what people will *use* seven hundred years in the future!"

His beneficent smile absorbing all arguments, Good explained, "Two reasons: first, if children tried to use lasers they could hurt themselves. . . ."

"But they can't buy lasers! People don't buy lasers for their kids. There aren't any laser toys."

Good waited for Gabriel to subside, then resumed: "Second, most states have very strict safety laws about using lasers. You wouldn't be able to employ them on the sound stage."

"But we weren't going to use real lasers! We were going to fake it with flashlights!"

Real lasers are too expensive, Montpelier added silently, from the slippery edge of sobriety.

"No, I'm sorry." Good's smile looked anything but that. "Lasers are on FINC's list of forbidden weapons and there's nothing anyone can do about it. Lasers are out. Have them use swords, instead."

"Swords!" Gabriel screamed. "Seven hundred years in the future, aboard an interstellar spaceship, you want them to use *swords*! Aaarrgghhhh. . . ."

Gabriel jumped up on the booth's bench and suddenly there was a butterknife in his hand. Good, sitting beside him, gave a startled yell and dived under the table. Gabriel clambered up on top of the table and started kicking Good's notes into shreds that were wafted into the air and sucked up into the ceiling vents.

"I'll give you swords!" he screamed, jumping up and down on the table like a spastic flamenco dancer. Montpelier's beer toppled into his lap.

Good scrambled out past Montpelier's legs, scuttled out of the booth on all fours, straightened up and started running for his life. Gabriel gave a war screech that couldn't be heard outside the booth, even though it temporarily deafened Montpelier, leaped off the table and took off in pursuit of the little censor, still brandishing his butterknife.

They raced past Connors and Brenda, who had just gotten up from their booth and were heading for the foyer.

"What in hell was *that*?" Connors shouted.

Brenda stared after Gabriel's disappearing, howling, butterknife-brandishing form. The waiters and incoming customers gave him a wide berth as he pursued Good out beyond the entryway.

"Apache dancers, I guess," Brenda said. "Part of the floorshow. Very impromptu."

Connors shook his head. "Never saw nuthin' like them back in Texas and we got plenty Apaches."

"No, I suppose not."

"Hey," he said, remembering. "You were gonna make a phone call fer me."

Since their table was not soundproofed, Earnest heard Gabriel's cries for blood and vengeance before he saw what was happening. He turned to watch the censor fleeing in panic and the enraged writer chasing after him.

No one else at the table took notice: Dulaq was snoring peacefully; Gloria and Rita were making love with their eyes, fingertips and toes.

Earnest smiled. *The little bastard's finished now, for sure. I won't even have to phone Finger about him. The show is mine.*

14: The Exodus

It was snowing.

Toronto International Jetport looked like a scene from *Doctor Zhivago*. Snowbound travelers slumped on every bench, chair and flat surface where they could sit or lie down. Bundled in their overcoats because the terminal building was kept at a minimum temperature ever since Canada had decided to Go Independent on Energy, the travelers slept or grumbled or moped, waiting for the storm to clear and the planes to fly again.

Ron Gabriel stood at the floor-to-ceiling window of Gate 26, staring out at the wind-whipped snow that was falling thickly on the other side of the double-paned glass. He could feel the cold seeping through the supposedly vacuum-insulated window. The cold, gray bitterness of defeat was seeping into his bones. The Unimerican jetliner outside was crusted over with snow; it was beginning to remind Gabriel of the ancient woolly mammoths uncovered in the ice fields of Siberia.

He turned and surveyed the waiting area of Gate 26. Two hundred eleven people sitting there, going slowly insane with boredom and uncertainty. Gabriel had already made dates with seventeen of the likeliest-looking girls, including the chunky security guard who ran the magnetic weapons detector.

He watched her for a moment. She was sitting next to the walkthrough gate of her apparatus, reading a comic book. Gabriel wondered how bright she could be, accepting a date from a guy she

160

had just checked out for the flight to Los Angeles. *Maybe she's planning to come to L.A.,* he thought. Then he wondered briefly why he had tried to make the date with her, when he was leaving Toronto forever. He shrugged. *Something to do. If we have to stay here much longer, maybe I can get her off into. . . .*

"Ron!"

He swung around at the sound of his name.

"Ron! Over here!"

A woman's voice. He looked beyond the moribund waiting travelers, following the sound of her voice to the corridor outside the gate area.

It was Brenda. And Bill Oxnard. Grinning and waving at him.

Gabriel left his trusty suitcase and portable typewriter where they sat and hurried through the bundled bodies, crumpled newspapers, choked ashtrays and tumbled suitcases of the crowd, out past the security girl—who didn't even look up from her *Kookoo Komix*—and out into the corridor.

"Hey, what're you two doing here? You're not trying to get out of town, are you?"

"No," Brenda said. "We wanted to say goodbye to you at the hotel, but you'd already left."

"I always leave early," Gabriel said.

"And when we heard that the storm was expected to last several hours and the airport was closed down, we figured you might like some company," Oxnard explained.

"Hey, that's nice of you. Both of you."

"We're sorry to see you leave, Ron," Brenda said; her throaty voice sounded sincere.

Gabriel shrugged elaborately. "Well . . . what the hell is left for me to stay here? They've shot the guts out of my scripts and they won't let me do diddely-poo with the other writers and the whole *idea* of the show's been torn to shreds."

"It's a lousy situation," Oxnard agreed.

Brenda bit her lip for a moment, then—with a *damn the torpedoes* expression on her face—she said, "I'm glad you're going, Ron."

He looked at her. "Thanks a lot."

"You know I don't mean it badly. I'm glad you found the strength to break free of this mess."

"I had a lot of help," Gabriel said, "from Finger and Earnest and the rest of those bloodsuckers."

Brenda shook her head. "That's not what I'm talking about. I thought Rita really had you twisted around her little finger."

"She did," Gabriel admitted. "But I got untwisted."

"Good for you," Brenda said. "She's trouble."

Oxnard said, "I just hate to see you getting screwed out of the money you ought to be getting."

"Oh, I'm getting all the money," Gabriel said. "They can't renege on that . . . the Screen Writers Guild would start napalming Titanic if they tried anything like that. I'll get paid for both the scripts I wrote. . . ."

"But neither one's going to be produced," Oxnard said. "Earnest has scrapped them both."

"So what? I'll get paid for 'em. And I've been getting my regular weekly check as Story Editor. And they still have to pay me my royalties for each show, as the Creator."

With a smile, Brenda asked, "You're going to let them keep your name on the credits?"

"Hell no!" Gabriel grinned back, but it was a Pyrrhic triumph. "They'll have to use my Guild-registered pen name: Victor Lawrence Talbot Frankenstein."

"Oh no!" Brenda howled.

Oxnard frowned. "I don't get it."

"Frankenstein and the Wolfman," Gabriel explained. "I save that name for shows that've been screwed up. It's my way of telling friends that the show's a clinker, a grade B horror movie."

"His friends," Brenda added, giggling, "and everybody in the industry."

"Oh." But Oxnard still looked as if he didn't really understand.

Laughing at the thought of his modest revenge, Gabriel said, "Lemma grab my bags and take you both to dinner."

"The restaurants are closed," Oxnard said. "We checked. They ran out of food about an hour ago."

Gabriel held up one hand, looking knowledgeable: "Have no fear. I know where the aircrews have their private cafeteria. One of the stewardesses gave me the secret password to get in there."

Oxnard watched the little guy scamper back through the

now-dozing security girl's magnetic detector portal and head for his bags, by the window. It was still snowing heavily.

"Victor Lawrence Talbot Frankenstein?" he muttered.

Brenda said to him, "It's the only satisfaction he's going to get out of this series."

"He's getting all that money. . . ."

She rested a hand on his shoulder and said, "It's not really all that much money, compared to the time and effort he's put in. And . . . well, Bill . . . suppose your new holographic system won the Nobel Prize. . . ."

"They don't give Nobels for inventions."

"But just suppose," Brenda insisted. "And then one of the people who decide on the Prize comes to you and says they're going to name Gregory Earnest as the inventor. You'll get the money that goes with the Prize, but he'll get the recognition."

"Ohh. Now I see."

Gabriel came back, lugging his suitcase and typewriter. As they started down the corridor, Oxnard took the typewriter from him.

"Thanks."

"Nothing to it."

Brenda said, "Looks like we'll be here a long time."

"Good," said Oxnard. "It'll give me a chance to ask you some questions about a new idea of mine."

"What's that?" Gabriel asked.

Oxnard scratched briefly at his nose. "Oh, it's just .a few wild thoughts I put together . . . but it might be possible to produce a three-dee show without using any actors. You. . . ."

"What?" Gabriel looked startled. Brenda pursed her lips.

Oxnard nodded as they walked. "After watching how pitiful Dulaq is as an actor, I got to thinking that there's no *fundamental* reason why you couldn't take one holographic picture of him—a still shot—and then use a computer to electronically move his image any way you want to . . . you know, make him walk, run, stand up, sit down. Some of the work they've been doing at the VA with hemiplegics. . . ."

Gabriel stopped and dropped his suitcase to the floor. Brenda and Oxnard took a step or two more, then turned back toward him.

"Don't say anything more about it," Gabriel warned.

"Why not?" Oxnard looked totally surprised at his reaction. "You could do away with. . . ."

"He's right," Brenda agreed. "Forget about it. You'll produce nothing but trouble."

Oxnard stared at them both. "But you could lower the costs of producing shows enormously. You wouldn't have to hire any act. . . ."

Gabriel put a hand over his mouth. "For Chrissake, you wanna start a revolution in L.A.? Every actor in the world will come after you, with guns!"

Oxnard shrugged as Gabriel took his hand away. "It's just an idea . . . might be too expensive to work out in real-time." He sounded hurt.

"It would cause more trouble than it's worth," Brenda said, as they resumed walking. "Believe me, a producer would have to be utterly desperate to try a scheme like that."

HONOLULU PINEAPPLES WIN EIGHTH STRAIGHT,
38-6
QB Gene Toho Passes
For Three Scores

Gregory Earnest stood beside the reclining plush barber chair, watching the skinny little old man daub Francois Dulaq's rugged features with makeup.

"What is it this time, Francois?" he asked, barely suppressing his growing impatience.

Dulaq's eyes were closed while the makeup man carefully filled in the crinkles at the corners and painted over the bags that had started to appear under them.

"I gotta leave early t'day. Th'team's catchin' the early plane to Seattle."

Earnest felt startled. "I thought you were taking the special charter flight, later tonight. You can still be in Seattle tomorrow morning, in plenty of time for the game."

"Naw . . . I wanna go wit' th'guys. They're startin' t'razz me about bein' a big TV star . . . and de coach ain't too happy, neither. Sez I oughtta get t'th'practices . . . my scorin's off and th'guys're gettin' a little sore at me."

"But we can't shoot your scenes in just a few hours," Earnest protested.

"Sure ya can."

Earnest grabbed the nearest thing at hand, a tissue box, and banged it viciously on the countertop. Dulaq opened one eye and squinted at him, in the mirror.

"Francois, you've got to *understand*," Earnest said. "We've stripped your scenes down as far as we can. We haven't given you anything more complicated to say than 'Let's go,' or 'Oh, no you don't.' We're dubbing all the longer speeches for you. But you've *got* to let us photograph you! You're the *star*, for goodness' sake! The people have to *see* you on the show!"

"I ain't gonna be a star of nuthin' if I don't start scorin' and th'team don't start winnin'."

Earnest's mind spun furiously. "Well, I suppose we *could* use Fernando to stand in for the long shots and the reverse angles, when your back's to the camera."

"He still limpin'?"

"A little. That was some fight scene."

"Dat's th'only fun I've had since we started dis whole show."

The makeup man pursed his lips, inspected his handiwork and then said, "Okay, *mon ami*. That's the most I can do for you."

Dulaq bounded up from the chair.

"Come on," Earnest said, "you're already late for the first scene."

As they left the makeup room and headed down the darkened corridor toward the studio, Dulaq put his arm around Earnest's shoulders. "Sorry I gotta buzz off, but th'team's important, y'know."

"I know," Earnest said, feeling dejected. "It's just . . . well, I thought we were going to have dinner tonight."

Dulaw squeezed him. "Don' worry. I'll be back Wensay night. I'll take d'early plane. You meet me at th' airport, okay?"

Earnest brightened. "All right. I will." And he thrilled to the powerful grip he was in.

"But you can't walk out on us!" Brenda pleaded.

Mitch Westerly was slowly walking along the windswept parking lot behind Badger's square red-brick studio building. The night was Arctic cold and dark; even the brilliant stars seemed to radiate cold light.

"It's h . . . hopeless," Westerly said.

His head was bent low, chin sunk into the upraised collar of his mackinaw, bands stuffed into the pockets. The wind tousled his long hair. Brenda paced along beside him, wrapped in an ankle-length synthetic fur coat that was warmed electrically.

"You can't give up now," Brenda said. "You're the only shred of talent left in the crew! You're the one who's been holding this show together. If you go. . . ."

Westerly pulled one gloved hand out of his pocket. Under the bluish arclamps the leather looked strange, otherwordly. The hand was trembling, shaking like the strengthless hand of a palsied old man.

"See that?" Westerly said. "The only way I can get it to stop . . . make my whole body shop shaking . . . is to pop some cat. Nothing less will do the trick anymore."

"Cat? But I thought . . ."

"I kicked it once . . . in the mountains, far away from here. But I'm right back on it again."

Brenda looked up at the director's face. It looked awful and not merely because of the lighting. "I didn't know, Mitch. How could. . . ."

It took an effort to keep his teeth from chattering. Westerly plunged his hand back into his pocket and resumed walking.

"How can anybody stay straight in this nuthouse?" he asked. "Dulaq is bouncing in and out of the studio whenever he feels like it. Half the time we have to shoot around him or use a double. Rita's spending most of her time with that snake from FINC . . . I think she's posing for pictures for him. He told me he's an amateur photographer."

Brenda huffed, "Oh for god's sake!"

"And when she's on the set all she wants to do is look glamorous. She can't act for beans."

"But you've gotten four shows in the can."

"In four weeks, yeah. And each week my cat bill goes up. Earnest is making a fortune off me."

"Earnest? He's supplying you with cat?"

"It's all legal . . . he tells me."

"Mitch . . . can you stay for just another three weeks? Until we get the first seven shows finished?"

He shook his head doggedly. "I'd do it for you, Brenda . . . if I could. But I know what I went through the last time with cat. If I don't stop now, I'll be really hooked. Bad. It's me or the show . . . another three weeks will kill me. Honest."

She said nothing.

"Earnest has a couple of local people who can direct the other three segments. Hell, the way things are going, anybody could walk off the street and do it."

Brenda asked, "Where will you go? What will you do?"

"To the mountains, I guess."

"Katmandu again?"

He shrugged. "Maybe. I'd like to try Aspen, if Finger will let me off the hook. I owe some debts. . . ."

"I'll take care of that," Brenda said firmly. "B.F. will let you go, don't worry."

He looked at her from under raised eyebrows. "Can you really swing it for me?"

Brenda said, "Yes. I will . . . but what will you do in Aspen?"

He almost smiled. "Teach, maybe. There's a film colony there . . . lots of eager young kids."

"That would be good," Brenda said.

He stopped walking. They were at his car. "I hate to leave you in this mess, Brenda. But I just can't cut it anymore."

"I know," she said. "Don't worry about it. You're right, the show's a disaster. There's no sense hanging on."

He reached out and grasped her by the shoulders. Lightly. Without pulling her toward him. "Why are you staying?" he asked. "Why do you put up with all this bullshit?"

"Somebody's got to. It's my job."

"Ever think of quitting?"

"Once every hour, at least."

"Want to come to Aspen with me?"

She stepped closer to him and let her head rest against his chest. "It's a tempting thought. And you're very sweet to ask me. But I can't."

"Why not?"

"Reasons. My own reasons."

"And they're none of my business, right?"

She smiled up at him. "You've got enough problems. You don't need mine. Go on, go off to the mountains and breathe clean air and forget about this show. I'll square it with B.F."

Abruptly, he let go of her and reached for the car door. "Can I drop you off at the hotel?"

"I've got my own car." She pointed to it, sitting alone and cold looking a few empty rows down the line.

"Okay," he said. "Goodbye. And thanks."

"Good luck, Mitch."

She walked to her car and stood beside it as he gunned his engine and drove off.

PINEAPPLES CLINCH PLAYOFF SLOT
AS TOHO LEADS 56-13 MASSACRE

It'll look like Orson Welles, Gregory Earnest told himself as he strode purposefully onto the set. *Script by Gregory Earnest. Produced by Gregory Earnest. Directed by Gregory Earnest.*

He stood there for a magnificent moment, clad in the traditional dungarees and tee shirt of a big-time director, surrounded by the crew and actors who stood poised waiting for his orders.

"Very well," he said to them. "Let's do this one *right.*"

Four hours later he was drenched with perspiration and longing for the safety of his bed.

Dulaq had just delivered the longest speech in his script:

"Oh yeah? We'll see about dat!"

He stood bathed in light, squinting at the cue cards that had his next line printed in huge red block letters, while the actor in the scene with him backed away and gave his line:

"Rom, we're going to crash! The ship's out of control!"

Dulaq didn't answer. He peered at the cue card, then turned toward Earnest and bellowed, "What th'hell's dat word?"

"Cut!" Earnest yelled. His throat was raw from saying it so often.

"Which one?" the script girl asked Dulaq.

"Dat one . . . wit' de 'S.'"

"*Stabilize,*" the girl read.

Dulaq shook his head and muttered to himself, "Stabilize. Stabilize. Stabilize."

(°) (°) (°)

This is getting to be a regular routine, Brenda told herself. *I feel like the Welcome Wagon Lady . . . in reverse.*

She was at the airport again, sitting at the half-empty bar with Les Montpelier. His travelbags were resting on the floor between their stools.

"I don't understand why you're staying," Montpelier said, toying with the plastic swizzle stick in his Tijuana Teaser.

"B.F. asked me to," she said.

"So you're going to stick it out until the bloody end?" he asked rhetorically. "The last soldier at Fort Zinderneuf."

She took a sip of her vodka gimlet. "Bill Oxnard still comes up every weekend. I'm not completely surrounded by idiots."

Montpelier shook his head, more in pity than in sorrow. "I could ask B.F. to send somebody else up here . . . hell, there's no real reason to have anybody here. The seventh show is finished shooting. All they have to do now is the editing. No sense starting the next six until we get the first look at the ratings."

"The editing can be tricky," Brenda said. "These people that Earnest has hired don't have much experience with three-dee editing."

"They don't have much experience with anything."

"They work cheap, though."

Montpelier lifted his glass. "There is that. I'll bet this show cost less than any major network presentation since the Dollar Collapse of Eighty-Four."

"Do you think that there's any chance the show will last beyond the first seven weeks?" Brenda asked.

"Are you kidding?"

"Thank god," she said. "Then I can go home as soon as the editing's finished."

The P.A. system blared something unintelligible about a flight to Los Angeles, Honolulu and Tahiti.

"That's me," Montpelier said. "I'd better dash." He started fumbling in his pocket for cash.

"Go on, catch your plane," Brenda said. "I'll take care of the tab."

"Gee, thanks."

"Give B.F. my love."

"Will do." He grabbed his travelbags and hurried out of the bar.

Brenda turned from watching him hurry out the doorway to the three-dee set behind the bar. The football game was on. Honolulu was meeting Pittsburgh and the Pineapples' star quarterback, Gene Toho, was at that very minute throwing a long pass to a player who was racing down the sideline. He caught the ball and ran into the endzone. The referee raised both arms to signal a touchdown.

Brenda raised her glass. "Hail to thee, blithe spirit," she said, and realized she was slightly drunk.

The guy on the stool at her left nudged her with a gentle elbow. "Hey, you a Pineapples fan?"

He wasn't bad looking, if you ignored the teeth, Brenda decided. She smiled at him. "Perforce, friend. Perforce."

Even though he knew better than anyone else exactly what to expect, the sight still exhilarated Bill Oxnard.

He was sitting in the darkened editing room—more a closet than a real room. He knew that what he was watching was a holographic image of a group of actors performing a teleplay. (A poor teleplay, but that didn't matter much, really.)

Yet what he saw was Francois Dulaq, life-sized, three-dimensional, full, real, solid, standing before him. He was squinting a little and seemed to be staring off into space. Oxnard knew that he was actually trying to read his cue cards. He wore an Elizabethan costume of tights, tunic and cape. A sword dangled from his belt and got in his way whenever he tried to move. His boots clumped on the wooden deck of the set. But he was as solid as real flesh, to the eye.

"You!" Dulaq was saying, trying to sound surprised. "You're here!"

"You" was Rita Yearling, who in her own overly heated way, was every bit as bad an actor as Dulaq. But who cared? All she had to do was try to stand up and breathe a little. Her gown was metallic and slinky; it clung in all the right places, which was everywhere on her body. She was wearing a long flowing golden wig and her child-innocent face gave the final touch of maddening desirability to her aphrodisiacal anatomy.

"I have waited for you," she panted. "I have crossed time and space to be with you. I have renounced my family and my home because I love you."

"Caught up with you at last!" announced a third performer, stepping out of the shadows where the holo image ended. This one was dressed very much like Dulaq, complete with sword, although his costume was blood red whereas Dulaq's was (what else?) true blue.

"You're coming back with me," the actor recited to Rita Yearling. "Our father is lying ill and dying, and only the sight of you can cure him."

"Oh!" gasped Rita, as she tried to stuff both her fists in her mouth.

"Take yer han's off her!" Dulaq cried, even though the other actor had forgotten to grasp Rita's arm.

"We can dub over that," an engineer muttered in the darkness beside Oxnard.

"Don't try to interfere, Montague dog," said the actor. "Stand back or I'll blast you." But instead of pulling out the laser pistol that was in the original script, he drew his sword. It flexed deeply, showing that it was made of rubber.

"Oh yeah?" adlibbed Dulaq, And he drew his rubber sword.

They swung at each other mightily, to no avail. The engineers laughed and suddenly reversed the tape. The fight went backwards, and the two heroes slid their swords back into their scabbards. Halfway. Then the tape went forward again and they fought once more. Back and forth. It looked ludicrous. It *was* ludicrous and Oxnard joined in the raucous laughter of the editing crew.

"Lookit the expression on Dulaq's face!"

"He's trying to hit Randy's sword and he keeps missing it!"

"Hey, hey, hold it . . . right there . . . yeah. Take a look at that terrific profile."

"Cheez . . . is she *built*!"

Oxnard had to admit that structurally, Rita was as impressive as the Eiffel Tower—or perhaps the Grand Teton Mountains.

"A guy could bounce to death off those!"

"What a way to go!"

"C'mon, we got work to do. It's almost quittin' time."

The fight ran almost to its conclusion and then suddenly the figures got terribly pale. They seemed to blanch out, like figures in an overexposed snapshot. The scene froze with Dulaq pushing his sword in the general direction of his antagonist, the other actor holding his sword down almost on the floor so Dulaq could stab him and Rita in the midst of a stupefyingly deep breath.

"See what I mean?" came the chief engineer's voice, out of the darkness. "It does that every couple minutes."

Oxnard looked down at the green glowing gauges on the control board in front of him. "I told them not to light the set so brightly," he said. "You don't need all that candlepower with laser imaging."

"Listen," said the chief engineer, "if they had any smarts, would they be doin' this for a living?"

Oxnard studied the information on the gauges.

"Can we fix it?" one of the editors asked. Oxnard smelled pungent smoke and saw that two of the assistants were lighting up in the dimness of the room.

"We'll have to feed the tape through the quality control computer, override the intensity program and manually adjust the input voltage," Oxnard said.

The chief engineer swore under his breath. "That'll take all humpin' night"

"A few hours, at least."

"There goes dinner."

Oxnard heard himself say, "You guys don't have to hang around. I can do it myself."

He could barely make out the editor's sallow, thin face in the light from the control board. "By yourself? That ain't kosher."

"Union rules?"

"Naw . . . but it ain't fair for you to do our work. You ain't gettin' paid for it."

Oxnard grinned at him. "I've got nothing else to do. Go on home. I'll take care of it and you can get back to doing the real editing tomorrow."

One of the assistants walked out into the area where the holographic images stood. He wasn't walking too steadily. Taking the joint from his mouth, he blew smoke in Dulaq's "face."

"Okay, tough guy," he said to the stilled image. "If you're so tough, let's see you take a swing at me. G'wan . . . I dare ya!" He stuck his chin out and tapped at it with an upraised forefinger. "Go on . . . right here on the button. I dare ya!"

Dulaq's image didn't move. "Hah! Chicken. I thought so."

The guy turned to face Rita's image. He walked all around her, almost disappearing from Oxnard's view when he stepped behind her. Oxnard could see him, ghostlike, through Rita's image. The other assistant drew in a deep breath and let it out audibly. "Boy," he said, with awe in his voice, "they really are three-dimensional, aren't they? You can walk right around them."

"Too bad you can't pinch 'em," said the chief engineer.

"Or do anything else with 'em," the assistant said.

Oxnard lost track of time. He simply sat alone at the control desk, working the buttons and keys that linked his fingers with the computer tape and instruments that controlled what stayed on the tape.

It was almost pleasant, working with the uncomplaining machinery. He shut off the image-projector portion of the system, so that he wouldn't have to see or hear the dreadful performances that were on the tape. He was interested in the technical problem of keeping the visual quality of the images constant; that he could do better by watching the gauges than by watching the acting.

All of physics boils down to reading a dial, he remembered from his undergraduate days. He chuckled to himself.

"And all physicists are basically loners," he said aloud. *Not because they want to be. But if you spend enough time reading dials, you never learn how to read people.*

Someone knocked at the door. Almost annoyed, Oxnard called, "Who is it?" without looking up from the control board.

Light spilled across his field of view as the door opened. "What are you doing here so late?"

He looked up. It was Brenda, her lean, leggy form silhouetted in the light from the hallway.

"Trying to make this tape consistent, on the optical quality side," he said. Then, almost as an afterthought, "What about you? What time is it?"

"Almost nine. I had a lot of paperwork to finish."

"Oh." He took his hands off the control knobs and gestured to her. "Come on in. I didn't realize I'd been here so long."

"Aren't you going back to L.A. tomorrow?" Brenda asked. She stepped into the tiny room, but left the door open behind her.

He nodded. "Yes. That's why I thought I'd stick with this until the job's done. The editors can't handle this kind of problem. They're good guys, but they'd probably ruin the tape."

"Which show are you working on?" Brenda asked, pulling up a stool beside him.

He shrugged. "I don't know. They all look alike to me."

Brenda agreed. "Will you be at it much longer?"

"Almost finished . . . another ten-fifteen minutes or so."

"Can I buy you dinner afterward?" she asked.

He started to say no, but held up. "I'll buy you some dinner."

"I can charge it off to Titanic. Let B.F. buy us both dinner."

With a sudden grin, he agreed.

He worked in silence for a few minutes, conscious of her looking over his shoulder, smelling the faint fragrance of her perfume, almost feeling the tickling of a stray wisp of her long red hair.

"Bill?"

"What?" Without looking up from the control board.

"Why do you keep coming up here every weekend?"

"To make sure the equipment works okay."

"Oh. That's awfully good of you."

He clicked the power off and looked up at her. "That's a damned lie," he admitted, to himself as much as to her. "I could stay down at Malibu and wait for you to have some trouble. Or send one of my technicians."

Brenda's face didn't look troubled or surprised. "Then why?"

"Because I like being with you," he said.

"Really?"

"You know I do."

She didn't look away, didn't laugh, didn't frown. "I hoped you did. But you never said a word. . . ."

Suddenly his hands were embarrassingly awkward appendages. They wouldn't stay still.

"Well," he said, scratching at his five o'clock shadow, "I guess I'm still a teenager in some ways . . . retarded . . . I was afraid . . . afraid you wouldn't be interested in me."

"You were wrong," she said simply.

She leaned toward him and his hands reached for her and he kissed her. She felt warm and safe and good.

They decided to have dinner in his hotel room. Oxnard felt giddy, as if he were hyperventilating or celebrating New Year's Eve a month early. As they drove through the dark frigid night toward the hotel, he asked:

"The one thing I was afraid of was that you'd walk out on the show, like everybody else has."

"Oh, I couldn't do that," Brenda said, very seriously.

"Why not?"

"B.F. wouldn't let me."

"You mean you allow him to run your whole life? He tells you to freeze your . . . your nose off here in Toronto all winter, on a dead duck of a show, and you do it?"

She nodded. "That's right."

He pulled the car into the hotel's driveway as he asked, "Why don't you just quit? There are lots of other studios and jobs. . . ."

"I can't quit Titanic."

"Why not? What's Finger got on you?"

"Nothing. Except that he's my father and I'm the only person in the world that he can really trust."

"He's your *father*?"

Brenda grinned broadly at him. "Yes. And you're the only person in the whole business who knows it. So please don't tell anyone else."

Oxnard was stunned.

He was still groggy, but grinning happily, as they walked arm-in-arm through the hotel lobby, got into an elevator and headed for his room. Neither of them noticed the three-dee set in the lobby; it was tuned to the evening news. A somber-faced sports reporter was saying:

"There's no telling what effect Toho's injury will have on the play-off chances of the Honolulu Pineapples. As everyone knows, he's the league's leading passer."

The other half of the Folksy News Duo, a curly haired anchorperson in a gingham dress, asked conversationally, "Isn't it unusual for a player to break his leg in the shower?"

"That's right, Arlene," said the sports announcer. "Just one of those freak accidents. A bad *break*," he said archly, "for the Pineapples and their fans."

The woman made a disapproving clucking sound. "That's terrible."

"It certainly is. They're probably going crazy down in Las Vegas right now, refiguring the odds for the playoff games."

15: The Warning

"You don't understand!" Bernard Finger shouted. "Every cent I had was tied up in that lousy football team! I'm broke! Ruined!"

He was emptying the drawers of his desk into an impossibly thin attache case. Most of the papers and mememtoes—including a miniature Emmy given him as a gag by a producer, whom Finger promptly fired—were missing the attache case and spilling across the polished surface of the desk or onto the plush carpet.

The usually impressive office reminded Les Montpelier of the scene in a war movie where the general staff has to beat a fast retreat and everybody's busy stripping the headquarters and burning what they can't carry.

"But you couldn't have taken everything out of Titanic's cash accounts," Montpelier said, trying to remain calm in the face of Finger's panic.

"Wanna bet?" Finger was bent over, pulling papers out of the bottommost drawer, discarding most of them and creating a miniature blizzard in the doing.

Montpelier found himself leaning forward tensely in his chair. "But we still get our paychecks. The accounting department is still paying its bills. Isn't it?"

Finger straightened up and eyed him with a look of scorn for such naivete. "Sure, sure. You know Morrie Witz, down in accounting?"

"Morrie the Mole?"

"Who else? He worked out a system for me. We keep enough in

the bank for two weeks of salaries and bills. Everything else we've been investing in the Pineapples. Every time they win, we bet on 'em again. The odds keep going down, but we keep making sure money. Better than the stock market."

"Then you must have a helluva cash reserve right now," Montpelier said.

"It's already bet!" Finger bawled. "And the Pineapples play the Montana Sasquatches this afternoon. . . ." He glanced at the clock on his littered desk. "They're already playing."

"Shall I turn on the game?" Montpelier asked, starting to get up from his chair.

"No! I can't bear to watch. Without Toho they're sunk." Montpelier eased back into the chair. "Yes!" Finger burst. "Turn it on. I can't stand not knowing!"

He went back to rummaging through the desk drawers as Montpelier walked across the room to the control panel for the life-sized three-dee set in the corner.

"The Pineapples still have their defensive team intact," Montpelier reasoned. "And Montana's not that high-scoring a team. . . ."

He found the right channel and tuned in the game. The far corner of the office dissolved into a section of a football field. A burly man in a Sasquatch uniform was kneeling, arms outstretched, barking out numbers. The crowd rumbled in the background. It was raining and windy; it looked cold in Montana.

The camera angle changed to an overhead shot and Montpelier saw that the Sasquatches were trying to kick a field goal. The ball was snapped, the kicker barely got the kick past a pair of onrushing Pineapple defenders, who ruined *their* orange and yellow uniforms by sprawling in the mud.

Again the camera angle changed, to show the football sailing through the uprights of the goal post. The announcer said, "It's gooood!" as the referee raised both arms over his head.

Finger groaned.

"It's only a field goal," Montpelier said.

"So as the teams prepare for the kickoff," the announcer said cheerily, "the score is Montana seventeen, Honolulu zero."

With a gargling sound, Finger pawed through the attache case.

He grabbed a bottle of pills as he yelled, "Turn it off! Turn it off!" and poured half the bottle's contents down his throat.

Montpelier turned the game off, just catching a view of the scoreboard clock. Only eight minutes of the first quarter had elapsed.

He turned to Finger. "What are you going to do?"

His face white, Titanic's boss said softly, "Get out of town. Get out of the country. Get off the planet, if I can. Maybe the lunar colony would be a safe place for me . . . if I could qualify. I've got a bad heart, you know."

Like an ox, Montpelier thought. Aloud, he asked, "But you've been through bankruptcy proceedings before. Why are you getting so upset over this one?"

Raising his eyes to an unhelpful heaven, Finger said, "The other bankruptcy hearings were when we owed money to *banks.* Or to the government. What we owe now, we owe to the mob. When they foreclose, they take your head home and mount it on the goddamn wall!"

"The gamblers. . . ."

Finger wagged his head. "Not the gamblers. I'm square with them. The bankers who backed us on 'The Starcrossed.' It's their money I've been betting. When the show flops they're gonna want their money back. With interest."

"Ohhh."

"Yeah, ohhh." Finger knuckled his eyes. "Turn the game on again. Maybe they're doing something. . . ."

The three-dee image solidified, despite annoying flickers and shimmers, to show an orange-and-yellow Pineapple ball carrier break past two would-be tacklers, twist free of another Sasquatch defender and race down the sidelines. The crowd was roaring and Finger was suddenly on his feet, screaming.

"Go! Go! Go, you black sonofabitch!"

There was only one Sasquatch left in the scene, closing in on the Pineapple runner. They collided exactly at the Montana ten yard line. He twisted partially free, and as he began to fall, another Sasquatch pounced on him. The ball squirted loose.

"Aarrghh!"

What seemed like four hundred men in muddied uniforms piled on top of each other. There was a long moment of breathless suspense while the referees pulled bodies off the mountain of rain-soaked flesh.

Finger stood frozen, his fists pressed into his cheeks.

The bottom man in the pile was a Sasquatch. And under him was the ball.

"Turn it off! Turn it off!"

They spent the rest of the afternoon like that, alternately turning on the three-dee, watching the Sasquatches hurt the Pineapples, and turning off the three-dee. Finger moaned, he fainted, he swallowed pills. Montpelier went out for sandwiches; on Sunday the building's cafeterias were closed.

He idly wondered how far the bankers' revenge would go. *If they can't get B.F., will they come after me?* He tried to put the thought aside, but ugly scenes from Mafia movies kept crawling into his skull.

Finger wolfed down his sandwich as if it were his last meal. They turned the game on one final time, and the Sasquatches were ahead by 38-7 with less than two minutes to play. Finger started calling airlines.

He set up seven different flights for himself, for destinations as diverse as Rio de Janeiro and Ulan Bator.

"I'll dazzle them with footwork," he joked weakly. His face looked far from jovial.

The phone chimed. With a trembling hand, Finger touched the ON button. The same corner that had showed the football game now presented a three-dee image of a gray-templed man sitting a a desk. He looked intelligent, wealthy, conservative and powerful. His suit was gray, with a vest. The padded chair on which he sat was real leather, Montpelier somehow sensed. The wall behind him was panelled in dark mahogany. A portrait of Nelson Rockefeller hung there.

"Mr. Finger," he said in a beautifully modulated baritone. "I'm pleased to find you in your office this afternoon. My computer doesn't seem to have your home number. Working hard, I see."

"Yes," Finger said, his voice quavering just the slightest bit. "Yes . . . you know how it is in this business, heh-heh."

The man smiled without warmth.

"I, uh . . . I don't think I know you," Finger said.

"We have never met. I am an attorney, representing a group of gentlemen who have invested rather substantial sums in Titanic Productions, Incorporated."

"Oh. Yes. I see."

"Indeed."

"The gentlemen who're backing 'The Starcrossed.'"

The man raised a manicured forefinger. "The gentlemen are backing Titanic Productions, not any particular show. In a very real sense, Mr. Finger, they have invested in *you*. In your business acumen, your administrative capabilities, your . . . integrity."

Finger swallowed hard. "Well, eh, 'The Starcrossed' is the show that we've sunk their . . . eh, invested their money into. It goes on the air in three weeks. That's the premiere date, second week of January. Friday night. Full network coverage. It's a good spot, and. . . ."

"Mr. Finger."

Montpelier had never seen B.F. stopped by such a quiet short speech.

"Yessir?" Finger squeaked.

"Mr. Finger, did you happen to watch the Montana Sasquatch football game this afternoon?"

"Uh. . . ." Finger coughed, cleared his throat. "Why, um, I *did* take a look at part of it, yes."

The man from New York let a slight frown mar his handsome features. "Mr. Finger, the bankers whom I represent have some associates who—quite frankly—I find very distasteful. These, ah, associates are spreading an ugly rumor to the effect that you have been betting quite heavily on the Honolulu professional football team. Quite heavily. And since Honolulu lost this afternoon, my clients thought it might be wise to let you know that this rumor has them rather upset."

"Upset," Finger echoed.

"Yes. They fear that the money they have invested in Titanic Productions has been channeled into the hands of. . . ." he showed his distaste quite visibly, ". . . bookies. They fear that you have lost all their money and will have nothing to show for their investment. That would make them very angry, I'm afraid. And justifiably so."

Finger's head bobbed up and down. "I can appreciate that."

"The proceedings that they would institute against you would be so severe that you might be tempted to leave the country or disappear altogether."

"Oh, I'd never. . . ."

"A few years ago, in a similar situation, a man who tried to cheat them became so remorseful that he committed suicide. He somehow managed to shoot himself in the back of the head. Three times."

What little color was left in Finger's face drained away completely. He sagged in his chair.

"Mr. Finger, are you all right? Does the thought of violence upset you?"

Finger nodded weakly.

"I'm terribly sorry. It's raining here in New York and I tend to get morbid on rainy Sunday afternoons. Please forgive me."

Finger raised a feeble hand. "Think nothing of it."

"Back to business, if you don't mind. Mr. Finger, there is a series called 'The Starcrossed'? And it will premier on the second Friday in January?"

"Eight p.m." Montpelier said as firmly as possible.

"Ah. Thank you, young man. This show does represent the investment that my clients have made?"

"That's right, it does," Finger said, his voice regaining some strength. But not much.

"That means," the New York lawyer went on, remorselessly, "that you have used my client's money to acquire the best writers, directors, actors and so forth . . . the best that money can buy?"

"Sure, sure."

"Which in turn means that the show will be a success. It will bring an excellent return on my clients' investment. Titanic Productions will make a profit and so will my clients. Is that correct?"

Sitting up a little straighter in his chair, Finger hedged, "Well now, television is a funny business. Nobody can *guarantee* success. I explained to. . . ."

"Mr. Finger." And again B.F. stopped cold. "My clients are simple men, at heart. If 'The Starcrossed' is a success and we all make money, all well and good. If it is not a success, then they will investigate just how their money was spent. If they find that Titanic did not employ the best possible talent or that the money was used in some other manner—as this regrettable betting rumor suggests, for instance—then they will hold you personally responsible."

"Me?"

"Do you understand? *Personally* responsible."

"I understand."

"Good." The lawyer almost smiled. "Now if you would do us one simple favor, Mr. Finger?"

"What?"

"Please stay close to your office for the next few weeks. I know you probably feel that you are entitled to a long vacation, now that your show is . . . how do they say it in your business? 'In the can'? At any rate, try to deny yourself that luxury for a few weeks. My clients will want to confer with you as soon as public reaction to 'The Starcrossed' is manifested. They wouldn't want to have to chase you down in some out-of-the-way place such as Rio de Janeiro or Ulan Bator."

Finger fainted.

1b: The Reaction

On the second Friday in January, twenty-odd members of the New England Science Fiction Association returned to their clubroom after their usual ritual Chinese dinner in downtown Boston. The clubroom was inside the lead walls of what once had housed MIT's nuclear reactor—until the local Cambridge chapter of Ecology Now! had torn the reactor apart with their bare hands, a decade earlier, killing seventeen of their members within a week from the radiation poisoning and producing a fascinating string of reports for the obstetrics journals ever since.

The clubroom was perfectly safe now, of course. It had been carefully decontaminated and there was a trusty scintillation counter sitting on every bookshelf, right alongside musty crumbling copies of *Astounding Stories of Super Science*.

The NESFA members were mostly young men and women, in their twenties or teens, although on this evening they were joined by the President Emeritus, a retired lawyer who was regaling them with his Groucho Marx imitations.

"Okay, knock it off!" said the current president, a slim, long-haired brunette who ran the City of Cambridge's combined police, fire and garbage control computer system. "It's time for the new show."

They turned on the three-dee in the corner and arranged themselves in a semicircle on the floor to see the first episode of "The Starcrossed."

But first, of course, they saw three dozen commercials: for bathroom bowl cleaners, bras, headache remedies, perfumes, rectal thermometers, hair dyes, and a foolproof electronic way to cheat on your school exams. Plus new cars, used cars, foreign cars, an airline commercial that explained the new antihijacking system (every passenger gets his very own Smith & Wesson .38 revolver!), and an oil company ad dripping with sincerity about the absolute need to move the revered site of Disneyland so that "we can get more oil to serve *you* better."

The science fiction fans laughed and jeered at all the commercials, especially the last one. They bicycled, whenever and wherever the air was safe enough to breathe.

Then the corner of the room where the three-dee projector cast its images went absolutely black. The fans went silent with anticipation. Then a thread of music began, too faint to really pick out the tune. A speck of light appeared in the middle of the pool of blackness. Then another. Two stars, moving toward each other. The music swelled.

"Hey, that tune is 'When You Wish Upon a Star!'"

"Sssshhh." Nineteen hisses.

The two stars turned out to be starships and bold letters spelled out "The Starcrossed" over them. The fans cheered and applauded.

Two minutes later, after another dozen commercials, they were gaping.

"Look at how *solid* they are!"

"It's like they're really here in the room. No scintillations at all."

"It's a damned-near perfect projection."

"I wish we had a life-sized set."

"You can reach out and touch them!"

"I wouldn't mind touching *her*!"

"Or him. He's got muscles. Not like the guys around here."

"And she's got . . ."

Twelve hisses, all from female throats, drowned him out.

Fifteen minutes later, they were still gaping, but now their comments were:

"This is pretty slow for an opening show."

"It's pretty slow, period."

"That hockey player acts better in the Garden when they call a foul on him."

"Shuddup. I want to watch Juliet breathe."

Halfway into the second act they were saying:

"Who wrote this crud?"

"It's *awful*!"

"They must be dubbing Romeo's speeches. His mouth doesn't sync with the words."

"Who cares? The words are *dumb*."

They laughed. They groaned. They threw marshmallows at the solid-looking images and watched the little white missiles sail right through the performers. When the show finally ended:

"What a wagonload of crap!"

"Well, at least the girl was good-looking."

"Good-looking? She's sensational!"

"But the story. Ugh!"

"What story?"

"There was a story?"

"Maybe it's supposed to be a children's show."

"Or a spoof."

"It wasn't funny enough to be a spoof."

"Or intelligent enough to be a children's show. Giant amoebas in space!"

"It'll set science fiction back ten years, at least."

"Oh, I don't know," the President Emeritus said, clutching his walking stick. "I thought it was pretty funny in places."

"In the wrong places."

"One thing, though. That new projection system is terrific. I'm going to scrounge up enough money to buy a life-sized three-dee. They've finally worked all the bugs out of it."

"Yeah."

"Right. Let's get a life-sized set for the clubroom."

"Do we have enough money in the treasury?"

"We do," said the treasurer, "if we cancel the rocket launch in March."

"Cancel it," the president said. "Let's see if the show gets any better. We can always scratch up more money for a rocket launch."

In Pete's Tavern in downtown Manhattan, the three-dee set was life-sized. The regulars sat on their stools with their elbows on the bar and watched "The Starcrossed" actors galumph across the corner where the jukebox used to be.

After the first few minutes, most of them turned back to the bar and resumed their drinking.

"*That's* Francois Dulaq, the hockey star?"

"Indeed it is, my boy."

"Terrible. Terrible."

"Hey, Kenno, turn on the hockey game. At least we can see some action. This thing stinks."

But one of the women, chain smoking while sipping daiquiris and petting the toy poodle in her lap, stared with fascination at the life-sized three-dimensional images in the corner. "What a build on him," she murmured to the poodle.

In the Midwest the show went on an hour later.

Eleven ministers of various denominations stared incredulously at Rita Yearling and immediately began planning sermons for Sunday on the topic of the shamelessness of modern women. They watched the show to the very end.

The cast and crew of *As You Like It* caught the show during a rehearsal at the Guthrie Theatre in Minneapolis. They decided they didn't like it at all and asked their director to pen an open letter to Titanic Productions, demanding a public apology to William Shakespeare.

The science fiction classes at the University of Kansas—eleven hundred strong—watched the show in the University's Gunn Amphitheater. After the first six minutes, no one could hear the dialogue because of the laughing, catcalls and boos from the sophisticated undergraduates and grad students. The professor who held the Harrison Chair and therefore directed the science fiction curriculum decided that not hearing the dialogue was a mercy.

The six-man police force of Cisco, Texas, voted Rita Yearling "The Most Arresting Three-Dee Personality."

The Hookers Convention in Reno voted Francois Dulaq "Neatest Trick of the Year."

The entire state of Utah somehow got the impression that the end of the world had come a step closer.

((•)) ((•)) ((•))

In Los Angeles, the cadaverous young man who wrote television criticism for the *Free Press-News-Times* smiled as he turned on his voice recorder. Ron Gabriel had stolen three starlets from him in the past year. Now was the moment of his revenge.

He even felt justified.

The editor-in-chief of the venerable *TV Guide*, in his Las Vegas office, shook his head in despair. "How in the world am I going to put a good face on this piece of junk?" he asked a deaf heaven.

In Oakland, the staff of the most influential science fiction newsletter watched the show to its inane end—where Dulaq (playing Rom, or Romeo) improvises a giant syringe from one of his starship's rocket tubes and kills the space-roving Giant Amoeba with a thousand-liter shot of penicillin.

Charles Brown III heaved a mighty sigh. The junior editors, copyreaders and collators sitting at his feet held their breath, waiting for his pronouncement.

"Stinks," he said simply.

High on a mountainside in the Cascade Range, not far from Glacier Park, a bearded writer clicked off his three-dee set and sat in the darkness of his mist-enshrouded chalet. For many minutes he simply sat and thought.

Then he snapped his fingers and his voice recorder came rolling out of its slot on smoothly oiled little trunnions.

"Take a letter," he said to the simple-minded robot and its red ON light winked with electrical pleasure. "No, make it a telegram. To Ron Gabriel. The 'puter has his address in its memory. Dear Ron: Have plenty of room up here in the hills if you need to get away from the flak. Come on up. The air's clean and the women are dirty. What more can I say? Signed, Herb. Make it collect."

And in Bernard Finger's home in the exclusive Watts section of Greater Los Angeles, doctors shuttled in and out, like substitute players for the Honolulu Pineapples, manfully struggling to save the mogul of Titanic Productions from what appeared to be—from the symptoms—the world's first case of manic convulsive paranoid cardiac insufficiency, with lockjaw on the side.

BARD SPINS AS "STARCROSSED" DRAGS
Variety

NEW THREE-DEE TECHNIQUE IS ONLY SOLID FEATURE OF "STARCROSSED"
NY Times-Herald-Voice

CAPSULE REVIEW
By *Gerrold Saul*

"The Starcrossed," which premiered last night on nationwide network three-dee, is undoubtedly the worst piece of alleged drama ever foisted on the viewers.

Despite the gorgeous good looks of Rita Yearling and the stubborn handsomeness of hockey star Frankie Dulaq, the show has little to offer. Ron Gabriel's script—even disguised under a whimsical penname—has all the life and bounce of the proverbial lead dirigible. While the sets were adequate and the costumes arresting, the story made no sense whatsoever. And the acting was nonexistent. Stalwart though he may be in the hockey rink, Dulaq's idea of drama is to peer into the cameras and grimace.

The technical feat of producing really solid three-dimensional images was impressive. Titanic Productions' new technique will probably be copied by all the other studios, because it makes everything else look pale and wan by comparison.

If only the script had been equal to the electronics.
LA Free Press-News-Times

TV GUIDE
America's Oldest and Most Respected Television Magazine

Contents
The Starcrossed:" Can a Science Fiction Show Succeed by Spoofing Science Fiction?
Technical Corner: New Three-Dee Projection Technique

Heralds End of "Blinking Blues"
The New Lineups: Networks Unveil "Third Season" Shows,
and Prepare for "Fourth Season" in Seven Weeks
A Psychologist Warns: Portraying Love in Three-Dee Could
Confuse Teenagers
Nielsen Reports: "Kongo's Mayhem" and "Shoot-Out" Still
Lead in Popularity

MITCH WESTERLY, MYSTERY MAN OF TELEVISION
Playperson

WHY RITA YEARLING CRIED WHEN SHE FLEW TO
TORONTO
TV Love Stars

DULAQ NOT SCORING, CANADIAN MAPLE STARS
NOT WINNING
Sporting News

CAN A GAY PORTRAY A STRAIGHT ON TV? AND IF
SO, WHY?
Liberty

NEW THREE-DEE PROJECTION SYSTEM FULLY SUC-
CESSFUL
Scintillation-Free Images Result from
Picosecond Control Units Developed by
Oxnard Laboratory in California

Dr. Oxnard Claims System Can Be
Adapted to 'Animate' Still Photos;
Obviate Need for Actors in TV
Electronics News

17: The Outcome

Bill Oxnard grimaced with concentration as he maneuvered his new Electric TR into Ron Gabriel's driveway. Ordinarily it would have been an easy task, but the late winter rainstorm made visibility practically nil and there was a fair-sized van parked at the curb directly in front of the driveway.

The front door of the house was open and a couple of burly men in coveralls were taking out the long sectional sofa that had curled around Gabriel's living room. They grunted and swore under their breaths as they swung their burden around the Electric TR. The sofa was so big that if they had dropped it on the sportscar, they would have flattened it.

Brenda looked upset as she got out of the righthand seat. "They're taking his *furniture!*" She dashed into the house.

Oxnard was a step behind her. It only took three long strides to get inside the foyer, but the rain was hard enough to soak him, even so.

There were no lights on inside the house. The furniture movers had left a hand torch glowing in the living room. Oxnard watched them reenter the house, trailing muddy footprints and dripping water, to grab the other chairs in the living room.

Brenda said, "Bill! And they've turned off his electricity!" She was very upset and Oxnard found himself feeling pleased with her concern, rather than jealous over it *She's really a marvelous person,* he told himself.

They looked around the darkened house for a few minutes and finally found Ron Gabriel sitting alone in the kitchen, in candlelight.

"Ron, why didn't you tell us?" Brenda blurted.

Gabriel looked surprised and, in the flickering light of the lone candle, a bit annoyed.

"Tell you what?"

"We would have helped you, wouldn't we, Bill?"

"Of course," Oxnard said. "If you're broke, Ron, or run out of credit. . . ."

"What're you talking about?" Gabriel pushed himself up from the table. He was wearing his old Bruce Lee robe.

"We've been following the reviews of 'The Starcrossed,'" said Brenda. "We saw what a panning the scripts took. They're blaming you for everything. . . ."

"And when we saw them taking away your furniture. . . ."

"And no electricity. . . ."

A lithe young girl walked uncertainly into the kitchen, dressed in a robe identical to Gabriel's. The candlelight threw coppery glints from her hair, which flowed like a cascade of molten red-gold over her slim shoulders.

With a *you guys are crazy* look, Gabriel introduced, "Cindy Steele, this is Brenda Impanema and Bill Oxnard, two of my loony friends."

"Hello," said Cindy, in a tiny little voice.

Brenda smiled at her and Oxnard nodded.

"We *were* going to have a quiet little candlelight dinner," Gabriel said, "just the two of us. Before the Ding-Dong Furniture Company came in with my new gravity-defying float-chair. And the Salvation Army came by to pick up my old living room furniture, which I donated to them. And my friends started going spastic for fear that I was broke and starving."

"Is that what. . . ." Brenda didn't quite believe it.

But Oxnard did. He started laughing. "I guess we jumped to the wrong conclusion. Come on," he held out a hand to Brenda, "we've got a candlelight dinner of our own to see to."

Gabriel's eyebrows shot up. "Yeah? Really?" He came around the table and looked at the two of them closely. "Son of a gun." He grinned.

They walked out to the foyer together, the four of them, Gabriel between Oxnard and Brenda, Cindy trailing slightly behind, twirling a curl of hair in one finger.

"Hey look," Gabriel said. "Come on back after dinner. For dessert. Got a lot to tell you."

"Oh, I don't think. . . ." Brenda began.

"We'll be back in a couple of hours," Oxnard said. "We've got a lot to tell you, too."

"Great. Bring back some pie or something."

"And give us at least three hours," Cindy said, smiling and walking the fingers of one hand across the back of Gabriel's shoulders. "I'm a slow cooker."

It was just after midnight when Gabriel, Brenda and Oxnard tried out the new floatchairs. They were like an arrangement of airfoam cushions out of the Arabian Nights, except that they floated a dozen centimeters above coppery disks that rested on the floor.

"It's like sitting on a cloud!" Brenda said, snuggling down on the cushions as they adjusted to fit her form.

"Takes a lot of electricity to maintain the field, doesn't it?" Oxnard asked.

"You bet," snapped Gabriel. "And you clowns thought they'd turned off my power."

"Where's Cindy?" asked Brenda.

Gabriel gave a tiny shrug. "Probably fell asleep in the whirlpool bath. She does that, sometimes. Nice kid, but not too bright."

"So what's your news?" Oxnard asked, anxious to tell his own.

Leaning back in his cushions, Gabriel said, "You know all the flak they've been throwing at me about the scripts for 'The Starcrossed'? Well my *original* script—the one that little creepy censor and Earnest tore to shreds—is going to get the Screen Writer's award next month as the best dramatic script of the year."

"Ron, that's great!"

Gabriel crowed, "And the Guild is asking the Canadian Department of Labor to sue Badger for using child labor—the high school kids who wrote scripts without getting paid!"

"Can they do that?"

Nodding, Gabriel said, "The lawyers claim they can and they're naming Gregory Earnest as a codefendant, along with Badger Studios."

"The suit won't affect Titanic, will it?" Brenda asked, looking around.

"Can't. It's limited to Canadian law."

"That's good; B.F.'s had enough trouble over 'The Starcrossed.'"

"Nothing he didn't earn, sweetie," Gabriel said.

"Maybe so," Brenda said. "But enough is enough. He'll be getting out of the hospital next week and I don't want him hurt any more."

Gabriel shook his head. "You're damned protective of that louse."

Oxnard glanced at Brenda. She controlled herself perfectly. He knew what was going through her mind: *He may be a louse, but he's the only louse in the world who's my father.*

"Has the show been cancelled yet?" Gabriel asked.

"No," Brenda said. "Its being renewed for the remainder of the season."

"What?"

Oxnard said, "Same reaction I had. Wait'll you hear why."

"What's going on?" Gabriel asked, suddenly a-quiver with interest.

"Lots," Brenda said. "Titanic is receiving about a thousand letters a week from the viewers. Most of them are science fiction fans complaining about the show; but they have to *watch* it to complain about it. The Nielsen ratings have been so-so, but there's been a good number of letters asking for pictures of Rita and personal mail for her. She's become the center of a new Earth Mother cult—most of the letters are from pubescent boys."

"My god," Gabriel moaned.

"Goddess," corrected Oxnard.

"Also," Brenda went on, "Rita's apparently got her talons into Keith Connors, the TNT man. So the show's assured of a sponsor for the rest of the season. She's got him signing commitments 'til his head's spinning."

With a rueful nod, Gabriel admitted, "She can do that."

"The New York bankers seem pleased. The show is making money. The critics hate it, of course, but it's bringing in some money."

"I'll be damned," Gabriel said.

"Never overestimate the taste of the American public," Brenda said.

Oxnard added, "And the show's bringing money into my lab, as well. People are seeing how good the new system is and they're showering us with orders. We're working three shifts now and I'm expanding the staff and adding more floor space for production."

Gabriel gave an impressed grunt.

"What Bill doesn't seem to realize," Brenda said, "is that it's really his holographic system that's created so much interest in 'The Starcrossed.' Nobody'd stare at Rita Yearling for long if she didn't look so solid."

"I don't know about that," Oxnard protested.

"It's true," Brenda said. "All the networks and production companies have placed orders for the new system. Everybody'll have it by next season."

"Then there goes Titanic's edge over the competition," Gabriel said, sounding satisfied with the idea.

"Not quite," Oxnard said.

"What do you mean?"

How to phrase this? he wondered. Carefully, Oxnard said, "Well . . . I made a slip of the tongue to a reporter from an electronics newspaper, about computerizing the system so you can animate still photos. . . ."

"You mean that thing about getting rid of the actors?"

"Somehow B.F. heard about it while he was recuperating from his seizure," Brenda took over, "and made Bill an offer to develop the system for Titanic."

"So I'm going to work with him on it," Oxnard concluded.

Gabriel's face froze in a scowl. "Why? Why do anything for that lying bastard?"

Oxnard shot a glance at Brenda, then replied, "He was sick. Those New York bankers were pressuring him. So I agreed to work with him on it. It impressed the bankers, helped make them happier with a small return on 'The Starcrossed.'" *Call it a present to a prospective father-in-law,* he added silently.

"You oughtta have your head examined," Gabriel said. "He'll just try to screw you again."

"I suppose so," Oxnard agreed cheerfully.

But Gabriel chuckled. "I think I'm going to drop a little hint about this to some of my acting friends. They've got a guild, too. . . ."

Brenda said, "Do me a favor, Ron? Wait a month . . . until he's strong enough to fight back."

"Why should I?"

"For me," she said.

He stared at her. "For you?"

"Please."

He didn't like it, that was clear. But he muttered, "Okay. One month. But no longer than that."

Brenda gave him her best smile. "Thanks, Ron. I knew you were just a pussycat at heart."

Gabriel shook his head. "It's just not *fair*! Dammit, Finger goes around screwing everybody in sight and comes up smelling like orchids. Every goddamned time! He works you to death, Brenda, sticks you with all the shit jobs. . . ."

"That's true," she admitted.

"Leaves me high and dry. . . ."

"You got your award," Oxnard said.

"Can't eat awards. I need work! There's nothing coming in except a few little royalties and residuals. And your mother-humping B.F. has spread the word all over town that I'm too cranky to work with."

Oxnard broke in, "Come to work with me, Ron."

Gabriel's eyes widened. "What?"

"Sure," Oxnard said. "Listen to me, both of you. Why should you have to put up with all this lunacy and nonsense? Ron, how long can you stand to be trampled by idiots like Earnest and that Canadian censor? Come to work with me! I need a good writer to direct our advertising and public relations staffs. You can be a consultant . . . work one day a week at the lab and spend the rest of the time free to write the books you've always wanted to write."

Before Gabriel could answer, Oxnard turned to Brenda. "And you too. You're a top-flight administrator, Brenda. Come to work with me. Why should you give yourself ulcers and high blood pressure over some dumb TV show? We can be a team, a real team—the three of us."

She looked shocked.

Oxnard turned back to Gabriel. "I mean it, Ron. You'd enjoy the work, I know." He looked back and forth, from Gabriel to Brenda and back again. "Well? How about it? Will you both come to work at Oxnard Labs?"

In unison they replied, "What? And quit show business?"

June 2007

Introduction to "Crisis of the Month"

"Crisis of the Month" began with my wife's griping about the hysterical manner in which the news media report on the day's events. Veteran newscaster Linda Ellerbee calls the technique "anxiety news." Back in journalism school (so long ago that spelling was considered important) I was taught that "good news is no news." Today's media takes this advice to extremes: no matter what the story, there is a down side to it that can be emphasized.

So when my darling and very perceptive wife complained about the utterly negative way in which the media presented the day's news I quipped, "I can see the day when science finally finds out how to make people immortal. The media will do stories about the sad plight of the funeral directors."

My wife recognizes an idea when she hears one, even if I don't. She immediately suggested, "Why don't you write a story about that?"

Thus the origin of "Crisis of the Month."

Crisis of the Month

While I crumpled the paper note that someone had slipped into my jacket pocket, Jack Armstrong drummed his fingers on the immaculately gleaming expanse of the pseudomahogany conference table.

"Well," he said testily, "ladies and gentlemen, don't *one* of you have a possibility? An inkling? An idea?"

No one spoke. I left the wadded note in my pocket and placed both my hands conspicuously on the table top.

Armstrong drummed away in abysmal silence. I guess once he had actually looked like The All-American Boy. Now, many facelifts and body remodelings later, he looked more like a moderately well-preserved manikin.

"Nothing at all, gentleman and ladies?" He always made certain to give each sex the first position fifty percent of the time. Affirmative action was a way of life with our Boss.

"Very well then. We will Delphi the problem."

That broke the silence. Everyone groaned.

"There's nothing else to be done," the Boss insisted. "We must have a crisis by Monday morning. It is now . . . " he glanced at the digital readout built into the table top, " . . . three-eighteen p.m. Friday. We will not leave this office until we have a crisis to offer."

We knew it wouldn't do a bit of good, but we groaned all over again.

The Crisis Command Center was the best-kept secret in the world. No government knew of our existence. Nor did the people, of course. In fact, in all the world's far-flung news media, only a select handful of the topmost executives knew of the CCC. Those few, those precious few, that band of brothers and sisters—they were our customers. The reason for our being. They paid handsomely. And they protected the secret of our work even from their own news staffs.

Our job, our sacred duty, was to select the crisis that would be the focus of worldwide media attention for the coming month. Nothing more. Nothing less.

In the old days, when every network, newspaper, magazine, news service, or independent station picked out its own crises, things were always in a jumble. Sure, they would try to focus on one or two sure-fire headline-makers: a nuclear powerplant disaster or the fear of one, a new disease like AIDS or Chinese Rot, a war, terrorism, things like that.

The problem was, there were so many crises springing up all the time, so many threats and threats of threats, so much blood and fire and terror, that people stopped paying attention. The news scared the livers out of them. Sales of newspapers and magazines plunged toward zero. Audiences for news shows, even the revered network evening shows, likewise plummeted.

It was Jack Armstrong—a much younger, more handsome and vigorous All-American Boy—who came up with the idea of the Crisis Command Center. Like all great ideas, it was basically simple.

Pick one crisis each month and play it for all it's worth. Everywhere. In all the media. Keep it scary enough to keep people listening, but not so terrifying that they'll run away and hide.

And it worked! Worked to the point where the CCC (or Cee Cubed, as some of our analysts styled it) was truly the command center for all the media of North America. And thereby, of course, the whole world.

But on this particular Friday afternoon, we were stumped. And I had that terrifying note crumpled in my pocket. A handwritten note, on paper, no less. Not an electric communication, but a secret, private, dangerous seditious note, meant for me and me alone, surreptitiously slipped into my jacket pocket.

"Make big $$$," it scrawled. "Tell all to Feds."

I clasped my hands to keep them from trembling and wondered who, out of the fourteen men and women sitting around the table, had slipped that bomb to me.

Boss Jack had started the Delphi procedure by going down the table, asking each of us board members in turn for the latest news in her or his area of expertise.

He started with the man sitting at his immediate right, Matt Dillon. That wasn't the name he had been born with, naturally; his original name had been Oliver Wolchinsky. But in our select little group, once you earn your spurs (no pun intended) you are entitled to a "power name," a name that shows you are a person of rank and consequence. Most power names were chosen, of course, from famous media characters.

Matt Dillon didn't look like the marshal of Dodge City. Or even the one-time teen screen idol. He was short, pudgy, bald, with bad skin and an irritable temper. He looked, actually, exactly as you would expect an Oliver Wolchinsky to look.

But when Jack Armstrong said," We shall begin with you," he added, "Matthew."

Matt Dillon was the CCC expert on energy problems. He always got to his feet when he had something to say. This time he remained with his round rump resting resignedly on the caramel cushion of his chair.

"The outlook is bleak," said Matt Dillon. "Sales of the new space-manufactured solar cells are still climbing. Individual homes, apartment buildings, condos, factories—everybody's plastering their roofs with them and generating their own electricity. No pollution, no radiation, nothing for us to latch onto. They don't even make noise!"

"Ah," intoned our All-American Boy, "but they must be ruining business for electric utility companies. Why not a crisis there?" He gestured hypnotically, and put on an expression of Ratheresque somberness, intoning, "Tonight we will look at the plight of the electrical utilities, men and women who have been discarded in the stampede for cheap energy."

"Trampled," a voice from down the table suggested.

"Ah, yes. Instead of discarded. Thank you." Boss Jack was never one to discourage creative criticism.

But Marshal Matt mewed, "The electric utility companies are doing just fine; they invested in the solar cell development back in '05. They saw the handwriting in the sky."

A collective sigh of disappointment went around the table.

Not one to give up easily, our Mr. Armstrong suggested, "What about oil producers, then? The coal miners?"

"The last coal miner retired on full pension in '08," replied Matt dolefully. "The mines were fully automated by then. Nobody cares if robots are out of work; they just get reprogrammed and moved into another industry. Most of the coal robots are picking fruit in Florida now."

"But the Texas oil and gas . . . ."

Matt headed him off at the pass. "Petroleum prices are steady. They sell the stuff to plastics manufacturers, mostly. Natural gas is the world's major heating fuel. It's clean, abundant and cheap."

Gloom descended on our conference table.

It deepened as Boss Jack went from one of our experts to the next.

Terrorism had virtually vanished in the booming world economy.

Political scandals were depressingly rare: with computers replacing most bureaucrats there was less cheating going on in government, and far fewer leaks to the media.

The space program was so successful that no less than seven governments of spacefaring nations—including our own dear Uncle Sam—had declared dividends for their citizens and a tax amnesty for the year.

Population growth was nicely levelling off. Inflation was minimal. Unemployment was a thing of the past, with an increasingly roboticized workforce encouraging humans to invest in robots, accept early retirement, and live off the productivity of their machines.

The closest thing to a crisis in that area was a street brawl in St. Peterrsburg between two retired Russian factory workers—aged thirty and thirty-two – who both wanted the very same robot. Potatoes that were much too small for our purposes.

There hadn't been a war since the International Peacekeeping Force had prevented Fiji from attacking Tonga, nearly twelve years ago.

Toxic wastes, in the few remote regions of the world were they still could be found, were being gobbled up by genetically-altered bugs (dubbed Rifkins, for some obscure reason) that happily died once they had finished their chore and dissolved into harmless water, carbon dioxide, and ammonia compounds. In some parts of the world the natives had started laundry and cleaning establishments on the sites of former toxic waste dumps.

I watched and listened in tightening terror as the fickle finger of fate made its way down the table toward me. I was low man on the board, the newest person there, sitting at the end of the table between pert Ms. Mary Richards (sex and family relations were her specialty) and dumpy old Alexis Carrington-Colby (nutrition and diets—it was she who had, three months earlier, come up with the blockbuster of the "mother's milk" crisis).

I hoped desperately that either Ms. Richards or Ms. Carrington-Colby would offer some shred of hope for the rest of the board to nibble on, because I knew I had nothing. Nothing except that damning damaging note in my pocket. What if the Boss found out about it? Would he think I was a potential informer, a philandering fink to the feds?

With deepening despair I listened to flinty-eyed Alexis offer apologies instead of ideas. It was Mary Richards' turn next, and my heart began fluttering unselfishly. I liked her, I was becoming quite enthusiastic about her, almost to the point of asking her romantic questions. I had never dated a sex specialist, or much of anyone, for that matter. Mary was special to me, and I wanted her to succeed.

She didn't. There was not crisis in sex or family relations.

"Mr. James," said the Boss, like a bell tolling for a funeral.

I wasn't entitled to a power name, since I had only recently been appointed to the board. My predecessor, Marcus Welby, had keeled over right at this conference table the previous month when he realized that there was no medical crisis in sight. His heart broke, literally. It had been his fourth one, but this time the rescue team was just a shade too late to pull him through again.

Thomas K. James is hardly a power name. But it was the one my parents had bestowed on me, and I was determined not to disgrace it. And in particular, not to let anyone know that someone in this conference room thought I was corruptible.

"Mr. James," asked a nearly-weeping All-American Boy, "is there anything on the medical horizon—anything at all—that may be useful to us?"

It was clear that Boss Armstrong did not suspect me of incipient treason. Nor did he expect me to solve his problem. I did not fail him in that expectation.

"Nothing worth raising an eyebrow over, sir, I regret to say." Remarkably, my voice stayed firm and steady, despite the dervishes dancing in my stomach.

"There are no new diseases," I went on, " and the old ones are all in rapid retreat. Genetic technicians can correct every identifiable malady in the zygotes, and children are born healthy for life." I cast a disparaging glance at Mr. Cosby, our black environmentalist, and added, "Pollution-related diseases are so close to zero that most disease centers around the world no longer take statistics on them."

"Addiction!" he blurted, the idea apparently springing into his mind unexpectedly. "There must be a new drug on the horizon!"

The board members stirred in their chairs and looked hopeful. For a moment.

I burst their bubble. "Modern chemotherapy detoxifies the addict in about eleven minutes, as some of us know from first-hand experience." I made sure not to stare at Matt Dillon or Alexis Carrington-Colby, who had fought bouts with alcohol and chocolate, respectively. "And, I must unhappily report, cybernetic neural programming is mandatory in every civilized nation in the world; once an addictive personality manifests itself, it can be reprogrammed quickly and painlessly."

The gloom around the table deepened into true depression, tinged with fear.

Jack Armstrong glanced at the miniature display screen discreetly set into the table top before him, swiftly checking on his affirmative actions, then said, "Ladies and gentleman, the situation grows more desperate with each blink of the clock. I suggest we take a five-minute break for R&R (he meant relief and refreshment) and then come back with some *new ideas!*"

He fairly roared out the last two words, shocking us all.

I repaired to my office—little more than a cubicle, actually, but it had a door that could be shut. I closed it carefully and hauled the unnerving note out of my pocket. Smoothing it on my desk top, I read it again. It still said:

"Make big $$$. Tell all to Feds."

I wadded it again and with trembling hands tossed it into the disposal can. It flashed silently into healthful ions.

"Are you going to do it?"

I wheeled around to see Mary Richards leaning against my door. She had entered my cubicle silently and closed the door without a sound. At least, no sound I had heard, so intent was I on that menacing message.

"Do what?" Lord, my voice cracked like Henry Aldrich.

Mary Richards (nee Stephanie Quaid) was a better physical proximation to her power name than anyone of the board members, with the obvious exception of our revered Boss. She was the kind of female for whom the words cute, pert, and vivacious were created. But beneath those skin-deep qualities she had the ruthless drive and calculated intelligence of a sainted Mike Wallace. Had to. Nobody without the same could make it to the CCC board. If that sounds self-congratulatory, so be it. A real Mary Richards, even a Lou Grant, would never get as far as the front door of the CCC.

"Tell all to the Feds," she replied sweetly.

The best thing I could think of was, "I don't know what you're talking about."

"The note you just ionized."

"What note?"

"The note I put in your pocket before the meeting started."

"You?" Until that moment I hadn't known I could hit high C.

Mary positively slinked across my cubicle and draped herself on my desk, showing plenty of leg through her slitted skirt. I gulped and slid my swivel chair into the corner.

"It's okay, there's no bugs operating in here. I cleared your office this morning."

I could feel my eyes popping. "Who are you?"

Her smile was all teeth. "I'm a spy, Tommy. A plant. A deep agent. I've been working for the Feds since I was a little girl, rescued from the slums of Chicago by the Rehabilitation Corps from what would have undoubtedly been a life of gang violence and prostitution."

"And they planted you here?"

"They planted me in Cable News when I was a fresh young thing just off the Rehab Farm. It's taken me eleven years to work my way up to the CCC. We always suspected some organization like this was manipulating the news, but we never had the proof . . . ."

"Manipulating!" I was shocked at the word. "We don't manipulate."

"Oh?" She seemed amused at my rightful ire. "Then what do you do?"

"We select. We focus. We manage the news for the benefit of the public."

"In my book, Tommy old pal, that is manipulation. And it's illegal."

"It's . . . out of the ordinary channels," I granted.

Mary shook her pretty chestnut-brown tresses. "It's a violation of FCC regulations, it makes a mockery of the antitrust laws, to say nothing of the SEC, OSHA, ICC, WARK and a half a dozen other regulatory agencies."

"So you're going to blow the whistle on us."

She straightened up and sat on the edge of my desk. "I can't do that, Tommy. I'm a government agent. An *agent provocateur*, I'm sure Mr. Armstrong's lawyers will call me."

"Then, what . . . ."

"You can blow the whistle," she said smilingly. "You're a faithful employee. Your testimony would stand up in court."

"Destroy," I spread my arms in righteous indignation, "all this?"

"It's illegal as hell, Tom," said Mary. "Besides, the rewards for being a good citizen can be very great. Lifetime pension. Twice what you're making here. Uncle Sam is very generous, you know. We'll fix you up with a new identity. We'll move you to wherever you want to live: Samoa, Santa Barbara, St. Thomas, even Schenectady. You could live like a retired financier."

I had to admit, "That is . . . generous."

"And," she added, shyly lowering her eyes, "of course I'll have to retire too, once the publicity of the trial blows my cover. I won't have the same kind of super pension that you'll get, but maybe . . . ."

My throat went dry.

Before I could respond, though, the air-raid siren went off, signaling that the meeting was reconvening.

I got up from my chair, but Mary stepped between me and the door.

"What's your answer, Thomas?" she asked, resting her lovely hands on my lapels.

"I . . . " gulping for air," . . . don't know."

She kissed me lightly on the lips. "Think it over, Thomas dear. Think hard."

It wasn't my thoughts that were hardening. She left me standing in the cubicle, alone except for my swirling thoughts, spinning through my head like a tornado. I could hear the roaring in my ears. Or was that simply high blood pressure?

The siren howled again, and I bolted to the conference room and took my seat at the end of the table. Mary smiled at my and patted my knee, under the table.

"Very well," said Jack Armstrong, checking his display screen, "gentleman and ladies. I have come to the conclusion that if we cannot find a crisis anywhere in the news," and he glared at us, as if he didn't believe there wasn't a crisis out there somewhere, probably right under our noses, "then we must manufacture a crisis."

I had expected that. So had most of the other board members, I could see. What went around the table was not surprise but resignation.

Cosby shook his head wearily, "We did that last month, and it was a real dud. The Anguish of Kindergarten. Audience response was a negative four point four. Negative!"

"Then we've got to be more creative!" snapped The All-American Boy.

I glanced at Mary. She was looking at me, smiling her sunniest smile, the one that could allegedly turn the world on. And the answer to the whole problem came to me with that blinding flash that marks true inspiration and minor epileptic seizures.

This wasn't epilepsy. I jumped to my feet. "Mr. Armstrong! Fellow board members!"

"What is it, Mr. James?" Boss Jack replied, a hopeful glimmer in his eyes.

The words almost froze in my throat. I looked down at Mary, still turning out megawatts of smile at me, and nearly choked because my heart had jumped into my mouth.

But only figuratively. "Ladies and gentlemen," (I had kept track, too), "there is a spy among us from the Federal Regulatory Commissions."

A hideous gasp arose, as if they had heard the tinkling bell of a leper.

"This is no time for levity, Mr. James," snapped the Boss. "On the other hand, if this is an attempt at shock therapy to stir the creative juices . . . ."

"It's real!" I insisted. Pointing at the smileless Mary Richards, I said, "This woman is a plant from the Feds. She solicited my cooperation. She tried to bribe me to blow the whistle on the CCC!"

They stared. They snarled. They hissed at Mary. She rose coolly from her chair, made a little bow, blew me a kiss, and left the conference room.

Armstrong was already on the intercom phone. "Have security detain her and get our legal staff to interrogate her. Do it now!"

Then the Boss got to his feet, way down there at the other end of the table, and fixed me with his steeliest gaze. He said not a word, but clapped his hands together, once, twice . . .

And the entire board stood up for me and applauded. I felt myself blushing, but it felt good. Warming. My first real moment in the sun.

The moment ended too soon. We all sat down and the gloom began to gray over my sunshine once more.

"It's too bad, Mr. James, that you didn't find a solution to our problem rather than a pretty government mole."

"Ah, but sir," I replied, savoring the opportunity for *le mot just*, "I have done exactly that."

"What?"

"You mean . . . ?"

"Are you saying that you've done it?"

I rose once more, without even glancing at the empty chair at my left.

"I have a crisis, sir." I announced quietly, humbly.

Not a word from any of them. They all leaned forward, expectantly, hopefully, yearningly.

"The very fact that we—the leading experts in the field—can find no crisis is in itself a crisis," I told them.

They sighed, as if a great work of art had suddenly been unveiled.

"Think of the crisis management teams all around the world who are idle! Think of the psychologists and the therapists who stand ready to help their fellow man and woman, yet have nothing to do! Think of the vast teams of news reporters, camera persons, editors, producers, publishers, even golfers, the whole vast panoply of men and women who have dedicated their lives to bringing the latest crisis into the homes of every human being on this planet—with nothing more to do than report on sports and weather!"

They leaped to their feet and converged on me. They raised me to their shoulders and joyously carried me around the table, shouting praises.

Deliriously happy, I thought to myself, I won't be at the foot of the table anymore. I'll move up. One day, I'll be at the head of the table, where The All-American Boy is now. He's getting old, burnt out. I'll get there. I'll get there!

And I knew what my power name would be. I'd known it from the start, when I'd first been made the lowliest member of the board. I'd been saving it, waiting until the proper moment to make the change.

My power name would be different, daring. A name that bespoke true power, the ability to command, the vision to see far into the future. And it wouldn't even require changing my real name that much. I savored the idea and rolled my power name through my mind again as they carried me around the table. Yes, it would work. It was right.

I would no longer be Thomas K. James. With the slightest, tiniest bit of manipulation my true self would stand revealed: James T. Kirk.

I was on my way.

Introduction to "The Great Moon Hoax"

This one you can blame on Norman Spinrad.

Norm is one of the best writers in the science fiction field, and a man who combines deep intelligence with a droll sense of humor.

In 1992 Norm invited me to contribute to an anthology he was putting together, *Down in Flames*. In his own words, the basic idea of the anthology was to "satirize, destroy, take the piss out of, overturn the basic premises of . . . your own universe." In other words, Norm wanted a story that would be the antithesis of my usual carefully-researched, scientifically-accurate fiction.

Norm's anthology never came to fruition, but I took his challenge and decided to write a story that "explains" just about everything from NASA's dullness to UFOs to—well, read it and see.

The Great Moon Hoax
or
A Princess of Mars

I leaned back in my desk chair and just plain stared at the triangular screen.

"What do you call this thing?" I asked the Martian.

"It is an interociter," he said. He was half in the tank, as usual.

"Looks like a television set," I said.

"Its principles are akin to your television, but you will note that its picture is in full color, and you can scan events that were recorded in the past."

"We should be watching the President's speech," said Prof. Schmidt.

"Why? We know what he's going to say. He's going to tell Congress that he wants to send a man to the Moon before Nineteen-Seventy."

The Martian shuddered. His name was a collection of hisses and sputters that came out to something pretty close to Jazzbow. Anyhow, that's what I called him. He didn't seem to mind. Like me, he was a baseball fan.

We were sitting in my Culver City office, watching Ted Williams' last ballgame from last year. Now *there* was a baseball player. Best damned hitter since Ruth. And as independent as Harry Truman. Told the rest of the world to go to hell whenever he felt like it. I admired him for that. I had missed almost the whole season last year; the Martians had taken me on safari with them. They were always doing little favors like that for me; this interociter device was just the latest one.

"I still think we should be watching President Kennedy," Schmidt insisted.

"We can view it afterward, if you like," said Jazzbow, diplomatically. As I said, he had turned into quite a baseball fan and we both wanted to see the Splendid Splinter's final home run.

Jazzbow was a typical Martian. Some of the scientists still can't tell one from another, they look so much alike, but I guess that's because they're all cloned rather than conceived sexually. Mars is pretty damned dull that way, you know. Of course, most of the scientists aren't all that smart outside of their own fields of specialization. Take Einstein, for example. Terrific thinker. He believes if we all scrapped our atomic bombs the world would be at peace. Yah. Sure.

Anyway, Jazzbow is about four foot nine with dark leathery skin, kind of like a football that's been left out in the sun too long. The water from the tank made him look even darker, of course. Powerful barrel chest, but otherwise a real spidery build, arms and legs like pipestems. Webbed feet, evolved for walking on loose sand. Their hands have five fingers with opposable thumbs, just like ours, but the fingers have so many little bones in them that they're as flexible as an octopus' tentacles.

Martians would look really scary, I guess, if it weren't for their goofy faces. They've got big sorrowful limpid eyes with long feminine eyelashes, like a camel; their noses are splayed from one cheek to the other; and they've got these wide lipless mouths stretched into a permanent silly-looking grin, like a dolphin. No teeth at all. They eat nothing but liquids. Got long tongues, like some insects, which might be great for sex if they had any, but they don't and anyway they usually keep their tongues rolled up inside a special pouch in their cheeks so they don't startle any of us earthlings. How they talk with their tongues rolled up is beyond me.

Anyway, Jazzbow was half in the tank, as I said. He needed the water's buoyancy to make himself comfortable in earthly gravity.

Otherwise he'd have to wear his exoskeleton suit and I couldn't see putting him through that just so we could have a face-to-face with Prof. Schmidt.

The professor was fidgeting unhappily in his chair. He didn't give a rat's ass about baseball, but at least he could tell Jazzbow from the other Martians. I guess it's because he was one of the special few who'd known the Martians ever since they had first crash-landed in New Mexico back in Forty-six.

Well, Williams socked his home run and the Fenway Park fans stood up and cheered for what seemed like an hour and he never did come out of the dugout to tip his cap for them. Good for him! I thought. His own man to the very end. That was his last time on a ball field as a player. I found I had tears in my eyes.

"*Now* can we see the President?" Schmidt asked, exasperated. Normally he looked like a young Santa Claus, round and red-cheeked, with a pale blond beard. He usually was a pretty jolly guy, but just now his responsibilities were starting to get the better of him.

Jazzbow snaked one long, limber arm out of the water and fiddled with the controls beneath the inverted triangle of the interociter's screen. JFK came on the screen in full color, in the middle of his speech to the joint session of Congress:

"I believe that this nation should commit itself to achieving the goal, before this decade is out, of landing a man on the Moon and returning him safely to the Earth. I believe we should go to the Moon."

Jazzbow sank down in his water tank until only his big eyes showed and he started noisily blowing bubbles, his way of showing that he was upset.

Schmidt turned to me. "You're going to have to talk him out of it," he said flatly.

I had not voted for John Kennedy. I had instructed all of my employees to vote against him, although I imagine some of them disobeyed me out some twisted sense of independence.

Now that he was President, though, I felt sorry for the kid. Eisenhower had let things slide pretty badly. The Commies were infiltrating the Middle East and of course they had put up the first artificial satellite and just a couple weeks ago had put the first man into space: Yuri something-or-other. Meanwhile young Jack

Kennedy had let that wacky plan for the reconquest of Cuba go through. I had *told* the CIA guys that they'd need strong air cover, but they went right ahead and hit the Bay of Pigs without even a Piper Cub over them. Fiasco.

So the new President was trying to get everybody's mind off all this crap by shooting for the Moon. Which would absolutely destroy everything we'd worked so hard to achieve since that first desperate Martian flight here some fifteen years earlier.

I knew that *somebody* had to talk the President out of this Moon business. And of all the handful of people who were in on the Martian secret, I guess that the only one who could really deal with the White House on an eye-to-eye level was me.

"Okay," I said to Schmidt. "But he's going to have to come out here. I'm not going to Washington."

It wasn't that easy. The President of the United States doesn't come traipsing across the country to see an industrial magnate, no matter how many services the magnate has performed for his country. And my biggest service, of course, he didn't know anything about.

To make matters worse, while my people were talking to his people, I found out that the girl I was grooming for stardom turned out to be a snoop from the goddamned Internal Revenue Service. I had had my share of run-ins with the Feds, but using a beautiful starlet like Jean was a low blow even for them. A real crotch shot.

It was Jazzbow who found her out, of course.

Jean and I had been getting along very nicely indeed. She was tall and dark-haired and really lovely, with a sweet disposition and the kind of wide-eyed innocence that makes life worthwhile for a nasty old S.O.B. like me. And she loved it, couldn't get enough of whatever I wanted to give her. One of my hobbies was making movies; it was a great way to meet girls. Believe it or not, I'm really very shy. I'm more at home alone in a plane at twenty thousand feet than at some Hollywood cocktail party. But if you own a studio, the girls come flocking.

Okay, so Jean and I are getting along swell. Except that during the period when my staff was dickering with the White House staff, one morning I wake up and she's sitting at the writing desk in my bedroom, going through my drawers. The desk drawers, that is.

I cracked one eye open. There she is, naked as a Greek goddess and just as gorgeous, rummaging through the papers in my drawers. There's nothing in there, of course. I keep all my business papers in a germtight fireproof safe back at the office.

But she had found *something* that fascinated her. She was holding it in front of her, where I couldn't see what was in her hand, her head bent over it for what seemed like ten minutes, her dark hair cascading to her bare shoulders like a river of polished onyx.

Then she glanced up at the mirror and spotted me watching her.

"Do you always search your boyfriends' desks?" I asked. I was pretty pissed off, you know.

"What is this?" She turned and I saw she was holding one of my safari photos between her forefinger and thumb, like she didn't want to get fingerprints on it.

Damn! I thought. I should've stashed those away with my stag movies.

Jean got up and walked over to the bed. Nice as pie she sat on the edge and stuck the photo in front of my bleary eyes.

"What is this?" she asked again.

It was a photo of a Martian named Crunchy, the physicist George Gamow, James Dean and me in the dripping dark jungle in front of a brontosaurus I had shot. The Venusian version of a brontosaurus, that is. It looked like a small mountain of mottled leather. I was holding the stun rifle Crunchy had lent me for the safari.

I thought fast. "Oh, this. It's a still from a sci-fi film we started a few years ago. Never finished it, though. The special effects cost too much."

"That's James Dean, isn't it?"

I peered at the photo as if I was trying to remember something that wasn't terribly important. "Yeah, I think so. The kid wanted more money than I wanted to spend on the project. That's what killed it."

"He's been dead for five or six years."

"Has it been that long?" James Dean was alive and having the time of life working with the Martians on Venus. He had left his acting career and his life on earth far behind him to do better work than the President's Peace Corps could even dream about.

"I didn't know he did a picture for you," she said, her voice dreamy, ethereal. Like every other woman her age she had a crush on James Dean. That's what drove the poor kid to Venus.

"He didn't," I snapped. "We couldn't agree on terms. Come on back to bed."

She did, but in the middle of it my damned private phone rang. Only five people on earth knew that number and one of them wasn't human.

I groped for the phone. "This better be important," I said.

"The female you are with," said Jazzbow's hissing voice, "is a government agent."

Oh yeah, the Martians are long-distance telepaths, too.

So I took Jean for a drive out to the desert in my Bentley convertible. She loved the scenery, thought it was romantic. Or so she said. Me, I looked at that miserable dry Mojave scrubland and thought of what it could become: blossoming farms, spacious tracts of housing where people cooped up in the cities could raise their kids, glamorous shopping malls. But about all it was good for now was an Air Force base where guys like Chuck Yeager and Scott Crossfield flew the X-planes and the Martians landed their saucers every now and then. After dark, of course.

"Just look at that sunset," Jean said, almost breathless with excitement, maybe real, maybe pretended. She *was* an actress, after all.

I had to admit the sunset was pretty. Red and purple glowing brighter than Technicolor.

"Where are we going?" she kept on asking, a little more nervous each time.

"It's a surprise." I had to keep on going until it was good and dark. We had enough UFO sightings as it was, no sense taking a chance on somebody getting a really good look. Or even worse, a photograph.

The stars came out, big and bright and looking close enough to touch. I kept looking for one in particular to detach itself from the sky and land on the road beside us. All that stuff about saucers shining green rays on cars or planes and sucking them up inside themselves is sheer hooey. The Martians don't have anything like that. Wish they did.

Pretty soon I see it.

"Look!" says Jean. "A falling star!"

I didn't say anything, but a couple of minutes later the headlights pick up the saucer sitting there by the side of the road, still glowing a little from the heat of its re-entry from orbit.

"Don't tell me you've driven me all the way out here to see another movie set," Jean said, sounding disappointed. "This isn't your big surprise, is it?"

"Not quite," I said, pulling up beside the saucer's spindly little ladder.

She was pretty pissed off. Even when two of the Martians came slithering down the ladder she still thought it was some kind of a movie stunt. They had to move pretty slow and awkwardly because of the gravity; made me think of the monster movies we made. Jean was definitely not impressed.

"Honestly, Howard, I don't see why—"

Then one of the Martians put its snake-fingered hands on her and she gave a yelp and did what any well-trained movie starlet would do. She fainted.

Jazzbow wasn't in the ship, of course. The Martians wouldn't risk a landing in Culver City to pick him up, not even at night. Nobody but Prof. Schmidt and me knew he was in my office suite there. And the other Martians, of course.

So I got Jazzbow on the ship's interociter while his fellow Martians draped the unconscious Jean on one of their couches. Her skirt rucked up nicely, showing off her legs to good advantage.

"They're not going to hurt her any, are they?" I asked Jazzbow.

"Of course not," his image answered from the inverted triangular screen. "I thought you knew us better than that."

"Yeah, I know. You can't hurt a fly. But still, she's just a kid . . . "

"They're merely probing her mind to see how much she actually knows. It will only take a few minutes."

I won't go into all the details. The Martians are extremely sensitive about their dealings with other living creatures. Not hurt a fly? Hell, they'd make the Dalai Lama look like a bloodthirsty maniac.

Very gently, like a mother caressing her sleeping baby, three of them touched her face and forehead with those tentacle-like fingers. Probing her mind. Some writer got wind of the technique second- or third-hand and used it on television a few years later. Called it a Velcro mind-melt or something like that.

"We have for you," the ship's science officer told me, "good news and bad news."

His name sounded kind of like Snitch. Properly speaking, every Martian is an "it," not a "him" or a "her." But I always thought of them as males.

"The good news," Snitch said to me, "is that this female knew nothing of our existence. She hadn't the faintest suspicion that Martians exist or that you are dealing with them."

"Well, she does now," I grumbled.

"The bad news," he went on, with that silly grin spread across his puss, "is that she is acting as an undercover agent for your Internal Revenue Service—while she's between acting jobs."

Aw hell.

I talked it over with Jazzbow. Then he talked in Martian with Snitch. Then all three of us talked together. We had evolved a Standard Operating Procedure for situations like this, when somebody stumbled onto our secret. I didn't much like the idea of using it on Jean, but there wasn't much else we could do.

So, reluctantly, I agreed. "Just be damned careful with her," I insisted. "She's not some hick cop who's been startled out of his snooze by one of your cockamamie malfunctioning saucers."

Their saucers were actually pretty reliable, but every once in a while the atmospheric turbulence at low altitude would get them into trouble. Most of the sightings happened when the damned things wobbled too close to the ground.

Jazzbow and Snitch promised they'd be extra-special careful.

Very gently, the Martians selectively erased Jean's memory so that all she remembered the next morning, when she woke up a half a mile from a Mojave gas station, was that she had been abducted by aliens from another world and taken aboard a flying saucer.

The authorities wanted to put her in a nut house, of course. But I sent a squad of lawyers to spring her, since she was under contract to my movie studio. The studio assumed responsibility for her, and my lawyers assured the authorities that she was about to star in a major motion picture. The yokels figured it had all been a publicity stunt and turned her loose. I actually did put her into a couple of starring roles, which ended her career with the IRS, although I figured that not even the Feds would have had anything to do with Jean after the tabloids headlined her story about being abducted by flying saucer aliens. I took good care of her, though. I even married her, eventually. That's what comes from hanging around with Martians.

See, the Martians have a *very* high ethical standard of conduct. They cannot willingly hurt anybody or anything. Wouldn't step on an ant. It's led to some pretty near scrapes for us, though. Every now and then somebody stumbles onto them and the whole secret's in jeopardy. They could wipe the person's brain clean, but that would turn the poor sucker into a zombie. So they selectively erase only the smallest possible part of the sucker's memory.

And they always leave the memory of being taken into a flying saucer. They tell me they have to. That's part of their moral code, too. They're constantly testing us—the whole human race, that is— to see if we're ready to receive alien visitors from another world. And to date, the human race as a whole has consistently flunked every test.

Sure, a handful of very special people know about them. I'm pretty damned proud to be among that handful, let me tell you. But the rest of the human race, the man in the street, the news reporters and preachers and even the average university professor—they either ridicule the very idea that there could be any kind of life at all on another world or they get scared to death of the possibility. Take a look at the movies we make!

"Your people are sadly xenophobic," Jazzbow told me more than once, his big liquid eyes looking melancholy despite that dumbbell clown's grin splitting his face.

I remembered Orson Welles' broadcast of *The War of the Worlds* back in Thirty-eight. People got hysterical when they thought Martians had landed in New Jersey, although why anybody would want to invade New Jersey is beyond me. Here I had real Martians zipping all over the place and they were gentle as butterflies. But no one would believe that; the average guy would blast away with his twelve-gauge first and ask where they came from afterward.

So I had to convince the President that if he sent astronauts to the Moon, it would have catastrophic results.

Well, my people and Kennedy's people finally got the details ironed out and we agreed to meet at Edwards Air Force Base, out in the Mojave. Totally secret meeting. JFK was giving a speech in LA that evening at the Beverly Wiltshire. I sent a company helicopter to pick him up there and fly him over to Edwards. Just him and two of his aides. Not even his Secret Service bodyguards; he didn't care much for having those guys lurking around him, anyway. Cut down on his love life too much.

We met in Hangar Nine, the place where the first Martian crew was stashed back in Forty-six, pretty battered from their crash landing. That's when I first found out about them. I was asked by Prof. Schmidt, who looked like a very agitated young Santa Claus back then, to truck in as many refrigeration units as my company could lay its hands on. Schmidt wanted to keep the Martians comfortable, and since their planet is so cold he figured they needed mucho refrigeration. That was before he found out that the Martians spend about half their energy budget at home just trying to stay reasonably warm. They loved southern California! Especially the swimming pools.

Anyway, there I am waiting for the President in good old Hangar Nine, which had been so Top Secret since Forty-six that not even the base commander's been allowed inside. We'd partitioned it and decked it out with nice furniture and all the modern conveniences. I noticed that Jazzbow had recently had an interociter installed. Inside the main living area we had put up a big water tank for Jazzbow and his fellow Martians, of course. The place kind of resembled a movie set: nice modern furnishings, but if you looked past the ten-foot-high partitions that served as walls you saw the bare metal support beams crisscrossing up in the shadows of the ceiling.

Jazzbow came in from Culver City in the same limo that brought Prof. Schmidt. As soon as he got into the hanger he unhooked his exoskeleton and dived into the water tank. Schmidt started pacing nervously back and forth on the Persian carpeting I had put in. He was really wound up tight: letting the President in on this secret was an enormous risk. Not for us, so much as for the Martians.

It was just about midnight when we heard the throbbing motor sound of a helicopter in the distance. I walked out into the open and saw the stars glittering like diamonds all across the desert sky. How many of them are inhabited? I wondered. How many critters out there are looking at our Sun and wondering if there's any intelligent life there?

Is there any intelligent life in the White House? That was the big question, far as I was concerned.

Jack Kennedy looked tired. No, worse than that, he looked troubled. Beaten down. Like a man who had the weight of the world on his shoulders. Which he did. Elected by a paper-thin majority, he was having hell's own time getting Congress to vote for his programs. Tax relief, increased defense spending, civil rights—they were all dead in the water, stymied by a Congress that wouldn't do spit for him. And now I was going to pile another ton and a half on top of all that.

"Mr. President," I said as he walked through the chilly desert night from the helicopter toward the hangar door. I sort of stood at attention: for the office, not the man, you understand. Remember, I voted for Nixon.

He nodded at me and made a weary smile and stuck out his hand the way every politician does. I let him shake my hand, making a mental note to excuse myself and go to the washroom as soon as decently possible.

As we had agreed, he left his two aides at the hangar door and accompanied me inside all by himself. He kind of shuddered.

"It's cold out there, isn't it?" he said.

He was wearing a summer-weight suit. I had an old windbreaker over my shirt and slacks.

"We've got the heat going inside," I said, gesturing him through the door in the first partition. I led him into the living area and to the big carpeted central room where the water tank was. Schmidt followed behind us so close I could almost feel his breath on my neck. It gave me that crawly feeling I get when I realize how many millions of germs are floating through the air all the time.

"Odd place for a swimming tank," the President said as soon as we entered the central room.

"It's not as odd as you think," I said. Jazzbow had ducked low, out of sight for the time being.

My people had arranged two big sofas and a scattering of comfortable armchairs around a coffee table on which they had set up a fair-sized bar. Bottles of every description, even champagne in its own ice bucket.

"What'll you have?" I asked. We had decided that, with just the three of us humans present, I would be the bartender.

Both the President and Schmidt asked for scotch. I made the drinks big, knowing they would both need them.

"Now what's this all about?" Kennedy asked after his first sip of the booze. "Why all this secrecy and urgency?"

I turned to Schmidt, but he seemed to be petrified. So absolutely frozen that he couldn't even open his mouth or pick up his drink. He just stared at the President, overwhelmed by the enormity of what we had to do.

So I said, "Mr. President, you have to stop this Moon program."

He blinked his baggy eyes. Then he grinned. "Do I?"

"Yessir."

"Why?"

"Because it will hurt the Martians."

"The Martians, you said?"

"That's right. The Martians," I repeated.

Kennedy took another sip of scotch, then put his glass down on the coffee table. "Mr. Hughes, I had heard that you'd gone off the deep end, that you've become a recluse and something of a mental case—"

Schmidt snapped out of his funk. "Mr. President, he's telling you the truth. There *are* Martians."

Kennedy gave him a "who are you trying to kid" look. "Professor Schmidt, I know you're a highly respected astronomer, but if you expect me to believe there are living creatures on Mars you're going to have to show me some evidence."

On that cue, Jazzbow came slithering out of the water tank. The President's eyes goggled as old Jazzie made his painful way, dripping on the rug, to one of the armchairs and half collapsed into it.

"Mr. President," I said, "may I introduce Jazzbow of Mars. Jazzbow, President Kennedy."

The President just kept on staring. Jazzbow extended his right hand, that perpetual clown's grin smeared across his face. With his jaw hanging open, Kennedy took it in his hand. And flinched.

"I assure you," Jazzbow said, not letting go of the President's hand, "that I am truly from Mars."

Kennedy nodded. He believed it. He had to. Martians can make you see the truth of things. Goes with their telepathic abilities, I guess.

Schmidt explained the situation. How the Martians had built

their canals once they realized that their world was dying. How they tried to bring water from the polar ice caps to their cities and farm lands. It worked, for a few centuries, but eventually even that wasn't enough to save the Martians from slow but certain extinction.

They were great engineers, great thinkers. Their technology was roughly a century or so ahead of ours. They had invented the electric light bulb, for example, during the time of our French and Indian War.

By the time they realized that Mars was going to dry up and wither away despite all their efforts, they had developed a rudimentary form of space flight. Desperate, they thought that maybe they could bring natural resources from other worlds in the solar system to revive their dying planet. They knew that Venus, beneath its clouds, was a teeming Mesozoic jungle. Plenty of water there, if they could cart it back to Mars.

They couldn't. Their first attempts at space flight ended in disasters. Of the first five saucers they sent toward Venus, three of them blew up on takeoff, one veered off course and was never heard from again, and the fifth crash-landed in New Mexico—which is a helluva long way from Venus.

Fortunately, their saucer crash-landed near a small astronomical station in the desert. A young graduate student—who eventually became Prof. Schmidt—was the first to find them. The Martians inside the saucer were pretty banged up, but three of them were still alive. Even more fortunately, we had something that the Martians desperately needed: the raw materials and manufacturing capabilities to mass-produce flying saucers for them. That's where I had come in, as a tycoon of the aviation industry.

President Kennedy found his voice. "Do you mean to tell me that the existence of Martians—living, breathing, intelligent Martians—has been kept a secret since Nineteen Forty-six? More than fifteen years?"

"It's been touch and go on several occasions," said Schmidt. "But, yes, we've managed to keep the secret pretty well."

"Pretty well?" Kennedy seemed disturbed, agitated. "The Central Intelligence Agency doesn't know anything about this, for Christ's sake!" Then he caught himself, and added, "Or, if they do, they haven't told me about it."

"We have tried very hard to keep this a secret from all the politicians of every stripe," Schmidt said.

"I can see not telling Eisenhower," said the President. "Probably would've given Ike a fatal heart attack." He grinned. "I wonder what Harry Truman would've done with the information."

"We were tempted to tell President Truman, but—"

"That's all water over the dam," I said, trying to get them back onto the subject. "We're here to get you to call off this Project Apollo business."

"But why?" asked the President. "We could use Martian space-craft and plant the American flag on the Moon tomorrow morning!"

"No," whispered Jazzbow. Schmidt and I knew that when a Martian whispers, it's a sign that he's scared shitless.

"Why not?" Kennedy snapped.

"Because you'll destroy the Martians," said Schmidt, with real iron in his voice.

"I don't understand."

Jazzbow turned those big luminous eyes on the President. "May I explain it to you . . . the Martian way?"

I'll say this for Jack Kennedy. The boy had guts. It was obvious that the basic human xenophobia was strong inside him. When Jazzbow had first touched his hand Kennedy had almost jumped out of his skin. But he met the Martian's gaze and, not knowing what would come next, solemnly nodded his acceptance.

Jazzbow reached out his snaky arm toward Kennedy's face. I saw beads of sweat break out on the President's brow but he sat still and let the Martian's tentacle-like fingers touch his forehead and temple.

It was like jumping a car battery. Thoughts flowed from Jazzbow's brain into Kennedy's. I knew what those thoughts were.

It had to do with the Martians' moral sense. The average Martian has an ethical quotient about equal to St. Francis of Assisi. That's the *average* Martian. While they're only a century or so ahead of us technologically, they're light-years ahead of us morally, socially, ethically. There hasn't been a war on Mars in more than a thousand years. There hasn't even been a case of petty theft in centuries. You can walk the avenues of their beautiful, gleaming cities at any time of the day or night in complete safety. And since their planet is so desperately near absolute depletion, they just about worship the smallest blade of grass.

If our brawling, battling human nations discovered the fragile, gentle Martian culture there would be a catastrophe. The Martians would be swarmed under, shattered, dissolved by a tide of politicians, industrialists, real estate developers, evangelists wanting to save their souls, drifters, grifters, con men, thieves petty and grand. To say nothing of military officers driven by xenophobia. It would make the Spanish Conquest of the Americas look like a Boy Scout Jamboree.

I could see from the look in Kennedy's eyes that he was getting the message. "*We* would destroy *your* culture?" he asked.

Jazzbow had learned the human way of nodding. "You would not merely destroy our culture, Mr. President. You would kill us. We would die, all of us, very quickly."

"But you have the superior technology . . ."

"We could never use it against you," said Jazzbow. "We would lay down and die rather than deliberately take the life of a paramecium."

"Oh."

Schmidt spoke up. "So you see, Mr. President, why this Moon project has got to be called off. We can't allow the human race *en masse* to learn of the Martians' existence."

"I understand," he murmured.

Schmidt breathed out a heavy sigh of relief. Too soon.

"But I can't stop the Apollo project."

"Can't?" Schmidt gasped.

"Why not?" I asked.

Looking utterly miserable, Kennedy told us, "It would mean the end of my administration. For all practical purposes, at least."

"I don't see—"

"I haven't been able to get a thing through Congress except the Moon project. They're stiffing me on everything else: my economics package, my defense build-up, civil rights, welfare—everything except the Moon program has been stopped dead in Congress. If I give up on the Moon I might as well resign the presidency."

"You are not happy in your work," said Jazzbow.

"No, I'm not," Kennedy admitted, in a low voice. "I never wanted to go into politics. It was my father's idea. Especially after my older brother got killed in the war."

A dismal, gloomy silence descended on us.

"It's all been a sham," the President muttered. "My marriage is a mess, my presidency is a farce, I'm in love with a woman who's married to another man—I wish I could just disappear from the face of the Earth."

Which, of course, is exactly what we arranged for him.

It was tricky, believe me. We had to get his blonde *inamorata* to disappear, which wasn't easy, since she was in the public eye just about as much as the President. Then we had to fake his own assassination, so we could get him safely out of the way. At first he was pretty reluctant about it all, but then the Berlin Wall went up and the media blamed *him* for it and he agreed that he wanted out—permanently. We were all set to pull it off but the Cuban Missile Crisis hit the fan and we had to put everything on hold for more than a month. By the time we had calmed that mess down he was more than ready to leave this Earth. So we arranged the thing for Dallas.

We didn't dare tell Lyndon Johnson about the Martians, of course. He would've wanted to go to Mars and annex the whole damned planet. To Texas, most likely. And we didn't have to tell Nixon; he was happy to kill the Apollo program—after taking as much credit for the first lunar landing as the media would give him.

The toughest part was hoodwinking the astronomers and planetary scientists and the engineers who built spacecraft probes of the planets. It took all of Schmidt's ingenuity and the Martians' technical skills to get the various *Mariner* and *Pioneer* probes jiggered so that they would show a barren dry Venus devastated by a runaway greenhouse effect instead of the lush Mesozoic jungle that really exists beneath those clouds. I had to pull every string I knew, behind the scenes, to get the geniuses at JPL to send their two *Viking* landers to the Martian equivalents of Death Valley and the Atacama Desert in Chile. They missed the cities and the canals completely.

Schmidt used his international connections too. I didn't much like working with Commies, but I've got to admit the two Russians scientists I met were okay guys.

And it worked. Sightings of the canals on Mars went down to zero once our faked *Mariner 6* pictures were published. Astronomy students looking at Mars for the first time through a telescope thought they were victims of eyestrain! They *knew* there were no canals there, so they didn't dare claim they saw any.

So that's how we got to the Moon and then stopped going. We set up the Apollo program so that a small number of Americans could plant the flag and their footprints on the Moon and then forget about it. The Martians studiously avoided the whole area during the four years that we were sending missions up there. It all worked out very well, if I say so myself.

I worked harder than I ever had before in my life to get the media to downplay the space program, make it a dull, no-news affair. The man in the street, the average xenophobic Joe Six-Pack forgot about the glories of space exploration soon enough. It tore at my guts to do it, but that's what had to be done.

So now we're using the resources of the planet Venus to replenish Mars. Schmidt has a tiny group of astronomers who've been hiding the facts of the solar system from the rest of the profession since the late Forties. With the Martians' help they're continuing to fake the pictures and data sent from NASA's space probes.

The rest of the world thinks that Mars is a barren lifeless desert and Venus is a bone-dry hothouse beneath its perpetual cloud cover and space in general is pretty much of a bore. Meanwhile, with the help of Jazzbow and a few other Martians, we've started an environmental movement on Earth. Maybe if we can get human beings to see their own planet as a living entity, to think of the other animals and plants on our own planet as fellow residents of this spaceship Earth rather than resources to be killed or exploited—maybe then we can start to reduce the basic xenophobia in the human psyche.

I won't live long enough to see the human race embrace the Martians as brothers. It will take generations, centuries, before we grow to their level of morality. But maybe we're on the right track now. I hope so.

I keep thinking of what Jack Kennedy said when he finally agreed to rig project Apollo the way we did, and to arrange his own and his girlfriend's demises.

"It is a far, far better thing I do, than I have ever done," he quoted.

Thinking of him and Marilyn shacked up in a honeymoon suite on Mars, I realized that the remainder of the quote would have been totally inappropriate: "it is a far, far better rest that I go to, than I have ever known."

But what the hell, who am I to talk? I've fallen in love for the first time. Yeah, I know. I've been married several times but this time it's real and I'm going to spend the rest of my life on a tropical island with her, just the two of us alone, far from the madding crowd.

Well, maybe not the whole rest of my life. The Martians know a lot more about medicine than we do. Maybe we'll leave this Pacific island where the Martians found her and go off to Mars and live a couple of centuries or so. I think Amelia would like that.

Introduction to "The Supersonic Zeppelin"

I worked for a number of years in the aerospace industry, most of that time at a high-powered research laboratory in Massachusetts. Our lab specialized in studying the physics of high-temperature gases. We were known world-wide as hot air specialists.

I saw firsthand how great ideas can be shot down for totally dumb reasons. And how dumb ideas can gain a momentum of their own and cost the taxpayers billions of dollars while they accomplish nothing.

"The Supersonic Zeppelin" is somewhere inbetween those extremes. It's a fully feasible piece of technology that will never get to fly. But it was fun writing the story and thinking about those fabulous days of yesteryear when we were going to the Moon and thinking great thoughts.

And pushing the envelope on hubris, while we were at it.

The Supersonic Zeppelin

Author's note: While this is a work of fiction, the concept of the Busemann biplane is real.

Let's see now. How did it all begin?

A bunch of the boys were whooping it up in the Malamute Saloon—no, that's not right; actually it started in the cafeteria of the Anson Aerospace plant in Phoenix.

Okay, then, how about:

There are strange things done in the midnight sun by the men who moil for gold—well, yeah, but it was only a little after noon when Bob Wisdom plopped his loaded lunch tray on our table and sat down like a man disgusted with the universe. And anyway, engineers don't moil for gold; they're on salary.

I didn't like the way they all looked down on me, but I certainly didn't let it show. It wasn't just that I was the newbie among them: I wasn't even an engineer, just a recently-graduated MBA assigned to work with the Advanced Planning Team, aptly acronymed APT. As far as they were concerned I was either a useless appendage forced on them, or a snoop from management sent to provide info on which of them should get laid off.

Actually, my assignment was to get these geniuses to come up with a project that we could sell to somebody, anybody. Otherwise, we'd all be hit by the iron ball when the next wave of layoffs started, just before Christmas.

Six shopping weeks left, I knew.

"What's with you Bob?" Ray Kurtz asked. "You look like you spent the morning sniffing around a manure pile."

Wisdom was tall and lanky, with a round face that was normally cheerful, even in the face of Anson Aerospace's coming wave of cutbacks and layoffs. Today he looked dark and pouchy-eyed.

"Last night I watched a TV documentary about the old SST."

"The *Concorde*?" asked Kurtz. He wore a full bushy beard that made him look more like a dog-sled driver than a metallurgical engineer.

"Yeah. They just towed the last one out to the Smithsonian on a barge. A beautiful hunk of flying machine like that riding to its final resting place on a converted garbage scow."

That's engineers for you. Our careers were hanging by a hair and he's upset over a piece of machinery.

"Beautiful, maybe," said Tommy Rohr. "But it was never a practical commercial airliner. It could never fly efficiently enough to be economically viable."

For an engineer, Rohr was unnervingly accurate in his economic analyses. He'd gotten out of the dot-com boom before it burst. Of the five of us at the lunch table, Tommy was the only one who wasn't worried about losing his job—he had a much more immediate worry: his new trophy wife and her credit cards.

"It's just a damned shame," Wisdom grumbled. "The end of an era."

Kurtz, our bushy-bearded metallurgist, shook his graying head. "The eco-nuts wouldn't let it fly supersonic over populated areas. That ruined its chances of being practical."

"The trouble is," Wisdom muttered as he unwrapped a soggy sandwich, "you can build a supersonic aircraft that doesn't produce a sonic boom."

"No sonic boom?" I asked. Like I said, I was the newcomer to the APT group.

Bob Wisdom smiled like a sphinx.

"What's the catch?" asked Richard Grand in his slightly Anglified accent. He'd been born in the Bronx, but he'd won a Rhodes scholarship and came back trying to talk like Sir Stafford Cripps.

The cafeteria was only half filled, but there was still a fair amount of clattering and yammering going on all around us. Outside the picture window I could see it was raining cats and elephants, a real monsoon downpour. Something to do with global warming, I'd been told.

"Catch?" Bob echoed, trying to look hurt. "Why should there be a catch?"

"Because if someone could build a supersonic aircraft that didn't shatter one's eardrums with its sonic boom, old boy, obviously someone could have done it long before this."

"We could do it," Bob said pleasantly. Then he bit it into his sandwich.

"Why aren't we, then?" Kurtz asked, his brows knitting.

Bob shrugged elaborately as he chewed on his ham and five-grain bread.

Rohr waggled a finger at him. "What do you know that we don't? Or is this a gag?"

Bob swallowed and replied, "It's just simple aerodynamics."

"What's the go of it?" Grand asked. He got that phrase from reading a biography of James Clerk Maxwell.

"Well," Bob said, putting down the limp remains of the sandwich, "there's a type of wing that a German aerodynamicist named Adolph Busemann invented back in the 1920s. It's a sort of biplane configuration, actually. The shock waves that cause a sonic boom are cancelled out between the two wings."

"No sonic boom?"

"No sonic boom. Instead of flat wings, like normal, you need to wrap the wings around the fuselage, make a ringwing."

"What's a ringwing?" innocent li'l me asked.

Bob pulled a felt-tip pen from his shirt pocket and began sketching on his paper placemat.

"Here's the fuselage of the plane." He drew a narrow cigar shape. "Now we wrap the wing around it, like a sleeve. See?" He drew what looked to me like a tube wrapped around the cigar. "Actually it's two wings, one inside the other, and all the shock waves that cause the sonic boom get cancelled out. No sonic boom."

The rest of us looked at Bob, then down at the sketch, then up at Bob again. Rohr looked wary, like he was waiting for the punch line. Kurtz looked like a puzzled Karl Marx.

"I don't know that much about aerodynamics," Rohr said slowly, "but this is a Busemann biplane you're talking about, isn't it?"

"That's right."

"Uh-huh. And isn't it true that a Busemann biplane's wings produce no lift?"

"That's right," Bob admitted, breaking into a grin.

"No lift?" Kurtz snapped.

"Zero lift."

"Then how the hell do you get it off the ground?"

"It won't fly, Orville," Bob Wisdom said, his grin widening. "That's why nobody's built one."

The rest of us groaned while Bob laughed at us. An engineer's joke, in the face of impending doom. We'd been had.

Until, that is, I blurted out, "So why don't you fill it with helium?"

The guys spent the next few days laughing at me and the idea of a supersonic zeppelin. I have to admit, at that stage of the game I thought it was kind of silly, too. But yet . . . .

Richard Grand could be pompous, but he wasn't stupid. Before the week was out he just happened to pass by my phonebooth-sized cubicle and dropped in for a little chat, like the lord of the manor being gracious to a stable hand.

"That was rather clever of you, that supersonic zeppelin quip," he said as he ensconced himself in a teeny wheeled chair he had to roll in from an empty cubicle.

"Thanks," I noncommittalled, wondering why a senior engineer would give a compliment to a junior MBA.

"It might even be feasible," Grand mused. "Technically, that is."

I could see in his eyes the specter of Christmas-yet-to-come and the layoffs that were coming with it. If a senior guy like Grand was worried, I thought, I ought to be scared purple. Could I use the SSZ idea to move up Anson Aerospace's hierarchical ladder? The guys at the bottom were the first ones scheduled for layoffs, I knew. I badly needed some altitude, and even though it sounded kind of wild, the supersonic zeppelin was the only foothold I had to get up off the floor.

"Still," Grand went on, "it isn't likely that management would go for the concept. Pity, isn't it?"

I nodded agreement while my mind raced. If I could get management to take the SSZ seriously, I might save my job. Maybe even get a promotion. But I needed an engineer to propose the concept to management. Those suits upstairs wouldn't listen to a newly-minted MBA; most of them were former engineers themselves who'd climbed a notch or two up the organization.

Grand sat there in that squeaky little chair and philosophized about the plight of the aerospace industry in general and the bleak prospects for Anson Aerospace in particular.

"Not the best of times to approach management with a bold, innovative concept," he concluded.

Omigod, I thought. He's talked himself out of it! He was starting to get up and leave my cubicle.

"You know," I said, literally grabbing his sleeve, "Winston Churchill backed a lot of bold, innovative ideas, didn't he? Like, he pushed the development of tanks in World War I, even though he was in the navy, not the army."

Grand gave me a strange look.

"And radar, in World War II," I added.

"And the atomic bomb," Grand replied. "Very few people realize it was Sir Winston who started the atomic bomb work, long before the Yanks got into it."

The Yanks? I thought. This from a Jewish engineer from the Bronx High School for Science.

I sighed longingly. "If Churchill were here today, I bet he'd push the SSZ for all it's worth. He had the courage of his convictions, Churchill did."

Grand nodded, but said nothing and left me at my desk. The next morning, though, he came to my cubicle and told me to follow him.

Glad to get away from my claustrophobic work station, I headed after him, asking, "Where are we going?"

"Upstairs."

Management territory!

"What for?"

"To broach the concept of the supersonic zeppelin," said Grand, sticking out his lower lip in imitation of Churchillian pugnaciousness.

"The SSZ? For real?"

"Listen, my boy, and learn. The way this industry works is this: you grab onto an idea and ride it for all it's worth. I've decided to hitch my wagon to the supersonic zeppelin, and you should too."

I should too? Hell, I thought of it first!

John Driver had a whole office to himself and a luscious, sweet-tempered executive assistant of Greek-Italian ancestry, with almond-shaped dark eyes and lustrous hair even darker. Her name was Lisa, and half the male employees of Anson Aerospace fantasized about her, including me.

Driver's desk was big enough to land a helicopter on, and he kept it immaculately clean, mainly because he seldom did anything except sit behind it and try to look important. Driver was head of several engineering sections, including APT. Like so many others in Anson, he had been promoted to his level of incompetency: a perfect example of the Peter Principle. Under his less-then-brilliant leadership APT had managed to avoid developing anything more advanced than a short-range drone aircraft that ran on ethanol. It didn't fly very well, but the ground crew used the corn-based fuel to make booze that would peel the paint off a wall just by breathing at it from fifteen feet away.

I let Grand do the talking, of course. And, equally of course, he made Driver think the SSZ was his idea instead of mine.

"A supersonic zeppelin?" Driver snapped, once Grand had outlined the idea to him. "Ridiculous!"

Unperturbed by our boss' hostility to new ideas, Grand said smoothly, "Don't be too hasty to dismiss the concept. It may have considerable merit. At the very least I believe we could talk NASA or the Transportation Department into giving us some money to study the concept."

At the word "money" Driver's frown eased a little. Driver was lean-faced, with hard features and a gaze that he liked to think was piercing. He now subjected Grand to his piercingest stare.

"You have to spend money to make money in this business," he said, in his best *Forbes* magazine acumen.

"I understand that," Grand replied stiffly. "But we are quite willing to put some of our own time into this—until we can obtain government funding."

"Your own time?" Driver queried.

We? I asked myself. And immediately answered myself, Damned right. This is *my* idea and I'm going to follow it to the top. Or bust.

"I really believe we may be onto something that can save this company," Grand was purring.

Driver drummed his manicured fingers on his vast desk. "All right, if you feel so strongly about it. Do it on your own time and come back to me when you've got something worth showing. Don't say a word to anyone else, understand? Just me."

"Right, Chief." I learned later that whenever Grand wanted to flatter Driver he called him Chief.

"Our own time" was aerospace industry jargon for bootlegging hours from legitimate projects. Engineers have to charge every hour they work against an ongoing contract, or else their time is paid by the company's overhead account. Anson's management—and the accounting department—was very definitely against spending any money out of the company's overhead account. So I became a master bootlegger, finding charge numbers for my APT engineers. They accepted my bootlegging without a word of thanks, and complained when I couldn't find a valid charge number and they actually had to work on their own time, after regular hours.

For the next six weeks Wisdom, Rohr, Kurtz and even I worked every night on the supersonic zeppelin. The engineers were doing calculations and making simulator runs in their computers. I was drawing up a business plan, as close to a work of fiction as anything on the Best Sellers list. My social life went to zero, which was—I have to admit—not all that much of a drop. Except for Driver's luscious executive assistant, Lisa, who worked some nights to help us. I wished I had the time to ask her to dinner.

Grand worked away every night, too. On a glossy set of illustrations to use as a presentation.

We made our presentation to Driver. The guys' calculations, my business plan, and Grand's images. He didn't seem impressed, and I left the meeting feeling pretty gunky. Over the six weeks I'd come to like the idea of a supersonic zeppelin, an SSZ. I really believed it was my ticket to advancement. Besides, now I had no excuse to see Lisa, up in Driver's office.

On the plus side, though, none of the APT team was laid off. We went through the motions of the Christmas office party with the rest of the undead. Talk about a survivor's reality show!

I was moping in my cubicle the morning after Christmas when my phone beeped and Driver's face came up on my screen.

"Drop your socks and pack a bag. You're going with me to Washington to sell the SSZ concept."

"Yessir!" I said automatically. "Er . . . when?"

"Tomorrow, bright and early."

I raced to Grand's cubicle, but he already knew about it.

"So we're both going," I said, feeling pretty excited.

"No, only you and Driver," he said.

"But why aren't you—"

Grand gave me a knowing smile. "Driver wants all the credit for himself if the idea sells."

That nettled me, but I knew better than to argue about it. Instead, I asked, "And if it doesn't sell?"

"You get the blame for a stupid idea. You're low enough on the totem pole to be offered up as a sacrificial victim."

I nodded. I didn't like it, but I had to admit it was a good lesson in management. I tucked it away in my mind for future reference.

I'd never been to Washington before. It was chilly, gray and clammy; no comparison to sunny Phoenix. The traffic made me dizzy, but Driver thought it was pretty light. "Half the town's on holiday vacations," he told me as we rode a seedy, beat-up taxicab to the magnificent glass and stainless steel high-rise office building that housed the Transportation Department.

As we climbed out of the smelly taxi I noticed the plaque on the wall by the revolving glass doors. It puzzled me.

"Transportation and Urban Renewal Department?" I asked. "Since when . . ."

"Last year's reorganization," Driver said, heading for the revolving door. "They put the two agencies together. Next year they'll pull them apart, when they reinvent the government again."

"Welcome to TURD headquarters," said Tracy Keene, once we got inside the building's lobby.

Keene was Anson Aerospace's crackerjack Washington

representative, a large round man who conveyed the impression that he knew things no one else knew. Keene's job was to find new customers for Anson from among the tangle of government agencies, placate old customers when Anson inevitably alienated them, and guide visitors from home base through the Washington maze. The job involved grotesque amounts of wining and dining. I had been told that Keene had once been as wiry and agile as a Venezuelan shortstop. Now he looked to me like he was on his way to becoming a Sumo wrestler. And what he was gaining in girth he was losing in hair.

"Let's go," Keene said, gesturing toward the security checkpoint that blocked the lobby. "We don't want to be late."

Two hours later Keene was snoring softly in a straightbacked metal chair while Driver was showing the last of his Powerpoint images to Roger K. Memo, Assistant Under Director for Transportation Research of TURD.

Memo and his chief scientist, Dr. Alonzo X. Pencilbeam, were sitting on one side of a small conference table, Driver and I on the other. Keene was at the end, dozing restfully. The only light in the room came from the little projector, which threw a blank glare onto the wan yellow wall that served as a screen now that the last image had been shown.

Driver clicked the projector off. The light went out and the fan's whirring noise abruptly stopped. Keene jerked awake and instantly reached around and flicked the wall switch that turned on the overhead lights. I had to admire the man's reflexes.

Although the magnificent TURD building was sparkling new, Memo's spacious office somehow looked seedy. There wasn't enough furniture for the size of it: only a government-issue steel desk with a swivel chair, a half-empty bookcase, and this slightly wobbly little conference table with six chairs that didn't match. The walls and floors were bare and there was a distinct echo when anyone spoke or even walked across the room. The only window had vertical slats instead of a curtain, and it looked out on a parking building. The only decoration on the walls was Memo's doctoral degree, purchased from some obscure "distance learning" school in Mississippi.

Driver fixed Memo with his steely gaze across the conference table. "Well, what do you think of it?" he asked subtly.

Memo pursed his lips. He was jowly fat, completely bald, wore glasses and a rumpled gray suit.

"I don't know," he said firmly. "It sounds . . . unusual . . . "

Dr. Pencilbeam was sitting back in his chair and smiling benignly. His PhD had been earned in the 1970s, when newly-graduated physicists were driving taxicabs on what they glumly called "Nixon fellowships." He was very thin, fragile looking, with the long skinny limbs of a preying mantis.

Pencilbeam dug into his jacket pocket and pulled out an electronic game. Reformed smoker, I thought. He needs something to do with his hands.

"It certainly looks interesting," he said in a scratchy voice while his game softly beeped and booped. "I imagine it's technically achievable . . . and lots of fun."

Memo snorted. "We're not here to have fun."

Keene leaned across the table and fixed Memo with his best *here's something from behind the scenes* expression. "Do you realize how the White House would react to a sensible program for a supersonic transport? With the *Concorde* gone, you could put this country into the forefront of air transportation again."

"Hmm," said Memo. "But . . . "

"Think of the jobs this program can create. The President is desperate to improve the employment figures."

"I suppose so . . . "

"National prestige," Keene intoned knowingly. "Aerospace employment . . . balance of payments . . . gold outflow . . . the President would be terrifically impressed with you."

"Hmm," Memo repeated. "I see . . . "

I could see where the real action was, so I wangled myself an assignment to the company's Washington office as Keene's special assistant for the SSZ proposal. That's when I started learning what money and clout—and the power of influence—are all about.

As the months rolled along, we gave lots of briefings and attended lots of cocktail parties. I knew we were on the right track when no less than Roger K. Memo invited me to accompany him to one of the swankiest parties of the season. Apparently he thought that since I was from Anson's home office in Phoenix I must be an engineer and not just another salesman.

The party was in full swing by the time Keene and I arrived. It was nearly impossible to hear your own voice in the swirling babble of chatter and clinking glassware. In the middle of the sumptuous living room the Vice President was demonstrating his golf swing. Several Cabinet wives were chatting in the dining room. Out in the foyer, three Senators were comparing fact-finding tours they were arranging for themselves to the Riviera, Bermuda, and American Samoa, respectively.

Memo never drank anything stronger than ginger ale, and I followed his example. We stood in the doorway between the foyer and the living room, hearing snatches of conversation among the three junketing Senators. When the trio broke up, Memo intercepted Senator Goodyear (R., Ohio) as he headed toward the bar.

"Hello, Senator!" Memo shouted heartily. It was the only way to be heard over the party noise.

"Ah . . . hello." Senator Goodyear obviously thought that he was supposed to know Memo, and just as obviously couldn't recall his name, rank, or influence rating.

Goodyear was more than six feet tall, and towered over Memo's paunchy figure. Together they shouldered their way through the crowd around the bar, with me trailing them like a rowboat being towed behind a yacht. Goodyear ordered bourbon on the rocks, and therefore so did Memo. But he merely held onto his glass while the Senator immediately began to gulp at his drink.

A statuesque blonde in a spectacular gown sauntered past us. The Senator's eyes tracked her like a battleship's range finder following a moving target.

"I hear you're going to Samoa," Memo shouted as they edged away from the bar, following the blonde.

"Eh . . . yes," the Senator answered cautiously, in a tone he usually reserved for news reporters.

"Beautiful part of the world," Memo shouted.

The blonde slipped an arm around the waist of one of the young, long-haired men and they disappeared into another room. Goodyear turned his attention back to his drink.

"I said," Memo repeated, standing on tiptoes, "that Samoa is a beautiful place."

Nodding, Goodyear replied, "I'm going to investigate ecological conditions there . . . my committee is considering legislation on ecology, you know."

"Of course. Of course. You've got to see things firsthand if you're going to enact meaningful legislation."

Slightly less guardedly, Goodyear said, "Exactly."

"It's a long way off, though," Memo said.

"Twelve hours from LAX."

"I hope you won't be stuck in economy class. They really squeeze the seats in there."

"No, no," said the Senator. "First class all the way."

At the taxpayers' expense, I thought.

"Still," Memo sympathized, "It must take considerable dedication to undergo such a long trip."

"Well, you know, when you're in public service you can't think of your own comforts."

"Yes, of course. Too bad the SST isn't flying anymore. It could have cut your travel time in half. That would give you more time to stay in Samoa . . . investigating conditions there."

The hearing room in the Capitol was jammed with reporters and camera crews. Senator Goodyear sat in the center of the long front table, as befitted the committee chairman. I was in the last row of spectators, as befitted the newly-promoted junior Washington representative of Anson Aerospace Corp. I was following the industry's routine procedure and riding the SSZ program up the corporate ladder.

All through the hot summer morning the committee had listened to witnesses: my former boss John Driver, Roger K. Memo, Alonzo Pencilbeam and many others. The concept of the supersonic zeppelin unfolded before the news media and started to take on definite solidity in the rococo-trimmed hearing chamber.

Senator Goodyear sat there solemnly all morning, listening to the carefully rehearsed testimony and sneaking peeks at the greenery outside the big sunny window. Whenever he remembered the TV cameras he sat up straighter and tried to look lean and tough. I'd been told he had a drawer full of old Clint Eastwood flicks in his Ohio home.

Now it was his turn to summarize what the witnesses had told the committee. He looked straight into the bank of cameras, trying to come on strong and determined, like a high plains drifter.

"Gentlemen," he began, immediately antagonizing the women in the room, "I believe that what we have heard here today can mark the beginning of a new program that will revitalize the American aerospace industry and put our great nation back in the forefront of international commerce—"

One of the younger Senators at the far end of the table, a woman, interrupted:

"Excuse me, Mr. Chairman, but my earlier question about pollution was never addressed. Won't the SSZ use the same kind of jet engines that the *Concorde* used? And won't they cause just as much pollution?"

Goodyear glowered at the junior member's impudence, but controlled his temper well enough to say only, "Em . . . Dr. Pencilbeam, would you care to comment on that question?"

Half-dozing at one of the front benches, Pencilbeam looked startled at the mention of his name. Then he got to his feet like a carpenter's ruler unfolding, went to the witness table, sat down and hunched his bony frame around the microphone there.

"The pollution from the *Concorde* was so minimal that it had no measurable effect on the stratosphere. The early claims that a fleet of SSTs would create a permanent cloud deck over the northern hemisphere and completely destroy the ozone layer were never substantiated."

"But there were only a half-dozen *Concordes* flying," said the junior Senator. "If we build a whole fleet of SSZs—"

Before she could go any farther Goodyear fairly shouted into his microphone, "Rest assured that we are well aware of the possible pollution problem." He popped his P's like artillery bursts. "More importantly, the American aerospace industry is suffering, employment is in the doldrums, and our economy is slumping. The SSZ will provide jobs and boost the economy. Our engineers will, I assure you, find ways to deal with any and every pollution problem that may be associated with the SSZ."

I had figured that somebody, sooner or later, would raise the question of pollution. The engineers back in Phoenix wanted to look into the possibilities of using hydrogen fuel for the SSZ's jet engines, but I figured that just the mention of hydrogen would make people think of the old *Hindenberg*, and that would scuttle the program right there and then. So we went with ordinary turbojet engines that burned ordinary jet fuel.

But I went a step farther. In my capacity as a junior (and rising) executive, I used expense-account money to plant a snoop in the organization of the nation's leading ecology freak, Mark Sequoia. It turned out that, unknown to Sequoia, Anson Aerospace was actually his biggest financial contributor. Politics make strange bedfellows, doesn't it?

You see, Sequoia had fallen on relatively hard times. Once a flaming crusader for ecological salvation and environmental protection, Sequoia had made the mistake of letting the Commonwealth of Pennsylvania hire him as the state's Director of Environmental Protection. He had spent nearly five years earnestly trying to clean up Pennsylvania, a job that had driven four generations of the original Penn family into early Quaker graves. The deeper Sequoia buried himself in the solid waste politics of Pittsburgh, Philadelphia, Chester, Erie and other hopelessly corrupted cities, the fewer dedicated followers and news media headlines he attracted. After a very credible Mafia threat on his life, he quite sensibly resigned his post and returned to private life, scarred but wiser. And alive.

When the word about the SSZ program reached him, Sequoia was hiking along a woodland trail in Fairmont Park, Philadelphia, leading a scraggly handful of sullen high school students through the park's soot-ravaged woodlands on a steaming August afternoon. They were dispiritedly picking up empty beer cans and gummy prophylactics— and keeping a wary eye out for muggers. Even full daylight was no protection against assault. And the school kids wouldn't help him, Sequoia knew. Half of them would jump in and join the fun.

Sequoia was broad-shouldered, almost burly. His rugged face was seamed by weather and news conferences. He looked strong and fit, but lately his back had been giving him trouble and his old trick knee . . .

He heard someone pounding up the trail behind him.

"Mark! Mark!"

Sequoia turned to see Larry Helper, his oldest and therefore most trusted aide, running along the gravel path toward him, waving a copy of the *Daily News* over his head. Newspaper pages were slipping from his sweaty grasp and fluttering off into the bushes.

"Littering," Sequoia muttered in a tone sometimes used by archbishops when facing a case of heresy.

"Some of you kids," said Sequoia in his most authoritative voice, "pick up those newspaper pages."

A couple of the students lackadaisically ambled after the fluttering sheets.

"Mark, look here!" Helper skidded to a gritty stop on the gravel and breathlessly waved the front page of the newspaper. "Look!"

Sequoia grabbed his aide's wrist and took what was left of the newspaper from him. He frowned at Helper, who cringed and stepped back.

"I . . . I thought you'd want to see . . . "

Satisfied that he had established his dominance, Sequoia turned his attention to the front page's blaring headline.

"Supersonic *zeppelin*?"

Two nights later, Sequoia was meeting with a half-dozen men and women in the basement of a prosperous downtown church that specialized in worthy causes capable of filling the pews upstairs.

Once Sequoia called his meeting I was informed by the mole I had planted in his pitiful little group of do-gooders. As a newcomer to the scene, I had no trouble joining Sequoia's Friends of the Planet organization, especially when I FedEx'd them a personal check for a thousand dollars—for which Anson Aerospace reimbursed me, of course.

So I was sitting on the floor like a good environmental activist while Sequoia paced across the little room. There was no table, just a few folding chairs scattered around, and a locked bookcase stuffed with tomes about sex and marriage. I could tell just from looking at Sequoia that the old activist flames were burning inside him again. He felt alive, strong, the center of attention.

"We can't just drive down to Washington and call a news conference," he exclaimed, pounding a fist into his open palm. "We've got to do something dramatic!"

"Automobiles pollute, anyway," said one of the women, a comely redhead whose dazzling green eyes never left Sequoia's broad, sturdy-looking figure.

"We could take the train; it's electric."

"Power stations pollute."

"Airplanes pollute, too."

"What about riding down to Washington on horseback! Like Paul Revere!"

"Horses pollute."

"They do?"

"Ever been around a stable?"

"Oh."

Sequoia pounded his fist again. "I've got it! It's perfect!"

"What?"

"A balloon! We'll ride down to Washington in a non-polluting balloon filled with helium. That's the dramatic way to emphasize our opposition to this SSZ monster."

"Fantastic!"

"Marvelous!"

The redhead was panting with excitement. "Oh, Mark, you're so clever. So dedicated." There were tears in her eyes.

Helper asked softly, "Uh . . . does anybody know where we can get a balloon? And how much they cost?"

"Money is no object," Sequoia snapped, pounding his fist again. Then he wrung his hand; he had pounded too hard.

When the meeting finally broke up, Helper had been given the task of finding a suitable balloon, preferably one donated by its owner. I had volunteered to assist him. Sequoia would spearhead the effort to raise money for a knockdown fight against the SSZ. The redhead volunteered to assist him. They left the meeting arm in arm.

I was learning the Washington lobbying business from the bottom up, but rising fast. Two weeks later I was in the White House, no less, jammed in among news reporters and West Wing staffers waiting for a presidential news conference to begin. TV lights were glaring at the empty podium. The reporters and camera crews shuffled their feet, coughed, talked to one another. Then:

"Ladies and gentlemen: the President of the United States."

We all stood up and applauded as she entered. I had been thrilled to be invited to the news conference. Well, actually it was Keene who'd been invited and he brought me with him, since I was the Washington rep for the SSZ project. The President strode to the podium and smiled at us in what some cynics had dubbed her rattlesnake mode. I thought she was being gracious.

"Before anything else, I have a statement to make about the tragic misfortune that has overtaken one of our finest public figures, Mark Sequoia. According to the latest report I have received from the Coast Guard—no more than ten minutes ago—there is still no trace of his party. Apparently the balloon they were riding in was blown out to sea two days ago, and nothing has been heard from them since.

"Now let me make this perfectly clear. Mr. Sequoia was frequently on the other side of the political fence from my administration. He was often a critic of my policies and actions, policies and actions that I believe in completely. He was on his way to Washington to protest our new supersonic zeppelin program when this unfortunate accident occurred.

"Mr. Sequoia opposed the SSZ program despite the fact that this project will employ thousands of aerospace engineers who are otherwise unemployed and untrainable. Despite the fact that the SSZ program will save the American dollar on the international market and salvage American prestige in the technological battleground of the world.

"And we should keep in mind that France and Russia have announced that they are studying the possibility of jointly starting their own SSZ effort, a clear technological challenge to America."

Gripping the edges of the podium tighter, the President went on, "Rumors that his balloon was blown off course by a flight of Air Force jets are completely unfounded, the Secretary of Defense assures me. I have dispatched every available military, Coast Guard, and Civil Air Patrol plane to search the entire coastline from Cape Cod to Cape Hatteras. We will find Mark Sequoia and his brave though misguided band of ecofr . . . er, activists—or their remains."

I knew perfectly well that Sequoia's balloon had not been blown out to sea by Air Force jets. They were private planes: executive jets, actually.

"Are there any questions?" the President asked.

The Associated Press reporter, a hickory-tough old man with

thick glasses and a snow-white goatee, got to his feet and asked, "Is that a Versace dress you're wearing? It's quite becoming."

The President beamed. "Why, thank you. Yes, it is . . . "

Keene pulled me by the arm. "Let's go. We've got nothing to worry about here."

*

I was rising fast, in part because I was willing to do the legwork (and dirty work, like Sequoia) that Keene was too lazy or too squeamish to do. He was still head of our Washington office, in name. I was running the SSZ program, which was just about the only program Anson had going for itself, which meant that I was running the Washington office in reality.

Back in Phoenix, Bob Wisdom and the other guys had become the nucleus of the team that was designing the SSZ prototype. The program would take years, we all knew, years in which we had assured jobs. If the SSZ actually worked the way we designed it, we could spend the rest of our careers basking in its glory.

I was almost getting accustomed to being called over to the West Wing to deal with bureaucrats and politicians. Still, it was a genuine thrill when I was invited into the Oval Office itself.

The President's desk was cleared of papers. Nothing cluttered the broad expanse of rosewood except the telephone console, a black-framed photograph of her late husband (who had once also sat at that desk), and a gold-framed photograph of her daughter on her first day in the House of Representatives (D., Ark.).

She sat in her high-backed leather chair and fired instructions at her staff.

"I want the public to realize," she instructed her media consultant, "that although we are now in a race with the Russians and the French, we are building the SSZ for sound economic and social reasons, not because of competition from overseas."

"Yes, Ma'am," said the media consultant.

She turned to the woman in charge of Congressional liaison. "And you'd better make damned certain that the Senate appropriations committee okays the increased funding for the SSZ prototype. Tell them that if we don't get the extra funding we'll fall behind the Ivans and the Frogs.

"And I want you," she pointed a manicured finger at the research director of TURD, "to spend every nickel of your existing SSZ money as fast as you can. Otherwise we won't be able to get the additional appropriation out of Congress."

"Yes, Ma'am," said Roger K. Memo, with one of his rare smiles.

"But, Madam President," the head of the Budget Office started to object.

"I know what you're going to say," the President snapped at him. "I'm perfectly aware that money doesn't grow on trees. But we've *got* to get the SSZ prototype off the ground, and do it before next November. Take money from education, from the space program, from the environmental superfund—I don't care how you do it, just get it done. I want the SSZ prototype up and flying by next summer, when I'm scheduled to visit Paris and Moscow."

The whole staff gasped in sudden realization of the President's masterful plan.

"That right," she said, smiling slyly at them. "I intend to be the first Chief of State to cross the Atlantic in a supersonic zeppelin."

Although none of us realized its importance at the time, the crucial incident, we know now, happened months before the President's decision to fly the SSZ to Paris and Moscow. I've gone through every scrap of information we could beg, borrow or steal about that decisive day, reviewing it all time and again, trying to find some way to undo the damage.

It happened at the VA hospital in Hagerstown, a few days after Mark Sequoia had been rescued. The hospital had never seen so many reporters. There were news media people thronging the lobby, lounging in the halls, bribing nurses, sneaking into elevators and even surgical theaters (where several of them fainted). The parking lot was a jumble of cars bearing media stickers and huge TV vans studded with antennas.

Only two reporters were allowed to see Mark Sequoia on any given day, and they were required to share their interviews with all the others in the press corps. Today the two—picked by lot—were a crusty old veteran from Fox News and a perky young blonde from *Women's Wear Daily*.

"But I've told your colleagues what happened at least a dozen times," mumbled Sequoia from behind a swathing of bandages.

He was hanging by both arms and legs from four traction braces, his backside barely touching the crisply sheeted bed. Bandages covered eighty percent of his body and all of his face, except for tiny slits for his eyes, nostrils and mouth.

The Fox News reporter held his palm-sized video camera in one hand while he scratched at his stubbled chin with the other. On the opposite side of the bed, the blonde held a similar videocorder close to Sequoia's bandaged face.

She looked misty-eyed. "Are . . . are you in much pain?"

"Not really," Sequoia answered bravely, with a slight tremor in his voice.

"Why all the traction?" asked Fox News. "The medics said there weren't any broken bones."

"Splinters," Sequoia answered weakly.

"Bone splinters!" gasped the blonde. "Oh, how awful!"

"No," Sequoia corrected. "Splinters. Wood splinters. When the balloon finally came down we landed in a clump of trees just outside Hagerstown. I got thousands of splinters. It took most of the surgical staff three days to pick them all out of me. The chief of surgery said he was going to save the wood and build a scale model of the *Titanic* with it."

"Oh, how painful!" The blonde insisted on gasping. She gasped very well, Sequoia noted, watching her blouse.

"And what about your hair?" Fox News asked.

Sequoia felt himself blush underneath the bandages. "I . . . uh . . . I must have been very frightened. After all, we were aloft in that stupid balloon for six days, without food, without anything to drink except a six pack of Perrier. We went through a dozen different thunderstorms . . . "

"With lightning?" the blonde asked.

Nodding painfully, Sequioa replied, "We all thought we were going to die."

Fox News frowned. "So your hair turned white from fright. There was some talk that cosmic rays did it."

"Cosmic rays? We never got that high. Cosmic rays don't have any effect on you until you get really up there, isn't that right?"

"How high did you go?"

"I don't know," Sequoia answered. "Some of those updrafts in the thunderstorms pushed us pretty high. The air got kind of thin."

"But not high enough to cause cosmic ray damage."

"Well, I don't know . . . maybe . . . "

"It'd make a better story than just being scared," said Fox News. "Hair turned white by cosmic rays. Maybe even sterilized."

"Sterilized?" Sequoia yelped.

"Cosmic rays do that, too," Fox News said. "I checked."

"Well, we weren't *that* high."

"You're sure?"

"Yeah . . . well, I don't think we were that high. We didn't have an altimeter with us . . . "

"But you could have been."

Shrugging was sheer torture, Sequoia found.

"Okay, but those thunderstorms could've lifted you pretty damned high."

Before Sequoia could think of what to answer, the door to his private room opened and a horse-faced nurse said firmly, "That's all. Time's up. Mr. Sequoia must rest now. After his enema."

"Okay, I think I've got something to hang a story on," Fox News said with a satisfied grin. "Now to find a specialist in cosmic rays."

The blonde looked thoroughly shocked and terribly upset. "You . . . you don't think you were really sterilized, do you?"

Sequoia tried to make himself sound worried and brave at the same time. "I don't know. I just . . . don't know."

Late that night the blonde snuck back into his room, masquerading as a nurse. If she knew the difference between sterilization and impotence she didn't tell Sequoia about it. For his part, he forgot about his still-tender skin and the traction braces. The morning nurse found him unconscious, one shoulder dislocated, most of his bandages rubbed off, his skin terribly inflamed, and a goofy grin on his face.

I knew that the way up the corporate ladder was to somehow acquire a staff that reported to me. And, in truth, the SSZ project was getting so big that I truly needed more people to handle it. I mean, all the engineers had to do was build the damned thing and make it fly. I had to make certain that the money kept flowing, and that wasn't easy. An increasingly large part of my responsibilities as the *de facto* head of the Washington office consisted of putting out fires.

"Will you look at this!"

Senator Goodyear waved the morning *Post* at me. I had already read the electronic edition before I'd left my apartment that morning. Now, as I sat at Tracy Keene's former desk, the senator's red face filled my phone screen.

"That Sequoia!" he grumbled. "He'll stop at nothing to destroy me. Just because the Ohio River melted his houseboat, all those years ago."

"It's just a scare headline," I said, trying to calm him down. "People won't be sterilized by flying in the supersonic zeppelin any more than they were by flying in the old *Concorde*."

"I know it's bullshit! And you know it's bullshit! But the god-damned news media are making a major story out of it! Sequoia's on every network talk show. I'm under pressure to call for hearings on the sterilization problem!"

"Good idea," I told him. "Have a Senate investigation. The scientists will prove that there's nothing to it."

That was my first mistake. I didn't get a chance to make another.

I hightailed it that morning to Memo's office. I wanted to see Pencilbeam and start building a defense against this sterilization story. The sky was gray and threatening. An inch or two of snow was forecast, and people were already leaving their offices for home, at ten o'clock in the morning. Dedicated government bureaucrats and corporate employees, taking the slightest excuse to knock off work.

The traffic was so bad that it had actually started to snow, softly, by the time I reached Memo's office. He was pacing across the thinly carpeted floor, his shoes squeaking unnervingly in the spacious room. Copies of *The Washington Post, The New York Times* and *Aviation Week* were spread across his usually immaculate desk, but his attention was focused on his window, where we could see fluffy snowflakes gently drifting down.

"Traffic's going to get worse as the day goes on," Memo muttered.

"They're saying it'll only be an inch or so," I told him.

"That's enough to paralyze this town."

Yeah, especially when everybody jumps in their cars and starts fleeing the town as if a terrorist nuke is about to go off, I replied silently.

Aloud, I asked, "What about this sterilization business? Is there any substance to the story?"

Memo glanced sharply at me. "They don't need substance as long as they can start a panic."

Dr. Pencilbeam sat at one of the unmatched conference chairs, all bony limbs and elbows and knees.

"Relax, Roger," Pencilbeam said calmly. "Congress isn't going to halt the SSZ program. It means too many jobs, too much international prestige. And besides, the President has staked her credibility on it."

"That's what worries me," Memo muttered.

"What?"

But Memo's eye was caught by movement outside his window. He waddled past his desk and looked down into the street below.

"Oh, my God . . . "

"What's going on?" Pencilbeam unfolded like a pocket ruler into a six-foot-long human and hurried to the window. Outside, in the thin mushy snow, a line of somber men and women were filing along the street past the TURD building, bearing signs that screamed:

STOP THE SSZ!

DSON'T STERILIZE THE HUMAN RACE

SSZ MURDERS UNBORN CHILDREN

ZEPPELINS GO HOME!

"Isn't that one with the sign about unborn children a priest?" Pencilbeam asked.

Memo shrugged. "Your eyes are better than mine."

"Ah-hah! And look at this!"

Pencilbeam pointed a long, bony finger farther down the street. Another swarm of people were advancing on the building. They also carried placards:

SSZ FOR ZPG

ZEPPELINS SI! BABIES NO!

ZEPPELINS FOR POPULATION CONTROL

UP THE SSZ

Memo sagged against the window. "This . . . this is awful."

The Zero Population Growth group marched through the thin snowfall straight at the environmentalists and anti-birth-control pickets. Instantly the silence was shattered by shouts and taunts. Shrill female voices battled against rumbling baritones and bassos. Placards wavered. Bodies pushed. Someone screamed. One sign struck a skull and then bloody war broke out.

Memo, Pencilbeam and I watched aghast until the helmeted TAC squad police doused the whole tangled mess of them with riot gas, impartially clubbed men and woman alike and carted everyone off, including three bystanders and a homeless panhandler.

*

The Senate hearings were such a circus that Driver summoned me back to Phoenix for a strategy session with Anson's top management. I was glad to get outside the Beltway, and especially glad to see Lisa again. She even agreed to have dinner with me.

"You're doing a wonderful job there in Washington," she said, smiling with gleaming teeth and flashing eyes.

My knees went weak, but I found the courage to ask, "Would you consider transferring to the Washington office? I could use a sharp executive assistant—"

She didn't even let me finish. "I'd love to!"

I wanted to do handsprings. I wanted to grab her and kiss her hard enough to bruise our lips. I wanted to, but Driver came out of his office just at that moment, looking his jaw-jutting grimmest.

"Come on, kid. Time to meet the top brass."

The top brass was a mixture of bankers and former engineers. To my disgust, instead of trying to put together a strategy to defeat the environmentalists, they were already thinking about how many men and women they'd have to lay off when Washington pulled the plug on the SSZ program.

"But that's crazy!" I protested. "The program is solid. The President herself is behind it."

Driver fixed me with his steely stare. "With friends like that, who needs enemies?"

I left the meeting feeling very depressed, until I saw Lisa again. Her smile could light up the world.

Before heading back to Washington to fight Sequoia's sterilization propaganda, I looked up my old APT buddies. They were in the factory section where the SSZ was being fabricated.

The huge factory assembly bay was filled with the aluminum skeleton of the giant dirigible. Great gleaming metal ribs stretched from its titanium nosecap to the more intricate cagework of the tail fins. Tiny figures with flashing laser welders crawled along the ribbing like maggots cleaning the bones of some noble whale.

Even the jet engines sitting on their carrying pallets dwarfed human scale. Some of the welders held clandestine poker games inside their intake cowlings, Bob Wisdom told me. The cleaning crews kept quiet about the spills, crumbs and other detritus they found in them night after night. I stood with Bob, Ray Kurtz, Tommy Rohr and Richard Grand beside one of those huge engine pods, craning our necks to watch the construction work going on high overhead. The assembly bay rang to the shouts of working men and women, throbbed with the hum of machinery, clanged with the clatter of metal against metal.

"It's going to be some Christmas party if Congress cancels this project," Kurtz muttered gloomily.

"Oh, they wouldn't dare cancel it now that the Women's Movement is behind it," said Grand, with a sardonic little smile.

Kurtz glared at him from behind his beard. "You wish. Half those idiots in Congress will vote against us just to prove they're pro-environment."

"Actually, the scientific evidence is completely on our side," Grand said. "And in the long run, the weight of evidence prevails."

He always acts as if he knows more than anybody else, I thought. But he's dead wrong here. He hasn't the foggiest notion of how Washington works. But he sounds so damned sure of himself! It must be that phony accent of his.

"Well, just listen to me, pal," said Wisdom, jabbing a forefinger at Grand. "I've been working on that secretary of mine since the last Christmas party, and if this project falls through and the party is a bust that palpitating hunk of femininity is going to run home and cry instead of coming to the party!"

Grand blinked at him several times, obviously trying to think of the right thing to say. Finally he enunciated, "Pity."

But I was thinking about Lisa. If the SSZ is cancelled, Driver won't let her transfer to the Washington office. There'd be no need to hire more staff for me. There'd be no need for me!

I went back to Washington determined to save the SSZ from this stupid sterilization nonsense. But it was like trying to stop a tsunami with a floor mop. The women's movement, the environmental movement, the labor unions, even Leno and Letterman got into the act. The Senate hearings turned into a shambles; Pencilbeam and the other scientists were ignored while movie stars testified that they would never fly in an SSZ because of the dangers of radiation.

The final blow came when the President announced that she was not going to Paris and Moscow, after all. Urgent problems elsewhere. Instead, she flew to Hawaii for an economic summit of the Pacific nations. In her subsonic Air Force One.

The banner proclaiming HAPPY HOLIDAYS! drooped sadly across one wall of the company cafeteria. Outside in the late afternoon darkness, lights glimmered, cars were moving and a bright full moon shone down on a rapidly-emptying parking lot.

Inside the Anson Aerospace cafeteria was nothing but gloom. The Christmas party had been a dismal flop, primarily because half the company's work force had received layoff notices that morning. The tables had been pushed to one side of the cafeteria to make room for a dance floor. Syrupy holiday music oozed out of the speakers built into the acoustic tile of the ceiling. But no one was dancing.

Bob Wisdom sat at one of the tables, propping his aching head in his hands. Ray Kurtz and Tommy Rohr sat with him, equally dejected.

"Why the hell did they have to cancel the project two days before Christmas?" Rohr asked rhetorically.

"Makes for more pathos," Kurtz growled.

"It's pathetic, all right," Wisdom said. "I've never seen so many women crying at once. Or men, for that matter."

"Even Driver was crying, and he hasn't even been laid off," Rohr said.

"Well," Kurtz said, staring at the half-finished drink in front of him, "Seqouia did it. He's a big media hero again."

"And we're on the bread line," said Rohr.

"You got laid off?" I asked.

"Not yet—but it's coming. This place will be closing its doors before the fiscal year ends."

"It's not that bad," said Wisdom. "We still have the Air Force work. As long as they're shooting off cruise missiles, we'll be in business."

Rohr grimaced. "You know what gets me? The way the whole project was scrapped, without giving us a chance to complete the big bird and show how it'd work. Without a goddamned chance."

Kurtz said, "Congressmen are scared of people getting sterilized."

"Not really," I said. "They're scared of not being on the right bandwagon."

All three of them turned toward me.

Rohr said, "Next time you dream up a project, pal, make it underground. Something in a lead mine. Or deeper still, a gold mine. Then Congress won't have to worry about cosmic rays."

Wisdom tried to laugh, but it wouldn't come.

"You know," I said slowly, "you just might have something there."

"What?"

"Where?"

"A supersonic transport—in a tunnel."

"Oh for Chri—"

But Wisdom sat up straighter in his chair. "You could make an air-cushion vehicle go supersonic. If you put it in a tunnel you get away from the sonic boom and the air pollution."

"The safety aspects would be better, too," Kurtz admitted. Then, more excitedly, "And pump the air out of the tunnel, like a pneumatic tube!"

Rohr shook his head. "You guys are crazy. Who the hell's going to build tunnels all over the country?"

"There's a lot of tunnels already built," I countered. We could adapt them for the SSST."

"SSST?"

"Sure," I answered, grinning for the first time in weeks. "Supersonic subway train."

They stared at me. Rohr pulled out his PDA and started tapping on it. Wisdom got that faraway look in his eyes. Kurtz shrugged and said, "Why the hell not?"

I got up and headed for the door. Supersonic subway train. That's my ticket. I'm going back to Washington, I knew. And this time I'll bring Lisa with me.

Introduction to "Vince's Dragon"

No matter how serious the problem under consideration, it is always amenable to humor. Sometimes laughter can accomplish more than moralizing. In 1729, for example, Jonathan Swift's "A Modest Proposal" applied the scalpel of satire to the heartbreaking despair racking Ireland at that time.

Modern (and future) crime is a serious matter. But we don't have to take it completely seriously all the time. "Vince's Dragon" is unserious in two ways. First, it is a fantasy, which by nature is a form of literature that disdains to deal with the real world, and therefore need not be considered to be very serious.

Second, the characters in this story are deliberately drawn to show the absurd side of the underworld. Let s face it: Most of the guys I knew in South Philadelphia who ended up in the Mafia were not the best and brightest lights of the community. They were driven by ruthless greed and an utter disregard for the rights of others. They could be fearsome, and they often were. But they were unconsciously funny a lot of the time, too.

"The Godfather" and "The Sopranos" don't show you the whole story.

Vince's Dragon

The thing that worried Vince about the dragon, of course, was that he was scared that it was out to capture his soul.

Vince was a typical young Family man. He had dropped out of South Philadelphia High School to start his career with the Family. He boosted cars, pilfered suits from local stores, even spent grueling and terrifying hours learning how to drive a big trailer rig so he could help out on hijackings.

But they wouldn't let him in on the big stuff.

"You can run numbers for me kid," said Louie Bananas, the onearmed policy king of South Philly.

"I wanna do somethin' big," Vince said, with ill-disguised impatience. "I wanna make somethin' outta myself."

Louie shook his bald, bulletshaped head. "I dunno, kid. You don't look like you got th' guts."

"Try me! Lemme in on th' sharks."

So Louie let Vince follow Big Balls Falcone, the loan sharks' enforcer, for one day. After watching Big Balls systematically break a guy's fingers, one by one, because he was ten days late with his payment, Vince agreed that loansharking was not the business for him.

Armed robbery? Vince had never held a gun, much less fired one. Besides, armed robbery was for the heads and zanies, the stupid and desperate ones. *Organized* crime didn't go in for armed robbery. There was no need to. And a guy could get hurt.

After months of wheedling and groveling around Louie Bananas' favorite restaurant, Vince finally got the break he wanted.

"Okay, kid, okay," Louie said one evening as Vince stood in a corner of the restaurant watching him devour linguine with clams (white sauce). "I got an openin' for you. Come here."

Vince could scarcely believe his ears.

"What is it, *Padrone*? What? I'll do anything!"

Burping politely into his checkered napkin, Louie leaned back in his chair and grabbed a handful of Vince's curly dark hair with his one hand, pulling Vince's ear close to his mouth.

Vince, who had an unfortunate allergy to garlic, fought hard to suppress a sneeze as he listened to Louie whisper, "You know that ol' B&O warehouse down aroun' Front an' Washington?"

"Yeah." Vince nodded as vigorously as he could, considering his hair was still in Louie's iron grip.

"Torch it."

"Burn it down?" Vince squeaked.

"Not so loud, *chidrool!*"

"Burn it down?" Vince whispered.

"Yeah."

"But that's arson."

Louie laughed. "It's a growth industry nowadays. Good opportunity for a kid who ain't afraid t' play with fire."

Vince sneezed.

It wasn't so much of a trick to burn down the rickety old warehouse, Vince knew. The place was ripe for the torch. But to burn it down without getting caught, that was different.

The Fire Department and Police and, worst of all, the insurance companies all had special arson squads who would be sniffing over the charred remains of the warehouse even before the smoke had cleared.

Vince didn't know anything at all about arson. But, desperate for his big chance, he was willing to learn.

He tried to get in touch with Johnnie the Torch, the leading local expert. But Johnnie was too busy to see him, and besides Johnnie worked for a rival Family, 'way up in Manayunk. Two other guys that Vince knew, who had something of a reputation in the field, had mysteriously disappeared within the past two nights.

Vince didn't think the library would have any books on the subject that would help him. Besides, he didn't read too good.

So, feeling very shaky about the whole business, very late the next night he drove a stolen station wagon filled with jerry cans of gasoline and big drums of industrial paint thinner out to Front Street.

He pushed his way through the loosely nailed boards that covered the old warehouse's main entrance, feeling little and scared in the darkness. The warehouse was empty and dusty, but as far as the insurance company knew, Louie's fruit and vegetable firm had stocked the place up to the ceiling just a week ago.

Vince felt his hands shaking. *If I don't do a good job, Louie'll send Big Balls Falcone after me.*

Then he heard a snuffling sound.

He froze, trying to make himself invisible in the shadows.

Somebody was breathing. And it wasn't Vince.

Keerist, they didn't tell me there was a night watchman here!

"I am not a night watchman."

Vince nearly jumped out of his jockey shorts.

"And I'm not a policeman, either, so relax,"

"Who . . . ?" His voice cracked. He swallowed and said again, deeper, "Who are you?"

"I am trying to get some sleep, but this place is getting to be a regular Stonehenge. People coming and going all the time!"

A bum, Vince thought. A bum who's using this warehouse to flop . . .

"And I am not a bum!" the voice said sternly.

"I didn't say you was!" Vince answered. Then he shuddered, because he realized he had only thought it.

A glow appeared, across the vast darkness of the empty warehouse. Vince stared at it, then realized it was an eye. A single glowing, baleful eye with a slit of a pupil, just like a cat's. But this eye was the size of a bowling ball!

"Wh . . . wha . . . ?

Another eye opened beside it. In the light from their twin smolderings, Vince could just make out a scaly head with a huge jaw full of fangs.

He did what any man would do. He fainted.

When he opened his eyes he wanted to faint again. In the eerie moonlight that was now filtering through the old warehouse's broken windowpanes, he saw a dragon standing over him.

It had a long, sinuous body covered with glittering green and bluish scales, four big paws with talons on them the size of lumberjacks' saws. Its tail coiled around and around, the end twitching slightly all the way over on the other side of the warehouse.

And right over him, grinning down toothily at him, was this huge fanged head with the giant glowing cat's eyes.

"You're cute," the dragon said.

"Huh?"

"Not at all like those other bozoes Louie sent over here the past couple of nights. They were older. Fat, blubbery men."

"Other guys . . . ?"

The dragon flicked a forked tongue out between its glistening white fangs. "Do you think you're the first arsonist Louie's sent here? I mean, they've been clumping around here for the past several nights."

Still flat on his back, Vince asked, "Wh . . . wh . . . what happened to them?"

The dragon hunkered down on its belly and seemed, incredibly, to *smile* at him. "Oh, don't worry about them. They won't bother us." The tongue flicked out again and brushed Vince's face. "Yes, you are *cute!*"

Little by little, Vince's scant supply of courage returned to him. He kept speaking with the dragon, still not believing this was really happening, and slowly got up to a sitting position.

"I can read your mind," the dragon was saying. "So you might as well forget about trying to run away."

"I . . . uh, I'm supposed to torch this place," Vince confessed.

"I know," said the dragon. Somehow, it sounded like a female dragon.

"Yes, you're right," she admitted. "I am a female dragon. As a matter of fact, all the dragons that you humans have ever had trouble with have been females."

"You mean like St. George?" Vince blurted.

"That pansy! Him and his silly armor. Aunt Ssrishha could have broiled him alive inside that pressure cooker he was wearing. As it was, she got to laughing so hard at him that her flame went out."

"And he killed her."

"He did not!" She sounded really incensed, and a little wisp of smoke trickled out of her left nostril. "Aunt Ssrishha just made herself invisible and flew away. She was laughing so hard she got the hiccups."

"But the legend . . ."

"A human legend. More like a human public relations story. Kill a dragon! The human who can kill a dragon hasn't been born yet!"

"Hey, don't get sore. I didn't do nuthin."

"No. Of course not." Her voice softened. "You're cute, Vince."

His mind was racing. Either he was crazy or he was talking with a real, firebreathing dragon.

"Uh . . . what's your name?"

"Ssrzzha," she said. "I'm from the Polish branch of the dragon family "

" Shh . . . Zz . . . " Vince tried to pronounce.

"You may call me 'Sizzle,' " the dragon said, grandly.

"Sizzle. Hey, that's a cute name."

"I knew you'd like it."

If I'm crazy, they'll come and wake me up sooner or later, Vince thought, and decided to at least keep the conversation going.

"You say all the dragons my people have ever fought were broads . . . I mean, females?"

"That's right, Vince. So you can see how silly it is, all those human lies about our devouring young virgins."

"Uh, yeah. I guess so."

"And the bigger lies they tell about slaying dragons. Utter false-hoods."

"Really?"

"Have you ever seen a stuffed dragon in a museum? Or dragon bones? Or a dragon's head mounted on a wall?"

"Well . . . I don't go to museums much."

"Whereas I could show you some very fascinating exhibits in certain caves, if you want to see bones and heads and . . . "

"Ah, no, thanks. I don't think I really wanna see that," Vince said hurriedly.

"No, you probably wouldn't."

Ben Bova

"Where's all the male dragons? They must be *really* big."

Sizzle huffed haughtily and a double set of smoke rings wafted past Vince's ear.

"The males of our species are tiny! Hardly bigger than you are. They all live out on some islands in the Indian Ocean. We have to fly there every hundred years or so for mating, or else our race would die out. "

"Every hundred years! You only get laid once a century?"

"Sex is not much fun for us, I'm afraid. Not as much as it is for you, but then you're descended from monkeys, of course. Disgusting little things. Always chattering and making messes. "

"Uh, look . . . Sizzle. This's been fun an' it was great meetin' you an' all, but it's gettin' late and I gotta go now, and besides . . . "

"But aren't you forgetting why you came here?"

Truth to tell, Vince had forgotten. But now he recalled, "I'm supposed t' torch this warehouse."

"That's right. And from what I can see bubbling inside your cute little head, if you don't burn this place down tonight, Louie's going to be very upset with you."

"Yeah, well, that's my problem, right? I mean, you wanna stay here an' get back t' sleep, right? I don't wanna bother you like them other guys did, ya know? I mean, like, I can come back when you go off to th' Indian Ocean or somethin' . . ."

"Don't be silly, Vince," Sizzle said, lifting herself ponderously to her four paws. "I can sleep anywhere. And I'm not due for another mating for several decades, thank the gods. As for those other fellows . . . well, they annoyed me. But you're cute!"

Vince slowly got to his feet, surprised that his quaking knees held him upright. But Sizzle coiled her long, glittering body around him, and with a grin that looked like a forest made of sharp butcher knives, she said:

"I'm getting kind of tired of this old place, anyway. What do you say we belt it out?"

"Huh?"

"I can do a much better job of torching this firetrap than you can, Vince cutie, " said Sizzle. "And I won't leave any telltale gasoline fumes behind me."

"But . . ."

"You'll be completely in the clear. Anytime the police come near, I can always make myself invisible."

"Invisible?"

"Sure. See?" And Sizzle disappeared.

"Hey, where are ya?"

"Right here, Vince." The dragon reappeared in all its glittering hugeness.

Vince stared, his mind churning underneath his curly dark hair.

Sizzle smiled at him. "What do you say, cutie? A life of crime together? You and I could do wonderful things together, Vince. I could get you to the top of the Family in no time."

A terrible thought oozed up to the surface of Vince's slowly simmering mind. "Uh, wait a minute. This is like I seen on TV, ain't it? You help me, but you want me to sell my soul to you, right?"

"Your soul? What would I do with your soul?"

"You're workin' for th' devil, an' you gimme three wishes or somethin' but in return I gotta let you take my soul down t' hell when I die."

Sizzle shook her ponderous head and managed to look slightly affronted. "Vince I admit that dragons and humans haven't been the best of friends over the millennia, but we do not work for the devil. I'm not even sure that he exists. I've never seen a devil; have you?"

"No, but . . ."

"And I'm not after your soul, silly boy."

"You don't want me t' sign nuthin'?"

"Of course not."

"An' you'll help me torch this dump for free?"

"More than that, Vince. I'll help you climb right up to the top of the Family. We'll be partners in crime! It'll be the most fun I've had since Aunt Hsspss started the Chicago fire."

"Hey, I just wanna torch this one warehouse!"

"Yes, of course."

"No Chicago fire or nuthin' like that."

"I promise."

It took several minutes for Vince to finally make up his mind and say, "Okay, let's do it."

Sizzle cocked her head slightly to one side. "Shouldn't you be out of the warehouse first, Vince?"

"Huh? Oh yeah, sure."

"And maybe drive back to your home, or—better yet—over to that restaurant where your friends are."

"Whaddaya mean? We gotta torch this place first."

"I'll take care of that, Vince dearie. But wouldn't it look better if you had plenty of witnesses around to tell the police they were with you when the warehouse went up?"

"Yeah . . . " he said, feeling a little suspicious.

"All right, then," said Sizzle. "You get your cute little body over to the restaurant and once you're safely there I'll light up this place like an Inquisition pyre."

"How'll you know—"

"When you get to the restaurant? I'm telepathic, Vince."

"But how'll I know—"

"When the claptrap gets belted out? Don't worry, you'll see the flames in the sky!" Sizzle sounded genuinely excited by the prospect.

Vince couldn't think of any other objections. Slowly, reluctantly, he headed for the warehouse door. He had to step over one of Sizzle's saberlong talons on the way.

At the doorway, he turned and asked plaintively, "You sure you ain't after my soul?"

Sizzle smiled at him. "I'm not after your soul, Vince. You can depend on that."

The warehouse fire was the most spectacular anyone had seen in a long time, and the police were totally stymied about its cause. They questioned Vince at length, especially since he had forgotten to get rid of the gasoline and paint thinner in the back of the stolen station wagon. But they couldn't pin a thing on him, not even car theft, once Louie had Big Balls Falcone explain the situation to the wagon's unhappy owner.

Vince's position in the Family started to rise. Spectacularly.

Arson became his specialty. Louie gave him tougher and tougher assignments and Vince would wander off a night later and the job would be done. Perfectly.

He met Sizzle regularly, sometimes in abandoned buildings, sometimes in empty lots. The dragon remained invisible then, of course, and the occasional passerby got the impression that a sharply dressed young man was standing in the middle of a weedchoked, bottlestrewn empty lot, talking to thin air.

More than once they could have heard him asking, "You really ain't interested in my soul?"

But only Vince could hear Sizzle's amused reply, "No, Vince. I have no use for souls, yours or anyone else's."

As the months went by, Vince's rapid rise to Family stardom naturally attracted some antagonism from other young men attempting to get ahead in the organization. Antagonism sometimes led to animosity, threats, even attempts at violence.

But strangely, wondrously, anyone who got angry at Vince disappeared. Without a trace, except once when a single charred shoe of Fats Lombardi was found in the middle of Tasker Street, between Twelfth and Thirteenth.

Louie and the other elders of the Family nodded knowingly. Vince was not only ambitious and talented. He was smart. No bodies could be laid at his doorstep.

From arson, Vince branched into loan sharking, which was still the heart of the Family's operation. But he didn't need Big Balls Falcone to terrify his customers into paying on time. Customers who didn't pay found their cars turned into smoking wrecks. Right before their eyes, an automobile parked at the curb would burst into flame.

"Gee, too bad," Vince would say. "Next time it might be your house," he'd hint darkly, seeming to wink at somebody who wasn't there. At least, somebody no one else could see. Somebody very tall, from the angle of his head when he winked.

The day came when Big Balls Falcone himself, understandably put out by the decline in his business, let it be known that he was coming after Vince. Big Balls disappeared in a cloud of smoke, literally.

The years rolled by. Vince became quite prosperous. He was no longer the skinny, scared kid he had been when he had first met Sizzle. Now he dressed conservatively, with a carefully tailored vest buttoned neatly over his growing paunch, and lunched on steak and lobster tails with bankers and brokers.

Although he moved out of the old neighborhood row house into a palatial ranch style single near Cherry Hill, over in Jersey, Vince still came back to the Epiphany Church every Sunday morning for

Mass. He sponsored the church's Little League baseball team and donated a free Toyota every year for the church's annual raffle.

He looked upon these charities, he often told his colleagues, as a form of insurance. He would lift his eyes at such moments. Those around him thought he was looking toward heaven. But Vince was really searching for Sizzle, who was usually not far away.

"Really Vince," the dragon told him, chuckling, "you still don't trust me. After all these years. I don't want your soul. Honestly I don't."

Vince still attended church and poured money into charities.

Finally Louie himself, old and frail, bequeathed the Family fortunes to Vince and then died peacefully in his sleep, unassisted by members of his own or any other Family. Somewhat of a rarity in Family annals.

Vince was now *capo* of the Family. He was not yet forty, sleek, hair still dark, heavier than he wanted to be, but in possession of his own personal tailor, his own barber, and more women than he had ever dreamed of having.

His ascension to *capo* was challenged, of course, by some of Louie's other lieutenants. But after the first few of them disappeared without a trace, the others quickly made their peace with Vince.

He never married. But he enjoyed life to the full.

"You're getting awfully overweight, Vince," Sizzle warned him one night, as they strolled together along the dark and empty waterfront where they had first met, "Shouldn't you be worrying about the possibility of a heart attack?"

"Naw," said Vince. "I don't get heart attacks, I give 'em!" He laughed uproariously at his own joke.

"You're getting older, Vince. You're not as cute as you once were, you know."

"I don't hafta be *cute*, Sizzle. I got the power now. I can look and act any way I wanna act. Who's gonna get in my way?"

Sizzle nodded, a bit ruefully. But Vince paid no attention to her mood.

"I can do anything I want! " he shouted to the watching heavens. "I got th' power and the rest of those dummies are scared to death of me. Scared to death!" He laughed and laughed.

"But Vince," Sizzle said, "I helped you to get that power."

"Sure, sure. But I got it now, an' I don't really need your help anymore. I can get anybody in th' Family to do whatever I want!"

Dragons don't cry, of course, but the expression on Sizzle's face would have melted the heart of anyone who saw it.

"Listen," Vince went on, in a slightly less bombastic tone, "I know you done a lot to help me, an' I ain't gonna forget that. You'll still be part of my organization, Sizzle old girl. Don't worry about that."

But the months spun along and lengthened into years, and Vince saw Sizzle less and less. He didn't need to. And secretly, down inside him, he was glad that he didn't have to.

I don't need her no more, and I never signed nuthin' about givin' away my soul or nuthin'. I'm free and clear!

Dragons, of course, are telepathic.

Vince's big mistake came when he noticed that a gorgeous young redhead he was interested in seemed to have eyes only for a certain slicklooking young punk. Vince though about the problem mightily, and then decided to solve two problems with one stroke.

He called the young punk to his presence, at the very same restaurant where Louie had given Vince his first big break.

The punk looked scared. He had heard that Vince was after the redhead.

"Listen kid," Vince said gruffly, laying a heavily beringed hand on the kid's thin shoulder. "You know the old clothing factory up on Twenty-eighth and Arch? "

"Y . . . yessir," said the punk, in a whisper that Vince could barely hear.

"It's a very flammable building, dontcha think?"

The punk blinked, gulped, then nodded. "Yeah. It is. But . . . "

"But what?"

His voice was trembling, the kid said, "I heard that two-three different guys tried beltin' out that place. An' they . . . they never came back!"

"The place is still standin', ain't it?" Vince asked severely.

"Yeah."

"Well, by tomorrow morning, either it ain't standin' or you ain't standin'. *Capisce*?"

The kid nodded and fairly raced out of the restaurant. Vince grinned. One way or the other, he had solved a problem, he thought.

The old factory burned cheerfully for a day and a half before the Fire Department could get the blaze under control. Vince laughed and phoned his insurance broker.

But that night, as he stepped from his limousine onto the driveway of his Cherry Hill home, he saw long coils of glittering scales wrapped halfway around the house.

Looking up, he saw Sizzle smiling at him.

"Hello Vince. Long time no see."

"Oh, hi Sizzle ol' girl. What's new?" With his left hand, Vince impatiently waved his driver off. The man backed the limousine down the driveway and headed for the garage back in the city, goggle eyed that The Boss was talking to himself.

"That was a real cute fellow you sent to knock off the factory two nights ago," Sizzle said, her voice almost purring.

"Him? He's a punk."

"I thought he was really cute."

"So you were there, huh? I figured you was, after those other guys never came back."

"Oh Vince, you're not cute anymore. You're just soft and fat and ugly."

"You ain't gonna win no beauty contests yourself, Sizzle."

He started for the front door, but Sizzle planted a huge taloned paw in his path. Vince had just enough time to look up, see the expression on her face, and scream.

Sizzle's forked tongue licked her lips as the smoke cleared.

"Delicious," she said. "Just the right amount of fat on him. And the poor boy thought I was after his *soul*!"

Introduction to "The Angel's Gift"

Everybody from Goethe to the high school kid next door has written a story about a deal with the devil: you know, a tale in which a man sells his soul in exchange for worldy wealth and power. Sometimes the story ends happily, as in Stephen Vincent Benét's "The Devil and Daniel Webster." More often it's a tragedy, such as "Faust."

Here's a story about a man making a deal with an angel. He has to give up all his worldy wealth and power in order to save his soul. I believe that this story explains the seemingly inexplicable fall of a former President of the United States.

Sort of.

The Angel's Gift

He stood at his bedroom window, gazing happily out at the well-kept grounds and manicured park beyond them. The evening was warm and lovely. Dinner with the guests from overseas had been perfect; the deal was going smoothly, and he would get all the credit for it. As well as the benefits.

He was at the top of the world now, master of it all, king of the hill. The old dark days of fear and failure were behind him now. Everything was going his way at last. He loved it.

His wife swept into the bedroom, just slightly tipsy from the champagne.

Beaming at him, she said, "You were magnificent this evening, darling."

He turned from the window, surprised beyond words. Praise from her was so rare that he treasured it, savored it like expensive wine, just as he had always felt a special glow within his breast on those extraordinary occasions when his mother had vouchsafed him a kind word.

"Uh . . . thank you," he said.

"Magnificent, darling," she repeated. "I am so proud of you!"

His face went red with embarrassed happiness.

"And these people are so much nicer than those Latin types," she added.

"You . . . you know, you were . . . you *are* . . . the most beautiful woman in this city," he stammered. He meant it. In her gown of gold lame and with her hair coiffed that way, she looked positively regal. His heart filled with joy.

She kissed him lightly on the cheek, whispering into his ear, "I shall be waiting for you in my boudoir, my prince."

The breath gushed out of him. She pirouetted daintily, then waltzed to the door that connected to her own bedroom. Opening the door, she turned back toward him and blew him a kiss.

As she closed the door behind her, he took a deep, sighing, shuddering breath. Brimming with excited expectation, he went directly to his closet, unbuttoning his tuxedo jacket as he strode purposefully across the thickly carpeted floor.

He yanked open the closet door. A man was standing there, directly under the light set into the ceiling.

"Wha . . . ?"

Smiling, the man made a slight bow. "Please do not be alarmed, sir. And don't bother to call your security guards. They won't hear you."

Still fumbling with his jacket buttons, he stumbled back from the closet door, a thousand wild thoughts racing through his mind. An assassin. A kidnapper. A newspaper columnist!

The stranger stepped as far as the closet door. "May I enter your room, sir? Am I to take your silence for assent? In that case, thank you very much."

The stranger was tall but quite slender. He was perfectly tailored in a sky-blue Brooks Brothers three-piece suit. He had the youthful, innocent, golden-curled look of a European terrorist. His smile revealed perfect, dazzling teeth. Yet his eyes seemed infinitely sad, as though filled with knowledge of all human failings. Those icy blue eyes pierced right through the man in the tuxedo.

"Wh . . . what do you want? Who are you?"

"I'm terribly sorry to intrude this way. I realize it must be a considerable shock to you. But you're always so busy. It's difficult to fit an appointment into your schedule." His voice was a sweet, mild tenor, but the accent was strange. East coast, surely. Harvard, no doubt.

"How did you get in here? My security . . . "

The stranger gave a slightly guilty grin and hiked one thumb ceilingward. "You might say I came in through the roof."

"The roof? Impossible!"

"Not for me. You see, I am an angel."

"An . . . angel?"

With a self-assured nod, the stranger replied, "Yes. One of the Heavenly Host. Your very own guardian angel, to be precise."

"I don't believe you."

"You don't believe in angels?" The stranger cocked a golden eyebrow at him. "Come now. I can see into your soul. You do believe."

"My church doesn't go in for that sort of thing," he said, trying to pull himself together.

"No matter. You do believe. And you do well to believe, because it is all true. Angels, devils, the entire system. It is as real and true as this fine house you live in." The angel heaved a small sight. "You know, back in medieval times people had a much firmer grasp on the realities of life. Today . . . " He shook his head.

Eyes narrowing craftily, the man asked, "If you're an angel, where are your wings? Your halo? You don't look anything like a real angel."

"Oh." The angel seemed genuinely alarmed. "Does that bother you? I thought it would be easier on your nervous system to see me in a form that you're accustomed to dealing with every day. But if you want . . . "

The room was flooded with a blinding golden light. Heavenly voices sang. The stranger stood before the man robed in radiance, huge white wings outspread, filling the room.

The man sank to his knees and buried his face in his hands. "Have mercy on me! Have mercy on me!"

He felt strong yet gentle hands pull him tenderly to his feet. The angel was back in his Brooks Brothers suit. The searing light and ethereal chorus were gone.

"It is not in my power to show you either mercy or justice," he said, his sweetly youthful face utterly grave. "Only the Creator can dispense such things."

"But why . . . who . . . how . . . " he babbled.

Calming him, the angel explained, "My duty as your guardian angel is to protect your soul from damnation. But you must cooperate, you know. I cannot *force* you to be saved."

"My soul is in danger?"

"In danger?" The angel rolled his eyes heavenward. "You've just about handed it over to the enemy, gift-wrapped. Most of the millionaires you dined with tonight have a better chance to attain salvation than you have, at the moment. And you know how difficult it is for a rich man."

The man tottered to the wingback chair next to his king-sized bed and sank into it. He pulled the handkerchief from his breast pocket and mopped his sweaty face.

The angel knelt beside him and looked up into his face pleadingly. "I don't want to frighten you into a premature heart seizure, but your soul really is in great peril."

"But I haven't done anything wrong! I'm not a crook. I haven't killed anyone or stolen anything. I've been faithful to my wife."

The angel gave him a skeptical smile.

"Well . . . " He wiped perspiration from his upper lip. "Nothing serious. I've always honored my mother and father."

Gently, the angel asked, "You've never told a lie?"

"Uh, well . . . nothing big enough to . . . "

"You've never cheated anyone?"

"Um."

"What about that actor's wife in California? And the money you accepted to swing certain deals. And all the promises you've broken?"

"You mean things like that—they count?"

"Everything counts," the angel said firmly. "Don't you realize that the enemy has your soul almost in his very hands?"

"No. I never thought—"

"All those deals you've made. All the corners you've cut." The angel suddenly shot him a piercing glance. "You haven't signed any documents in blood, have you?"

"No!" His heart twitched. "Certainly not!"

"Well, that's something, at least."

"I'll behave," he promised. "I'll be good. I'll be a model of virtue."

"Not enough," the angel said, shaking his golden locks. "Not nearly enough. Things have gone much too far."

His eyes widened with fear. He wanted to argue, to refute, to debate the point with his guardian angel, but the words simply would not force their way through his constricted throat.

"No, it is not enough merely to promise to reform," the angel repeated. "Much stronger action is needed."

"Such as . . . what?"

The angel got to his feet, paced across the room a few steps, then turned back to face him. His youthful visage brightened. "Why not? If *they* can make a deal for a soul, why can't we?"

"What do you mean?"

"Hush!" The angel seemed to be listening to another voice, one that the man could not hear. Finally the angel nodded and smiled. "Yes. I see. Thank you."

"What?"

Turning back to the man, the angel said, "I've just been empowered to make you an offer for your soul. If you accept the terms, your salvation is assured."

The man instantly grew wary. "Oh no you don't. I've heard about deals for souls. Some of my best friends—"

"But this is a deal to *save* your soul!"

"How do I know that?" the man demanded. "How do I know you're really what you say you are? The devil has power to assume pleasing shapes, doesn't he?"

The angel smiled joyfully. "Good for you! You remember some of your childhood teachings."

"Don't try to put me off. I've negotiated a few tricky deals in my day. How do I know you're really an angel, and you want to save my soul?"

"By their fruits ye shall know them," the angel replied.

"What are you talking about?"

Still smiling, the angel replied, "When the devil makes a deal for a soul, what does he promise? Temporal gifts, such as power, wealth, respect, women, fame."

"I have all that," the man said. "I'm on top of the world, everyone knows that."

"Indeed."

"And I didn't sign any deals with the devil to get there, either," he added smugly.

"None that you know of," the angel warned. "A man in your position delegates many decisions to his staff, does he not?"

The man's face went gray. "Oh my God, you don't think . . . "

With a shrug, the angel said, "It doesn't matter. The deal that I offer guarantees your soul's salvation, if you meet the terms."

"How? What do I have to do?"

"You have power, wealth, respect, women, fame." The angel ticked each point off on his slender, graceful fingers.

"Yes, yes, I know."

"You must give them up."

The man lurched forward in the wingchair. "Huh?"

"Give them up."

"I can't!"

"You must, if you are to attain the Kingdom of Heaven."

"But you don't understand! I just can't drop everything! The world doesn't work that way. I can't just . . . walk away from all this."

"That's the deal," the angel said. "Give it up. All of it. Or spend eternity in hell."

"But you can't expect me to . . . " He gaped. The angel was no longer in the room with him. For several minutes he stared into empty air. Then, knees shaking, he arose and walked to the closet. It too was empty of strange personages.

He looked down at his hands. They were trembling.

"I must be going crazy," he muttered to himself. "Too much strain. Too much tension." But even as he said it, he made his way to the telephone on the bedside table. He hesitated a moment, then grabbed up the phone and punched a number he had memorized months earlier.

"Hello, Chuck? Yes, this is me. Yes, yes, everything went fine tonight. Up to a point."

He listened to his underling babbling flattery into the phone, wondering how many times he had given his power of attorney to this weakling and to equally venal deputies.

"Listen, Chuck," he said at last. "I have a job for you. And it's got to be done right, understand? Okay, here's the deal—" He winced inwardly at the word. But, taking a deep manly breath, he plunged ahead. "You know the Democrats are setting up their campaign quarters in that new apartment building—what's it called, Watergate? Yeah. Okay. Now I think it would serve our purposes very well if we bugged the place before the campaign really starts to warm up . . . "

There were tears in his eyes as he spoke. But from far, far away, he could hear a heavenly chorus singing.

Introduction to "A Slight Miscalculation"

This story was literally cooked up over a bowl of mulligatawny soup.

Back before she married Lester Del Rey and became one of the most innovative and successful book editors in the history of science fiction, Judy-Lynn Benjamin was managing editor of *Galaxy* magazine. (Or, as Robert Blocka slyly put it, she was "the man-aging editor.") Judy-Lynn and I had lunch in one of Manhattan's Indian restaurants and started talking about the dire news media fears of *the Big One*: an earthquake along the San Andreas Fault that would knock California into the Pacific Ocean.

I muttered a "what if" kind of idea. Judy-Lynn laughed heartily and told me to write the story for *Galaxy*.

But the joke was on me. When I sent the story in, *Galaxy*'s editor in chief, knowing me as the author of scientifically accurate stories, demanded to know the scientific basis behind my story.

I sold the story elsewhere, much to Judy-Lynn's chagrin. And mine.

A Slight Miscalculation

Nathan French was a pure mathematician. He worked for a research laboratory perched on a California hill that overlooked the Pacific surf, but his office had no windows. When his laboratory earned its income by doing research on nuclear bombs, Nathan doodled out equations for placing men on the Moon with a minimum expenditure of rocket fuel. When his lab landed a fat contract for developing a lunar flight profile, Nathan began worrying about air pollution.

Nathan didn't look much like a mathematician. He was tall and gangly, liked to play handball, spoke with a slight lisp when he got excited and had a face that definitely reminded you of a horse. Which helped him to remain pure in things other than mathematics. The only possible clue to the nature of his work was that lately he had started to squint a lot. But he didn't look the slightest bit nervous or high strung, and he still often smiled his great big toothy, horsy smile.

When the lab landed its first contract (from the State of California) to study air pollution, Nathan's pure thoughts turned—naturally—elsewhere.

"I think it might be possible to work out a method of predicting earthquakes," Nathan told the laboratory chief, kindly old Dr. Moneygrinder.

Moneygrinder peered at Nathan over his half-lensed bifocals. "Okay, Nathan, my boy," he said heartily. "Go ahead and try it. You know I'm always interested in furthering man's understanding of his universe."

When Nathan left the chief's sumptuous office, Moneygrinder hauled his paunchy little body out of its plush desk chair and went to the window. *His* office had windows on two walls: one set overlooked the beautiful Pacific; the other looked down on the parking lot, so the chief could check on who got to work at what time.

And behind the parking lot, which was half-filled with aging cars (business had been deteriorating for several years), back among the eucalyptus trees and paint-freshened grass, was a remarkably straight little ridge of ground, no more than four feet high. It ran like an elongated step behind the whole length of the laboratory grounds and out past the abandoned pink stucco church on the crest of the hill. A little ridge of grass-covered earth that was called the San Andreas Fault.

Moneygrinder often stared at the Fault from his window, rehearsing in his mind exactly what to do when the ground started to tremble. He wasn't afraid, merely careful. Once a tremor had hit in the middle of a staff meeting. Moneygrinder was out the window, across the parking lot, and on the far side of the Fault (the eastern, or "safe" side) before men half his age had gotten out of their chairs. The staff talked for months about the astonishing agility of the little waddler.

A year, almost to the day, later the parking lot was slightly fuller and a few of the cars were new. The pollution business was starting to pick up since the disastrous smog in San Clemente. And the laboratory had also managed to land a few quiet little Air Force contracts—for six times the amount of money it got for the pollution work.

Moneygrinder was leaning back in his plush desk chair, trying to look both interested and noncommittal at the same time, which was difficult to do, because he never could follow Nathan when the mathematician was trying to explain his work.

"It's a thimple matter of transposing the progression," Nathan was lisping, talking too fast because he was excited as he scribbled equations on Moneygrinder's fuchsia-colored chalkboard with nerve-ripping squeaks of the yellow chalk.

"You thee?" Nathan said at last, standing beside the chalkboard.

It was totally covered with his barely legible numbers and symbols. A pall of yellow chalk dust hovered about Nathan.

"Um . . . " said Moneygrinder. "Your conclusion, then . . . ?"

"It's perfectly clear," Nathan said. "If you have any reasonable data base at all, you can not only predict when an earthquake will hit and where, you can also predict its intensity."

Moneygrinder's eyes narrowed. "You're sure?"

"I've gone over it with the CalTech geophysics people. They agree with the theory."

"Hmmm." Moneygrinder tapped the desktop with his pudgy fingers. "I know this is a little outside your area of interest, Nathan, but . . . ah, can you really predict actual earthquakes? Or is this all theoretical?"

"Sure you can predict earthquakes," Nathan said, grinning like Mr. Ed, the talking horse. "Like next Thursday's."

"Next Thursday's?"

"Yeth. There's going to be a major earthquake next Thursday."

"Where?"

"Right here. Along the Fault."

"Ulp!"

Nathan tossed the stubby remainder of his chalk into the air nonchalantly, but missed the catch and it fell to the carpeted floor.

Moneygrinder, slightly paler than the chalk, asked, "A major quake, you say?"

"Uh-huh."

"Did . . . did the CalTech people agree with your prediction?"

"No," said Nathan, frowning slightly. "They claim I've got an inverted gamma factor in the fourteenth set of equations. I've got the computer working on it right now."

Some of the color returned to Moneygrinder's flabby cheeks. "Oh . . . I see. Well, let me know what the computer says."

"Sure."

The next morning, as Moneygrinder stood behind the gauzy drapes of his office window watching the cars pull up, his phone rang. His secretary had put in a long night, he knew, and she wasn't in yet. Pouting, Moneygrinder went over to the desk and answered the phone himself.

It was Nathan. "The computer still agrees with the CalTech boys.

But I think the programming's slightly off. Can't really trust computers. They're only as good as the people who feed them data, you know."

"I understand," Moneygrinder said. "Well, keep working on it."

He chuckled as he hung up. "Good old Nathan. Great at theory, but hopeless in the real world."

Still, when his secretary finally showed up and brought him his morning coffee and pill and nibble on the ear, he said thoughtfully:

"Maybe I ought to talk with those bankers in New York after all."

"But you said that you wouldn't need their money now that business is picking up," she purred.

He nodded bulbously. "Yes, but still . . . arrange a meeting with them for next Thursday. I'll leave Wednesday afternoon. Stay the weekend in New York."

She stared at him. "But you said we'd . . . "

"Now, now. Business comes first. You take the Friday afternoon jet and meet me at the hotel."

Smiling, she answered, "Yes, Cuddles."

Matt Climber had just come back from a Pentagon lunch when Nathan's phone call reached him.

Climber had worked for Nathan several years earlier. He had started as a computer programmer, assisting Nathan. In two years he had become a section head and Nathan's direct superior. (On paper only; nobody bossed Nathan, he worked independently.) When it became obvious to Moneygrinder that Climber was heading his way, the lab chief helped his young assistant to get a government job in Washington. Good experience for an up-and-coming executive.

"Hi, Nathan, how's the pencil-pushing game?" Climber shouted into the phone as he glanced at his calendar appointment pad. There were three interagency conferences and two staff meetings scheduled for this afternoon.

"Hold it now, slow down," Climber said, sounding friendly but looking grim. "You know people can't understand you when you talk too fast."

Thirty minutes later Climber was leaning back in his chair, feet on his desk, tie loosened, shirt collar open, and the first two meetings of his afternoon's schedule crossed off.

"Now let me get this straight, Nathan," he said into the phone.

"You're predicting a major quake along the San Andreas Fault next Thursday afternoon at two-thirty p.m. Pacific Standard Time. But the CalTech people and even your own computer don't agree with you?"

Another ten minutes later Climber said, "Okay, okay . . . sure, I remember when we'd screw up the programming once in a while. But you made mistakes, too. Okay, look—tell you what, Nathan. Keep checking. If you find out definitely that the computer's wrong and you're right, call me right away. I'll get to the President himself, if we have to. Okay? Fine. Keep in touch."

He slammed the phone back onto its cradle and his feet back on the floor, all in one weary motion.

Old Nathan's really gone 'round the bend, Climber told himself. *Next Thursday. Hah! Next Thursday. Hmmm . . .*

He leafed through his calendar pages. Sure enough, he had a meeting with the Boeing people in Seattle next Thursday.

If there is a major quake the whole damned West Coast might slide into the Pacific. Naw . . . don't be silly. Nathan's cracking up, that's all. Still . . . how far north does the Fault go?

Climber leaned across his desk and tapped the intercom button.

"Yes, Mr. Climber?" came his secretary's voice.

"That conference with Boeing on the hypersonic ramjet transport next Thursday," Climber began, then hesitated a moment. But, with absolute finality, he said, "Cancel it."

Nathan French was not a drinking man, but by Tuesday of the following week he went straight from the laboratory to a friendly little bar that hung on a rocky ledge over the surging Pacific.

It was a strangely quiet Tuesday afternoon, so Nathan had the undivided attention of both the worried-looking bartender and the freshly-painted hooker who worked the early shift in a low-cut black cocktail dress and overpowering perfume.

"Cheez, I never seen business so lousy as yesterday and today," the bartender complained. He was fidgeting around the bar, with nothing to do. The only dirty glass in the place was Nathan's, and he was holding onto it because he liked to chew the ice cubes.

"Yeah," said the hooker. "At this rate I'll be a virgin again by the end of the week."

Nathan didn't reply. His mouth was full of ice cubes, which he crunched in absent-minded cacophony. He was still trying to figure out why he and the computer didn't agree on the fourteenth set of equations. Everything else checked out perfectly: time, place, force level on the Richter scale. But the vector, the directional value—somebody was still misreading the programming instructions. That was the only possible answer.

"The stock market's dropped through the floor," the bartender said darkly. "My broker says Boeing's gonna lay off half their people. That ramjet transport they was gona build is getting' scratched. And the lab up the hill is getting' bought out by some East Coast banks." He shook his head.

The hooker, sitting beside Nathan with her elbows on the bar and her Styrofoam bra sharply profiled, smiled at him and said, "How about it, big guy? Just so I don't forget how to, huh?"

With a final crunch on the last ice cube, Nathan said, "Um, excuse me. I've got to get check that computer program."

By Thursday morning Nathan was truly upset. Not only was the computer still insisting that he was wrong about equation fourteen, but none of the programmers had shown up for work. Obviously, one of them—maybe all of them—had sabotaged his program. But why?

He stalked up and down the hallways of the lab searching for a programmer, somebody, anybody—but the lab was virtually empty. Only a handful of people had come in, and after an hour or so of wide-eyed whispering among themselves in the cafeteria over coffee, they started to sidle out to the parking lot and get into their cars and drive away.

Nathan happened to be walking down a corridor when one of the research physicists—a new man, from a department Nathan never dealt with—bumped into him.

"Oh, excuse me," the physicist said hastily, as he started to head for the door down at the end of the hall.

"Wait a minute," Nathan said, grabbing him by the arm. "Can you program a computer?"

"Uh, no, I can't."

"Where is everybody today?" Nathan wondered aloud, still holding the man's arm. "Is it a national holiday?"

"Man, haven't you heard?" the physicist asked, goggle-eyed. "There's going to be an earthquake! The whole damned state of California is going to slide into the Pacific Ocean!"

"Oh, that."

Pulling his arm free, the physicist scuttled down the corridor. As he got to the door he shouted over his shoulder, "Get out while you can! East of the Fault! The roads are jamming up fast!"

Nathan frowned. "There's still an hour or so," he said to himself. "And I still think the computer's wrong. I wonder what the tidal effects on the Pacific Ocean would be if the whole state collapsed into it?"

Nathan didn't really notice that he was talking to himself. There was no one else to talk to.

Except the computer.

He was sitting in the computer room, still poring over the stubborn equations, when the rumbling started. At first it was barely audible, like very distant thunder. Then the room began to shake and the rumbling grew louder.

Nathan glanced at his wristwatch: two-thirty-one.

"I knew it!" he said gleefully to the computer. "You see? And I'll bet the rest of it is right, too, including equation fourteen."

Going down the hallway was like walking through the passageway of a storm-tossed ship. The floor and walls were swaying violently. Nathan kept his feet despite some awkward lurches here and there.

It didn't occur to him that he might die until he got outside. The sky was dark, the ground heaving, the roaring deafened him. A violent gale was blowing dust everywhere, adding its shrieking fury to the earth's tortured groaning.

Nathan couldn't see five feet ahead of him. With the wind tearing at him and the dust stinging his eyes, he couldn't tell which way to go. He knew the other side of the Fault meant safety, but which way was it?

Then there was a biblical crack of lightning and the ultimate grinding, screaming, ear-shattering roar. A tremendous shock wave knocked Nathan to the ground and he blacked out. His last thought was, "I was right and the computer wrong."

When he woke up the Sun was shining feebly through a gray overcast. The wind had died away. Everything was strangely quiet.

Nathan climbed stiffly to his feet and looked around. The lab building was still there. He was standing in the middle of the parking lot; the only car in sight was his own Volvo, caked with dust.

Beyond the parking lot, where the eucalyptus trees used to be, was the edge of a cliff, where still-steaming rocks and raw earth tumbled down to a foaming sea.

Nathan staggered to the cliff's edge and looked out across the water, eastward. And realized that the nearest land was Europe.

"Son of a bitch," he said with unaccustomed vehemence. "The computer was right after all."

Cyberbooks

To Ginny and John, Eldene and Bill:
shipmates and treasured friends.
And to Barbara and the Rock.

Introduction to Cyberbooks

I've been writing science fiction long enough so that some of my fiction has become fact. Take *Cyberbooks*, for example. When I wrote this novel, in the late 1980s, electronic books were nothing more than a glimmer in the eyes of a few engineers. Today they are being peddled in shopping malls and catalogues.

But predicting a technological innovation is easy. What makes *Cyberbooks* interesting, to me, is the way the novel depicts the book publishing industry's reaction to the technological innovation.

The truth is, you see, that *Cyberbooks* is a satire of the New York-based book publishing industry. The novel came about because Tom Doherty, publisher of Tor Books, enjoyed my earlier satirical novel, *The Starcrossed*. "You should do a novel about the publishing industry," he insisted. "I could tell you stories!"

Well, everybody in the business has hair-raising (or stomach-turning) stories to tell about the publishing industry. I have a few myself. Many of them have been woven into the warp and woof of *Cyberbooks*.

For years, young wannabe writers who've read *Cyberbooks* would ask me tearfully, "The industry in New York isn't as bad as you paint it in your novel, is it?"

"No of course not," I always assure them. "It's worse."

Spring, Book 1

Murder One

The first murder took place in a driving April rainstorm, at the corner of Twenty-first Street and Gramercy Park West.

Mrs. Agatha Marple, eighty-three years of age, came tottering uncertainly down the brownstone steps of her town house, the wind tugging at her ancient red umbrella. She had telephoned for a taxi to take her downtown to meet her nephew for lunch, as she had every Monday afternoon for the past fourteen years.

The Yellow Cab was waiting at the curb, its driver imperturbably watching the old lady struggle with the wind and her umbrella from the dry comfort of his armored seat behind the bulletproof partition that separated him from the potential homicidal maniacs who were his customers. The meter was humming to itself, a sound that counterbalanced nicely the drumming of rain on the cab's roof; the fare was already well past ten dollars. He had punched the destination into the cab's guidance computer: Webb Press, just off Washington Square. A lousy five-minute drive; the computer, estimating the traffic at this time of day and the weather conditions, predicted the fare would be no more than forty-nine fifty.

Briefly he thought about taking the old bat for the scenic tour along the river; plenty of traffic there to slow them down and run up the meter. Manny at the garage had bypassed the automated alarm systems in all the cab's meters, so the fares never knew when the drivers deviated from the computer's optimum guidance calculations. But this old bitch was too smart for that; she would refuse to pay and insist on complaining to the hack bureau on the two-way. He had driven her before, and she was no fool, despite her age. She was a lousy tipper, too.

She finally got to the cab and tried to close the umbrella and open the door at the same time. The driver grinned to himself. One of his little revenges on the human race: keep the doors locked until *after* they try to get in. They break their fingernails, at least. One guy sprained his wrist so bad he had to go to the hospital.

Finally the cabbie pecked the touchpad that unlocked the right rear door. It flew open and nearly knocked the old broad on her backside. A gust of wet wind flapped her gray old raincoat.

"Hey, c'mon, you're gettin' rain inside my cab," the driver hollered into his intercom microphone.

Before the old lady could reply, a man in a dark blue trenchcoat and matching fedora pulled down low over his face splashed through the curbside puddles and grabbed for the door.

"I'm in a hurry," he muttered, trying to push the old woman out of the taxi's doorway.

"How dare you!" cried Mrs. Marple, with righteous anger.

"Go find a garbage can to pick in," snarled the man, and he twisted Mrs. Marple's hand off the door handle.

She yelped with pain, then swatted at the man with her umbrella, ineffectually. The man blocked her feeble swing, yanked the umbrella out of her grasp, and knocked her to the pavement. She lay there in a puddle, rain pelting her, gasping for breath.

The man raised her red umbrella high over his head, grasping it in both his gloved hands. The old woman's eyes went wide, her mouth opened to scream but no sound came out. Then the man drove the umbrella smashingly into her chest like someone would pound a stake through a vampire's heart.

The old lady twitched once and then lay still, the umbrella sticking out of her withered chest like a sword. The man looked down at her, nodded once as if satisfied with his work, and then stalked away into the gray windswept rain.

True to the finest traditions of New York's hack drivers, the cabbie put his taxi in gear and drove away, leaving the old woman dead on the sidewalk. He never said a word about the incident to anyone.

One

It was a Hemingway kind of day: clean and bright and fine, sky achingly blue, sun warm enough to make a man sweat. A good day for facing the bulls or hunting rhino.

Carl Lewis was doing neither. In the air-conditioned comfort of the Amtrak Levitrain, he was fast asleep and dreaming of books that sang to their readers.

The noise of the train plunging into a long, dark tunnel startled him from his drowse. He had begun the ride that morning in Boston feeling excited, eager. But as the train glided almost silently along the New England countryside, levitated on its magnetic guide way, the warm sunshine of May streaming through the coach's window combined with the slight swaying motion almost hypnotically. Carl dozed off, only to be startled awake by the sudden roar of entering the tunnel.

His ears popped. The ride had seemed dreamily slow when it started, but now that he was actually approaching Penn Station it suddenly felt as if things were happening too fast. Carl felt a faint inner unease, a mounting nervousness, butterflies trembling in his middle. He put it down to the excitement of starting a new job, maybe a whole new career.

Now, as the train roared through the dark tunnel and his ears hurt with the change in air pressure, Carl realized that what he felt was not mere excitement. It was apprehension. Anxiety. Damned close to out-right fear. He stared at the reflection of his face in the train window: clear of eye, firm of jaw, sandy hair neatly combed, crisp new shirt with its blue MIT necktie painted down its front, proper tweed jacket with the leather elbow patches. He looked exactly as a brilliant young soft-ware composer should look. Yet he felt like a scared little kid.

The darkness of the tunnel changed abruptly to the glaring lights of the station. The train glided toward a crowded platform, then screeched horrifyingly down the last few hundred yards of its journey on old-fashioned steel wheels that struck blazing sparks against old-fashioned steel rails. A lurch, a blinking of the light strips along the ceiling, and the train came to a halt.

With the hesitancy known only to New Englanders visiting
Manhattan for the first time, Carl Lewis slid his garment bag from
the rack over his seat and swung his courier case onto his shoulder.
The other passengers pushed past him, muttering and grumbling
their way off the train. They shoved Carl this way and that until he
felt like a tumble weed caught in a cattle stampede.

Welcome to New York, he said to himself as the stream of
detraining passengers dumped him impersonally, indignantly,
demeaningly, on the concrete platform.

The station was so big that Carl felt as if he had shrunk to the size
of an insect. People elbowed and stamped their way through the
throngs milling around; the huge cavern buzzed like a beehive.
Carl felt tension in the air, the supercharged crackling high-stress
electricity of the Big Apple. Panhandlers in their traditional grubby
rags shambled along, each of them displaying the official city begging
permit badge. Grimy bag ladies screamed insults at the empty air.
Teenaged thugs in military fatigues eyed the crowds like predators
looking for easy prey. Religious zealots in saffron robes, in severe
black suits and string ties, even in mock space suits complete with
bubble helmets, sought alms and converts. Mostly alms. Police
robots stood immobile, like fat little blue fireplugs, while the tides of
noisy, smelly, angry, scampering humanity flowed in every direction
at once. The noise was a bedlam of a million individual voices acting
out their private dramas. The station crackled with fierce, hostile
anxiety.

Carl took a deep breath, clutched his garment bag tighter, and
clamped his arm closely over the courier case hanging from his
shoulder. He avoided other people's eyes almost as well as a native
Manhattanite, and threaded his way through the throngs toward the
taxi stand outside, successfully evading the evangelists, the beggars,
the would-be muggers, and the flowing tide of perfectly ordinary
citizens who would knock him down and mash him flat under their
scurrying shoes if he so much as missed a single step.

There were no cabs, only a curbside line of complaining jostling
men and women waiting for taxis. A robot dispatcher, not unlike
the robot cops inside the station, stood impassively at the head of
the line. While the police robots were blue, the taxi dispatcher's
aluminum skin was anodized yellow, faded and chipped, spattered

here and there with mud and other substances Carl preferred not to think about.

Every few minutes a taxi swerved around the corner on two wheels and pulled up to the dispatcher's post with a squeal of brakes. One person would get in and the line would inch forward. Finally Carl was at the head of the line.

"I beg your pardon, sir. Are you going uptown or downtown?" asked the man behind Carl.

"Uh, uptown—no, downtown." Carl had to think about Manhattan's geography.

"Excellent! Would you mind if I shared a cab with you? I'm late for an important appointment. I'll pay the entire fare."

The man was tiny, much shorter than Carl, and quite slim. He was the kind of delicate middle-aged man for whom the word *dapper* had been coined. He wore a conservative silver-gray business suit; the tie painted down the front of his shirt looked hand done and expensive. He was carrying a blue trenchcoat over one arm despite the gloriously sunny spring morning. Silver-gray hair clipped short, a toothy smile that seemed a bit forced on his round, wrinkled face. Prominent ears, watery brownish eyes. He appeared harmless enough.

The big brown eyes were pleading silently. Carl did not know how to refuse. "Uh, yeah, sure, okay."

"Oh, thank you! I'm late already." The man glanced at his wristwatch, then stared down the street as if he could make a cab appear by sheer willpower.

A taxi finally did come, and they both got into it.

"Bunker Books," said Carl.

The taxi driver said something that sounded like Chinese. Or maybe Sanskrit.

"Fifth Avenue and Eighth Street," said Carl's companion, very slowly and loudly. "The Synthoil Tower."

The cabbie muttered to himself and punched the address into his dashboard computer. The electronic map on the taxi's control board showed a route in bright green that seemed direct enough. Carl sat back and tried to relax.

But that was impossible. He was sitting in a Manhattan taxicab with a total stranger who obviously knew the city well. Carl looked out the window on his side of the cab. The sheer emotional energy level out there in the streets was incredible. Manhattan *vibrated*. It hummed and crackled with tension and excitement. It made Boston seem like a placid country retreat. Hordes of people swarmed along the sidewalks and streamed across every intersection. Taxis by the hundreds weaved through the traffic like an endless yellow snake, writhing and coiling around the big blue steam buses that huffed and chuffed along the broad avenue.

The women walking along the sidewalks were very different from Boston women. Their clothes were the absolutely latest style, tiny hip-hugging skirts and high leather boots, leather motorcycle jackets heavy with chains and lovingly contrived sweat stains. Most of the women wore their biker helmets with the visor down, a protection against mugging and smog as well as the latest fashion. The helmets had radios built into them, Carl guessed from the small whip antennas bobbing up from them. A few women went boldly bareheaded, exposing their long hair and lovely faces to Carl's rapt gaze.

The cab stopped for a red light and a swarm of earnest-looking men and women boiled out of the crowd on the sidewalk to begin washing the windshield, polishing the grillwork, waxing the fenders. Strangely, they wore well-pressed business suits and starched formal shirts with corporate logos on their painted ties. The taxi driver screamed at them through his closed windows, but they ignored his Asian imprecations and, just as the light turned green again, affixed a green sticker to the lower left-hand corner of the windshield.

"Unemployed executives," explained Carl's companion, "thrown out of work by automation in their offices."

"Washing cars at street corners?" Carl marvelled.

"It's a form of unemployment benefit. The city allows them to earn money this way, rather than paying them a dole. They each get a franchise at a specific street corner, and the cabbie must pay their charge or lose his license."

Carl shook his head in wonderment. In Boston you just stood in line all day for a welfare check.

"Bunker Books," mused his companion. "What a coincidence."

Carl turned his attention to the gray-haired man sitting beside him.

"Imagine the statistical chance that two people standing next to one another in line waiting for a taxi would have the same destination," the dapper older man said.

"You're going to Bunker Books, too?" Carl could not hide his surprise.

"To the same address," said the older man. "My destination is in the same building: the Synthoil Tower." He glanced worriedly at the gleaming gold band of his wristwatch. "And if we don't get through this traffic I am going to be late for a very important appointment."

The taxi driver apparently could hear their every word despite the bulletproof partition between him and the rear seat. He hunched over his wheel, muttering in some foreign language, and lurched the cab across an intersection despite a clearly red traffic light and the shrill whistling of a brown-uniformed auxiliary traffic policewoman. They swerved around an oncoming delivery truck and scattered half a dozen pedestrians scampering across the intersection. Carl and his companion were tossed against one another on the backseat. The man's blue trenchcoat slid to the filthy floor of the cab with an odd thunking sound.

"Who's your appointment with?" Carl asked, inwardly surprised at questioning a total stranger so brazenly—and with poor grammar, at that.

The older man seemed unperturbed by either gaffe as he retrieved his trenchcoat. "Tarantula Enterprises, Limited. Among other things, Tarantula owns Webb Press, a competitor of Bunker's, I should think."

Carl shrugged. "I don't know much about the publishing business. . . ."

"Ahh. You must be a writer."

"Nosir. I'm a software composer."

The rabbity older man made a puzzled frown. "You're in the clothing business?"

"I'm a computer engineer. I design software programs."

"Computers! That *is* interesting. Is Bunker revamping its inventory control system? Or its royalty accounting system?"

With a shake of his head, Carl replied, "Something completely different."

"Oh?"

In all of Carl's many telephone conversations with his one friend at Bunker Books a single point had been emphasized over and over. *Tell no one about this project,* the woman had whispered urgently. Whispered, as though they were standing in a crowded room rather than speaking through a scrambled, private, secure fiberoptic link. *If word about this gets out to the industry—don't say a word to anybody!*

"It's, uh, got to do with the editorial side of the business," he generalized.

"I see," said his companion, smiling toothily. "A computer program to replace editors. Not a very difficult task, I should imagine."

Stung to his professional core, Carl replied before he could think of what he was saying, "Nothing like that! There've been editing programs for twenty years, just about. Using a computer to edit manuscripts is easy. You don't need a human being to edit a manuscript."

"So? And what you are going to do is difficult?"

"Nobody's done it before."

"But you will succeed where others have failed?"

"Nobody's even tried to do this before," Carl said, with some pride.

"I wonder what it could be?"

Carl forced himself to remain silent, despite the voice inside his head urging him to reach into the courier case lying on the seat between them and pull out the marvel that he was bringing to Bunker Books. A slim case of plastic and metal, about the size of a paperback novel. With a display screen on its face that could show any page of any book in the history of printing. The first prototype of the electronic book. Carl's very own invention. His offspring, the pride of his genius.

The taxi lurched around a corner, then stopped so hard that Carl was thrown almost against the heavy steel-and-glass partition. His companion seemed to hold his place better, almost as if he had braced himself in advance. His trenchcoat flopped over Carl's courier bag with a heavy thunking sound that was lost in the squeal of the taxi's brakes.

"Synthoil Tower," announced the cab driver. "That's eighty-two even, with th' tip."

True to his word, the dapper gray-haired man slid his credit card into the slot in the bulletproof partition, patted Carl's arm briefly by way of farewell, then scampered to the imposing glass-and-bronze doors of the Synthoil building. It took a few moments for Carl to gather his two bags and extricate himself from the backseat of the taxi. The cabbie drummed his fingers on his steering wheel impatiently. As soon as Carl was clear of the cab, the driver pulled away from the curb, the rear door swinging shut with a heavy slam.

Carl gaped at the rapidly disappearing taxi. For a wild instant a flash of panic surged through him. Clutching at his courier case, though, he felt the comforting solidity of his prototype. It was still there, safely inside his case.

So he thought.

Reader's Report

Title: *The Terror from Beyond Hell*
Author: Sheldon Stoker
Category: Blockbuster horror
Reader: Priscilla Alice Symmonds

Synopsis: What's to synopsize? Still yet another trashy piece of horror that will sell a million copies hardcover. Stoker is *awful*, but he sells books.

Recommendation: Hold our noses and buy it.

Two

Lori Tashkajian's almond-shaped eyes were filled with tears. She was sitting at her desk in the cubbyhole that passed for an editor's office at Bunker Books, staring out the half window at the slowly disappearing view of the stately Chrysler Building.

Her tiny office was awash with paper. Manuscripts lay everywhere, some of them stacked in professional gray cartons with the printed labels of literary agents affixed to them, others in battered cardboard boxes that had once contained shoes or typing paper or even children's toys. Still others sat unboxed, thick wads of paper bound by sturdy elastic bands. Everywhere. On Lori's desk, stuffing the bookshelves along the cheap plastic partition that divided the window and separated her cubicle from the next, strewn across the floor between the partition and gray metal desk, piled high along the window ledge.

One of management's strict edicts at Bunker Books was that editors were not allowed to read on the job. "Reading is done by readers," said the faded memo tacked to the wall above Lori's desk. "Readers are paid to read. Editors are paid to package books that readers have read. If an editor finds it necessary to read a manuscript, it is the editor's responsibility to do the reading on her or his own time. Office hours are much too valuable to be wasted in reading manuscripts."

Not that she had time for reading, anyway. Lori ignored all the piled-up manuscripts and, sighing, watched the construction crew weld another I-beam into the steel skeleton that was growing like Jack's beanstalk between her window and her view of the distinctive art-deco spike of the Chrysler Building. In another week they would blot out the view altogether. The one beautiful thing in her daily grind was being taken away from her, inches at a time, erased from her sight even while she watched. Coming to New York had been a mistake. Her glamorous life in the publishing industry was a dead end; there were no men she would consider dating more than once; and now they were even taking the Chrysler Building away from her.

She was a strikingly comely young woman, with the finely chiselled aquiline nose, the flaring cheekbones, the full lips, the dark almond eyes and lustrous black hair of distant romantic desert lands. Her figure was a trifle lush for modern New York tastes, a touch too much bosom and hips for the vassals of Seventh Avenue and their cadaverous models. Her life was a constant struggle against junk food. Instead of this week's fashionable biker image, which would have made her look even more padded than she was naturally, Lori wore a simple sweater and denim skirt.

She sighed again, deeply. There was nothing left except the novel, and no one would publish it. Unless . . .

The novel. It was a work of pure art, and therefore would be totally rejected by the editorial board. Unless she could gain a position of power for herself. If only Carl . . .

The desk phone chimed. Lori blinked away her tears and said softly, "Answer answer." The command to the phone had to be given twice, as a precaution against setting off its voice-actuated computer during the course of a normal conversation.

"A Mr. Lewis to see you," said the phone. "He claims he has an appointment." Whoever had programmed the communications computer had built in the hard-nosed suspicion of the true New Yorker. Even its voice sounded nasty and nasal.

"Show him in," commanded Lori. Softly. On second thought she added, "No, wait. I'll come out and get him."

Carl could be the answer to all her problems. He was brilliant. His invention could propel Bunker Books to the top of the industry. And, having dated him more than once in Boston, Lori was willing to try for more. But Carl would never find his way through this rabbit warren of offices and corridors, Lori told herself as she made the three steps it took to get through the only clear path between her desk and her door. Carl could design electronic software that made MIT professors blink with pleasured surprise, but he got lost trying to cross the street. She hurried down the narrow corridor toward the reception area.

Sure enough, Carl stood blinking uncertainly at the first cross-hallway, trying to figure out the computer display screen on the wall that supposedly showed even the most obtuse visitor the precise directions to the office he or she was seeking. True to his engineering nature, Carl was peering at the wall fixture with its complex code of colored paths rather than asking any of the people scurrying along the corridors.

He looked exactly as she remembered him: tall, trim, handsome in a boyish sort of way. He carried a garment bag and a smaller one both slung over the same shoulder, rumpling his tweed jacket unmercifully and making him look like an ill-clothed hunchback.

"Carl! Hi!"

He looked up toward Lori, blinked, and his smile of recognition sent a thrill through her.

"Hi yourself," he replied, just as he had in the old days when they had both been students: he at MIT and she at Boston University.

Carl put out his right hand toward her, and Lori took it in hers. Instead of a businesslike handshake she stepped close enough to peck at his cheek in the traditional gushy, phony manner of the publishing industry. But the heavy bags started to slip off Carl's shoulder and somehow wrapped themselves around her. Lori found herself pressed against Carl, and the traditional peck became a full, warm-blooded kiss on his lips. Definitely not phony, at least on her part.

Somebody snickered. She heard a wolf whistle from down the hall. As they untangled, she saw that Carl's face was red as a May Day banner. She felt flustered herself.

"I . . . I'm sorry," Carl stammered, trying to straighten out the twisted shoulder straps of his bags.

Lori smiled and said nothing. She took him by the free arm and led him back toward her office.

"Did you bring it?" she asked as they strode down the corridor. It was barely wide enough for the two of them to pass through side by side. Lori had to press close to his tweed-sleeved arm.

He nodded. "It's right here."

"Wonderful."

As she pushed open the door to her cubbyhole, Lori's heart sank. It was such a tiny office, so shabby, so sloppy with all those damned manuscripts all over the place, schedules and cover proofs tacked to the walls. It seemed even smaller with Carl in it; he looked like a giant wading through a sea of paper.

But he said, "Wow, you've got an office all to yourself!"

"It's a little on the small side," she replied.

"I'm still sharing that telephone booth with Thompson and two freshmen."

Lori had not the slightest doubt that Carl was being sincere. There was not a dissembling bone in his body, she knew. That was his strength. And his weakness. She would have to protect him from the sharks and snakes, she knew.

"You can hang your garment bag on the back of the door," Lori told him as she picked a double armload of manuscripts off the only other chair in the office and plopped them onto the window ledge, atop the six dozen already there. What the hell, she thought. I can't see much out of the window now anyway.

"We don't have much time before the meeting starts," she said as she slid behind her desk and sat down.

"Meeting?" Carl felt alarmed. "What meeting? I thought—"

"The editorial board meeting. It's mandatory for all the editors. Every Tuesday and Thursday. Be there on time, or else. One of the silly rules around here."

Carl muttered, "I'm going to have to show this to your entire board of editors?"

Lori moved her shoulders in a semishrug that somehow stirred Carl's blood. He had not seen her in nearly two years; until just now he had not realized how much he had missed her.

"I wanted you to show it to me first," she was saying, "and then we'd go in and show the Boss. But now it's time for the drippy meeting, and I *have* to attend."

"It's my own fault," said Carl. "The train was late, and it took me longer to get a cab than I thought it would. I should have taken an earlier train."

"Can you show me how it works? Real quick, before the meeting starts?"

"Sure." Carl took the emptied chair and unzipped his courier case. From it he pulled a gray oblong box, about five inches by nine and less than an inch thick. Its front was almost entirely a dark display screen. There was a row of fingertip-sized touchpads beneath the screen.

"This is just the prototype," Carl said almost apologetically. "The production model will be slightly smaller, around four by seven, just about the size of a regular paperback book."

Lori nodded and reached out her hands to take the electronic book from its inventor.

The phone chimed. "Editorial board meeting starts in one minute," said the snappish computer voice. "All editors are required to attend."

With a sigh, Lori said, "Come on, you can show the whole editorial board."

"This'll only take a few seconds."

"I can't be late for the meeting. They count it against you when your next salary review comes up."

"They take attendance and mark you tardy?"

"You bet!"

Stuffing his invention back in the black case and getting to his feet, Carl said, "Sounds like kindergarten."

With a rueful smile, Lori agreed, "What do you mean, 'sounds like'?"

Twenty floors higher in the Synthoil Tower sprawled the offices of Webb Press, a wholly owned subsidiary of Tarantula Enterprises (Ltd.). The reception area was larger than the entire set of grubby editorial cubicles down at Bunker Books. Sweeping picture windows looked out on the majestic panorama of lower Manhattan: the financial district, the twin Trade Towers, the magnificent new Disneydome that covered most of what had once been the slums and tenements of the Lower East Side. Farther away stood the Statue of Liberty and the sparkling harbor.

Harold D. Lapin sat patiently on one of the many deep soft leather chairs arranged tastefully across the richly soft silk carpeting of the reception area. His blue trenchcoat lay neatly folded across the chair's gleaming chrome arm. Being the man he was, Lapin's interest was focused not on the stunningly beautiful red-haired receptionist sitting behind her glass desk, microskirted legs demurely crossed, nor even on the splendid view to be seen through the picture windows. Rather, he studied the intricate floral pattern of the heavy drapes that framed the windows, mentally tracing a path from the ceiling to the floor that did not cross a flower, leaf, or stem.

"Mr. Lapin?" came the dulcet tones of the receptionist.

He turned in his chair to look at her, and she smiled a practiced smile that suggested much and revealed nothing.

"Mr. Hawks will see you now."

As she spoke, a door to one side of her desk slid open soundlessly and an equally lovely woman appeared there. She nodded slightly. Like the receptionist she was red of hair, gorgeous of face and figure, and dressed in the microskirt and tailored blouse that seemed to be something of a uniform at Webb Press.

Lapin followed the young woman wordlessly along broad quiet corridors lined with exquisite paintings and an occasional fine small bronze on a pedestal. All the doors along the corridor were tightly closed; the brass nameplates on them were small, discreet, tasteful.

Power exuded from those doors. Lapin could feel it. There was money here, much money, and the power to do great things.

At the end of the corridor was a double door of solid oak bearing an equally simple nameplate: P. Curtis Hawks. Idly wondering what the "P." stood for, and why Hawks preferred his second name to his first, Lapin allowed himself to be ushered through the double doors, past a phalanx of desks and secretaries (all red-haired), into an inner anteroom where still another gorgeous red-haired young woman smiled up at him and gestured silently toward the unmarked door beyond her airport-sized desk.

Are they all mute? Lapin wondered. Does Hawks clone them, all these redheads?

The unmarked door opened of itself and Lapin stepped through. The sanctum sanctorum inside was somewhat smaller than he had imagined it would be, merely the size of a bus terminal or a minor cathedral. It was splendidly panelled in teak, however, and its floor-length windows opened onto a handsome terrace that looked out on the East River, the Brooklyn condo complex, and the slender grace of the Verrazano-Narrows Bridge. A massive teak desk took up one end of the room, its broad clean top supported by four carved elephants with real ivory tusks. The other corners of the huge office contained, respectively, a conference table that could seat twelve, an electronics center that rivalled anything in Cape Canaveral, and a billiard table with an ornate Tiffany lamp hanging above it.

Hawks was standing by the French windows, fists clenched together behind his back, with the morning sun streaming in so boldly that it made Lapin's eyes water to gaze upon the president of Webb Press.

"Well?" Hawks snapped, without turning to face his visitor.

Squinting somewhat painfully, Lapin said, "Mission accomplished, sir." He had been told by the man who had hired him that Hawks preferred military idioms.

Hawks spun around and clapped his hands together with a loud smack. "Good! Let's see what you got."

P. Curtis Hawks was a short, chubby man in his late fifties. His curly red hair was obviously a toupee to Lapin's refined eye. Hawks's face was round, puffy-cheeked, with eyes so small and set so deep beneath menacing russet brows that Lapin could not tell what color they were. The man had a plastic pacifier clamped between his teeth; it was colored brown and shaped like a cigar butt. He wore a sky-blue suit tailored to suggest a military uniform: epaulets, decorative ribbons over the left breast pocket, trousers creased to a razor's edge. Yet he did not look military; he looked like a beach ball that had been unexpectedly drafted.

Hawks gestured to the electronics center. Lapin placed his trench-coat neatly on the back of one of the six chrome chairs there, and slid an oblong black box from the coat's inner pocket.

"You know how to work a scanner?" Hawks growled. His voice was like a diesel engine's heavy rumbling, yet there was a trace of a whine in it.

"Yessir, of course," said Lapin. Without sitting, he slid his black box into a slot on the console, then studied the control keyboard for a brief moment.

Hawks paced back and forth and chewed on his pacifier. "Three-D X rays," he muttered. "Do you realize that with this one hologram we'll be able to save the corporation the trouble of buying out those assholes at Bunker Books?"

Tapping commands into the console, Lapin replied absently, "I had no idea so much was at stake." Then he found himself adding, "Sir."

"There's billions involved here. Billions."

The display screen before the two standing men glowed to life, and a three-dimensional picture took form.

"What in hell is *that*?" Hawks shouted.

Lapin gasped in sudden fear. Hanging in midair before his horrified eyes was a miniature three-dimensional picture of what appeared to be the rear axle of a New York taxicab, overlain with vague blurs of other things.

"You shitfaced asshole!" Hawks screamed. "You used too much power! The X rays went right through his goddamned device and took a picture of the goddamn cab's axle! I'll have you broken for this!"

The Writer

The Writer eagerly pawed through the mail box hanging at a precarious tilt from the door of his rusted, dilapidated mobile home. It was not a *very* mobile home; so far as he knew, it had not moved an inch off the cinderblocks on which it rested since years before he had bought it, and that had been almost a decade ago.

Automatically ducking his head to get through the low doorway, he let the screen door slam as he riffled through the day's mail. Four bills that he could not pay, six catalogues advertising goods he could not afford, and a franked envelope bearing the signature of his congress woman, who was being opposed in the upcoming primaries by the owner of a chain of hardware stores.

Nothing from Bunker Books! Exasperated, the Writer tossed all the envelopes and catalogues onto his narrow bunk, which was still a mess of twisted sheets from his thrashing, tossing sleeplessness the night before.

Six months! They've had the manuscript for six months now. He had checked off the days on the greasy calendar hanging above the sink. The pile of dirty dishes nearly obscured it, but the red *x*'s on the calendar showed how the days had marched, one after another, without a word from Bunker Books.

All the magazine articles he had studiously read in the town library said that the longer a publishing house held on to a manuscript, the more likely they were to eventually buy it. It meant that the manuscript had been liked by the first reader and passed on to the more important editors. They, of course, were so busy that you couldn't expect them to sit right down and read your manuscript. They were flooded with hundreds of manuscripts; thousands, more likely. It took time to get to the one that you had sent in.

But six months? The Writer had sent follow-up letters, servilely addressed to "First Reader" and "Editor for New Manuscripts." No response whatsoever. On one daring night, emboldened by several beers at Jumping Joe's Bar, he sent an urgent, demanding telegram to the Editor-in-Chief. It was never answered, either.

As he sat in the only unbroken chair in the cramped living room area and turned on the noontime news, the Writer felt close to despair. For all he knew, the manuscript had never even gotten to Bunker Books. Some wiseguy in the post office might have dumped it in a sewer, figuring it was too heavy to carry. He'd heard plenty of stories like that, especially around Christmastime.

On the TV screen the solemn yet bravely smiling face of the network anchorman was replaced by a scene somewhere in the Middle East. The U.S. secretary of state was back there, trying to get the Arabs and Jews to stop shooting at each other. Fat chance, thought the Writer.

But something the secretary of state said to the reporters caught his attention. "We must do everything we can do to bring about a satisfactory solution to the problem. No matter how slim the chances, we must not shrink from doing everything we can do."

It was as if the TV screen had gone blank after that. The Writer saw no more, heard no more. He stared off into a distant, personal infinity. He must do everything he can do, no matter how slim the chances.

Absolutely right! Instead of going to the fridge and pulling out a frozen dinner, the Writer stalked out the front door of the mobile home and got into his battered old GMota hatchback. He gunned the engine and drove out to the throughway heading north. Toward New York. They would probably fire him, back at the garbage recycling plant, when he didn't show up for work that night. The bill collectors would probably grab his mobile home and all its contents. So what? He was heading for New York, for Bunker Books, for his rendezvous with destiny.

He was already more than a hundred miles north when the tornado ripped through town. Suddenly his ex-home became *very* mobile and wound up in the bottom of the bay, seven miles from its original site. Police dredged the bay for three days without finding his body.

Three

As he sat in the stuffy conference room, Carl thought he had somehow fallen down a rabbit hole or plunged into another dimension. Here he was with the greatest invention to hit the publishing world since Gutenberg, and the people around the conference table were ignoring him completely. The table looked cheap, hard-used. Carl ran a fingertip across its top: wood-grained Formica.

As one of the female editors droned on endlessly, Carl leaned toward Lori, sitting next to him. "They're talking about *books*," he whispered.

With a small grin she whispered back, "Of course, silly. This is the editorial board meeting."

"But what about my presentation?"

Lori's eyes flicked to the empty chair at the head of the table. "Not until the Boss comes in."

"The boss isn't here?"

"Not yet."

Carl sank back in his chair. It creaked. Or is it my spine? he wondered. The chair was old and stiff and uncomfortable. He was sitting at the foot of the table, farthest from the conference room's only door, squeezed in beside Lori. The Formica table top was scratched and chipped, he noticed. The walls of the windowless conference room bore faded color prints from the covers of old Bunker books.

Eight other editors sat slumped in various attitudes of boredom and frustration. Four men, four women, plus the male editor-in-chief, a pudgy little fellow with a dirty white T-shirt showing beneath his unzipped leather jacket, a fashionable two-day growth of beard on his round little chinny-chin-chin, pop eyes, and thick oily lips. He reminded Carl of a scaly fish. The editors all were dressed in ultra-modish biker's black leathers with chains and studs, except for Lori in her simple golden-yellow sweater and midcalf denim skirt. A burst of sunshine in the midst of all the black gloom.

Editorial bored meeting, Carl said to himself. Then, with a mental shrug of his cerebral shoulders, he decided to pay attention to what the editors were saying. Maybe he could learn something about how the publishing business worked. It beat chewing his fingernails waiting for his moment to speak.

The editor sitting next to the chief, an enormous mountain of flesh, was droning like a Tibetan lama in a semitrance about Sheldon Stoker's latest horror novel. Her name was Maryann Quigly, and she gave every appearance of loathing her job.

"It's the same old tripe," she said in a voice that sounded totally exhausted, as if just the effort of getting up in the morning and dragging her bloated body to this meeting had almost overwhelmed her. "Blood, devil-worship, blood, supernatural doings, blood, and more blood. It's awful."

"But it sells," said Ashley Elton, the bone-thin, nasal-voiced editor sitting across the table from the lugubrious Ms. Quigly. Ashley Elton was not her real name: she had been born Rebecca Simkowitz, but felt that her parents should have given her a name that sounded more literary. Hence Ashley Elton. She was an intense, beady-eyed toothache of a woman with the pale pinched face and smudged black eye makeup of a Hollywood vampire. The living dead, Carl thought.

"Sure it sells," Maryann Quigly agreed, barely squeezing the words past her heavy-eyed torpor.

The editor-in-chief shook his wattles. "Stoker writes crap, all right, but it's *commercial* crap. It keeps this company afloat. If we ever lose him we all go pounding the pavements looking for new jobs."

Quigly sighed a long, pained, wheezing sigh.

"What'd we give him as an advance for his last book?" asked the editor-in-chief.

"One million dollars." Quigly drew out the words to such length that it took almost a full minute to say it.

"Offer him the same for this one."

"His agent will want more," snapped Ashley Elton (nee Simkowitz).

"Murray Swift," muttered the editor-in-chief. "Yep, he'll hold us up for a million two, at least." Turning back to Quigly, he instructed, "Offer a million even. Give us more room for negotiating."

One by one, the editors presented books that they thought the company should publish. Each presentation was made exactly the same way. The editor would give the book's title and author, and then a brief description of the category it fit into. Thus:

Jack Drain, the young ball of fire who sported a small Van Dyke on his receding chin, proposed *Taurus XII: The Return of the Bull.* "It's by Billy Bee Bozo, same as the other eleven in the series. Fantasy adventure, set in a distant age when men battled evil with swords and courage."

"And all the weemen have beeg breasts," said Concetta Las Vagas, the company's Affirmative Action "two-fer," being both Hispanic and female. There were those in Bunker Books who claimed she should be a "three-fer," since her skin was quite dark as well. There were also those who claimed that Concetta's idea of Affirmative Action was to say "*Si, si,*" to any postpubertal male. The standard line among the office gossips was that a man could get lucky in Las Vagas.

"Look who's talking about beeg breasts," mimicked Mark Martin, who wore a pale lemon silk T-shirt beneath his biker's leather jacket, and a tastefully tiny diamond on his left nostril.

Drain frowned across the table at Las Vagas. "There are women warriors in this one. Bozo's not as much of a male chauvinist as he used to be."

"There go his sales," somebody mumbled.

Ted Gunn, sitting next to Drain, perked up on his chair. Although he wore leathers and metal studs just like the rest of the editors, he gave off an aura of restless energy that announced he was a Young Man Headed for the Top. He was the only one in the conference room who smoked; his place at the table was fenced in by a massive stainless-steel ashtray smudged with a layer of gray ash and six crushed butts, and a pair of electronic air purifiers that sucked the smoke out of the air so efficiently that they could snatch up notepaper and even loose change.

"What have sales been like for the *Taurus* series lately?" Gunn asked.

Drain said, "Good. Damned good." But it sounded weak, defensive.

"Haven't his sales been dropping with every new book?"

"Not much."

"But if a series is effective," Gunn said, suddenly the sharp young MBA on the prowl, "his sales should be going up, not down."

That started a long, wrangling argument about the marketing department, the art director's choice of cover artists, the hard winter in the Midwest, and several other subjects that mystified Carl. What could all that have to do with the sales of books? Why didn't they all have pocket computers, so they could punch up the sales figures and have them in hard numbers right before their eyes?

Carl shook his head in bewilderment.

With great reluctance, P. Curtis Hawks entered the private elevator that ran from his spacious office to the penthouse suite of the Synthoil Tower. Lapin had been ushered away in the grip of two burly security men to learn the lessons of failure. Now Hawks had to report that failure to the Old Man.

Once he had enjoyed talking with the Old Man, gleaning the secret techniques of power and persuasion that had built Tarantula Enterprises into one of the world's largest multinational corporations. But ever since the takeover battle had started, the Old Man had seemed to recede from reality, to slide into a private world that was almost childlike. Senility, thought Hawks. Just when we need him most, his mind turns to Silly Putty.

He whacked the only button on the elevator's control board four times before the doors could close, like a true New Yorker, impatient, urgent, demanding. The doors swished shut and he felt the heavy acceleration of upward thrust. Years ago, when he had first become president of Tarantula's publishing subsidiary, whenever Hawks entered this elevator he had pictured himself as an astronaut blasting off to orbit. I could have been an astronaut, he told himself. If only I could have passed algebra in high school.

The ride was all too swift. Hawks felt a moment of lightness as the elevator slowed to a stop. ("Zero gravity," he used to say to himself. "We have achieved orbit.") The doors slid smoothly open. The office of Weldon W. Weldon, president and chief executive officer of Tarantula Enterprises (Ltd.) lay before him.

It was a jungle. The office had been turned into a tropical green-house. Or maybe a zoo. All sorts of lushly flowering shrubs were growing out of huge ceramic pots dotting the vast expanse of the Old

Man's office. Palm trees brushed their fronds against the ceiling. Raucous birds jeered from perches in the greenery, and Hawks heard a new sound—a hooting kind of howl that must have been a monkey or baboon or some equally noisome animal. Vines trailed along the incredibly expensive Persian carpeting. Hawks wrinkled his nose at the clashing, cloying scents of the jungle. For god's sake, look at the stains on the carpeting! Those goddamn birds!

There were snakes in those bushes, too, he knew. Poisonous snakes. The Old Man said he needed them for protection. Ever since the takeover struggle had started, he had become more and more paranoid. Said he was training them to guard him and attack strangers.

Wishing he had brought a machete, Hawks made his perilous way slowly through the Old Man's personal jungle. The heat and humidity were intolerable. Hawks's expensive silk suit was already soaked with perspiration. It dripped off the end of his pudgy nose and trickled along his belly and legs. His skull steamed under his toupee. He felt as if he were melting.

The old bastard changes the layout every day, he fumed to himself. One of these days I'm going to need a native guide to find his goddamned desk.

After nearly ten minutes of stalking around potted orchids and stepping over twisted vines (and hoping they were not snakes lying in wait), Hawks ducked under a low palm bole, turned a corner, and there in a clearing was the Old Man. Watering a row of Venus flytraps with a seltzer bottle.

Weldon W. Weldon sat in his powered chair, in his usual undertaker's black suit, a heavy plaid blanket tucked over his lap, blissfully spritzing the Venus flytraps. His back was to the approaching Hawks. A line from Shakespeare sprang into Hawks's mind: "Now might I do it, Pat."

Hawks had never understood who Pat was, and why he had no lines to speak in the scene. But he understood opportunity when he saw it. I could come up behind him, whisk the blanket off his lap, and smother him with it. Nobody would know, and I would be elected to replace him, Hawks told himself.

Then he saw the jaguar lying indolently in the corner by the picture windows. Its burning eyes were fastened on Hawks, and there was no chain attached to its emerald-studded collar. Hawks was not certain that anyone could train a snake to attack on command, but he had no doubts whatsoever about the jaguar. He swallowed his ambition. It tasted like bile. The sleek cat purred like the rumble of a heavy truck.

The president and chief executive officer of Tarantula Enterprises (Ltd.) spun his powered chair around to face Hawks. Weldon was old, stooped, wrinkled, totally bald, and confined to his powered chair since his massive coronary more than a year earlier. The coronary, of course, had come in the midst of Tarantula's battle to avoid an unfriendly takeover by Etna Industries, a multinational corporation headquartered in Sicily and reputed to be a wholly owned Mafia subsidiary. A decidedly unfriendly takeover bid. The struggle was still going on, the battlefields were the stock exchanges of New York, London, and Rome, the law courts of Washington and Palermo. This war had already cost Weldon his health. Maybe his sanity.

And there was no end in sight. The swarthy little men from Sicily had great persistence. And long memories. Hawks could *feel* the brooding Sicilians hovering over them, like dark angels of death, waiting for the chance to grab Tarantula in their rapacious claws.

"You didn't get it," the Old Man snapped. His voice was as sharp and scratchy as an icepick scraping along a chalk board.

"Not exactly," said Hawks from around his pacifier. His tone was meekly servile. He hated himself for it, but somehow in the face of the Old Man he always felt like a naughty little kid. Worse: an incompetent little kid.

"And what do you mean by that?" Weldon laid his seltzer bottle on the blanket across his lap and drove the chair over to his desk. Its electric motor barely buzzed, it was so quiet. The once immaculate expanse of Philippine mahogany was now a miniature forest of unidentifiable potted plants. Hawks had to sit at just the right angle to see his boss through a clearing in the greenery.

"The man we hired to copy the device used too strong an X-ray dose," Hawks confessed, feeling sheepish.

"And? And?"

"The hologram contains a complete three-dimensional picture of the device, but it's a very weak image. Blurred. Very difficult to make out any details."

Weldon snorted. His wizened old face frowned at Hawks. "I see," he sneered. "If I want a perfect three-D image of a taxicab's rear axle, you can get it for me. But not the device we're after."

Hawks felt a shudder of fright burn through him. He's bugged my office! He's been listening to everything that I do!

Pointing a crooked, shaking finger at Hawks, the old man commanded, "You get the best people in NASA, or the Air Force, or wherever to work on that fudged hologram. I want to see that device!"

Hawks swallowed again. Hard. "Yessir."

"And get somebody who knows what he's doing to make another copy of it. Steal the damned thing if you have to!"

"Right away, sir."

Weldon's frown relaxed slightly. He almost smiled, a ghastly sight. "Now listen, son," he said, suddenly amiable. "Don't you understand how important this device is? It's going to revolutionize the publishing industry."

"But publishing is such a small part of Tarantula," Hawks heard himself object. "Why bother . . ."

He stopped himself because the old man's smile faded into a grimace.

"How many times do I have to tell you," Weldon said sharply, "that publishing is the keystone to all of Tarantula's business lines? Control publishing and you control people's minds, their attitudes. Books and magazines and newspapers tell people what to think, how to vote, where to spend their money. How many idiots do you know who let the *Times* book reviews decide for them what's good reading and what isn't?"

"But what about TV?" Hawks asked, unfazed by the non sequitur. "And even radio . . ."

The old man snarled at him, making the jaguar's ears perk up. "Television? Are you serious?" He cackled. "Those Twinkies and egomaniacs get their ideas and their information from books and magazines and newspapers! Don't you understand that yet? Why do you think I put you in charge of our publishing subsidiary? Because I thought you were incompetent?"

That was exactly why Hawks thought he had been made president of Webb Press. But he remained silent as Weldon continued:

"Sure, Webb runs in the red every year. It's a good tax shelter for us; the more money Webb loses, the less taxes we pay. But the books Webb publishes are important to the rest of Tarantula. The magazines and newspapers even more so."

Hawks nodded to show he understood. He did not agree, of course, but if the Old Man thought publishing was that important, he was not going to argue.

"This device," Weldon went on, "this electronic book doohickey . . . it's the wave of the future. We've got to have it!"

"But—"

"Don't you understand?" Weldon's eyes began to shine, he seemed to vibrate with inner energy. "With electronic books we can undercut all the other publishers. We can corner the entire publishing industry!"

"Do you really think so?" Hawks felt entirely dubious. Clearly the Old Man's trolley was derailed.

Weldon's eyes were glowing now. His arms stretched out to encompass the world. Hawks almost thought he was going to rise out of his chair and walk.

"First we take over publishing here in the States," he said, his voice deep, powerful. "But that's just the spring freshet that precedes the flood. From the States we go to Japan. From Japan to Europe. Soon all the world will be ours! One publishing house, telling the whole world what to think!"

The Old Man sank back in his chair, panting with the exertion of his dynamic vision.

"I . . . I think I understand," Hawks murmured. And he almost did.

"This young engineer—what's his name?"

"Carl Lewis, sir."

"We've got to have his invention. One way or the other, we've got to have it!"

"I've already taken steps in that direction, sir."

Weldon scowled at him. "Such as?"

Feeling pleased as a puppy laying his master's slippers before the great man's feet, Hawks said, "I have arranged for one of our editors to be hired away from us by Bunker Books."

The Old Man's scowl melted into a crooked grin. "A spy in their camp, eh?"

"A Mata Hari, in fact."

"Ms. Dean, isn't it? Very attractive woman. Very formidable."

Again Hawks shuddered inwardly. He *has* bugged my office. He knows everything I'm doing.

"Well, if you don't have anything else to tell me, get on with your work. Get me that electronic book." Weldon made a shooing motion with his long-fingered, liver-spotted hands.

Hawks got up from his chair, dreading the trek through the Old Man's jungle. There were a lot of snakes between him and the elevator.

"Oh, one little thing more," the Old Man said, with a slight cackling that might have been laughter. "There's going to be a few changes at Webb. I've hired a new assistant for you."

Hawks turned back to face Weldon. He had to stand on tiptoe to see over the plants on his desk. "An assistant?" His voice nearly cracked with anxiety.

"Yes. A corporate systems engineer. What we used to call an efficiency expert in the old days."

"Corporate . . ." Hawks knew what the title meant: hatchet man.

"Gunther Axhelm." Weldon's wrinkled face was grinning evilly. "You may have heard of him."

Hawks's knees turned to water. Heard of him? Who hadn't heard of Axhelm the Axe, the man who single-handedly reduced General Motors to a museum with a staff of six, the man who fired four thousand management employees of AT&T in a single afternoon and drove Du Pont out of business altogether. He was coming to Webb! Might as well get in line for unemployment compensation now, before the rush.

"Don't get scared," the Old Man said, almost kindly.

"Scared? Me?"

"You're white as an albino in shock, son."

Hawks tried to control the fluttering of his heart. "Well, Axhelm's got quite a reputation. . . ."

"Nothing for you to worry about, son. I promise you. Just give him a free hand. It'll all work out for the best."

"Yessir."

"And get that electronic book for me! I want it in our hands. I want this brilliant young inventor on our team—or out of the picture altogether. Do you understand me?"

"Certainly, sir." Hawks saw the diamond-hard glint in the Old Man's eyes and decided that he would rather face the snakes.

Weldon W. Weldon watched his protégé slink away through the jungle foliage. "Brain the size of a walnut," he muttered to himself. "But he follows orders, like a good Nazi."

With a sigh, Weldon poked a bony finger at the floral design on one of the ceramic pots atop his desk. The plants were all plastic, beautiful fakes. The pot's curved surface turned milky, then steadied into a three-dimensional image of Tarantula's corporate organization chart.

Tapping a few more places here and there among the flower pots, Weldon got the display to show the distribution of stockholders in Tarantula. Although he himself was the largest individual stockholder, he only owned twelve percent of the company. There were others out there, selling out to the Sicilians.

It was a complicated situation. Tarantula was supposedly an independent corporation. But Synthoil Inc. owned a majority of the stock, and Tarantula was in fact controlled by that Houston-based corporation. Yet sizable chunks of stock were owned by other companies, too, such as Mozarella Bank & Trust—an obvious Mafia front.

The old man shook his head tiredly. The stockholders meeting coming up this November will determine the fate of the corporation, and I'm not even sure who the hell owns the company!

Reader's Report

Title: *Midway Diary*

Author: Ron Clanker (Capt., U.S.N., [Ret.])

Category: WWII historical fiction

Reader: Elizabeth Jane Rose

Synopsis: Tells the story of the Battle of Midway from the point of view of a young navy officer serving aboard a U.S. ship. He is in love with a Japanese-American woman who lives in Hawaii, which causes no end of troubles because we are at war with Japan at the time. I don't know much about WWII (I was an English major, of course), but his writing is vivid and there's not too much blood and machismo. The novel is really very romantic and sensitive in spite of all the war stuff.

Recommendation: Should be considered seriously by the editorial board.

Four

After two hours, Carl finally began to understand the way the editorial board worked, although it didn't seem to make any sense.

He had thought, from the little Lori had told him, that the purpose of the meeting was to decide which books Bunker would publish, out of all the manuscripts the editors had received since the last meeting. One by one, each editor seated around the conference table described a book manuscript that he or she believed should be published. The editor usually started with the author's name and a brief listing of the author's previous books. Then the editor spoke glowingly of the book's subject matter: "This one is *hot!*" was a typical remark. "A diet that allows you to eat all the chocolate you want!"

Not a word was said about the quality of the writing, nor of the ideas or philosophies the writers were writing about. The editors talked about each manuscript's category (whatever that was) and the author's track record. Are they talking about writers or racehorses? Carl wondered. After the first hour he decided that the editors viewed their writers as horses. Or worse.

That much he understood. But what followed confused Carl, at first. For no matter how enthusiastically a book was described by the editor presenting it, the rest of the editors seemed to go right to work to destroy it.

"His last two novels were duds," one of the other editors would say.

Or, "I can just picture the sales force trying to sell *that* in the Middle West."

"He's out of his category; he doesn't have a track record with mysteries."

"It's just another diet book. Even if it does work it'll get lost on the shelves."

Slowly it dawned on Carl that the real purpose of the editorial board meeting was not to decide which books Bunker would publish. It was to decide which they would *not* publish. He felt like a child watching a great aerial battle in which every plane in the sky would inevitably, inexorably, be shot down.

Except for the Sheldon Stoker horror novel, which everyone agreed was so terrible that it would sell millions of copies. Carl began to wonder how Thackeray or Graves or Hawthorne would get through an editorial board meeting. Not to mention Hesse or Hugo or Tolstoy. Not that he had read the works of those masters, of course; but he had seen dramatizations of their novels on public television.

As the second hour dragged on into the third, and Carl's stomach began to make anticipatory noises about lunch, the Moment of Truth moved down the table and finally arrived at Lori's chair.

"Well, Ms. Tashkajian," asked the editor-in-chief, "what priceless work of art do you have for us today?" Carl thought the mouth-breathing bastard was being awfully sarcastic.

Lori forced a smile, though, from her seat at the foot of the table and began to speak glowingly about a novel titled *Midway Diary*.

"But it's a first novel!" gasped Ted Gunn, once he realized that the author had written nothing earlier. "The guy's got no track record at all! How's the sales force going to tell how many copies he ought to sell if he's never had a book out there before?"

"It's a good novel," said Lori.

"Goods we get at a fabric store," giggled Gina Lucasta, who sat just to Lori's left. She was one notch above Lori in seniority, and she was not about to let the lowliest member of the editorial board move past her. She had started with the company as a receptionist, but her surly way with visitors, her propensity to cut off telephone calls at the switchboard, and her apparent inability to get even the simplest message to its intended recipient resulted in her being promoted to the editorial staff, where, it was felt by management, she could not do so much damage to the company.

Lori answered softly, "This novel has romance for the women and war action for men. Properly promoted, it could become a best-seller."

"By a first-timer?" Ted Gunn scoffed. "Do you know the last time a totally unknown writer made it to the best-seller list?"

"That was when the publishing house recognized that the book had terrific potential and backed it to the hilt," Lori said sweetly.

"It's a historical novel?" asked the editor-in-chief.

"World War Two."

"What page does the rape scene come on?"

Lori shook her head. "There isn't any rape scene. It's more romantic than a bodice ripper."

"A historical novel without a rape scene in it? Who'd buy it?"

Lori bit her lips and did not reply. Ashley Elton started to say, "Most women are offended by that kind of violence. Just because—"

But at that moment the door swung open and the Boss stepped into the room.

All the editors stood up. Kee-ripes, thought Carl as he reluctantly got to his feet, this is worse than kindergarten. But he realized that his buttocks had gone numb from sitting so long on the uncomfortable chair. It felt good to be off his backside.

The relief lasted only a moment. The Boss nodded a tight-lipped hello to the editorial board, cast a slightly raised eyebrow at Carl, and took the chair at the head of the table. The editor-in-chief held the chair for her as she daintily sat down.

The Boss was a slim blond woman of an age that Carl was hopelessly unable to fathom. More than thirty, less than sixty; that was all he could estimate. Her skin was glowing and flawless, like the finest porcelain. Her hair was cut short, almost boyish, but as impeccably coiffed as a TV ad. Although she obeyed the dictates of current fashion and wore a biker-type suit, it was all of pure white leather, both jacket and slacks, with a slightly frilly white blouse beneath. Where the others wore metal chains or studs, the Boss wore gold. Gold necklaces, several chains, and heavy gold bracelets on both wrists. Carl could not see (and probably would not have noticed, even if he had been close enough to see) the cold, hard glint of her eyes. They were the tawny fierce eyes of an eagle; they missed nothing, especially opportunities for making money.

The editor-in-chief, whose appearance looked even grubbier next to this saintly vision of white and gold, said to the Boss, "We're almost finished, Mrs. Bunker, but if you want us to review everything for you . . ."

"That won't be necessary," said Mrs. Bunker in a tiny china doll's voice that everyone strained to hear. "I have a few announcements to make."

Carl sensed tension crackle across the conference table. Several of the editors actually drew back in their chairs, as if trying to avoid some invisible sniper's bullet that was heading their way.

"First, the rumors that our company will be bought out by some multinational corporation are strictly rumors. Mr. Bunker has no intention of selling his company to anyone."

They relaxed so hard that Carl could feel the breeze of their sighs gusting past him at close to Mach 1.

"Second, our son P.T. Junior has graduated with honors from the Wharton School of Business—"

A round of "Ahhs" and clapping interrupted her. When it died down, Mrs. Bunker continued. "And will join the company as a special assistant to the publisher. You can expect him to attend the next editorial board meeting."

The congratulatory vibrations in the air vanished like the smoke from a birthday cake's candles.

"Third, we have been fortunate enough to obtain the services of one of the top editors in the business, Scarlet Dean. She has accepted our offer and will start here on Monday." The Boss allowed a satisfied smile to bend her lips slightly.

"She's leaving Webb Press?" asked one of the editors.

"But she was the head of their romance and inspirational lines!"

"I invited her to lunch a few weeks ago," said Mrs. Bunker, "and"—her smile broadened—"made her an offer she couldn't refuse."

"Wonderful!"

"Just what we needed!"

"A real coup!"

The congratulations buzzed around the table; everyone seemed anxious to get their word in. All except the editor-in-chief, who looked slightly puzzled.

Once the acclamations died down, Mrs. Bunker turned to the man and said softly, "I'm afraid we can't have two editors-in-chief, Max."

The man's stubbly jaw flapped several times, like a flounder gasping on the hard planks of a dock, but no sounds came out.

"I'd appreciate it if you'd clear out your office by the end of the day," said the Boss with the sweetness of a Borgia princess.

The man slumped back in his chair, his face white and lifeless, his eyes round and vacant. The rest of the editors looked away, as if fearing to be touched by his hollow-eyed stare. Carl felt hollow himself; he had never seen a public execution before.

Mrs. Bunker looked down the table, toward Carl. "Now then, Lori. Is this the young genius who's going to transform the publishing industry?"

With a visible swallow to clear her throat, Lori nodded and said, "This is Carl Lewis, assistant professor of software design at the Massachusetts Institute of Technology. He's brought us the prototype of the device that will become as important to the world as the printing press was."

"Let's see it," said the Boss with a slight smile. It looked to Carl as if she was amused by Lori's grandiose claim.

Carl got to his feet once again. As he unzipped his courier case he began to explain, "The concept of the electronic book is nothing new; people have been predicting it for years. What *is* new is that"—he pulled his invention out and held it up for them all to see—"here it is!"

Total disinterest. The editors did not react at all. It was if he had pulled out a bologna sandwich or a copy of the postal service's zip code guide. Nothing. Carl could not see Lori's beaming face, of course, because she was sitting beside him. And he did not know Mrs. Bunker well enough to detect the gold-seeking glitter in her eyes and the tiny, furtive dart of her tongue across her lower lip. The just fired editor-in-chief, of course, simply sat there like a dead fish, his mouth gaping open, his eyes staring at nothing.

Somewhat grimly, Carl went on with his prepared presentation. "More than ninety percent of a publisher's costs stem from moving megatonnages of paper across the country, from the paper mills to the printers, from the printers to the warehouses, from the warehouses to the wholesalers, from the wholesalers to the retail outlets."

Mrs. Bunker nodded slightly.

"I contend that publishers are in the information business, not the wood pulp and chemical industry. What you want to get into the hands of your readers is *information*—which does not necessarily have to be in the form of ink marks on paper."

Holding his device up for them all to see, Carl said, "This is an electronic book. It does away with the need for paper and ink."

"How does it work?" Lori prompted brightly in the silence of the rest of the editors.

Placing his device on the scarred top of the conference table, Carl explained, "Instead of printing books on paper, you 'print' them on miniature electro-optic wafers, like the diskettes used in computers, only smaller. This device in my hand allows you to read the book. The screen here shows you a full page. It can show illustrations as well as printed material; in fact, the quality of the pictures can be made better than anything you can achieve with the printed page."

"Can you show us?" Mrs. Bunker asked.

"Sure," replied Carl. "I've programmed one of my favorite children's books onto a wafer. It's called *Rain Makes Applesauce.* . . ."

Carl reached into his bag again and pulled out the tiny electro-optic wafer. It was barely the size of a postage stamp. "A wafer this size, incidentally, can hold more than a thousand pages of text."

Still no response whatsoever from the assembled editors. A few of them, however, glanced sideways toward the Boss, waiting to see her reaction and then follow suit.

Carl slid the electro-optic wafer into his device with the tap of a forefinger. "These touchpads work just about the same as a videocassette recorder's controls: start, stop, fast forward, reverse. You can also punch in a specific page number and the screen will go right to that page."

Holding the slim oblong box up so that they all could see its screen, Carl tapped the "start" button. Nothing happened.

"Shouldn't do that," he muttered, frowning. Carl touched it again. Still nothing appeared on the screen.

Suddenly perspiring, Carl pressed frantically on each of the touchpads in turn. The screen remained stubbornly blank.

Now the editors reacted. They laughed uproariously. They guffawed. All except the former editor-in-chief, who still sat there with his mouth hanging open and his eyes staring as sightlessly as a flounder on ice in a fish store display.

Murder Two

Rex Wolfe was walking his dog along Riverside Drive, pooper-scooper dutifully clutched in one hand, the leash attached to the toy terrier in his other. They made an incongruous pair, the fleshily ponderous yet utterly dignified old man and the nervously twitchy little dog. Wolfe was impeccably garbed in the old style: a hand-tailored pinstripe suit with vest, off-white classic shirt with a real collar, and a rep tie that he had knotted flawlessly himself.

Traffic along the drive was its usual hopeless snarl, taxis and trucks and buses honking impatiently, drivers screaming filthy admonitions at one another. Wolfe sighed an immense sigh. In all his long years he could not remember it otherwise. When the city had finally prohibited private automobiles from entering Manhattan, it had been hailed as the solution to the traffic problem. It was not. It simply made room for more trucks. And buses. The number of taxis remained constant, thanks to the political clout of the cabbies, but their fares skyrocketed.

The dog yapped scrappily at the traffic zooming by as Wolfe waited patiently for the traffic light to change. "Quiet, Archie," said Wolfe as a middle-aged matron stared distastefully at the dog.

But secretly Wolfe felt the dog was right: the drivers needed someone to set them straight.

He crossed the drive, with the little dog tugging at its leash. They looked like a tiny scooter towing an immense dirigible.

Once inside Riverside Park, Wolfe allowed the dog to run loose.

But he kept an eye on the animal as he ambled slowly northward, toward the ancient graffiti-covered edifice of Grant's Tomb. The dog, for its part, never wandered too far from its master as it scurried from lamppost to bench to wall to bush, sniffing out who had been around the old haunts lately.

"Ulysses S. Grant," Wolfe muttered to himself as he approached the pile of Victorian stonework. One of the great examples of the old Peter Principle. A hard-drinking farm boy who rose to command in the U.S. Army during the Civil War and literally saved the Union, only to be elected president, a task that was clearly beyond his powers. Promoted one step too far, elevated to the level of his incompetence. It was an old story, but a sad one still the same.

And now the final indignity. A tomb forgotten by everyone except the graffitists who regularly spattered it with their semi-literate proclamations of self: Gavilan 103; Shifty; The Bronx Avengers. What could possibly be worth avenging in the Bronx? Wolfe asked himself.

The only reply he got was a tremendous blow to the back of his head. Wolfe felt himself lifted off his feet, then hitting the concrete walk facedown with the crunching thud of breaking bones. There was no pain, only stunned surprise. Another enormous blow to his ribs rolled him over partially onto one side. Standing above him, silhouetted against the late afternoon sunlight, was a figure in some sort of a trenchcoat with a baseball bat raised above his head in both hands.

The ultimate fate of the native New Yorker, Wolfe thought. Mugged and murdered.

The bat crashed down again and everything went black.

Five

Carl Lewis sat broodingly hunched over his second beer in the noisy dark bar at the street level of the Synthoil Tower. Lori Tashkajian sat next to him in the cramped little booth, nursing a glass of white wine; the bench on the other side of the table held Carl's two bags. The bar was crowded with men and women at the end of the working day, starting to unwind from their tensions, the young ones looking for friends and possible mates for the evening; the older ones fortifying themselves before the rush to the homeward-bound trains and their more-or-less permanent mates.

"I just don't understand how it could have malfunctioned," Carl mumbled for approximately the seventy-fourth time in the past hour.

He had spent the afternoon in Lori's office, desperately examining his failed electro-optic book reader.

"It was fried," he repeated to Lori. "Darned near melted. Like somebody had put it in a microwave oven, or an X-ray machine."

"Maybe the airport security . . ."

"I came in by train, remember?" Carl said.

"Oh, yeah, that's right." Lori sipped at her wine, then suggested, "Maybe they have a security X-ray on the train?"

Carl shook his head. "If they did they wouldn't keep it a secret. And even if they did, it wouldn't be powerful enough to fry electro-optical circuitry."

"Can you fix it?" Lori asked.

"Sure."

"How quickly?"

He shrugged. "A day, two days. I'll have to replace most of the components, but that shouldn't be too tough."

"Can you do it overnight?"

"Overnight? Why?"

Lori grasped Carl's arm in both her hands. "We've got to get this across to the Boss before she comes to the conclusion that the idea's a dud."

Frowning unhappily, Carl said, "She's already come to that conclusion."

"No! While you were poking into your little machine in my office, I spent the afternoon in *her* office, pleading with her to give you another chance."

"You did?"

"She's willing to listen," said Lori, "but she certainly isn't enthusiastic."

"Can you blame her?" Carl felt seething anger in his guts, and something worse: self-disgust. How could I let this happen? My one big chance . . .

Yet Lori's face, in the dimness of the shadowy bar, was bright and eager. "We've got to get her before she cools off altogether. A lot of people are always bringing her ideas; there's a lot of pressure on her constantly. We've got to strike right away."

"Okay, but overnight—I don't know if I can do it that quick. I have to go back to my lab. . . ."

"Can't you do it here?"

"I need the components. And the tools."

"Gee," said Lori, "we're right next to NYU. Don't you think they'd have the stuff you need?"

"Maybe. But how do I get it? I don't know anybody there."

Lori pressed her lips together and turned to scan the crowded bar. "I hope he's still . . . yes! There he is."

Without another word she slid out of the booth, wormed her way through the crowd at the "meat market" of unattached singles jammed around the bar, and came out towing a wiry-looking man of about thirty-five or forty. He had a slightly puzzled grin on his face.

Sliding onto the booth's other bench, he pushed Carl's bags into a squashed mess. He had a thick mop of reddish hair that looked like a rusty Brillo pad, long lean arms that ended in oversized hands with long fingers that looked almost like talons. He held big mugs brimming with beer, one in each clawlike hand.

"Saves time going for refills," he said in answer to Carl's questioning gaze.

"Carl, this is Ralph Malzone; Ralph, Carl Lewis."

"I heard about your fiasco." Malzone said it jovially, as if he had heard and seen plenty of other fiascos, and even participated in a few of his own.

He released the beer mugs and reached across the table to shake Carl's hand. His grip was strong. And wet. He had a long, lopsided, lantern-jawed grinning face that seemed honest and intelligent. Carl immediately liked him, despite his opening line.

"Ralph is our director of sales," Lori said. "And our resident electronics whiz. Whenever a computer or anything else complicated breaks down, Ralph can fix it for us."

The wiry guy seemed to blush. "Yeah, but from what I hear, your gadget is way out of my league."

"Do you know where I might find a good electronics lab at NYU?" Carl asked.

"Nope. But maybe I could get you into one at my old alma mater, Columbia."

"I didn't know you were a Columbia graduate," Lori said, sounding surprised.

"Electrical engineering, '91," Malzone said amiably. "Then I went back three years ago and got the mandatory MBA. Only way to get promoted."

"How did you get into the publishing business?" Carl wondered aloud. "And sales, at that."

"Long story. You really don't want to hear it." He raised one of the mugs to his lips and drained half of it in a gulp.

"Can you really get Carl into a lab where he can fix his . . . his . . ."

"It's an electro-optical reader," said Carl.

Malzone knocked off the rest of the beer in mug number one and thunked it down on the table. "You're going to have to get a sexier name for the thing, pal. And, yeah, I can get you into the lab. I think. Lemme make a phone call."

He slid out of the booth with the graceful agility of a trained athlete.

Lori glanced at her wristwatch. "I'll have to be going in a few minutes," she said.

"Going? You're not coming along with me?"

"I'd love to, but I can't. I've got my other job to get to."

"Other job?" Carl felt stupid, hearing himself echo her words.

With a sad little smile Lori explained, "You don't think an editor's salary pays for living in New York, do you?"

"I . . ." Carl shrugged and waved his hands feebly.

"All the editors who live *in* the city have second jobs. It's either that or live in Yonkers or out on the Island someplace. Or New Jersey." She shuddered. "And then you have to get up before dawn and spend half the day travelling to and from your office."

Carl held himself back from replying. But he thought, I'm going to change all that. The electronic book is just the beginning. I'm going to revolutionize the whole business world, all of it. I'm going to put an end to senseless commuting and make the world safe for trees.

"Maryann Quigly weaves baskets and sells them to anybody she sink her hooks into," Lori was explaining. "Didn't you notice them all over the offices upstairs? And Mr. Perkins, the editor-in-chief— uh, the former editor-in-chief—he writes book reviews under several noms de plume and teaches literary criticism at the Old New School."

"What's going to happen to him now that he's lost his position at Bunker Books?" Carl wondered.

"Who? Perkins?" asked Malzone, pushing himself into the other side of the booth, two fresh beer mugs in his hands.

Both Carl and Lori nodded.

"That's all taken care of," Malzone said jovially. "He's landed a job at S&M as head of their juvenile line."

Lori gasped. "I thought Susan Mangrove . . ."

"She's out. They bounced her yesterday. Found out she had a four-year-old niece in Schenectady."

"No!"

"What's wrong with that?" Carl asked.

"She was a children's book editor," answered Ralph with glee. "One of the requirements of a children's book editor is that he, she, or it has never seen or dealt with a child. Ironclad rule."

"Don't listen to him," Lori snapped. Then, to Ralph, she asked, "So what's Susan going to do?"

"She's moving over to take Alex Knox's place at Ballantrye."

"Knox is gone?"

"Yep. He starts Monday as head of Webb's romance and inspirational line."

"Replacing Scarlet Dean."

"Who's taking Max's job, that's right," said Malzone.

Carl's head was spinning, and not from the beer. "It sounds like musical chairs."

"It is," Malzone said. "The average lifetime of an editor in this business is about two years. Some last longer than that, but a lot of 'em don't even hang in that long."

"Two years? Is that all?"

Malzone laughed. "Long enough. It takes roughly two years for the accounting department to figure out that the books the editor is putting out don't sell. Accounting sends word to management, and the poor dufo gets tossed out."

"That's not exactly true," Lori said.

"Close enough. Meanwhile, over at the competition's office across the street, they've just found out that one of their editors has been putting out books for the past two years that don't sell. So they deep-six him. The two unemployed editors switch places. Each one goes to work at the other's old office, where they'll be safe for another two years. And the two publicity departments put out media releases praising their new hire as the genius who's going to lead them out of the wilderness."

"You mean they'll keep on publishing books that don't sell?" asked Carl.

"Not exactly," Lori said.

"Exactly!" Malzone said with some fervor.

"But why does the publishing house keep on putting out books that don't sell?"

"Simple," replied Malzone, almost jovially. "The books are picked by the editors."

Lori started to protest. "Now wait . . ."

Halting her with a lopsided grin, Malzone went on, "The publishing community is like a small town. We all work in the same neighborhood, pretty much. Eat in the same restaurants. Editors move back and forth from one company to another. They all share pretty much the same values, have the same outlook on life." With sudden intensity, he added, "And the editors all publish the same sorts of books, the books that interest *them*."

Lori frowned slightly but said nothing.

"The editors all live in the New York area," Malzone continued. "They all work in a small neighborhood of Manhattan. They think that New York is America. And they publish books that look good in New York, but sink like lead turds once they cross the Hudson."

"They don't sell well?" Carl asked.

"Most books don't sell at all," said Malzone. "Ask the man who's stuck with the job of selling them."

Lori said, "Only a small percentage of the books published earn back the money originally invested in them. Most of them lose money."

"But how can an industry stay in business that way?" Carl asked. He felt genuinely perplexed.

Malzone laughed and quaffed down a huge gulp of beer. "Damned if I know, pal. Damned if I know."

Lori looked at her wristwatch again. "I've really got to go. See you tomorrow, Carl. In my office. Early as you can make it."

Carl got up to let her out of the booth. She reached up and bussed his cheek. He felt confused; did not know how to react, what to do.

"Uh . . . you didn't tell me what your second job is," he mumbled.

Lori smiled sweetly. "Same as it was when we met."

"Belly dancing?" Carl blurted.

Lifting one hand before her face in imitation of a veil, Lori said, "I am Yasmin, the Armenian Dervish. But only from nine to midnight, three nights a week."

Purchase Requisition 98021

Title of Work: *The Terror from Beyond Hell*
Author: Sheldon Stoker
Agent: Murray Swift
Editor: Scarlet Dean (upon arrival)
Contract terms: To be negotiated; offering will be same terms as Stoker's last book
Advance: To be negotiated; offering $1,000,000.00

Purchase Requisition 98022

Title of Work: *Midway Diary*
Author: Ron Clanker (Capt., U.S.N., [Ret.])
Agent: none
Editor: L. Tashkajian
Contract terms: Standard, all rights retained by Bunker Books
Advance: Minimum, $5,000, returnable

Six

Long after the end of the business day, P. Curtis Hawks remained in his office, sitting glumly at his desk, staring out the wide windows as Manhattan turned on its lights to greet the encroaching night.

Bugged my office, he kept repeating to himself as he chewed ceaselessly on his plastic cigar butt. The Old Man has bugged my office. My office. Bugged.

There were wheels within wheels here, he realized. The Old Man, up there in the dotty jungle he had turned his office into, was playing crazy, senile games. Hawks remembered from history when other great tyrants had gone mad: Ivan the Terrible, Hitler, Stalin— they had all gone on paranoid sprees of suspicion and wholesale murder. Even within the publishing industry right here in New York, Kordman and Dyson and even Wanly had all gone nuts toward the end; each one of them pulled their own houses down on top of them.

Weldon was clearly cracking up. One minute he wants to buy out Bunker, the next he doesn't. Then he wants this kid Lewis's invention copied, or stolen, or the guy himself snatched away from Bunker. It's crazy.

Why is the Old Man behaving this way? Hawks asked himself for the thousandth time that evening. Some electronic gadget that shows books on its screen can't be that important. Something else is going on; something he hasn't told me about.

Then it hit him, with the clarity and bone-chilling certainty of absolute truth. *He knows about the warehouse!* Hawks blanched with terror. *He knows about the warehouse!* There was no other explanation for it. The Old Man was toying with him, like a grinning Cheshire cat playing with a very tiny, very terrified mouse.

With a shaking hand, Hawks reached for the telephone. But as soon as his fingers touched the instrument he yanked them away as if they had been scorched by molten lava.

He's bugging my office. Damnation! He's probably tracing all my phone and computer traffic, too.

Pull yourself together, he commanded himself fiercely. You can't let yourself go to pieces. This is life or death, man! It's him against me! Hawks shifted the plastic cigar butt from one side of his mouth to the other.

He's out to get me. Just because of that goddamned warehouse the old bastard is after my ass. Hawks grunted with the realization of it. Despite years of the Old Man's calling him "son" and grooming him to take over the top slot at Tarantula, Hawks could not escape the conclusion that the only thing he was at the very top of was Weldon W. Weldon's personal hit list. One little mistake. That's all it takes in this business.

Well, two can play at that game, by god. If the senile old bastard wants to do away with me, I've got to do away with him first.

But how? he asked himself. There's nobody in the whole corporation that you can trust. Anybody might be a spy for the Old Man. You'll have to get outside help.

Which meant going to New Jersey and having a talk with the Beast from the East.

"... so I'm sitting there, just a skinny kid right out of the navy, it's my first job . . ."

Ralph Malzone was talking while Carl bent over the exposed innards of his electro-optical reader. They sat side by side at a laboratory bench strewn with tools, wires, and flea-sized electronic components. Both men wore disposable white lab coats and silly-looking hats made of paper. This was a clean-room facility, and they even had to put paper booties over their shoes before Malzone's friend would reluctantly allow them in.

Carl had a surgeon's magnifiers clamped over his eyes and a pair of ultrasensitive micromanipulators in his white-gloved hands as he operated on his failed machine, trying to bring the dead back to life.

Malzone was passing the time by recounting his early adventures as a route salesman for a magazine distribution company.

"So I'm sitting there in what passes for a waiting room, a crummy hallway piled high with old magazines waiting for the shredder. Just this one rickety bench; I think he stole it from a kids' playground. All of a sudden, from inside the guy's office I hear him holler, 'Nobody's gonna give *me* a fuckin' ultimatum!' And then a pistol shot!"

"Jeez," muttered Carl.

"Yeah. And this salesman comes whizzing out of the office like his pants are on fire. The owner walks out after him with a smoking Smith & Wesson in his hand!"

Carl grunted. He had just dropped an electro-optical chip out of the micromanipulator's tiny fingers. Malzone took it as a comment on his unfolding story.

"Now remember, *I* had been sent there to give him an ultimatum, too. The sonofabitch hadn't been paying any of his bills for months. So there he is, the smoking gun in his hand and fire in his eyes. And he sees me sitting there, just about to crap in my pants."

"Uh-huh." Carl picked up the chip and deftly inserted it where it belonged, at last.

"'Whaddaya you want?' he asks me, waving the gun in my general direction. Before I can answer, he says, 'You're the new kid from General, ain'tcha?' I sort of nod, and he tucks the gun in his pants and says, 'Come on, kid, I'll show you what this business is all about.' He takes me to the bar next door and we spend the rest of the afternoon drinking beer."

Without looking up at him, Carl asked, "Did he ever pay you what he owed?"

"Oh sure, eventually. He got to be one of the best customers on my route."

"That's good," said Carl.

Malzone's lanky face frowned slightly, but from behind his magnifiers Carl could no more see the expression on his face than a myopic dolphin could see the carvings of Mt. Rushmore. Malzone sank into silence. The two men were alone in the electronics lab. It was well after midnight. Silent and dim in the corridors beyond the lab's long windows. Silent and dim inside the clean room, too, except for the pool of intense light Carl had focused onto his work area from a swing-neck lamp.

The older man studied Carl intently as he worked. His stories about his youthful adventures in the sales end of the publishing business had been a way to pass the time, and to hide the terrible smoldering jealousy he felt burning in his guts. For wiry, grinning, gregarious Ralph Malzone was secretly, totally, hopelessly in love with Lori. He had never told her how he felt. He had never even worked up the courage to ask her for a date. But as he watched Carl working on electronic circuitry that was far beyond his own knowledge, Ralph realized that this guy was Lori's own age and they had known each other in Boston, before Lori had come to New York, before he had met her and fallen so hard for her. He heard someone sigh like a moonstruck moose. Himself.

"Maybe I should go out and get us a coupla beers," Malzone suggested.

"Not for me. Anyway, I think it's just about finished."

"Yeah?" The older man brightened.

Carl held his breath as he inserted the final filament lead. "Yeah," he said in a shaky whisper. "Yeah, I think that's it."

He straightened up painfully, his spine suddenly telling him that he had spent too many hours bent over his labor. Taking off the magnifiers, Carl blinked several times, then rubbed his eyes.

"Will it work now?" Malzone asked.

"It should."

Still, Carl's hands trembled slightly as he snapped the cover shut on the oblong case and turned it over so that its screen glinted in the lamp's powerful light.

He touched the first keypad with his index finger. The screen sprang to life instantly, glowing with color to reveal the title page of *Rain Makes Applesauce*.

Carl let out the breath he had not realized he'd been holding in. It worked. It worked!

He picked up the glowing box and offered it to Malzone, grinning. It looked much smaller in the sales manager's long-fingered, big-knuckled hands.

"What do I do?" Malzone asked.

"Just touch the green button to move ahead a page. Hold it down and it will riffle through the pages for you until you take your finger off. Then it'll stop. If you want a specific page, tap in the number on the little keyboard on the right."

Malzone spent several minutes paging back and forth. Looking over his shoulder, Carl saw that the screen was working fine: everything in clear focus. The illustrations looked beautifully sharp.

"Nice gadget," Malzone said at last, handing it back to Carl.

"Is that all you can say?"

Malzone hunched his shoulders. "It's an electronic way of looking at a book. Like a pocket TV, only you can see books with it instead of TV programs. Might make a nice fad gift for the Christmas season."

"But it's a lot more than that!" Carl said fervently. "This is going to replace books printed on paper! This is the biggest breakthrough since the printing press!"

"Nahhh." Malzone shook his head, his russet brows knitted. "It's a nice idea, but it's not going to replace books. Who'd buy a machine that's got to cost at least a hundred bucks when you can buy a hardcover book for fifty? And a paperback for less than ten?"

"Who would buy a hardcover or a paperback," Carl retorted, "when an electronic book will cost pennies?"

Malzone grunted, just as if someone had whacked him in the gut with a pool cue.

"Pennies?"

"Sure, the reader—this device, here—is going to cost more than a half-dozen books. But once you own one you can get your books electronically. Over the phone, if you like. The most expensive books there are will cost less than a dollar!"

"Now wait a minute. You mean . . ."

"No paper!" Carl exulted. "You don't have to chop down trees and make paper and haul tons of the stuff to the printing presses and then haul the printed books to the stores. You move electrons and photons instead of paper! It's cheap and efficient."

For a long moment Malzone said nothing. Then he sighed a very heavy sigh. "You're saying that a publisher won't need printers, paper, ink, wholesalers, route salesmen, district managers, truck drivers—not even bookstores?"

"The whole thing can be done electronically," Carl enthused. "Shop for books by TV. Buy them over the phone. Transmit them anywhere on Earth almost instantaneously, straight to the customer."

Malzone glanced around the shadows of the clean room uneasily. In a near whisper he told Carl, "Jesus Christ, kid, you're going to get both of us killed."

And deep within his innermost primitive self he thought, Maybe I ought to knock you off myself and save us both a lot of misery.

Typical Editor's Day

(Scheduled)

9:00 A.M.: Arrive in office.
9:05 A.M.: Read mail. Answer memos.
10:30 A.M.: Production meeting.

11:30 A.M.: Editorial board meeting.
12:30-1:30 P.M.: Lunch.
1:35 P.M.: Review readers' reports.
4:00 P.M.: Answer mail, phone calls.
5:00 P.M.: Leave for home, bringing manuscripts to read.

(Actual)

9:00 A.M.: Gobble breakfast.
9:05 A.M.: Catch train to office.
10:30 A.M.: Arrive office (tell them train was late).
10:35 A.M. Production meeting (argue with managing editor and art director).
11:15 A.M.: Coffee break.
11:30 A.M.: Editorial board meeting.
2:00 P.M.: Go to lunch (editorial board meeting ran late).
4:24 P.M.: Back from lunch with author and agent (cocktails, two bottles of wine plus brandy afterwards).
4:30-5:00 P.M.: Aspirin and Maalox.
5:00-6:30 P.M.: Catch up on office gossip.
6:30-7:30 P.M.: Drinks with the gang (why try to fight the rush hour?).
7:40 P.M.: Take train home (the Battle of Lexington Ave.).
8:45 P.M.: Fall asleep over TV dinner.
11:30 P.M.-12:30 A.M.: *The Tonight Show Starring Johnny Carson II.*

Seven

The following morning, a bleary-eyed Carl Lewis sat before Mrs. Alba Blanca Bunker, the publisher of Bunker Books. Her husband, of course, was sole owner of the company—almost. A few shares of stock were scattered here and there, but the controlling interest was firmly in the hands of Pandro T. Bunker, his wife, and his only son, P.T. Jr.

The Boss sat behind her petite desk, with Junior at his mother's side, a crafty little smile on his narrow-eyed face. Mrs. Bunker was, as usual, dressed entirely in white. Her office was all in white as well: the dainty Louis-Something-or-Other furniture was bleached white, the carpeting looked like softly tufted white angora wool, the walls and ceiling were white cream. Carl had once been trapped in a sudden blizzard in the (where else?) White Mountains years earlier, and the effect of the Boss's office was much the same. Whiteout. Almost snowblind.

But warmer. Much warmer. Golden sunlight streamed through the windows of the corner office. And Mrs. Bunker was smiling pleasantly as she tapped away at Carl's invention, happily reading *Rain Makes Applesauce* from beginning to end.

Absolute silence reigned. Not even the crackle of a page being turned, of course. Carl watched the almost childlike expression on Mrs. Bunker's face as she read through the delightful book and studied its fascinating illustrations. Junior peered over her shoulder now and then, but mostly he seemed to be staring at Carl as if trying to size him up. Carl felt that uncomfortable sensation a man gets when he's confronted by a determined haberdashery salesman.

Lori sat beside him, close enough almost to touch. Their chairs were delicate, graceful, yet surprisingly comfortable.

The suit Mrs. Bunker was wearing seemed identical to the one she wore the previous day, to Carl. Her jewelry was different, however, although still all gold. Junior wore jeans and a ragged biker's T-shirt, complete with artificial sweat and grease stains. Its front bore a Bunker Books logo. Lori was in a simple wide-yoked light tan dress that showed her smooth shoulders to advantage.

Carl felt distinctly grubby. He had grabbed a few hours' sleep in the hotel room that Bunker had provided, and then climbed back into the same slacks and tweed jacket he had worn the day before. Except for one change of underwear and shirt, that was all the clothes he had brought with him.

Mrs. Bunker finished *Rain Makes Applesauce* at last, and put Carl's reader down on the immaculate surface of her little desk.

"It's a beautiful book," she said. "I noticed from the copyright date that it's almost fifty years old. Is it in the public domain yet? Can we reprint it?"

Surprised by her question, Carl stammered, "Gosh, I . . . it never occurred to me that you would want . . ."

"That's not really why we're here, Mrs. Bee," said Lori with equal amounts of politeness and firmness in her voice.

"Oh. Of course. I just thought that if the book is in the public domain we could publish it without the expense of paying the author."

"Or the illustrator," Junior chimed in.

Mother turned a pleased smile upon son.

"But how did you like the electro-optical reader?" Carl blurted, unable to stand the suspense any further.

Mrs. Bunker smiled again, but differently. "It's *wonderful*. It's everything you said it would be. The pages are crisp and clear, and the illustrations come out *beautifully*. I've never seen such brilliant colors in print. Well—let's say seldom, instead of never."

Reaching into his jacket pocket, Carl pulled out a half dozen more wafers and spread them out on the Boss's desk.

"Here we have *War and Peace, Asimov's Guide to Everything*, this year's *World Almanac*"—he pointed each one out with his index finger—"and these three contain the complete novels of James Michener."

"Really? All in those little disks?" Mrs. Bunker asked.

"All in these six wafers," Carl agreed. "I could provide you with the complete *Encyclopedia Britannica* in a pocketful more. Or two of Victor Hugo's novels in a single wafer."

"Hugo? Who publishes him?" asked Mrs. Bunker.

"Hey, Mom," Junior replied, "he does plays. He was big on Broadway the year I was born. Don't you remember, Dad almost named me John Val John." He pronounced the name like a New Yorker, and favored his mother with a condescending smile that pitied her lack of literary lore.

Carl glanced at Lori, who kept a perfectly straight face.

"It's a wonderful invention," Mrs. Bunker said again, "and I think you're right—this can transform the publishing industry. I believe that Bunker Books can become the nation's number-one publisher if we move ahead swiftly with this."

Carl felt a surge of—what? Satisfaction. Relief. Joy. Justification for all the months he had spent half starving and working twenty hours a day to create the electro-optical marvel that rested modestly on the desk of this woman in white. He felt gratitude, too. For deep within him, buried in the innermost convolutions of his mind, there lurked a stubborn fear that his invention was worthless, that any half-trained TV repair man could have figured it out, that it was nothing but a toy without any real value whatsoever.

But she thinks it's great, Carl told himself. She thinks it's going to transform the publishing industry, he rejoiced triumphantly to that inner voice of fear.

And the voice answered, Maybe so. She also thinks Victor Hugo is a Broadway playwright.

Carl found that he had to swallow a lump in his throat before he could say, "I'm very pleased, Mrs. Bunker. How do you want to proceed from here?"

"Proceed?" Her face suddenly looked blank.

"Do we sign a consulting agreement, or do you want me to become a contractor to Bunker Books? What kind of payments will Bunker Books make for the invention? What rights do you want to purchase? That sort of thing."

With a glance toward her son, Mrs. Bunker answered, "I'm not empowered to make any commitments of that sort. Only Mr. Bunker himself can do that."

"Then I suppose I'll have to demonstrate the device to him," Carl said, reaching for the reader.

Mrs. Bunker put on a smile that showed some teeth. "Couldn't you let me borrow it overnight? I'll show it to my husband this evening."

With alarm bells tingling in every nerve, Carl slowly slid the reader to the edge of the desk and gripped it in both his hands. "This is the only prototype in existence. I'm afraid I can't let it out of my sight. I'd be glad to show it to Mr. Bunker myself. . . ."

Mrs. Bee bit her lower lip. "That may be difficult. He's such a busy man. . . ."

Holding the reader firmly in his lap, Carl gestured with his other hand to the six wafers still resting on the desk top. "I can let you show the wafers to him. To give him an idea of how small and cheap books can be made."

"But he won't be able to read them without your device, will he?"

"I'm afraid not."

"What's the matter, don't you trust us?" Junior asked. His tone was light enough, almost bantering. But there was no levity in his face.

Carl replied, "This isn't personal. I decided before I left Boston that I would not let the prototype out of my sight."

A cloud of silence dimmed the all-white office.

"I'd be glad to show it to Mr. Bunker personally," Carl repeated.

"I suppose that's what we'll have to do, then," said Mrs. Bunker. "I'll see what I can arrange."

Feeling vastly relieved, Carl shot to his feet. "Thank you! You won't regret it."

He put out his hand to her, still staunchly grasping the prototype in his left hand. She made a sweet smile without getting up from her chair and touched his hand briefly, like a queen dispensing a blessing. Junior's eyes never left the device until Carl tucked it back into his black courier case.

Lori and Carl got as far as the door. Mrs. Bunker called, "Oh, Lori, dear. Could you stay a moment longer? There's something I want to discuss with you."

Carl stepped outside into the busy corridor where editors and other unidentified frenzied objects were dashing about. Mrs. Bunker had no secretary, no outer office. Bunker Books was a tightly run ship where computers and communications were used in place of salaried employees, Carl realized. It's criminal to use human beings in lackey jobs like secretarial work, he told himself. Nothing but ostentatious show for the people who hire them and degrading drudgery for the people who take such jobs. Electrons work more efficiently. And cheaper. Any job that can be done twice the same way *ought* to be done by a machine.

Then why do they have editors? he asked himself. Computers can check a manuscript's spelling and grammar much more thoroughly than any human being can. What do editors do that computers can't?

His ruminations were interrupted by Lori's stepping through the Boss's office door and out into the corridor. A grim-faced gray-haired man clutching a long trailing sweep of narrow white sheets of paper fluttering behind him like the tail of a kite bolted past them like an underweight halfback being pursued by the first-string defense. He brushed so close to Lori that she jumped into Carl's arms.

"Who was that?" he asked, releasing her as the gray flash disappeared down the hall.

"Grenouille, the assistant managing editor," Lori said without moving from his side. "He's always in a rush."

Carl shook his head. "This is an odd place."

"Isn't it, though?" Lori laughed.

As they headed back toward her office, Lori said, "How's your hotel room?"

He shrugged. "It's a hotel room. Okay, I guess. It's walking distance to the office."

"My apartment's down in the Village. How about letting me cook you dinner tonight?"

"Fine!"

"And then you can come and watch me dance."

Carl tried to stop his face from reddening, but he could feel his cheeks turning hot. "Uh, okay, sure."

Lori grinned up at him.

Alba Blanca Bunker sat on the edge of the enormous round waterbed waiting for her husband. She was tired. It had been a hectic, exhausting day. The new line of historic novels was not selling well. It had seemed so *right*: a line of novels based on true history, the actual deeds and romantic exploits of some of history's greatest figures—Cary Grant, Lynn Redgrave, Willie Nelson, Barbara Walters. But despite a six-million-dollar publicity campaign, the books were moldering in the warehouses. Nobody seemed to want them.

She sighed deeply and lay back on the waterbed, allowing her filmy white peignoir to drape itself dramatically across the tiger-striped sheets. She studied the effect in the overhead mirror. This bedroom had been their fantasy place when they had first built this home out of a converted warehouse next to the Disneydome, years earlier. With voice command either she or her husband could convert the holographic decor from jungle to desert, from underwater to outer space. With a sad little smile she remembered how the circuitry had blown itself out in a shower of sparks during one particularly vocal bout of lovemaking.

Nothing like that had happened for many years now. The room was a cool forest green, the scent of pine in the whispering breeze, the bint of a full moon silvering the drawn draperies of the window.

She knew where her husband was. In his office talking to Beijing, trying desperately to nail down the deal that would open up the Chinese market. A billion potential customers! It could mean the salvation of Bunker Books.

Or could this MIT whiz kid be their salvation? His invention worked, there was no denying it. How much would he want for it? How much would it cost to start a whole new line of operations, electronic books instead of paper ones? *That's* why we need the China deal, she told herself, to provide the capital for developing the electronic book. Otherwise . . .

There was still the tender offer from Tarantula Enterprises. Pandro would never sell his company. Never. He had built it practically from scratch, with nothing but the ten million his father had loaned him. Bunker Books was *his* creation, and he would go to hell and burn eternally before he would sell the company or any part of it.

Still—if she could get him to pretend to consider the Tarantula offer, they might be able to raise some capital from a few insiders down on Wall Street. No, that wouldn't work. Pandro wouldn't stoop to such chicanery. He would plug ahead stubbornly trying to close the China deal with those elusive, wily orientals. She did not trust men who spoke so politely, yet never quite seemed to do what they said they would.

The electronic book. We've *got* to have it. And somehow find the money to develop it. Nothing else matters. It's either that or bankruptcy.

She lay perfectly still on the beautiful bed in the beautiful room, waiting for her husband to come to her while her mind searched out a way to avoid the yawning black abyss that was ready to swallow Bunker Books. No path appeared safe; there was no way out of the financial chasm awaiting them. Except perhaps the electronic book. Perhaps.

She fell asleep waiting for her husband to leave his work and come to bed. She dreamed of electronic books and showers of golden coins pattering gently over the two of them as they lay coiled in a passionate embrace.

Murder Three

John Watson was a professor of sociology at the New New School, at Central Park North. The neat rows of condominiums marched northward through Harlem, each lovingly renovated building flanked on both sides by blockwide vegetable gardens, also lovingly tended by the neighborhood residents. Watson could have taken considerable pride in the role he had played in turning Harlem into a model of peace and prosperity.

All his younger years he had battled the city, the state government, the feds, and the people of Harlem themselves. His enemies had been hopelessness and resistance to change: the indifference of the masses and the brutal opposition of the dope peddlers and slumlords and crooked city officials who made their millions out of the sweat and suffering of Harlem's people.

His allies had been the mothers who had seen their children killed by narcotics, or guns, or knives. And the brighter youngsters who sought a way out of the endless cycle of misery and poverty. They had little power. But they had guts and brains. Then John Watson hit upon a stroke of genius. He made allies of the building contractors and their associated trade unions. Rebuilding Harlem made jobs for nearly a generation of carpenters, plumbers, electricians, masons, truck drivers. It made hundreds of millions for the companies that employed them. The money came from taxes, of course: local, state, and federal. But the payoff, as John Watson spent twenty years explaining to appropriations committees, would be a Harlem that was productive, a Harlem that housed taxpayers, not welfare cases. Not criminals and diseased addicts.

Now, as he strolled along Martin Luther King Boulevard toward Rev. Jesse Jackson Park, Watson took no small measure of satisfaction in the happiness that he saw all around him. Harlem was not heaven; it was not even the Garden of Eden. But it was no longer the rotting, drug-infested ghetto that it had been when he was a child growing up in it.

It was a considerable shock, therefore, when a strange white man stepped out of a car parked in a clearly marked bus stop zone and sank a switchblade knife into John Watson's heart. He died almost instantly, while the white man got back into his car and calmly drove away. None of the stunned witnesses could provide the police with the car's license number, probably because the license plate had been carefully smeared with dirt beforehand.

It was a monument to John Watson's life work that this foul murder was treated as any other would be, both by the police and the media. Everyone was shocked. No one suggested that such an event was only to be expected in Harlem.

Eight

Carl sat sweating in the smoky Greek nightclub on Ninth Avenue, watching a fleshy half-naked young woman performing the artfully erotic oriental ritual known in the West as the belly dance.

The place was only half-full, but almost all of the customers were men. Most of them sat up at the bar itself, squinting through the haze of cigarette smoke and muttering an occasional "Yasoo!" at a particularly stimulating movement by the dancer up on the tiny platform that passed for a stage. A three-piece band—reedy clarinet, big-bellied stringed bouzouki, and the inevitable drums—played weaving snake charmer's music. Now and then the drummer would sing in a wavering, almost yodelling high-pitched tenor.

Carl sat alone at a table near the stage, close enough to smell the dancers' heavy perfumes and feel the breeze from their veils as they twirled about. Men staggered up to the edge of the stage now and then to press dollar bills into the dancer's bra or g-string. Carl had never seen that before. In Cambridge, where he had met Lori, the belly-dancing was more of an Armenian clan gathering. Everybody danced before the night was over, linking hands in a long human chain that wended around the restaurant and, sometimes, right out into the street.

But that had been in Cambridge. Now he was in New York. They played by different rules here. It had been a dizzying, stupefying couple of days. Now, as he sipped alternately at a water tumbler filled with milky iced ouzo and a tiny cup of powerful, muddy Greek coffee, Carl wondered how long it would take before P.T. Bunker, the founder and president of Bunker Books, would condescend to meet with him.

"Mrs. Bee wants me to entice you into turning the prototype over to her, so she can show it to Mr. Bee," Lori had told him in the cab as they rode to the club.

"She *what*?" Carl had snapped.

Patting his knee, Lori said soothingly, "Relax. I'm going to do no such thing. If P.T. Bunker wants to see your prototype, he'll have to see you along with it."

Carl felt his misgivings ease away. Slightly.

"It's just that it's almost impossible to get to see Mr. Bunker. He's so busy all the time."

"What about when he comes to the office?"

"He *never* comes to the office," Lori had said. "We never see him. Mrs. Bunker runs the office and he stays in their home down in the Lower East Side."

"That's a pretty posh neighborhood, isn't it?" Carl had asked. "Near the Disneydome and all."

Lori smiled bitterly. "Listen: I know plenty of starving writers, hungry artists, editors who have to take moonlighting jobs just to pay the rent on their studio apartments. But publishers live in posh neighborhoods and drink champagne every night."

No champagne for me, Carl told himself as he took another sip of the ouzo. It was powerful stuff, even iced. Strong flavor like licorice. The waiter had taken one look at Carl and decided he did not look Greek. When he brought the first ouzo, he also brought a stainless-steel bowl filled with ice cubes. "You don't drink it straight," he insisted. "You put ice in it. No friend of Yasmin's is going to throw up on this floor!"

The waiter was watching him now, from the shadows in the corner of the room, a dark scowl of suspicion on his swarthy mustachioed face. There was a table full of young, broad-shouldered men on that side of the stage, laughing and drinking and hollering to the dancer in Greek. They looked like stevedores from the nearby docks. Muscular types, shirts opened to their belt buckles to show off their hairy chests.

A crash from up near the bar made Carl swivel his head. The men up there, older, balder, paunchier, were laughing uproariously. One of them raised his emptied glass over his head and smashed it to the floor. Everybody laughed and applauded.

The ouzo should be relaxing me, Carl told himself. I ought to be loosening up, like everyone else. Instead he felt tense, wary, as if he had been trapped alone in a strange and dangerous land.

The dancer finished with a flourish and a hearty round of "Yasoos" and applause, then scurried offstage with dollar bills flapping from her costume.

The music died. Muttered conversations and occasional bursts of laughter were the only sounds in the club. Carl finished his glass of ouzo, then sipped carefully at the coffee. When he began to taste the mud at the bottom of the little cup, he put it down and signalled to the waiter.

The swarthy man was at his side like a shot. "Another coffee?"

"When does Yasmin come on?"

"She is next."

Carl pulled in a deep breath. His nose wrinkled at the acrid smell of cigarette smoke. "Another ouzo," he ordered.

"And coffee?"

"No. Just the ouzo."

"You don't like our coffee? Too strong for you?"

Carl looked up at him. "I love your coffee."

"Then I bring you another cup."

The man was being protective, Carl realized. "Okay. Another cup of coffee. And another glass of ouzo."

"Hokay."

The waiter also brought a glass full of ice cubes, with a fierce scowl that told Carl he would not tolerate his drinking the ouzo straight.

The band started tuning up again as Carl was pouring the clear liquor over the ice and watching it turn pale milky white, wondering what chemical reaction caused the change in color. Then the club's bass-heavy loudspeaker announced: "And now, our next Oriental dancer—Yasmin! The Armenian Dervish!"

It was Lori all right. She was beautiful. Bare flesh as smooth and flawless as the most perfect fantasy. She moved sensuously, sinuously, hips weaving a spell that soon had Carl breathing hard.

The first part of her dance was all right. The dancers all started with see-through veils that really hid nothing, but at least discouraged admirers from trying to stuff money into their costumes.

Carl gulped at his watered ouzo as slowly, tantalizingly, Yasmin removed her veils. She smiled at Carl as if to say she were dancing especially for him. But although his eyes were riveted on her, he could hear the raucous remarks coming from the table across the way.

Carl felt every nerve in him tightening. It's just their way, he told himself. They're not being crude or obscene. Still, as Lori danced, he found himself glaring at the table full of young stevedores.

She moved toward their side of the stage and, sure enough, one of the hairy grinning apes stood up and tucked a dollar bill in the g-string circling Lori's hips. She danced away from them, back toward Carl, bending over him slightly so that her breasts swayed with the music.

Carl was panting now. Then another one of the stevedores jumped up on the stage with a fistful of bills and started pushing them into Lori's bra. She looked slightly alarmed.

Before he could think, Carl was on the stage and pushing the young Greek away from her. The music stopped. All the other stevedores got to their feet, fists clenched. The mustachioed waiter dashed up onto the stage and stood between Carl and the others. The rest of the waiters gathered around.

Carl found himself being politely but firmly led by both arms out of the club and out into the street. His waiter shook his head sadly at him and said, "Not enough ice."

It was drizzling. Carl felt like a perfect idiot. And he also felt furious that there were men in there pawing Lori's body. And she was letting them do it! He started walking in the general direction of his hotel, letting the drizzling rain cool him off. He imagined it sizzling to steam as it struck his body, he felt so heated.

After what seemed like an hour's walking he found himself back at the same club. I must've walked around the block, he realized. Like a man lost in the desert, he had made a circle and returned to his starting point.

Briefly he wondered what would happen if the half dozen or so stevedores came out the door right at this instant. But instead, when the club's front door swung open, Lori stepped out, looking worried and slightly dishevelled, bundled in a beige raincoat.

"Carl!"

He started to say hello as casually as he knew how, but his throat was raw and it came out as a croaking "Hi."

"Whatever possessed you . . . ?"

"I got mad."

She did not seem angry. In fact, she was smiling. "You decided to protect my honor?"

"Something like that."

Almost, she laughed. But she caught herself. "Come on, you can walk me home." She pulled a miniature umbrella from her capacious shoulder bag and opened it. Carl had to snuggle very close to her just to keep his head under its tiny red canopy.

Quite seriously, Lori asked, "Don't you know that the waiters protect all the dancers? This is a respectable club; they don't allow any nasty stuff."

"Just feeling you up onstage, in front of everybody."

"That's nothing. It's like leaving a tip for the waiter."

"Do you enjoy having strange guys paw you?"

For a moment she said nothing. Then, in a small voice, Lori told him, "I'd enjoy it more if someone I knew very well pawed me."

Carl gulped and asked, "How far is it to your apartment?" It was a studio apartment on the second floor of an old redbrick high rise in the Gramercy Park area. Once the neighborhood had been prime real estate, but it had been going steadily downhill for a generation. Still, Lori assured Carl, the building was safe. The automated security system kept strangers from entering the lobby, and the bars on the windows discouraged burglars.

Carl did not notice the automated security system or the bars on the windows or anything other than Lori, the nearness of her, the warmth of her, the scent of her. In his mind he heard swirling reedy music and saw her dancing for him alone. They danced together, the oldest dance of all, entwined in each other on a foldout bed until he fell into an exhausted sleep.

Lori lay next to Carl's peacefully slumbering body. It smoldered like hot lava, and she pressed herself against him. He was out like a light, poor baby. Too much ouzo, she diagnosed. She smiled at the cracked ceiling in the shadows of her little apartment. The noise from the traffic of Third Avenue and the wailing sirens of the ambulances from the hospital across the way did not bother her now.

But something else did. The novel. *The* novel. The greatest piece of literature she had ever read, in manuscript. Not as good as Tolstoy or Proust or even Dickens, but as good as anything ever written in America. As good as Hemingway or Twain or Fitzgerald, even when he was sober. Better.

They'll never let me publish it. They'll say it's not commercial. It's not a *Thorn Birds* or a *Shogun*. It's merely the finest piece of literature written by any American since Christopher goddamn Columbus stumbled ashore. And there's no market for fine literature. That's what they'll say.

But, Lori told herself, if I bring them Carl's electronic book, if the company gets rich on the idea that I brought to them, then I'll have the power to publish what I want to. I'll be able to bring this great work of literature to print.

Carl groaned softly and shifted in the bed. Lori gazed at his naked body, still sheened with perspiration. I'm using you, she said silently to him. She felt a pang of remorse at the realization. But it's all in the service of great art, she rationalized, great literature.

And besides, she almost giggled, I think I really do love you, you big silly knight in shining armor.

Capt. Ron Clanker, U.S.N. (Ret.)
c/o Army/Navy Home
Chelsea MA 02150

Dear Capt. Clanker:

It is my great pleasure to tell you that Bunker Books will be happy to publish your novel, *Midway Diary*. As you will see in the enclosed contract forms, we offer you an advance of $5,000 against all rights to the work.

Let me offer my personal congratulations. I think you have written a fine, sensitive novel that still contains stirring action. It is the best such work I've read since Richard McKenna's *The Sand Pebbles*. I only hope it sells as well!

Sincerely yours,
Lori Tashkajian
Fiction Editor

Nine

Two men spent the rest of the week in an agony of suspense.

Carl Lewis felt like an astronaut lost in the dark vacuum of space, hanging weightless and alone, waiting for rescue. P.T. Bunker had agreed to see him, but not today. He was busy. Tomorrow. When the next day came, it was the same story. Sorry, Mr. Bunker is engaged in some very delicate negotiations and cannot be disturbed.

Mrs. Bunker was pleasant, even sweet, to Carl as he came by the office every day. Junior kept casting a shifty eye on Carl whenever they bumped into one another in the corridor. Each afternoon Carl went back to his hotel room, wondering if he should ask Lori to dinner, wondering if their night together was the result of ouzo or true love or just animal passion.

For her part, Lori did not mention their night of lovemaking, although she smiled at Carl warmly and cast him long-lashed glances as if she expected him to make the next move. And he was not certain what his next move should be.

So he waited for his moment with P.T. Bunker. And waited.

Twenty floors higher in the Synthoil Tower, P. Curtis Hawks anticipated the weekend with barely concealed frenzy. He was not waiting for someone else to make himself available. Hawks yearned

for the day, Saturday, when he did not have to be in the office. When
he could sneak out to New Jersey without the Old Man knowing it.
When he could start the machinery that would eventually remove
Weldon W. Weldon and install himself as CEO of Tarantula
Enterprises—the head spider.

Saturday dawned like a scene out of Edgar Allan Poe: dark and
dreary. Rain slanted down from black clouds. The perfect day for
sleeping late. But Hawks was up and out of his Westchester County
house by seven, leaving his lumpy overweight wife snoring soundly
in her bed, her usual tray full of tranquilizers on her night table in
easy reach.

It never occurred to Hawks that the same technology that could
turn his office into a veritable Hollywood sound studio could also
keep track of his private automobile. An electronic chip the size of a
fingernail paring could send a signal to a satellite orbiting more man
22,000 miles high, which in turn could pinpoint the car's position
anywhere in the Western Hemisphere. If Hawks had realized that, it
probably would have affected his driving.

As it was, he sped his heavy Citroën-Mercedes down practically
empty throughways in the dreary pelting rain, crossed the Hudson
on the Tappan Zee Bridge, and plunged into New Jersey. Within an
hour he was at the warehouse.

His warehouse. The primary storage area and distribution center
for Webb Press's books and magazines. Hawks's personal, concrete
monument to himself. His albatross.

It was a long, low, gray concrete structure, more reminiscent of the
bunkers and gun emplacements of the Siegfried Line than a publisher's
warehouse. Rows of big trucks, each emblazoned with the stylized
spiderweb of Webb Press on their flanks (and a small representation
of a tarantula at the edge of the web), lined the parking area. The
loading docks were shut tight. The place looked empty and deserted.

Hawks pulled his big sedan up to the front entrance, beneath the
marquee that he had personally designed. It was rusting already,
even though he had specified that it be made of stainless steel
throughout.

Ignoring the streaks of ignominy defacing his creation, Hawks
trudged the few feet from his car to the warehouse's front door,
huddled inside his trenchcoat against the gusting wet wind.

He pushed at the door. Locked.

He tapped at the security buzzer.

"Name, please?" asked the security computer in the hard, no-nonsense voice of a retired cop.

"Hawks. P. Curtis Hawks."

"Just a moment for voiceprint identification, please."

Hawks fidgeted in the rain that slanted in under the canopy. A leak in the supposedly stainless steel dripped into a puddle that spanned the front doorway like a miniature moat. Hawks's immaculate Argentinean boots, with their clever inner soles and heels that raised him two inches taller than he deserved, were getting soaked and ruined.

"I'm sorry, sir. Voiceprint does not match."

"Whattaya mean it doesn't match!" Hawks shouted at the little speaker grille. "I'm P. Curtis Hawks. I'm the president of this goddamn company! Open this fucking door or I'll replace you with a Radio Shack robot, you goddamn stupid mother—"

The computer's flat voice cut through. "Voiceprint identification accepted, sir."

The door popped open.

Muttering to himself, Hawks stepped through and out of the rain. Goddamn idiot computer doesn't recognize my voice unless I scream at it. Who the hell set up the voiceprint IDs, anyway?

Fuming and steaming, Hawks stomped through the carpeted reception area and pushed through a steel fire door. The warehouse spread out before him, silent and still, a vast windowless conglomeration of row after row of twenty-foot-high shelving on which rested huge cartons filled with nothing but books. Even taller piles of magazines, neatly baled and wrapped in impervious protective plastic, lay in long rows on the floor. They were not on shelves because there was not enough shelf space for both Webb Press's books *and* magazines. In his personal direction of the warehouse's design and construction, Hawks had badly underestimated the space needed to store all of Webb's many publications. The brand-new warehouse was far too small the day it opened.

And dangerous.

Hawks had insisted on a completely automated warehouse. "We have the technology," he had snapped. "Let's not be afraid to use it."

So there were no human workers in the warehouse, in theory. All the lifting and carrying and sorting was done by clever robots. In theory. Overhead conveyor belts whisked heavy cartons of books from one end of the warehouse to the other with swift, silent efficiency. The only people working there were up in the control center, where they pushed buttons from the comfort of padded chairs. In theory.

In practice the robots were not quite clever enough. They could not reach the shelves higher than ten feet off the concrete floor, and not even the most patient Japanese technicians could teach them to climb like monkeys. The warehouse operators had to hire teenagers and unemployed laborers for that. To keep the facts secret from higher management, these employees were listed in the personnel files as assistant truck drivers. Once the Teamsters got wind of that, of course, they had to be *paid* as assistant truck drivers.

Hawks's footsteps echoed off the concrete floor as he made his way across the warehouse toward the control center. Should have placed it on the same side of the building as the front entrance and reception area, he told himself. I'll know better next time.

He looked warily above him as he crossed the shadow of one of the overhead conveyor belts. It was not in operation, but still, caution was the watchword. At top speed the conveyors developed a slight wobble, just enough to send a heavy carton of books toppling down to the floor below now and then. The concrete was chipped where the cartons had landed. And there were several chalked outlines of human figures, workers who had been conked by falling cartons. Some wiseass Puerto Rican had started putting up little crosses at the spots where people had been killed, but Hawks had put a stop to *that*.

The warehouse was costing Webb a fortune. The accident insurance claims alone were enough to keep the company in the red. If the Old Man ever started wondering why so many assistant truck drivers were receiving accident benefits, Hawks might end up working in the warehouse himself.

All the more reason to get the Old Man out of the picture. For good.

With grim resolve, Hawks climbed the clanging metal stairs that led up to the control room. He pushed open the heavy, acoustically insulated door, and saw that the Beast from the East was already there, smiling at him.

Vinnie DeAngelo had won his nickname many years earlier, when he had been in charge of Webb's magazine circulation for the western region of the country. Headquartered in Denver, responsible for getting Webb's magazines prominently displayed on every newsstand between the Mississippi and the Pacific coast, Vinnie had instituted a reign of terror among wholesalers, distributors, truck drivers, and newsstand operators.

He looked fearsome. Six feet even, in every direction. Built like a block of concrete. Absolutely no neck at all; his shoulders grew out of his ears, which were strangely petite and a shell-like pink. A nose that had been broken so many times it looked like a hiker's trail twisting up a steep mountain. Ice-blue eyes. Reddish-brown hair. The control center, built to accommodate three operators at their consoles and at least two more supervisors behind them, seemed crowded with Vinnie in it.

"Hello, Mr. Hawks," said Vinnie. It sounded almost like an old Mickey Mouse cartoon.

The Beast had a high-pitched little-girl's voice that made people want to laugh when they first met him. Those who did laugh never repeated the error.

"Hello, Vinnie."

"What can I do for you?" asked the Beast.

"I need a favor."

"Such as?"

Hawks glanced around the control center. It was small: merely three electronic consoles and the padded chairs for them, plus two more empty chairs behind them. The wide windows looked out on the warehouse floor. The only door was at Hawks's back. The walls were softly padded to keep out the noise of the machines that clattered during the working day.

"It's time for the Old Man to retire."

For the first time in the years that Hawks had known the Beast, Vinnie's glacial blue eyes widened with surprise.

"The Old Man? Mr. Weldon?" He whispered the name.

Hawks nodded.

Vinnie shifted his ponderous bulk from one foot to the other. "Gee, I don't know. The Old Man . . ."

"It's got to be done. For the good of the company."

"He's already had a stroke, ain't he?"

"A heart attack."

"Maybe he'll pop off by himself soon."

"This can't wait for nature to take its course, Vinnie." Besides, Hawks thought, the old bastard will probably live long enough to bury us all. Especially me.

"Gee, I don't know," Vinnie repeated.

"I can make it worth the risks you'd be taking."

Hunching his massive shoulders, the Beast replied, "I'm already special assistant to the national manager of magazine circulation. I get more money than I can spend as it is."

"Name your price."

"The Old Man? Gee, I don't know. . . ."

"Name your price," Hawks repeated.

Glancing furtively around, as if afraid that someone was eavesdropping, Vinnie hesitated for agonizingly long moments. At last he said, "See, I met this guy a couple months ago. In the airport in Dallas. He was autographin' books. He's a writer. An author."

Hawks felt his brows knitting. What was the Beast after?

"An' we got to talking on the plane back to New York, an' he told me I ought to write my life story. You know, I'd tell it to him and he'd write it and we'd split the money."

"You want me to publish your autobiography?"

Sheepishly, the Beast nodded his massive head. "Yeah. That's it."

"Aren't you afraid that the police would read it?"

"I ain't done nothin' illegal. Nothin' they got witnesses for."

Hawks started to smile, but quickly suppressed it. Not wise to smile at the Beast; he might get the wrong idea.

"All right, Vinnie," said Hawks slowly, carefully. "I'm sure that Webb Press will be happy to publish your autobiography."

"And make it a best-seller."

"We'll do our best."

"It's gotta be a best-seller," said the Beast ominously.

"Well, your people in distribution would have more to say about that than I would," Hawks replied smoothly. "We'll start with a print run of fifteen thou—"

"A hunnert thousand. Hardcover."

"That's not necessary, Vinnie. Fifteen to start, and we can go back to press as soon as we see they're selling well enough to warrant another press run."

"A hunnert thousand," rumbled the Beast. "This writer guy said it can't be a best-seller unless you print a hunnert thousand hardcover."

"Oh, come on now," Hawks countered—cautiously. "What do writers know about the publishing business?"

Vinnie scowled, a look that many a man had taken to the grave with him.

"I'll tell you what," said Hawks, trying to keep his voice from trembling. "We'll do a first print run of fifty thousand. That'll be enough to get the book on *The New York Times* best-seller list all by itself. Okay?"

Vinnie thought it over for a while. Hawks could almost hear the laborious grinding of gears inside the Beast's thick skull. Finally, he stuck out his right hand and Hawks let the enormous paw engulf his own hand. Weldon W. Weldon is about to enter that big publishing house in the sky, Hawks congratulated himself as Vinnie pumped his arm nearly out of its socket.

Then he added, And I'm going to publish the autobiography of a goon.

The Writer

The Writer drove his battered GMota across the George Washington Bridge and into Manhattan that same rainy, dreary Saturday morning. But to him, the fabulous skyline of the city sparkled like Arthur's Camelot.

For hours he drove through the midtown streets, seeing with own eyes for the first time the legendary Saks Fifth Avenue windows, the Cathedral of St. Paul, the United Nations complex, the Empire State Building. It was breathtaking.

By midafternoon he was running out of gas, with no idea of where a gas station might be, practically no money in his pockets, and not a clue about where he might find a motel room. But he did see a police precinct station halfway down the block, with half a dozen blue-and-white police cars double-parked in the narrow street, blocking traffic almost completely.

He double-parked behind a police car, got out, and started into the station. Then he remembered he was now in New York City, the Big Apple, and sprinted back to lock the doors of his old hatchback.

Contrary to what he had been led to expect by watching hundreds of TV police shows, the precinct station house was drowsily quiet this Saturday morning. A few uniformed officers were standing off in the far corner of the room he entered, quietly talking together. Along the side wall stood four squat blue robots, silent and inert. The Writer paid careful attention to the equipment on the human police officers: pistols, stun wands, gas and concussion grenades, bulletproof vests, protective helmets with built-in radios and shatterproof sliding visors. Yes, he was in New York, all right.

The sergeant behind the desk was neither friendly nor gruff, just totally impersonal. He seemed to be looking *through* the writer instead of at him.

"Excuse me," said the Writer.

The desk sergeant sat up on a raised platform, like a judge. He seemed to take in the Writer's presence at a glance, his faded jeans and checkered polyester sports jacket. He made the barest perceptible motion of his head. Otherwise he remained as stolid as a robot.

"I just got into town, and I'm looking for a place to stay. Can you recommend—"

"Traveler's Aid," snapped the desk sergeant.

"'Scuse me?"

"Grand Central Concourse. Traveler's Aid."

The Writer scratched his head.

Leaning forward slightly and peering down at the writer, the desk sergeant said slowly and carefully, as if speaking to a retarded child, "Go to Grand Central Station. That's at Forty-second Street and Park Avenue. Ask any officer there and he, she, or it will direct you to the Traveler's Aid desk. The people there will help you to find a hotel. Understand?"

The Writer nodded vaguely.

The desk sergeant started to repeat his instructions, this time in Spanish: "*Vaya a Grand Central Estación . . .*"

The Writer backed away, muttering his thanks and wondering if the desk sergeant actually was a robot.

Outside, it was drizzling again. But that was nothing compared with what had happened to the Writer's faithful old hatchback. Vandals had taken all four wheels, popped the hood and stolen the battery, the distributor, and all four sparkplugs, jimmied the hatch and taken his only suitcase, ripped out the seats, the radio, and the hand-stitched snakeskin steering wheel cover that his mother had made for him many Christmases ago, and broken each and every one of the windows. In front of the police station.

The Writer gasped and gaped at the pillaged remains of his car. Then he noticed a piece of paper stuck in the one remaining windshield wiper. A ticket for double parking.

He sank down onto the curbstone and cried.

Ten

For the fiftieth time that cheerless Saturday Carl picked up the telephone, then slammed it back down again. He paced to the window of his sparse hotel room again and looked out at the rain. It spattered the puddles growing on the rooftops across the street, it slanted down onto the cars and pedestrians in the avenue far below. The city allowed private cars into Manhattan on weekends. They and the umbrellas along the sidewalks made a shifting patchwork of colors against the gray stones, gray streets, and gray skies of this somber Saturday.

So you slept with her, Carl said to himself. That doesn't mean anything. Not in this day and age. You're both consenting adults.

But what did you consent to? the other half of his brain asked. A one-night stand? Or do you love her? Would you want to marry her?

Not so fast! This is no time to talk about marriage. Don't even *think* about it. You're in no position to take on responsibilities like that.

But you've got a tricky situation here. You're here in New York because she got her company to invite you. If you go ahead with them on the electronic book project, you're going to have to work with her. How are you going to handle that?

You can't mix business and romance, Carl insisted stubbornly. That's the one thing I learned out of all the management courses I took. Office romances lead to disaster.

So it was just a one-night stand, eh?

It has to be.

Carl nodded, satisfied that he had thought the problem through and come to the correct conclusion. But his hand reached for the telephone, and he asked the information computer for Lori's number.

Lori was in the middle of her morning calisthenics. Saturday she could sleep late, then do the week's wash and her exercises at the same time. Instead of riding down to the basement laundry room on the elevator, she jogged the three flights down and back up again.

Not only was it better for her cardiovascular system and muscle tone, it avoided the jerk who lived on the ninth floor and seemed to lurk in the elevator, waiting for anything female to leer and lunge at.

She finished the deep bending routine and, wiping a sheen of perspiration from her face, was about to head downstairs again when the phone chimed.

Drat! she said to herself. If that's Momma she'll talk me blue in the face while the clothes wrinkle before I can get them into the dryer.

She touched the phone console's automatic answer button and heard the telephone's flat, emotionless voice say, "You have reached 999-5628. When you hear the tone, please leave your name, your number, and a brief message. Thank you. Please remember to wait for the tone."

Lori had one hand on the front door's knob when she recognized Carl's voice. "Uh, oh, Lori? This is Carl Lewis. I . . . I, uh, I'll call you back later."

She was at the phone before he could hang up.

"Carl? I'm here. It's me."

"Oh! I thought maybe I got a wrong number."

"No, that's just the answering program. It's not a good idea for a woman to use her own voice."

A long pause. Then, "I was wondering if you'd be free for dinner tonight."

Lori's first impulse was to say yes, and then explain that it would have to be early and brief, because she had to work and a belly dancer with a full belly was a belly dancer in trouble.

But she heard her voice replying, "Gee, I'm sorry, Carl. Not tonight. I have to work."

"Oh." Did he sound disappointed? Or relieved? Or some of each?

"How about brunch tomorrow?" she suggested. Brunch would be safer than dinner, she thought. Not so many complications afterward.

His voice brightened. "Sure. That'll be fine."

She gave him the name and address of a neighborhood restaurant. "Is one o'clock okay?" she asked.

"Sure. I've got nothing else to do."

"All right. I'll make the reservation. See you then."

And she sang to herself all the way down to the laundry room and back upstairs again.

Sunday morning was warm and bright, a perfect spring day in the city, like a scene from a Woody Allen film. The previous day's rain had washed the streets and the sky; everything seemed to sparkle as Lori walked from her apartment to the restaurant. People were actually smiling on the street and almost being polite to one another. A fantastic spring day in Manhattan.

Just what is it you expect of Carl? she asked herself. And she answered, grinning, Nothing. Not a damned thing. All I want is for him to be himself. And to stay near me.

That's *all* you want?

For now, she admitted. Carl is attractive, intelligent, a little shy, very gentle, very steady. Kind of old-fashioned. Not one of those macho beer-swilling clowns that this town is so full of. Or one of those phony name-dropping intellectuals who try to impress you with how much they know, and then take out a calculator to tote up the dinner check. I'm sick to death of them; the publishing business is filled with them.

And you think Carl's not like that?

Not at all like that. He got angry when those longshoremen were tucking money into my costume. He was ready to fight the whole crowd of them.

Foolish.

Gallant.

He was drunk.

But very lovable.

What was that word? Did you say "love"? Be careful girl, that's the way careers turn into pregnancies.

I know what I'm doing.

Do you?

Then she saw Carl sitting at one of the rickety tables on the sidewalk in front of the restaurant, and ended her dialogue with herself. He was staring off into some private vision, somber and serious, just gazing at nowhere as he sat there in the early afternoon sunlight. The Macy's Thanksgiving Day parade could have passed by and he wouldn't have noticed it. Still in that rumpled tweed jacket. But suddenly he did recognize Lori and his face brightened into a million-kilowatt smile. He stood up as she approached.

Carl saw Lori approaching and automatically got to his feet. She smiled brilliantly at him and he felt himself grinning back. In the warm spring sunlight she wore a sleeveless tan blouse and a knee-length skirt of darker brown. She seemed to glow, she looked so beautiful.

He held her chair for her as she sat down. The sunlight felt warm and good. Not even the foul-smelling diesel buses lumbering past on the avenue or the filthy bag lady rummaging through the dumpster on the corner could spoil the beauty of the moment.

They spoke about inconsequential matters at first: Would you rather sit out here or go indoors? Do you think the eggs Benedict would be better than the bagels and lox?

"What is lox, anyway?" Carl asked.

"A kind of smoked salmon."

"Oh. In the lab it's an abbreviation for liquid oxygen."

Lori laughed.

Carl ordered the eggs Benedict. After a tussle with her conscience, Lori skipped the bagels and rich cream sauces and settled for a salad. After the waiter had brought their trays, Carl started to say, "Lori—about what happened a couple of nights ago . . ."

She stopped him by placing her hand gently on his. "What happened, happened. It was lovely, and there's nothing we can do to change it. So let's just forget about it."

He looked into her dark eyes and saw that there was no regret, no anger, in them. "I don't think I can forget about it," he said. "I don't think I want to forget about it."

With a smile, Lori replied, "Okay. Neither do I. But let's just leave it as a nice memory. Let's not make it more important than it is."

Now he felt puzzled. Does that mean she doesn't care? Or is she trying to make me feel better about it?

"You're supposed to see Mr. Bunker tomorrow," she changed the subject.

"If he doesn't cancel out again."

"He'll see you," she said firmly, then added, "Sooner or later."

"What's he like?" Carl asked.

Lori shrugged her shoulders, a move that churned Carl's entire glandular system.

"I've never met him," she said.

"But you've seen him around the office, haven't you?"

"I told you, he never comes to the office. Honest. Mrs. Bee holds the title of publisher; she's in the office every day. Mr. Bee is the president and owner of the company. We never see him."

With an exasperated sigh, Carl asked, "What kind of a business is this, anyway? Nobody can do anything without Bunker's okay, and nobody gets to see him!"

"Publishing is unique," Lori admitted.

"It sure isn't anything like the business management courses I've taken."

She took a leaf of her salad and agreed. "What other business puts out a product that you can return for a full refund even after you've used it?"

"Huh?"

"No book sale is ever final. All the books we send out to the regional distributors and wholesalers, they're all taken on consignment. If they don't sell, they come back to us. If you buy a book in a store, you can return it a day or two later and they'll refund your money. The store management might argue, but they'll give your money back if you insist on it—and if the book is still in decent shape."

"But that's crazy! How can you tell what your sales are?"

"You can't. Not for a couple of years."

In the back of his mind Carl realized that his electronic book would change all that. He would bring the publishing business into the twenty-first century. By now, though, Lori had lapsed into tales of the editorial department.

". . . every year she would send us a manuscript, a totally unpublishable piece of junk," Lori was saying, "and every year we would send it back with a standard rejection form. You know, 'Dear Sir or Madam: Thank you for submitting the enclosed manuscript, but we find that it does not suit our needs at the present time.'"

Without waiting for Carl to ask what happened next, Lori went on, "So one year Arleigh Berkowitz—he's not with us anymore—he gets fed up with Mrs. Kranston and her terrible prose, so he writes her a really nasty letter: 'Stop bothering us with this rotten material! It's a waste of your time and ours!'"

"That must have hurt her feelings," Carl said.

"Are you kidding? We're talking about a would-be *writer*," Lori retorted. "She sent us a letter back in the return mail that said Arleigh's letter was the first personal response she's ever gotten from an editor, and she's so inspired she's going to work twice as hard. Now we get *two* unpublishable manuscripts a year from her, every spring and every fall."

Lori laughed, but Carl failed to see the humor. "And her stuff never gets better? She doesn't improve at all from one year to the next?"

"She doesn't learn a thing. I think it gets worse."

"You've read them?"

"We've all read them, at one time or another. They're *awful!*"

"It's a strange business, all right," Carl said. But in the back of his head he kept thinking, I'll change all this. Electronic books are going to totally change the publishing industry.

He mentally squared his shoulders in preparation for his meeting with P.T. Bunker, his rendezvous with destiny.

Telephone Transcript

"You have reached the Murray Swift Literary Agency. There are no humans at work over the weekend. Please leave your name and number and someone will get back to you first thing Monday morning."

"This is the Bunker Books automated message transmitter. Please have Mr. Swift call Ms. Scarlet Dean no later than three P.M. on Monday to discuss contract terms for Sheldon Stoker's new novel, *The Terror from Beyond Hell*."

"I am programmed to accept contract offers electronically. Please transmit the contract and state orally the amount of the advance being offered."

(Delay of four seconds.)

"Contract transmitted. Advance offered is one million dollars."

"Thank you. I am programmed to respond that the advance is too low. Mr. Swift will call you on Monday."

Eleven

Monday morning. The city stirred to life much as it did in O. Henry's time, bleary-eyed, reluctant. Gleaming silver subway trains streaked through their tunnels, their anodized surfaces immune to the spray paints and felt pens of even the most rabid graffitists. Inside the swaying, *swooshing* cars working men and women sat crammed in plastic seats, numbly inanimate, ignoring their fellow workers who stood jammed together shoulder to shoulder hanging by one arm from the overhead hand rails. Darwin smiled from the grave.

Most of the men read the sports sections of their newspapers. Most of the women read the fashion pages. After all, it was Monday, time for the latest new styles to appear. The columns were illustrated by color photographs showing the fashion of the week: the smoldering, sensuous, slutty look—tangled kinky hair, sloppy sweatshirts that exposed at least one shoulder, very tight knee-length skirts slitted to the hip, patterned stockings, and spike heels. Accessories included voluminous handbags that carried mace and tranquilizer dart guns.

The sports pages carried ads that showed subtle changes in last week's biker image: tear the sleeves off the leather jackets, add a new broad-brimmed hat, buy a pair of glitter gloves and elevator boots, and the new pimp image was yours, just in time to match your girlfriend's slutty look.

On the city's streets buses lumbered over potholes and detoured around repair crews, depositing streams of workers at every corner. The clothing stores were open early, of course, for those enterprising men and women who wanted to show off the new fashion first thing upon starting work.

Carl Lewis wore his usual corduroy slacks and tweed jacket as he walked through the sunny morning to the Synthoil Tower. Lori had taken him shopping after their brunch on Sunday, and he had bought some shirts and underwear and socks. But he had not yet worked up the nerve to try the flamingo-pink pimp slacks that the salesman had shown him as a special preview of the coming week's new style.

"You can be ahead of all your friends by buying now," the salesman had prompted.

While Lori could barely conceal her giggles, Carl had decided to remain behind.

A phone message inviting him to demonstrate his invention at the Monday morning editorial board meeting had been waiting for him when he returned to his hotel room after walking Lori back to her apartment. He had spent the night checking and double-checking the electro-optical reader, and then had slept with it under his pillow.

Now, with a small but discernible dent in his temple left by one of the reader's hard corners, he strode past fake bikers staring at the newest fashions in store windows, determined to make the editors realize that they were witnessing the dawn of an entirely new era in the history of publishing.

It's more than publishing, Carl reminded himself. Publishing is only the first step. Electro-optical communications is going to allow the human race to live in harmony with the whole Earth's ecology. No more chopping down forests to make paper. No more ignorance and poverty. The price for information will go down to the point where everyone on Earth can obtain all the knowledge they need. They won't even have to know how to read; the next improvement on my invention will be the talking book. The singing book. The device that speaks to you just like the village story teller or your own mother.

P. Curtis Hawks started the work week in the most unpleasant way imaginable. He found that Gunther Axhelm was waiting for him in his office when he arrived there, shortly after nine o'clock.

Since Hawks rode his private elevator from the underground parking garage directly to his office, neither his secretary nor his communications computer was able to warn him of the Axe's presence. Hawks stepped out of the elevator and saw a strange man leaning over the billiard table in the far corner of the spacious office.

"Who the hell are you?" Hawks grumbled, even while his brain (which was often slower than his tongue) told him that it could be no one other than the Old Man's newly hired hatchet man.

The tall, slim, blond stranger stood ramrod straight, the pool cue gripped in one hand like a rifle. He clicked his heels and made a curt bow.

"Sir. Permit me to introduce myself. I am Gunther Axhelm. Mr. Weldon ordered me to meet with you first thing this morning. I assumed that he meant nine A.M. precisely."

Hawks groaned inwardly. It was going to be a difficult relationship.

Hawks crossed to his desk and Axhelm carefully replaced the cue in its rack, then went to the padded leather chair in front of the desk and sat himself on it. Neither man offered to shake hands. Hawks took a long look at his new "assistant." Axhelm was long-limbed, athletic. Not an ounce of fat on him. His face was sculptured planes, sharp nose, slightly pointed chin, gray killer's eyes. Blond hair cut ruthlessly short. Instead of a business suit he wore a long-sleeved turtleneck shirt and form-fitting slacks. All in black. The uniform of a burglar.

"My assignment here," he began without preamble, "is to reduce the workforce by fifty percent before—"

"Fifty percent! That's impossible!"

Axhelm allowed a wintry smile to bend his lips slightly. "Sir. My assignment was given me directly by Mr. Weldon. He *is* the chief executive officer of Tarantula Enterprises, is he not? And therefore your superior."

"We can't cut fifty percent of the workforce," Hawks insisted. "We wouldn't be able to handle the work load with only half the people we have now."

Again the smile. "It is my intention to go further. I have examined the personnel files, and I believe it will be possible to cut perhaps seventy or even seventy-five percent."

Hawks gave a strangled little cry.

"Do not be alarmed, sir. Your position is quite secure."

That's what Macbeth told Banquo just before he hired the assassins, Hawks thought.

Leaning back in the leather chair, stretching his long legs casually, Axhelm explained, "You see, you have not taken complete advantage of the benefits of modern technology. You have computers, but you do not use them as fully as you could. For example—how many editors do you have on staff?"

"Um . . . thirty or so," Hawks guesstimated.

"Thirty-two, full time," corrected Axhelm, "and six part time. They can all be eliminated by a computer programmed to read incoming manuscripts and make selections based on criteria such as word length, subject matter, and writing quality."

"How can a computer judge writing quality?" snapped Hawks.

Axhelm's smile turned pitying. "Come now, sir. Programs capable of judging writing quality have been used in university examinations for nearly twenty years. Even high school teachers use such programs, rather than relying on their own faulty judgments."

"You can't use a program developed to grade freshman English compositions to judge the value of incoming manuscripts!"

"And why not?"

"Because the *quality* of the writing isn't really important! Take a look at the best-seller lists: none of those books would pass freshman English!"

Axhelm fell silent, stroking his chin absently with his, long, slim fingers.

"It's *salability* that counts," Hawks insisted. "And to determine salability you need human judgment."

"Is that why ninety-five percent of the books that Webb Press publishes lose money?"

Hawks grimaced, but countered, "It's the five percent that *make* money for us that count."

With a nod and a sigh, Axhelm said, "Then we must develop a computer program that can determine salability."

"Impossible!"

"Of course not. If your editors can do it, a computer program can be written to do it better. More efficiently. I will make that my first priority."

Hawks said nothing.

"In the meantime, we will begin reducing the workforce. Today."

At precisely eleven A.M. the eight editors of Bunker Books filed into their shabby conference room, with Carl Lewis and Ralph Malzone added to their number. The two men took seats on either side of Lori, down at the end of the table.

Mrs. Bunker's chair remained vacant, as did the chair for the editor-in-chief. But all the others were there: the mountainous Maryann Quigly, the cadaverous Ashley Elton, ferret-faced Jack Drain, Concetta Las Vagas (who needed hardly any change of clothes at all to look slutty), and the rest. Before anyone could say a word, P.T. Junior entered the conference room, dragging his own chair from his own office.

"My mother will be here in a minute or two," he announced, sitting at the head of the table. "She's chatting with the new editor-in-chief." He eyed them all with his sly, smirking look.

A murmur went around the table. Before it died away, Junior spoke up again.

"You know, I've been looking over the publishing business for some time now . . ."

"Yeah, the whole weekend," Ralph Malzone whispered.

Unperturbed, Junior was going on, ". . . and I see that there are some books that get onto the best-seller lists, and they make a lot of money."

None of the editors said a word. All eyes were focused on Junior.

"What we ought to do," he said with the fervor of true revelation, "is stick to those books! Just publish the best-sellers and forget all the other stuff!"

There was a long, *long* moment of utter silence. Then someone coughed. Another editor scraped his chair against the uncovered floor. Maryann Quigly emitted a loud, labored sigh.

Ted Gunn rose to the occasion. "Uh—Junior . . . that's exactly what we try to do. We don't *deliberately* publish books that lose money. You just don't know which books are going to become best-sellers beforehand."

Junior stared at him disbelievingly. "You don't?"

Gunn slowly shook his head.

"Oh," said Junior, with vast disappointment.

"Wait a minute, though," said Ralph Malzone. "In his own way, I think Junior's got a point there."

All eyes turned to the wiry sales manager questioningly. Malzone, trying to curry favor with the Boss's son? Carl saw the expression on Lori's face: somewhere between surprise and disgust.

"What I mean is this," Ralph explained. "Most of the books we publish are doomed to lose money before they even get into print."

"How can you—"

"We publish them on the theory of minimum success," Malzone said.

"The theory of minimum success?"

"Yeah. Take this new novel Lori's just bought, this Midway book. We're giving the author the minimum advance, and we're putting out the minimum investment in the book all the way down the line. When we print it, it's going to be the minimum number of copies."

"That's to minimize our risk," snapped Ted Gunn.

"Yeah. Sure. But it also minimizes our chances of making the book profitable."

Lori started to ask something, but Malzone went on before she could frame the words.

"We print a small number of copies, we don't spend money on advertising or promotion. The book flops and we lose money on it— or break even, at best."

"But it's up to your sales people to *sell* the book," Jack Drain pointed out.

Malzone made a sour grin. "Sure. They've got a hundred-some books per season to push, and you expect them to spend any effort on an also-ran? A book the editorial department thinks so little of that they only print a couple thousand copies? Come on! My people ain't stupid, for chrissakes. They're not going to waste their time on a book after you've convinced 'em it's going nowhere."

"But it's a good novel," Lori insisted.

"Doesn't matter," replied Malzone. "What's inside the covers doesn't really matter at all. Not when my sales people are out there trying to get the wholesalers and bookstore managers to order the title. None of those people read! They take a look at the cover and ask how many copies we've printed. If *we* don't show any faith in the book, they sure as hell don't buy it in any quantity."

"But . . ."

"And how in hell can you sell books that haven't been printed?" Malzone went on with some heat of passion coloring his lean cheeks. "Suppose your author gets on all the TV talk shows and a zillion people go rushing to the bookstores for his novel. And the stores only have a couple thousand copies of the book because that's all we've printed. You think those customers are going to wait six weeks—or six months—while we make up our minds to go back to press? The hell they will!"

"So the book bombs," said Lori, "and the writer gets blamed for writing an unsuccessful book."

"Hey, it's not *our* fault if a book doesn't sell! Why don't you . . ."

At that moment the door opened again and Mrs. Bunker entered, accompanied by Scarlet Dean. The argument ended like a light being switched off. Everyone snapped to their feet.

Mrs. Bunker was all in white, as always: she had bowed to the new slutty look only to the extent that her hair had been frizzed and her silk suit jacket had no blouse beneath it. Pearls adorned her throat, wrists, and earlobes.

Smiling, she said in her tiny voice, "I'm sure I really don't need to introduce Scarlet Dean. Even those few of you who haven't met her before know of her fine work at Webb and elsewhere. We're truly fortunate to have her join our team."

Still standing, the assembled editors gave their new chief a smattering of applause. Carl, noticing that Ralph Malzone smacked his hands together along with the rest of them, clapped a few times also.

Scarlet Dean was a vision in red. Tall and leggy, like a fashion model, her hair was flame, her eyes the green of a deep forest. She wore a sheath of fire-engine red adorned with spangles; Carl immediately thought of a circus trapeze artist. A rope of carnelians lay over her slim bosom. Her face had a slightly evil cast to it, the eyes darting from one person to another, the thin red lips twitching slightly in what might have been an attempt at a smile.

"Thank you," said Scarlet Dean. "Please—let's sit down and get to work." Her voice was low, sultry, suggestive. Despite himself, Carl felt a thrill of excitement stir him. He felt strangely stimulated and guilty, at the same time.

"I think the first order of business," the new editor-in-chief was saying, "is to let Mr. Lewis show us his wonderful new invention."

Suddenly all heads swivelled toward Carl. Feeling a flush of unexpected stage fright, Carl grasped the electro-optical reader in both his hands and got to his feet.

This time it was different. The device worked perfectly. Carl showed them pages from half a dozen different books. They oohed and aahed. Carl passed it around the table so that each editor could see for him- or herself how easy it was to use the device. Mrs. Bunker was smiling happily at him. All the editors beamed approvingly, now that they knew how the Boss felt about the subject. Lori, of course, was radiating delight and satisfaction. Even Ralph seemed to be pleased with the demonstration.

But Carl found himself ignoring all of them. He found that he was not looking at Mrs. Bunker, or any of the editors, not even Lori. His eyes were locked on Scarlet Dean, as if he were powerless to look elsewhere. She was smiling at him, a beguiling, bewitching little smile that perked the corners of her mouth and opened her lips just enough for the tip of her pink tongue to peek out at Carl. And her eyes were telling him that she would love to meet with him, alone, just the two of them with no one else.

He barely heard Mrs. Bunker when she announced that P.T. would definitely see him at five o'clock this afternoon, at the Bunker house.

Murder Four

Homicide Lieutenant Jack Moriarty knelt over the expired body of Nora Charleston, a grim look on his lean, weatherbeaten face.

"That's how they found her, Lieutenant," said the uniformed sergeant. "Musta been dead a couple days, at least."

Moriarty was glad of the head cold that had stuffed his sinuses so completely that he could smell nothing. Straightening painfully, his arthritis reminding him of his age, he asked, "Forensics been through the apartment yet?"

"They've finished with the living room, here. They're doin' the bedroom and bath now."

Moriarty surveyed the apartment. Once it had been very posh, but time had withered it all. The furniture was tattered, the carpeting threadbare. The old lady lying facedown on the living room rug was wearing what had once been an elegant robe. Now it looked frayed and hopelessly old-fashioned, like a faded photo from a high school yearbook.

"What do you think, Sergeant?" he asked the younger cop. "Burglary? Drugs?"

The sergeant pulled a long frown. "Nothing taken that we can see. No sign of forced entry. No struggle."

"Who called it in?"

"The super. He let himself in when he realized he hadn't seen her in a couple of days. Called the apartment on the intercom and got no answer. So he let himself in and found her layin' there."

Moriarty looked back to the frail body of Mrs. Charleston.

"Thought it was natural causes, at first," the sergeant continued. "She was ninety-nine years old, after all."

"Sonofabitch couldn't let her live out the full hundred," Moriarty muttered.

"She musta let him in. Door was shut when the super came in, but the inner locks weren't locked. She let him in, he conked her on the head, and walked out. No noise. No struggle. No fuss."

"We had another old lady knocked off for no discernible reason," said Moriarty. "Last month, down in Gramercy Park."

The sergeant said nothing.

"Wonder if there's any connection?" Moriarty made a mental note to check the homicide computer for similar recent murders and see if there was any common thread to them. Might be a nut case knocking off old ladies.

He glanced down at the body again. "Couldn't let her live out the full one hundred. Damned shame."

Twelve

Scarlet Dean managed to seat herself in the limousine exactly opposite the young inventor from MIT.

Her instructions from her former boss, P. Curtis Hawks, had been explicit: find out everything there is to know about the man and his invention. Although Hawks had not revealed his strategy to her, Scarlet had a good idea of what it was. If young Tom Edison's invention is actually as good as it appears to be, Webb Press will buy out Bunker Books, thereby acquiring the electronic book in the process. Failing that, they would buy out the inventor himself.

There were four of them in the limousine: herself and Mrs. Bunker side by side on the limo's ultraplush rear seat, and on the jumpseats facing them, the slightly exotic-looking young editor who had discovered the handsome inventor and the young man himself. He looked distinctly uncomfortable locked into the car with three attractive women gazing fondly at him.

Scarlet glanced at the editor and then at Mrs. Bunker. Mrs. Bee's eyes had dollar signs in them; she saw Carl Lewis as a way to make money for Bunker Books. The editor, Lori Something-or-other, was smiling admiringly at the man. Were they romantically involved? No matter, she would put an end to that quickly enough. If nothing else worked she could always fire the editor.

She probed Carl Lewis's eyes with her own. He blushed slightly and looked away. He's vulnerable, Scarlet told herself. He can be had.

She began to consider various possibilities. Of course, Bunker does not want to sell his company. Hawks may be planning an unfriendly takeover, but Bunker himself owns virtually all the stock. There are only a few shares outside the family, and the people who own them are not quick to sell. She knew; she had ordered her broker to quietly buy up as much Bunker stock as could be found. Result: none available. Not one share.

"The few percent that Bunker and his family don't personally own are held mostly by retirees," the broker had told her. "Old friends of Bunker's father and mother. They just won't sell."

The thing to do, then, is to get Lewis and his invention away from Bunker. Which means getting him away from this dark-haired editor. That shouldn't be too difficult. In less than a week I'll have him eating out of the palm of my hand—so to speak.

Then Scarlet Dean had her inspiration. If Carl Lewis is personally attached to *me*, I can write my own ticket with Hawks and Webb Press. Or any other publishing house in New York! In the world!

She turned up the wattage on her smile and was pleased to see Lewis squirm a little on the jumpseat.

The limousine crawled through Manhattan's late afternoon traffic and finally pulled up in front of what had once been a five-story tenement in the Lower East Side. Now it was one of long rows of posh town houses, each with its own marquee and private parking space at curbside. The law banning private autos in Manhattan did not apply to residents of the borough, naturally. Eighty percent of the private cars registered in Manhattan were limousines, which also seemed natural enough.

A live doorman helped Mrs. Bunker out of the limo and escorted her to the front door of the house. Carl got out next and helped Lori and Scarlet Dean, while the chauffeur slowly strolled around the monstrously long vehicle just in time to close the rear door.

Mrs. Bunker ushered her three guests up the sweeping marble

stairs and into the second-floor parlor, where still another live servant met them with a rolling cart laden with drinks.

"Please make yourselves comfortable," she said. "I'll go and tell P.T. that you're here."

Carl had never seen such splendor. The room was huge, richly carpeted, pillared with marble, panelled with rare Mayan tile. On the walls were hologram reproductions of the wonders of the world. Simply by turning around, Carl could look out upon the Sphinx guarding the great pyramids, or snow-capped Mt. Everest, or the original Disneyland romantically shrouded in sunset-pink smog.

Lori seemed equally impressed. "What a beautiful room," she murmured as the butler—she guessed he was the butler—poured her a diet cola.

Only Scarlet seemed to take it all in stride. "They found a good decorator," she said, and ordered a martini. Heading for the deep, fur-covered easy chair set before the fireplace hologram, she advised:

"Better relax and make yourselves comfortable. From what I know of P.T. Bunker, we have a considerable wait in store for us."

Mrs. Bunker, meanwhile, had gone to the splendid bedroom of their home. The master bedroom and the second-floor parlor were the only two rooms in the huge house that were decently furnished and decorated. The parlor, of course, was to impress visitors. The bedroom was for the two of them. The other rooms of the house were either bare and unused, or furnished with Spartan spareness. P.T.'s office, adjoining the bedroom, contained the same old pine desk that he had started with. Behind it was a magnificent hologram of the New York harbor. When P.T. talked with people by Picturephone, they saw the harbor and little else. And no visitor saw any part of the house other than the second-floor parlor.

They had intended to furnish the entire house just as sumptuously as the parlor and master bedroom. But running a business twenty-four hours a day saps one's energy and will. After a long, long day of frantic decisions and boring conferences, there just is no time or strength left to deal with decorators and painters.

Moreover, there was no money. Every cent the Bunkers had was tied up in the business. Being a middling-sized publishing house was a perilous existence. The big houses kept trying to buy out Bunker

Books, or squeeze the company into bankruptcy. The smaller houses constantly undersold them.

Alba checked out her appearance in the full-length mirror next to the big circular waterbed. She frowned slightly. The slutty look was not for her. She had heard a rumor that next week's fashion would emphasize elegance: the Fred and Ginger look, from what she had been able to glean. She looked forward to it.

With a glance at her gold wristwatch she called through the open door to the office, "Pandro, dear, the guests are here."

No reply.

Alba went to the doorway. P.T. Bunker sat alone at the ancient desk of his childhood, an old-fashioned pair of bifocals perched on his nose, one finger running down a long column of computer printout figures, a semidesperate expression on his face. It was still a ruggedly handsome face, despite the years of worry and responsibilities that had carved deep lines into it. Worse, those years of sitting behind a desk and directing the firm had brought about a certain sagging around the jawline. Even his broad shoulders and brawny arms seemed to be withering. And his bulging stomach was stretching the buttons on his sport shirt, she noticed.

"Pandro, darling, we have guests downstairs."

He looked up at her, peering over the bifocal rims. "Do you know," he said," that we've been losing money steadily on every category we publish, except for the self-help books." His voice was a sweet clear tenor, the voice of a born singer, a voice that should have led to the opera rather than conference calls with bankers in Beijing.

"Self-help books always sell, dear," Alba replied patiently. "The same awful people keep buying them, year after year."

"Don't the books actually help them?"

"Heavens, no! If they did, the entire category would have gone down the tubes ages ago."

Bunker wiped a bead of perspiration from the end of his nose. The office was uncomfortably warm. Windowless, totally undecorated except for the hologram view of the harbor, the stuffy little room held nothing but the desk and rows of aged filing cabinets. Despite the computer printouts that he was perusing, and despite the impressive array of electronic hardware on his desk, P.T. Bunker neither used nor trusted computers. Alba understood and sympathized; the poor dear had never learned to type, and it just would not be fair to expect him to embarrass himself trying to learn, since he was such an important and busy man.

"We shouldn't keep them waiting too long," she urged gently.

Bunker glanced at the calendar pad on his desk and the notes that his wife had written on it.

"Do I *have* to see these people?"

He had become a borderline agoraphobe, she knew. Over the years of his sweating and struggling to make Bunker Books profitable, he had slowly but steadily withdrawn into his own private, inner fortress. He trusted no one except his wife, and Alba wondered if the day would ever come when even she was shut out of his increasingly desperate broodings. He would much rather remain cooped up in this unhealthy little cell than come out and meet the people who had come to pay homage to him. He hardly ever left the house, and it was getting more and more difficult to get him to see anyone, even in the comfortable security of the downstairs parlor.

"You know I wouldn't bother you if it weren't important, dear."

"Why can't I talk to them over the Picturephone?" he asked unhappily.

"I think they might find that a little strange."

"We could tell them I'm . . . I'm . . ." His voice trailed off and faded away into silence.

"It's all right, darling," Alba said soothingly. "I'll be right beside you."

With an unhappy frown, P.T. Bunker got up from his desk. He wore only a pair of boxer trunks beneath his stylish open-neck sport shirt. Like a TV newscaster, Bunker had no need to clothe himself below his navel. Not as long as he remained behind his desk.

Now, however, he walked into the bedroom and began the ritual of showering, shaving, and dressing for company. He had been an impressive figure when Alba had first met him, nearly twenty years earlier. She had been an advertising copywriter for a small agency that still had its office on Madison Avenue. He had just started Bunker Books on the shoestring ten million his father had loaned him. It was love at first sight, a whirlwind courtship and marriage within a week. Never had either one of them regretted an instant of their life together. There had been hard times, businesswise, of course; in fact, the publishing business was *always* on hard times, it seemed. But Alba and Pandro loved each other with a steadfastness that defied all the strains and pressures of the lunatic world of publishing.

While he dressed she explained once again about Carl Lewis and the electronic book. Pandro cast her a skeptical look, but said nothing. Alba also reminded him that he would meet Scarlet Dean, their new editor-in-chief. He nodded and grunted as he tugged on his muscle suit.

It had been years since P.T. had taken the time to play tennis or swim in the four-lane pool they had built in the basement of their home. His once proud physique, with its flat stomach and powerful shoulders and arms, had slumped into middle-aged flabbiness. He avoided revealing this to the people with whom he did business over the Picturephone by wearing shirts that had impressive shoulder pads built into them.

But when he had to meet people in person, sterner measures were required. The muscle suit gave him the same athletic physique he had possessed decades ago. Once covered with a tight-fitting sport shirt and even tighter jeans, no one could tell that P.T.'s muscular build was made of plastic foam. He looked better than a matador, in Alba's eyes.

He complained about putting in his contact lenses, and worried that his toupee might have been askew. His cowboy boots returned the inch or so that had been taken away by years of bending over a desk. All in all, he looked handsome, trim, tanned, and ready to face the world—thanks to a touch of makeup and a constant stream of encouraging chatter from his wife.

Grasping her arm tightly, P.T. Bunker reluctantly entered the tiny elevator that took them down to the second floor. Alba reviewed the names of the people waiting to see him, and why they were there.

"This electronic book invention is very important, dear. It could mean the salvation of the company."

He nodded to show that he understood, but still he dreaded facing the people.

"Ralph Malzone has come up with a sexy name for the invention," Alba went on. "You know, we can't just call it the electronic book. We need a catchy name for it."

He nodded again. God, my stomach's turning itself inside out. I wish this was over and done with.

The elevator stopped and the door slid open automatically before Alba had a chance to tell him the name she had thought of. So she stood on tiptoes and whispered it into his ear.

To the three people waiting in the parlor, it looked as if Mrs. Bunker was whispering sweet nothings into the ear of the man she adored. He looked tight-lipped and slightly flustered. She smiled at their guests, as if somewhat embarrassed.

Carl's heart was thundering in his ribs. This is the big moment, he told himself. This is *it*. Go or no-go. This man holds the power of life and death over your invention.

Mrs. Bunker introduced her husband. As if in a dream, Carl took the prototype from his jacket pocket and showed P.T. Bunker how it worked. He watched in silence as Carl demonstrated with *The Illustrated Moby Dick*. Bunker said nothing. When Carl offered the device to him, Mrs. Bunker took it and played with it for a few minutes. They were all still standing, clustered around the great man a few steps in front of the elevator. No one had taken a chair.

"You see, darling?" said Mrs. Bunker. "It works beautifully."

Bunker finally made a single nod of his head as he handed the prototype back to Carl. "Okay. Looks good. We'll call it Cyberbooks."

And with that he turned abruptly and ducked back into the elevator, leaving Carl, Lori, Scarlet Dean, and his wife standing there gaping at his retreating back.

Summer, Book 11

The Writer

It was a blazing hot July day, the kind of molten heat and humidity that drives even the mildest man to thoughts of murder. An Ed McBain day in the city, where the detectives of the eighty-seventh precinct knew that each ring of the phone meant another body had met a meat cleaver.

The Writer had found a job. Not in the city. He could no more afford to live in Manhattan than he could fly to the moon by flapping his arms. His job, and his miserable one-room apartment, were in New Jersey. He could see Manhattan's skyline every day; see the myriad gleaming lights of the city each night. But he was separated from it by a river of poverty whose current was too strong for him to cross.

He worked in the warehouse of Webb Press, one of the dispensable men who were not supposed to be there, but who were needed because the automated machinery could not do what it had been designed to do, and ordinary expendable human beings were required to carry out the work of the imperfect machines.

Twice in the past month he had almost been killed by heavy cases of books falling from the wobbly overhead conveyor belts. Six times he and his fellow nonentities had spent whole work shifts searching the entire warehouse for cartons of books that had been misplaced by the robots. On one frightening occasion the entire workforce had to battle a robot that resisted having a truckload of books taken out to the loading dock. Somehow the robot got it into its minuscule electronic brain that its job was to protect the huge crates from being moved. While the Japanese-American foreman screamed in two languages, the men risked injury and death to duck beneath the robot's menacing arms, pry off its access panel, and turn it off.

Now the Writer worked at the most thankless job of them all: the furnace. Another stroke of some architect's genius, the furnace burned the books that were returned from the stores unsold. In the brilliant design of the automated warehouse, the furnace supplied heat for the winter months and electricity all year long. During the summer the electricity not only powered the lights and computers, it ran the air-conditioning system.

But the heat of the burning books overburdened the air-conditioning system, so the computer program that ran the warehouse's environmental controls shut down the air-conditioning and there was no way to override its dogmatic decision. The supervisors up in their control booth sneaked in a few room-sized air conditioners for themselves. The men and machines on the warehouse floor worked in summer's heat—supplemented by the flames of the book-burning furnace.

The Writer knew that he was going mad. He spent his days shovelling paperback books into the furnace's hungry red fire. He worked stripped down to his shorts, sweat streaming along his scrawny ribs and lanky arms and legs, blurring his vision. The heat made him feel dizzy, crazy. Like O'Neill's Hairy Ape, he began to shout aloud, "Who makes the warehouse work? I do! Who makes the publishing industry work? I do!"

The other men on the warehouse floor started to avoid him.

But the Writer never noticed, never cared. He knew that he was right. If these books were not destroyed there would be no room for the new books coming off the presses. The whole industry would grind to a halt, strangled to death on a glut of books. So he shovelled the paperbacks into the flames: romance novels, westerns, mysteries, cookbooks, diet books, revealing biographies, lying autobiographies, books about God, about sin, about how to get rich in just ninety days. He scooped them all up in his heavy black shovel and threw them into the baleful blood-red fiery furnace.

These were the bad books, the books that did not sell, the books that had been returned to the warehouse by the stores and the distributors.

Some of the books had been on store shelves for all of a week, some less. Some had never gotten to the shelves; their cartons came back to the warehouse unopened.

The Writer giggled as he worked. He cackled. These were *other writers'* books! If only he could burn enough of them, he told himself, there might one day be room in the world for his own book to be published. He scooped and threw, scooped and threw, making room for his own book and cackling madly all the while.

"Bad books! Bad books!"

Meanwhile, at the far end of the warehouse one of the robots trundled a newly opened carton of books to the inspection station next to the loading dock.

"Malfunction," it said in its limited vocabulary. "Malfunction."

The human inspector looked inside the box and turned pale.

Thirteen

Carl Lewis's life was being dominated by three strong women, and he was not certain that he disliked it.

Since that brief, weird moment nearly three months earlier when he had met P.T. Bunker and the great man had okayed the project—and named it—Carl had become a full-time consultant to Bunker Books. That is, he worked for the company exclusively but was not entitled to any of the fringe benefits or government-ordained insurance that a regular employee received.

That did not matter to Carl one whit. He was being paid handsomely enough to afford a three-room apartment for himself, in the same Gramercy Park building that Lori lived in. He worked all day every day of the week and most of every night. His social life consisted of an occasional lunch with Lori, or a dinner with Scarlet Dean, who insisted on being kept up-to-date on the Cyberbooks project.

Cyberbooks.

Carl liked the name that Bunker had come up with; he did not realize that it was Ralph Malzone's original idea. Nor did it occur to him that the name was now formally registered as a trademark belonging to Bunker Books, Inc. Carl just plugged away at the task of turning his prototype into a device that could be manufactured as inexpensively as possible, while still maintaining quality and reliability. His goal was to have the device on sale nationwide for the Christmas buying season, priced at less than $200.

It was at one of the dinners Scarlet Dean insisted on that he first heard about the cruise.

"Cruise?" Carl almost sputtered out the salad he had been chewing. "Why do I have to go on a cruise?"

They were in the Argenteuil, one of the oldest and finest restaurants of Manhattan. Although it seemed to be Scarlet's favorite place, the restaurant always made Carl feel uneasy. An expense account restaurant, like so many in midtown Manhattan. Too formal and grand for his simple tastes. The maître d' always made Carl feel as if he were a shabby hobo who had drifted into the restaurant by mistake, even when he wore the new suit that Scarlet had sent him and his formal shirt with the blue MIT tie painted on it.

Daintily spearing an ear of asparagus, Scarlet replied, "It's the company sales meeting. We've rented out the ocean liner for the week."

"A week? I can't take a week off. . . ."

Scarlet smiled soothingly and touched his hand with her own. "Relax, Carl. Relax. You won't have to take the time off your work. I know how important it is. It's vital! We'll fix you up with a workshop and a satellite communications link to the office here in New York."

Somewhat relieved, he muttered, "I've also got to be able to work with the guys in the factory."

"That too," Scarlet assured him. "Interactive picture, voice and data links. Don't worry about it."

But he replied, "I still don't see why I have to go. Why can't I stay here?"

"Two reasons: First, Mrs. Bunker will be on the cruise, and she doesn't want you to be out of her sight."

"Really?"

"Really. Second, the whole sales force will be aboard. We'll need you to demonstrate the Cyberbooks hardware to them. And it will be good for you to meet them all informally, talk with them, get them pumped up about Cyberbooks."

"Hmm. I suppose so," he admitted grudgingly.

"And besides," said Scarlet, "think how much fun it will be to be out on the ocean for a whole week. It's very romantic, you know."

He nodded absently. "Will Lori be there, too?"

Her smile fading just a little, Scarlet said, "Yes, of course. The whole editorial staff will be aboard."

Sitting at the bottom of his swimming pool, P. Curtis Hawks made two telephone calls that night. Although he was certain that all the phones in his expansive Westchester home had been bugged by the Old Man's minions, he had obtained a surplus U.S. Navy underwater communications system from a Washington friend in the munitions business. In his fishbowl helmet and wet suit, breathing canned air that smelled faintly of machine oil and carcinogenic plastic, Hawks knew that the ultralow frequency of this communications equipment was beyond the range of the Old Man's tapping.

His first call was to Scarlet Dean, at a prearranged time and place: the ladies' room of the Waldorf Astoria Hotel lobby, at precisely ten minutes before midnight. A little square area of his glass helmet glowed with strangely shifting colors, then her face came into focus two inches in front of his nose.

"Good evening, Ms. Dean."

She frowned slightly. "Your voice sounds strange. Like you're in an echo chamber or something. Are those bubbles coming out of your ear?"

"Never mind that," Hawks snapped. "What's going on over there?"

"The entire sales and editorial staffs will be on the cruise. And I've talked Mrs. Bunker into bringing young Tom Edison along, too."

"Tom Edison? Who in hell is—"

"The Cyberbooks inventor, Carl Lewis."

"Oh."

"They'll all be on the ship together. There's talk that P.T. Bunker will be coming along, too, but so far that's just unconfirmed rumor."

"Christ. If I had a submarine or a cruise missile I could wipe out the whole company."

"Not before I get the complete data for the Cyberbooks machine," Scarlet said.

Hawks nodded inside his helmet. "Yes. Right." Then a brilliant thought occurred to him. "*You* could sink the ship and get away in a lifeboat with the device!"

She seemed startled for a moment, but she quickly composed herself. "Mr. Hawks, I'm an editor first, and a spy for you second. I am not an underwater demolitions expert."

"Yes, of course, I understand," he mumbled, his mind filled with visions of the *Titanic* slipping beneath the ice-choked waves. He saw Bunker and his whole staff huddled on the slanting deck while the orchestra played "Nearer My God to Thee." Refuse to sell out to us, will you? Then down you go, Bunker, you and all your flunkies, down to a watery grave.

"Mr. Hawks?" Scarlet Dean's insistent voice broke into his fantasy.

"Eh? What?"

"You were—cackling, sir."

"Nonsense!" he snapped. "Must be something wrong with this phone link."

She said nothing.

"Get me the data on that Cyberbooks machine as quickly as you can. I don't care if you're in the middle of the ocean, as soon as you have the machine in your hands or a copy of its circuitry, send it to me over the special Tarantula communications satellite."

"Yes, sir," she replied. "Of course."

"Don't call me otherwise. I'll call you each night at this time."

Scarlet nodded and cut their link. The tiny picture of her face winked out, leaving Hawks nothing to see but the blue-green haze of his swimming pool, lit by its underwater lights. He sat at the bottom of the pool for several minutes, the only sound coming from the frothy bubbles of his breathing apparatus.

As soon as she transmits the data on the Cyberbooks device, I could sink the damned ship and be rid of Bunker altogether. And all the evidence. Then I could present the Cyberbooks concept as my own to the board of directors. If the Old Man is still around, that by itself should be enough to remove him and put me at the top of the heap.

He resolved to find a reliable terrorist group that had access to speedboats and anti-shipping missiles. Maybe some of the Atlantic City boys, he mused. Didn't they sink a gambling ship that refused to pay them protection, a few years back?

At precisely ten minutes after midnight Hawks made his second phone call. The miniature image of Vinnie DeAngelo's beefy face screwed up in amazement.

"Gee, you look funny, Mr. Hawks. Like your nose is too close to th' camera, you know?"

"Never mind that. How are you coming along on the special project?"

The Beast's eyes evaded Hawks's. "Like I told you, this is a tough one. I been dopin' it out, but it don't look no easier than when I started. He's got snakes, for Chrissakes. Poison snakes."

"He doesn't stay in his office all the time. He goes home to his apartment."

"Yeah, but he takes th' snakes with him. His chauffeur got bit a couple days ago. Damn near killed him."

Exasperated, Hawks snapped, "Then find a mongoose!"

"Huh? A what?"

"Never mind. Keep working at it. There's got to be a weak link in the Old Man's defenses. He's a senile cripple, for god's sake. There's *got* to be a way to get to him."

"Not while all those snakes are sneakin' around." The Beast shuddered.

Hawks fumed silently. "Stay with it. And, by the way, Vinnie, who was that outfit that sank the gambling boat off Atlantic City a few years ago?"

"Oh, you mean my cousin Guido."

Alba Blanca Bunker allowed the chauffeur to help her out of the long white limousine and stepped onto the concrete surface of the massive dock. It was a gray, mean, John O'Hara kind of day in New York, threatening rain. But there alongside the shabby, deteriorating two-story passenger terminal rose the magnificently sweeping lines of the SS *New Amsterdam,* the cruise liner that would carry them off on a week-long jaunt on the sunny ocean. She took a deep breath of tangy salt air. Actually, the tang in the air was from a garbage barge being hauled down the Hudson River by a chuffing tugboat.

Alba felt thrilled anyway. For more than a year she had been working on the dozens of different strings that led to this moment. Now everything seemed to be in place. The Cyberbooks project had reached the point where they could brief the sales force. The medical specialists had agreed to come along on the cruise on a contingency fee basis. And P.T. himself would arrive soon.

In fact, there he was! Alba saw the blue-and-white helicopter loaned for the occasion by the American Express office droning purposefully against the gray sky up the river toward the pier. She knew that P.T. did not like to fly, did not like to leave the womblike safety of his office and bedroom, but she hoped that the panoramic view of lower Manhattan and the harbor would inspire him and be the first step toward reinvigorating her husband, the man she loved.

He needs this ocean voyage, she told herself for the millionth time. I'm doing this for him.

She watched as the helicopter settled briefly on the roof of the passenger terminal, its big rotors *whooshing* up a clatter of dust and grit. Even from this distance she recognized P.T., stuffed into his muscle suit and a double-breasted blazer topped by a jaunty white yachting cap. He scurried quickly up the special gangplank and into the ship without turning to see if his wife was watching. The chopper took off again, as though eager to hurry back to its ordained task of hunting down deadbeats with overdue bills.

Alba had suppressed her sudden urge to wave to him, knowing how silly it would look to the other people gathering on the pier. She turned to the chauffeur and ordered him to begin unloading her voluminous trunks and suitcases. P.T. was safely ensconced in their private suite; the medical specialists and the rest of the company could begin boarding the ship now.

Ms. Lori Tashkajian
Fiction Editor
Bunker Books
Synthoil Tower
New York NY 10012

Dear Ms. Tashkajian:

Thank you so much for accepting *Midway Diary*! I'm so delighted I almost got out of my wheelchair and danced a jig! The signed contracts are enclosed. How soon will the book be published? You know, I am the last surviving man to have been in the Battle of Midway, and I'd like to at least see the book before I report to the Big Admiral up yonder.

Thank you again. You've made an old man very happy. The advance money will come in handy when next month's bills arrive.

Thanks once again,
Capt. R. Clanker, U.S.N. (Ret.)

P.S. Do you think we could make a movie out of the book?

Fourteen

The first night out of New York, the good ship *New Amsterdam* ran into a bit of foul weather. Nothing serious, merely a line of squalls that marked the leading edge of a weather front. Herman Melville would barely have noticed it. Yet the night resounded with the thump of landlubbers' bodies rolling out of their bunks.

Ralph Malzone leaned his scrawny forearms against the ship's rail and squinted out toward the bright, clean horizon. The morning was clear as crystal, the sun warm, the sea down to a light chop. Grinning dolphins rode along the ship's bow wave, gliding effortlessly up to the surface and disappearing beneath the sea, only to rise again glistening and sleek a few moments later.

Carl Lewis came up beside him and gripped the rail with white-knuckled hands.

"You okay?" Malzone asked.

"I think so. This is the first time I've been out of sight of land."

"You look a little green."

"I feel a little green," Carl admitted.

"Did you eat anything at dinner last night?"

"Not much."

"Keep it down?"

"Some of it."

Ralph chuckled. "Come on, kid. What you need is a decent breakfast."

Carl shook his head. "I'm not so sure. . . ."

"Trust me. I spent two years on destroyers. I've seen more upchucking than a men's room attendant at an ancient Roman banquet."

"Huh?"

"Don't worry about it. Every once in a while I forget that sales managers aren't supposed to know anything about literature. Neither are engineers."

"I read Classic Comics in my freshman English class," Carl said defensively.

Ralph sighed heavily and put an arm around the younger man's shoulders. "Come on, let's get some breakfast. You'll feel a lot better with something in your stomach."

Uncertainly, Carl let the sales manager lead him to the ship's dining room. It was a spacious, sumptuously appointed room, decorated in cool, soothing ocean greens and blues. Most of the tables were for four, a few for two, and only the captain's table big enough to hold eight or ten places.

Carl had to admit, half an hour later, that he did feel better. Some tomato juice, a couple of poached eggs, toast, and tea had revived him.

"You know a lot about a lot of things, don't you?" Carl asked.

Malzone shrugged his slim shoulders. "Mostly useless junk. How many times do you get the chance to help somebody get over a slight case of seasickness?"

Carl leaned back in his chair. The dining room was almost empty. Past Malzone's grinning face he could see the ocean through the ship's wide windows. The slight rise and fall of the horizon did not bother him at all now.

"Listen," Malzone said, his face growing serious. "I've been talking with my sales people, and I think you're in for some real problems."

"Problems?"

"Yeah. Y'see, what you're doing with this Cyberbooks idea, basically, is asking the sales force to learn a whole new way of doing their job. It's kinda like asking a clerk in a shoe store to start selling airplanes to the Pentagon."

Carl felt puzzled. "But selling Cyberbooks will be easy!"

Malzone made a lopsided grin that was almost a grimace. "No it won't. My sales people are used to dealing with book distributors, wholesalers, truck drivers, bookstore managers. If I understand the way Cyberbooks is going to work, we're going to be selling directly to the customer."

"That's right. We eliminate all those middle men."

"You eliminate most of my sales force."

"No, no! We'll need them to—"

"They won't change," Malzone said quietly. But very firmly. Hunching forward in his chair, leaning on his forearms until his head almost touched Carl's, he said in a low voice, "They've spent their careers in this business doing their jobs a certain way. They work on the road. They live in their cars. They're not going to give up everything and sit in front of a phone all day."

Carl felt a flare of anger at the pigheadedness Malzone was describing. But he saw that the sales manager was genuinely concerned, truly worried about the conflict that was about to break over his head.

"What should I do?" he heard himself ask.

Malzone's lips twitched in a smile that was over before it started. "Nothing much you can do. Tomorrow morning you show them how Cyberbooks works. Half the sales staff will jump overboard before lunchtime. The other half will try to throw you overboard."

"Terrific!"

"I'll handle them. That's my responsibility. I just wanted to warn you that they're not going to fall down and salaam at the end of your presentation."

"But they all know the basic idea already, don't they?"

"Yep. And they're loading their guns to convince Mrs. Bee that Cyberbooks won't work."

Carl felt worse than seasick. "Jeez . . ."

Malzone straightened up and made an expansive gesture with both hands. "Like I said, that's not your worry. It's mine."

"But the whole purpose of this voyage is to familiarize the editorial and sales staffs with Cyberbooks," Carl insisted.

Laughing, Malzone countered, "Not exactly. That's the *excuse* for this sea voyage, but it's not the real reason for it."

"I don't understand."

"Didn't you notice the big contingent of medical people who came aboard with us?"

"Is that who they are?" Carl had noticed several dozen men and women, elegantly groomed and well dressed, who had arrived at the pier in limousines and shining luxury cars. Obviously neither editors nor sales people. Even their expensive matched luggage had stood out in pointed contrast to the worn, shabby bags of the Bunker Books employees.

"Plastic surgeons," Malzone explained. "It's time for Mrs. Bee's facelift again. And several other people are going in for lifts and tucks and some body remodelling."

"Here on the ship?"

"Sure. They get the job done and the bruises are all healed up by the time we get back to New York. Everybody home says how great they look, how much good the ocean voyage did them. Nobody knows they had plastic surgery aboard ship."

"My god," said Carl. "A facelift cruise."

Thus it was that the following morning, when Carl made his presentation of Cyberbooks to the assembled sales staff, he stood before an audience of bruised and bandaged men and women. They were dressed casually, in shorts and sports tops for the most part. Nearly all of them wore dark glasses. Maryann Quigly was in a whole-body cast, wrapped in white plastic from chin to ankles as a result of a fat-sucking procedure that had drained fifty pounds from her, and the follow-up procedure of tightening her skin so that her body would not be wrinkled like a dieting elephant.

Mrs. Bunker sat in the first row of the ship's auditorium, wearing an elegant hooded jacket and dark glasses that effectively hid the bandages around her eyes and jawline. Carl felt as if he were addressing the survivors of the first wave of an infantry assault team that had been caught in a deadly ambush. There was more bandaging showing than human flesh.

Unbeknownst to Carl or anyone else except Mrs. Bunker, at that very moment P.T. Bunker was on the surgical table, undergoing the multiple procedures that would replace his middle-aged flab with firm young muscle, a transplant procedure that was still very much in the experimental phase.

Just about the only two people in Carl's audience who were not bandaged were Ralph Malzone and Lori Tashkajian. Even Scarlet Dean, slimly beautiful and meticulously dressed as she was, sported a pair of Band-Aids just behind her ears. She had combed her hair into a smooth upsweep, obviously relishing the opportunity to show the bandages rather than hide them.

Feeling somewhat shaken by all this, Carl launched into his demonstration of Cyberbooks. Standing alone on the little stage at the front of the ship's auditorium, he used not his original prototype, but a new model fresh from the manufacturing center. It was exactly the size of a paperback book, small enough to fit in Carl's hand easily.

". . . and as you can see," he was saying, holding up one of the minuscule program wafers, "we can package an entire novel, complete with better graphics than any printing press can produce, in a wafer small enough to tuck into your shirt pocket."

"And how do you *sell* these chips?" asked someone in the audience.

"Two ways," replied Carl. "The customer can buy the wafers from retail outlets, or can get them over the phone, recording the book he or she asks for on a blank wafer, the same way you record a telephone message or a TV show."

"What about copyright protection?" asked Mrs. Bunker. Her hood and oversized dark glasses reminded Carl of movie stars who pretended to avoid public recognition by a disguise so blatant you could not help but stare at it.

"The wafers cannot be copied," he answered. "Once a book is printed on a wafer, instructions for self-destruction are also printed into the text, so if someone tried to recopy the wafer it will erase itself completely."

"Until some ten-year-old hacker figures a way around the instructions," a voice grumbled.

Everybody laughed.

Carl shook his head. "I've had the nastiest kids in the Cambridge public school system try to outsmart the programming. They found a couple of loopholes that surprised me, but we've plugged them."

"You hope."

"I know," Carl shot back with some heat.

A man at the rear of the auditorium stood up, slowly. No bandages showed on him, but the careful way he moved convinced Carl that he must have had a tummy tuck done the day before, or worse.

"I'm just an old war-horse who's been workin' out in the field for damn near thirty years," he said in a rough voice deepened by a lifetime of cigarettes and alcohol. "I don't know anything about this electronics stuff. Hell, I got to get my nephew to straighten out my computer every time I glitch it up!"

The other sales people laughed.

"Now, what I wanna know is this: If this here invention of yours is gonna replace books printed on paper, what happens to the regional distributors, the warehouses, the truck drivers, and the bookstores?"

"The bookstores will still stay in business," Carl said. "They'll just carry electronic books instead of paper ones."

Maryann Quigly yelped from inside her body cast, "You mean there'll be no paper books at all?"

"Eventually electronic books will replace paper books entirely, yes," replied Carl.

"I ain't worried about eventually," the old salesman said. "I'm worried about this coming season. What do I tell the distributors in my area?"

"As far as Cyberbooks is concerned, you won't have to deal with them at all. You can show the line directly to the bookstores. We can supply them from the office in New York, over the telephone lines, with all the books they want."

A hostile muttering spread through the audience.

"In fact," Carl continued, raising his voice slightly, "the bookstores won't have to order any books in advance. They can phone New York when a customer asks for a Cyberbook and we can transmit it to them instantly, electronically."

The muttering grew louder.

"In other words," said the old war-horse, "first you're gonna replace the entire wholesale side of the business, and then you're gonna replace us!"

Carl's jaw dropped open.

Mrs. Bunker got to her feet and turned to face the salesman. "Woody—nobody could possibly replace you."

A ripple of laughter went through the group.

"Seriously," Mrs. Bunker continued, "we have got to learn how to adapt to this new innovation. That's why I've brought us all together on this ship, so we can hammer out the new ways of doing things that we're *all* going to have to learn."

"Mrs. Bee," retorted Woody hoarsely, "I been with you and P.T. for damn near thirty years. Through good times and lean. But it seems to me that this Cyber-thing is gonna mean you won't need us sales people. You won't need anything except a goddamned computer!"

"That's just not true," Mrs. Bunker snapped. "I don't care how the books are produced or distributed, they will not sell themselves. We will *always* need good, dedicated, experienced sales people. The techniques might change, the system may be altered, but your jobs will be just as important to this company with Cyberbooks as before. More important, in fact."

Ralph Malzone sprang to his feet. "Hey, listen, guys. How many times have you come to me complaining about this knuckleheaded distributor or some dopey truck driver who brings the books back for returns without even opening the cartons? Huh?"

They chuckled. Somewhat grudgingly, Carl thought.

"Well, with Cyberbooks you eliminate all the middlemen. You deal directly with the point of sales. And you don't have to carry six hundred pounds of paper around with you!"

The discussion went on and on. Carl stepped down from the stage and let Ralph and Mrs. Bunker argue with the sales force. The editors shifted uncomfortably on their seats, whether from irritation, boredom, or low-grade postsurgical pain, Carl could not tell.

The men and women of the sales force were clearly hostile toward Cyberbooks. Even when Mrs. Bunker explained to them that since sales were bound to increase, the company would have to hire more sales people, which meant that most of the present sales personnel would get promoted, they expressed a cynical kind of skepticism that bordered on mutiny.

The most telling counterthrust came from one of the women. "So we start selling Cyberbooks direct to the stores," she said in a nasal Bronx accent. "So what about our other lines? They'll still be regular paper books. How do you think the wholesalers are gonna behave when they see us going around them with the Cyberbooks, huh? I'll tell you just what they'll do: they'll say, 'You stop going behind our backs with these electrical books or we'll stop carrying Bunker Books altogether.' That's what they'll say!"

Telephone Transcript

"I can hear you clear as a bell, Scarlet."

"You ought to, for what Bunker's paying to have its own satellite communications link from ship to shore."

"I'm glad you're with Bunker now. Webb seems to be going downhill."

"Stop fishing for dirt, Murray. We're discussing the Stoker contract and that's all."

(Laughing.) "Okay, okay. The terms are acceptable, all except the split on the foreign rights. Sheldon wants ninety percent instead of eighty."

"Eighty-five is the best I can do."

"Okay, I'll talk him into eighty-five. But just for you. I wouldn't do it for anybody else."

"You're a sweetheart."

"Oh, yeah. The advance. It's still no bigger than his last contract."

"That's because his last book still hasn't earned out, Murray. His stuff is getting stale. The readers aren't buying it the way they used to."

"Not earned out yet? Are you sure?"

"Sad but true."

"Hmm. Well, I guess Sheldon can live with a million until the next royalty checks come in. In his tax bracket, it isn't so bad."

"The self-discipline will be good for him."

"But how about making it a two-book deal?"

"On the same contract? Two books?"

"Right. You know he can pump out another one in six months or less."

"I think he pumps them out in six *weeks* or less, doesn't he?"

"Whatever. Two books, two million up front, and the same terms we've been discussing."

"You've got a deal, Murray."

"Nice doing business with you. Have a pleasant cruise."

Fifteen

Walking through the vast offices of Webb Press is like walking through a mausoleum these days, thought P. Curtis Hawks. That damned Axhelm has depopulated the company. Where once there sat dozens of lovely red-haired lasses with dimpled knees and adoring eyes that followed his every gesture, now there was row upon row of empty desks.

Even worse, the Axe had brought in automated partitions for the editorial and sales offices. The amount of office space those people had now depended on how well their books were selling. "Psychological reinforcement," Axhelm had called it. What it meant was, if your sales figures for the week were good, your office got bigger, the goddamned walls spread out automatically, in response to the computer's commands.

But if your sales figures were down, the walls crept in on you. Your office shrank. It was like being in a dungeon designed by the insidious Dr. Fu Manchu: the walls pressed in closer and closer. Already one editor had cracked up completely and run screaming back home to her mother in the wilds of Ohio.

"The next step," Axhelm was saying as the two men surveyed the emptiness that had once been filled with doting redheads, "is to sell all this useless furniture and other junk." Eyeing Hawks haughtily, he added, "The teak panelling in your spacious office should be worth a considerable sum."

Hawks chomped hard on his pacifier. Maybe I should put Vinnie onto this sonofabitch instead of the Old Man, he thought.

"And then we move to smaller quarters," Axhelm went on. "Where the rents are more reasonable. Perhaps across the river, in Brooklyn Heights."

"Never!" Hawks exploded. "No publishing house could survive outside of Manhattan. It's impossible."

Axhelm looked down at his supposed superior with that damned pitying smile of his. "If you don't mind my saying so, sir, your grasp on what is possible and what is impossible seems not to be very strong."

"Now see here . . ."

"You said it would be impossible to run Webb Press with only one-third of the staff that was present when I joined the company. Yet look!" The Axe gestured toward the empty desks. "Two thirds of the personnel are gone and the company functions just as well. Better, even. More efficiently."

"Our sales are down."

"A temporary dip. Probably seasonal."

"Seasonal nothing!" Hawks almost spat the pacifier out of his mouth. "How can we sell books when two-thirds of our sales force has been laid off?"

"The remaining one-third is sufficient," said the Axe smugly.

"You're going to run the company into the ground," moaned Hawks.

Axhelm eyed the shorter man as if through a monocle. "My dear sir, the task given me by corporate management was to make Webb Press more efficient. I have pruned excess personnel and now I shall reduce costs further by moving the offices out of this overly expensive location. *Operating* the company is your responsibility, not mine. If you cannot show a profit even after I have reduced your costs so drastically, then I suggest that you tender your resignation and turn over the reins of authority to someone who can run an efficient operation."

Slowly, with the certainty of revealed truth dawning upon him, Hawks took the plastic cigar butt out of his mouth. So that's it, he said to himself. Axhelm wants to take over Webb Press. He wants my job. He wants my head as a trophy on his wall.

He said nothing aloud. But to himself, Hawks promised, I'm going to chop you down, you Prussian martinet. And I'm going to use your own methods to do it.

Sunset at sea. Scarlet Dean lay back on a deck chair, splendidly alone up on the topmost deck of the *New Amsterdam*, and watched the sun dip toward the horizon, blazing a path of purest gold across the sparkling waters directly toward her. It was if the huge glowing red sphere were trying to show her a path to wealth and happiness, she thought.

She knew she was in some danger. Not from anyone with Bunker Books. As far as she could tell they were all pleasantly incompetent nincompoops. Even Alba Bunker, who had a reputation for being the real brains behind the company, seemed totally unaware of what a tiger she had by the tail in Cyberbooks. Just about the only person who seemed to understand what was going on, really, was the sales manager. Ralph Malzone. A wiry, intense kind of guy. And a lot smarter than he pretended to be.

The danger came from Hawks and his temper. The man had no patience. God knows what demons are after his hide, Scarlet told herself. But it wouldn't be beyond him to order someone to sink this ship and drown everyone on it.

Including me.

But he won't do that unless and until he has the Cyberbooks machine in his grubby little paws. Or will he? Does he see Cyberbooks as a threat? Does he think he'd be better off putting the whole problem at the bottom of the Atlantic?

On the other hand, she thought, suppose I had control of Cyberbooks. Me. Myself. I could write my own ticket with Webb Press. Or with any publishing house in New York. I could probably get the top publishers together to buy me off, pay me millions to suppress the invention. I could retire for life.

Or start my own company. Take their money and then go to Japan and start a Cyberbooks company there. She smiled to herself. Or Singapore, even better. I could live like a queen in the Far East. The Dragon Lady. Empress of worldwide publishing. What a trip!

To do that, though, I'll have to get our young inventor to trust me. He's got to come along with me, at least at the beginning. The machine means nothing without the inventor to show others how to build it.

Scarlet realized, with a start, that she was sitting up tensely in the deck chair, every nerve taut with anticipation. She forced herself to lean back in the chair as she thought about Carl Lewis.

Lori Tashkajian is after him, she knew. Probably in love with him. Certainly the little twit understands that Carl is the key to her personal success. I'll have to pry Carl loose from her. More important, I'll have to pry him loose from his work. He's married to his damned invention, Scarlet realized. Oblivious to everything else. Lori is practically throwing herself at him and he just glides along without seeing it.

He's susceptible, though. I could see that the first time I met him. The tongue-tied engineer type. I'll have to be much more aggressive than Lori's been. His type calls for special measures.

Scarlet practiced smiling, alone up there on the top deck, while the sun slid slowly toward the gleaming red-gold sea and the sky turned to majestic flame.

Lori and Carl were standing side by side at the ship's rail, just one deck below Scarlet Dean's solitary perch.

"Isn't the sunset beautiful?" she murmured.

"So are you," Carl said. And she was, with the sea breeze caressing her shimmering ebony hair and the blazing red glory of the setting sun on her face. Lori wore a sleeveless white frock. In the last light of the sunset it glowed like cloth of gold.

She acknowledged his compliment with a smile, then looked back toward the sea.

"I think you and I are the only people on board," Carl went on, "who haven't had any plastic surgery done on them."

Lori giggled. "That's true enough! Have you seen Ted Gunn? Hair implants and artificial bone in his legs to make him two inches taller. Even Concetta has had her breasts and backside lifted."

Carl chuckled. "The one that gets me is Quigly. The pain she must have gone through!"

"And now she's eating five meals a day," Lori said, "even before the bandages come off! She'll be the same weight at the end of this cruise as she was at the beginning."

"But think of the great time she's having," Carl countered.

They both laughed. Then he said, "You don't need plastic surgery. You're gorgeous just as you are."

"I'm overweight. . . ."

"You're perfect."

"No I'm not."

"Yes you are."

"Carl, I'm far from perfect." Lori's face grew so serious that he did not reply. Then she went on, "In fact, I have a confession to make. I've been using you, Carl—for my own purposes."

"I don't understand."

She looked into his steady blue-gray eyes, a turmoil of conflicting emotions raging within her. As if beyond her conscious control, her voice said, "Carl, back in my office there's a manuscript. . . ."

"There's hundreds of "em!"

"This is serious," Lori insisted. "One of those manuscripts is by a completely unknown writer. Nothing the author has written before has ever been published. And it's *good*, Carl! It's better than good. It's a masterpiece. It's raw, even crude in places. It's an unpolished gem. But it's a masterpiece. I want to publish it."

"So?" It was obvious from his puzzled expression that Carl did not understand the problem.

"It doesn't fit into any of the marketing categories. It's not a mystery, or a Gothic, or an historical novel. It's just the finest piece of American literature I've ever read. I get tears in my eyes whenever I think about it, that's how good it is. Pulitzer Prize, at least. Maybe the Nobel."

"Then why don't you publish it?"

"No New York publisher would touch it. It's a thousand manuscript pages long. It's not category. It's *literature*. That's the kiss of death for a commercial publishing house. They don't publish literature because literature doesn't make money."

"But if it's so good . . ."

"That's got nothing to do with it," Lori said, almost crying. "Quality doesn't sell books. Can you imagine the sales people on this ship going out and selling *Crime and Punishment* or *Bleak House*?"

Carl's expression turned thoughtful. "Didn't I read someplace that every publisher in New York turned down *Gone With the Wind* at one time or another?"

Nodding, Lori said, "Yes. And for twelve years none of them would touch *Lost Horizon*. There's a long list of great novels that nobody wanted to publish."

"But they all got into print eventually."

"But how many others didn't?" Lori almost shouted with a vehemence that surprised her. "How many truly fine novels have never been published because the people in this business are too blind or stupid to see how great they are? How many really great authors have gone to their graves totally unknown, their work turned to dust along with them?"

"My god, you're trembling."

Lori rested her head against Carl's shoulder. "It's a fine novel, a great work of art. And it's going to die without seeing the light of day—unless . . ."

"Unless what?" he asked, folding his arms around her.

"Unless we can make a success of Cyberbooks. Then they'll let me take a chance on an unknown, on a work of literature. I need to be able to tell Mrs. Bunker that the price of my bringing you to her is letting me publish this novel."

"That makes sense, I guess."

She pushed slightly away from him, enough to be able to look up into his eyes. "But don't you understand? I'm using you! I'm not interested in your invention just for its own sake. I want it to be a success so that I can have the power to publish this book!"

Carl smiled at her. "Okay. So what? I'm using you too, aren't I? Using you to get me inside a big New York publishing house so I can get my invention developed. Otherwise I'd still be sitting in some publisher's waiting room, wouldn't I?"

"But that's not the same. . . ."

"Listen to me. Cyberbooks can help you in more ways than one. How big is this great novel of yours? A thousand pages? How much would it cost to print a book that long?"

"A fortune," Lori admitted.

"With Cyberbooks it won't cost any more than a regular-sized book. And the retail price of the novel will be less than five dollars."

Lori brightened. "I hadn't even thought about that part of it. I was still thinking in terms of printing the novel on paper."

"Come on." He crooked a finger under her chin. "Cheer up. You help me bring Cyberbooks to life and I'll help you get your novel published. That's what the biologists call a symbiotic relationship."

Dabbing away the tears at the corner of her eyes, Lori allowed Carl to lead her along the deck toward the hatch that opened into the dining salon. Neither of them noticed Scarlet Dean, leaning over the railing of the deck just above where they had been standing, a knowing little smile curving her narrow red lips.

Murder Five

Miles Archer was an ex-police officer. A retired homicide detective, in fact. He had even been named after a detective. A small, unremarkable man who had gray hair by the time he was thirty, Archer had cracked many cases during his long distinguished career with the NYPD simply by the fact that hardly anyone could recognize the steel-trap mind behind his bland, utterly forgettable facade.

"He must have known he was being followed," said the uniformed cop.

Lt. Moriarty nodded. "Yeah. Miles would never have wandered up an alley like this for no reason."

Moriarty's steely gaze swept up and down the narrow alley. It was littered with paper, but otherwise clean enough. They were down in the financial district, near Wall Street. No winos huddled in the alleys here. Brokers might sneak martinis into their Thermos jugs, but they went home to posh suburbia after the day's frenzied work.

Archer's slight body lay facedown, where it had fallen, rumpled gray trenchcoat twisted around him, in front of a rusted metal door that led into the rear of a high-rise office building. The alley dead-ended at the brick rear wall of another high rise. A third skyscraper formed the other side of the narrow alley. Moriarty sniffed disdainfully; there was no garbage or urine smell to the alley. It seemed unnatural to him.

The forensics team was taking holographic pictures and lifting samples of litter from the area around the body. One of the team members was scanning the alleyway with an infrared detector for latent footprints. The binocularlike black detector steamed slightly as the summer evening's heat boiled away some of its liquid nitrogen coolant.

"He figured somebody was following him," Moriarty reconstructed the event aloud, "and ducked up here to see if whoever it was would come in too."

"And the perpetrator did follow him," said the cop in blue.

Moriarty nodded. "Must've been one person, and not a rough-looking type at all. Miles wasn't the kind for personal heroics. He must've thought whoever he was being followed by was lightweight enough for him to face down by himself."

"He made a mistake."

"The last one he'll ever make."

"Uh, Lieutenant . . ." The uniformed cop hesitated. "You don't think maybe he was deliberately meeting somebody here, do you?"

"In an alley?"

"They do a lot of designer drugs around here. Those brokers got a lot of money to throw around."

Moriarty dismissed the idea with a shake of his head. "Not Miles. He didn't even drink."

"Then what was he doing down in the financial district? He lived in Queens, didn't he?"

"He set up his own business after retiring from the force," said Moriarty. "Might have been down here on a case."

The cop went silent. Moriarty continued, thinking aloud, "I'll get the records from his office and see what he was working on. Must be a connection there." He watched as the medical team gently lifted the inert body onto a stretcher and carried it to the ambulance waiting at the head of the alley, lights flashing.

"You think there's a connection with the other Retiree Murders?" the uniformed policeman asked.

Moriarty looked sharply at him. "Is that what they're calling 'em? 'Retiree Murders'?"

"In the newspapers, yeah. And on TV. This makes the fifth one, doesn't it?"

"That's right. But I don't think their murders have anything to do with their being retired. Hell, the Social Security clerks aren't going around bumping off their clients."

The cop shrugged and started up the alley. Their work here was finished. Moriarty followed behind him, thinking, I ran the other four through the computer to look for correlations. The only thing the victims had in common was that they were elderly, retired, and living off pensions, Social Security, and the income from a few odd shares of stocks.

Sixteen

Weldon W. Weldon frowned balefully at the computer's holographic display. It showed a graphic presentation of the owners of Tarantula's stock, twisted threads of colored lines that weaved and interlinked in a three-dimensional agony of confusion. Like a tangled mess of spaghetti. Like a pit of snakes slithering over and around one another. Or the snarled, twining stems of jungle vines struggling to find the sun.

He snorted in self-derision as he glanced from the display to the rotting jungle that infested his once immaculate office. Leaning forward in his powered wheelchair, he squinted at the display and tapped commands on the remote controller he held in one hand.

Who the hell really owns Tarantula? Ever since the Sicilians had started their takeover effort, that one question had burned through Weldon's brain like a laser beam cutting through naked flesh.

I don't have enough of the stock to stop them by myself, although I've climbed over the twenty-five percent mark. Synthoil is the largest single shareholder, that much is clear. The sky-blue line threading through the heart of the display was General Conglomerates, which owned eight percent of Tarantula. Are they in with the Sicilians? Not likely, Weldon thought, although you could never be entirely certain. The Benevolent International Brotherhood of Bureaucrats, a kinked muddy-brown line, owned twelve percent. Twelve percent! And the BIBB is a *known* Mafia subsidiary. Damnation.

And then there was the blood-red line pulsing through the others like an aorta: Rising Sun Electronics. They already had seventeen percent and were busily buying more. Weldon had encouraged the

Japanese to buy Tarantula stock. Better in their hands than the Sicilians'. Play the Nips against the Wops, he had cackled to himself. But now the Japanese share of the company was becoming large enough to be a threat of its own.

The rest of the ownership was in the hands of individuals, thank god. Ordinary men and women who each owned a few shares apiece. Thousands of them. How would they vote at November's stockholders' meeting? Most of 'em never vote at all, never even send in their proxies, bless them. Then *I* vote their stock for them.

But what would they do if some smarmy jerkoff with olive oil in his hair offers to buy their stock at ten percent above the current market value? I'd have to make them a better offer, and the only way to do that is to liquidate half the company's assets to generate the cash for such a buy-back. Once Axhelm's finished with Webb Press I'll have to turn him loose on other divisions of the corporation. The old man sighed heavily. It can't be helped. We can't fight through an unfriendly takeover bid without spattering some blood on the floor, he thought grimly.

Maryann Quigly and Ashley Elton sat forlornly in the afterdeck lounge at the stern of the SS *New Amsterdam*. It was nearly midnight, and Quigly was working her way through her fifth meal of the day, a dainty snack of steak, french-fried potatoes, custard pie, and malted milk. Elton was nursing a tall concoction made of various rums and fruit juices.

The lounge was beautifully decorated in deep blue and silver, with glittering wall panels of faceted crystal that could be turned into giant display screens for video presentations. Beyond the curving windows that overlooked the ship's stern, the *New Amsterdam*'s churning wake glistened against the placid moonlit ocean. The muted strains of dance music from the main salon wafted through the afterdeck lounge.

"All these men on board," murmured the cadaverous Ms. Elton, "and not one of them has asked us even for a dance."

"I couldn't dance in this body cast," Quigly said through a mouthful of french fries. "It itches all over. I think they made it too tight for me."

Elton had availed herself of the plastic surgeons to transplant some of her gluteus maximus to her pectoral area. There was hardly enough meat on her to make any difference, but she felt better for it, although for the time being she had to sit on an inflated plastic ring, like a hemorrhoid victim.

"Well, I can dance, but nobody's asked me," she whined.

Maryann stuffed half the custard pie into her mouth. The after-deck lounge was almost empty. The evening floor show had ended an hour ago, and now most of the ambulatory men and women aboard the ship were in the main salon, dancing to the syntho-rock music of a robot band.

"Don't feel bad about it," Maryann advised her colleague. "All the men on this cruise are either macho or gay."

"Yeah, I suppose so. Still, you'd think . . ." Ashley Elton's voice trailed off wistfully.

"That's not important," said Quigly, reaching for her malted milk. "What's important is this Cyberbooks deal."

"Yeah. What do you think of it?"

Quigly's eyes, small and deepset in folds of flesh that not even the cosmetic surgeons had been able to remove, shifted evasively. "It bothers me," she said.

"Me too."

"There's too many computers in this business already," muttered Quigly, glancing around to see if anyone was close enough to over-hear. No one was. No one was sitting within thirty feet of them.

"Yeah. Did you see what they did at Webb Press? They've got computers doing just about *everything* now. Only three editors left in the whole house! They've got to do everything!"

"Who has time to do anything?" Quigly puffed out a weary sigh, then polished off the rest of her malted.

"I sure don't," admitted Elton. "What with meetings and meetings and more meetings, I'm lucky if I open the morning mail."

With a ponderous shake of her head, Quigly said slowly, "A book ought to have *pages*. It ought to be made out of paper."

"Yeah. Something you can curl up with in bed at night."

"Not some electronic box."

"It's so cold!"

"It isn't right," Quigly insisted. "Books should be made out of paper. That's the way they were meant to be made."

"Wrong, girls."

The two women jerked with guilty surprise. Standing over them was Woodrow Elihu Balogna, known to all as Woody Baloney, sales rep for the upper Midwest region.

"Books," Woody said genially, waving a cigarette in a grand gesture, "were meant to be made out of clay tablets—or maybe papyrus scrolls."

"Pass the bread," Elton announced ritualistically, "here comes the Baloney."

Woody pulled out the empty chair and sat himself carefully on it, sighing out a puff of smoke as he settled down.

"You know this is a no-smoking area," Elton said peevishly. "All indoor spaces on this ship are no-smoking."

"Yeah, but what the hell. You girls won't fink on me, will you?"

"They should have transplanted a human brain into your skull instead of just giving you a tummy tuck," Quigly chimed in.

"And you're adorable too," croaked Woody in his husky voice, a big grin on his weatherbeaten face. But he stubbed the cigarette out in the crumb-littered plate that had once held Quigly's custard cream pie.

He was a big man, and once had been handsome in a rawboned sort of way. But years of alcohol, cigarettes, sleeping in motels, and pounding his head against the ingrained obstinacy of wholesalers and jobbers had ravaged him. His face was seamed and scarred like the Grand Canyon, and scruffy with a day's growth of gray stubble. He wore a faded gray sweatshirt and patched jeans that hung loosely on his suddenly gangly frame.

"What you should have done," Ashley Elton said more seriously, "was let them give you a facelift. You're still handsome, underneath all those wrinkles."

Woody tilted his head back and guffawed. "Now, can you just picture me waltzing into Duluth Distributing's warehouse looking all prettied up! They'd throw me out on my ass!"

Maryann Quigly refused to smile. She waited for Woody's whoops to die down, then said, "Don't you go telling anybody what we were saying about the Cyberbooks idea. Just because—"

"Hey, I'm with you," Woody assured her. "I think this smart-aleck inventor is going to get us all thrown out of work. We gotta find a way to stop him."

Quigly's porcine little eyes widened. "You mean it?"

"It's him or us, that's the way I feel about it."

"But Mrs. Bunker . . ." whispered Elton.

"We gotta convince her that this Cyberbooks gadget is a mistake, a flop, a disaster. We gotta make her see that if she tries to market Cyberbooks it'll ruin the company."

"But her mind's already made up," Elton countered, "the other way."

"Then we've got to make her reverse her decision," said Quigly.

"But how?"

"That's the hard part," Woody admitted, his grin fading.

P. Curtis Hawks was standing at the sweeping windows of his spacious office, staring hard across the river toward Brooklyn.

The goddamned Junker bastard wants to move us to Brooklyn! He shook his head for the ten-thousandth time. Brooklyn. It's the end of the world.

He had to admit, however, that Gunther Axhelm's pruning was already showing results. The latest quarterly profit and loss statement on his desk was considerably better than it had been in years. The operation was actually in the black for the first time since the Reagan memoirs had swept the world with their candid charm and naively brutal insights.

Sales were slipping, but that was to be expected when the sales force had been reduced from two hundred men and women to a single voice-activated computer and a fleet of roboticized trucks. They would pick up again, Hawks fervently prayed, once the wholesalers got accustomed to seeing robots instead of human beings. The big chain stores, where the really massive orders came from, had not even noticed the difference. Book orders went from their computers to Webb's computer as smoothly as snakes slithering on banana oil.

Offsetting the downtrend in sales was the even larger downtrend in costs. The Old Man upstairs must be happy with the situation, Hawks told himself. He hasn't bothered me in weeks. Then he frowned. Or maybe he just doesn't want to see me anymore. Maybe Axhelm's axe is going to stab *me* in the back, too.

The warehouse. The goddamned, mother-humping, sonofabitching warehouse. So far I've been able to keep Axhelm's beady little eyes off it. But how long can I hold out? How long can I keep him from finding out what a fiasco the damned warehouse is?

His desk phone chimed.

"Answer answer," he called out, thinking that the goddamned phones were just like most goddamned people, you had to tell them everything twice.

"Sir," came the mechanical voice of his computer (where once there had been an achingly lovely red-haired lass), "Engineer Yakamoto is waiting to see you."

Oh Christ, thought Hawks. Just what I need. Yakamoto. Something else has gone wrong at the warehouse.

With a reluctant, shivering sigh, Hawks told the computer to let the Japanese warehouse manager enter his office.

Hideki Yakamoto was pure Japanese. He had come over from Osaka as a field engineer to oversee the installation of the robotic equipment at the warehouse. When it became apparent that he was the only man on the continent of North America who could make the robots function the way they should, Hawks had insisted to his parent company, Rising Sun Electronics, that they allow him to remain at the warehouse as supervisor. Rising Sun, happy to have a spy inside the Tarantula organization, allowed itself to be reluctantly persuaded.

Yakamoto, small, wiry, round-faced, clad in a Saville Row three-piece summerweight suit, bowed from the waist and inhaled through his teeth with a sharp hiss meant to express his unworthiness to breathe the same air as his illustrious superior. Hawks found himself bowing back. Not that he wanted to, his body just seemed to bow whenever the little Nip did it to him.

Annoyed at himself, he snapped, "What's wrong, Yakamoto?"

The Japanese engineer said blandly, "Nothing that cannot be put right by the wealth of knowredge that you possess. I am ashamed to bother you with what must be a small detail . . ."

"Come to the point, dammit!" Hawks went to his desk and stood behind it. It made him feel safer.

Yakamoto bowed again. "It is shameful for me to intrude on your extremery busy schedule . . ."

"What is it?" Hawks fairly screamed.

Yakamoto braced himself. Standing at rigid attention, he said, "The grue, sir."

"The grue? What grue?"

"The grue used to bind the pages of the books together, sir."

"You mean *glue*! Well, what about it?"

Yakamoto closed his eyes, as if standing before a firing squad. "It evaporates, sir."

"What?"

"The grue evaporates while the books are in their packing cases. When the cases are open, there is nothing in them but roose pages and covers."

Hawks sank heavily into his padded chair. "Oh, my sweet baby Jesus."

Yakamoto said nothing, he just stood there with his fists clenched by his sides, eyes squeezed shut. He did not even seem to be breathing.

"How many . . . cases . . ."

Without opening his eyes, "This month's entire print run, sir. We began receiving compraints from stores and warehouses rast week. Whenever a case is opened—nothing but roose pages, fluttering rike butterflies in the summer breezes."

"Spare me the goddamned poetry!" Hawks snapped.

"I have taken the liberty of firing a comprete report in your personal computer system," Yakamoto said, "so that you have all the details avairable at your industrious fingertips. However, I felt it necessary for me to tell you of this catastrophe in person."

Hawks grunted and reached out a reluctant hand to access the data. His screen soon showed the gory details. Millions of dollars' worth of books, reduced to millions of loose pages. Tens of millions of pages. Hundreds of millions . . .

He groaned. We're ruined. Absolutely ruined.

Yakamoto was making strange, gargling sounds. Hawks looked up. Is he trying to commit suicide, right here in my office?

No, the man was merely trying to get Hawks's attention by repeatedly clearing his throat.

"Don't tell me there's more," Hawks moaned.

Yakamoto stood rigidly silent.

"Well?"

"You told me not to tell you," the Japanese engineer said pleadingly.

"Tell me!" Hawks snapped. "Tell me all of it! Every goddamned ball-breaking detail. Give it to me, all of it. Then we can both jump out the frigging window!"

Yakamoto bowed as if to say, *You asked for it.* "Apparently, exalted sir, the grue used to bind the books decomposes into a psychedelic gas. When the crates are opened, whoever is within ten feet becomes intoxicated—they have immediate and invoruntary 'head trips' that approximate the effects of taking a sizable dose of harrucinogen."

Hawks felt his breakfast making its burning way up his digestive tract, toward his throat. Glue sniffing! With the effects of LSD!

"And . . ." Yakamoto said as quietly as a dove gliding through tranquil air.

"Still more?"

Barely nodding, Yakamoto said, "Those who have been affected by the narcotic nature of the residual gas from the faired grue are initiating rawsuits against Webb Press. Several such riabirity suits have already been fired against the company."

"Several? How many?"

With a pained expression, Yakamoto replied, "Seven hundred thirty-four, as of this morning."

Hawks slammed both palms down on his desk and hauled himself to his feet. "That's it! Hara-kiri! That's the only road left open to us, Yakamoto!" He strode toward the sliding glass partition that led to the terrace. "It's a fifty-story drop. That ought to do the job."

Yakamoto did not stir from where he stood. "Most respected and brave sir, it is not my place to kill myself over this matter. I had nothing to do with putting this unfaithful grue on the books. It is not my responsibility."

Hawks stopped with one hand on the handle of the sliding glass partition.

"Wait a minute," he said. "You're right. I didn't order any new kind of glue for binding the books."

Yakamoto said softly, "Still, it is your responsibility, sir."

"Is it? We've been binding books by the zillions for years without this kind of trouble. Who the hell ordered different glue? I'll nail his balls to the wall!"

Suddenly a happy thought penetrated Hawks's consciousness, and he broke into a slight grin. As eagerly as a teenaged boy reaching for a condom, he jumped back onto his desk chair and sent his fingers flying across the computer keyboard.

"Yes!" he shouted triumphantly after several frenzied minutes. "Yes! Yes! Yes!"

Yakamoto stood motionless, but his face showed unbearable curiosity.

"Axhelm ordered the new glue!" Hawks crowed. "The wise-ass ordered it because it's half a cent per thousand cheaper!"

While his faithful Japanese engineer watched incredulously, Hawks flung himself on the carpet and laughed hysterically.

The Writer

The Writer cringed in terror in the farthest corner of the warehouse. They had all gone mad. Wildly, murderously mad.

His fellow employees—the bedraggled men and few equally unattractive women who worked the warehouse floor, those human dregs who daily risked life and sanity to do jobs that gleaming robots could not handle—they were capering and gibbering, ripping open the cartons that they were supposed to be neatly stacking, tearing out loose pages of books and flinging them high into the air until the entire warehouse looked like a blizzard was raging through it.

They sang. They screamed with laughter. They danced through the paper snowfall and howled with animal glee. Several heaps of paper the size of mating couples were twitching and shuddering here and there across the warehouse floor. Even the Japanese supervisors, who had raced down from the control booth shouting and gesticulating, were now capering through the littered warehouse, eyeglasses askew, reeling for all the world as if they were dead drunk.

"C'mon, pal! Don' be 'fraid!" One of the grimy-faced women was bending over the Writer, her faded blouse pulled open and her meager breasts hanging free.

With wordless terror, the Writer scrabbled away from her until his back was pressed against the concrete wall and he could retreat no farther.

The woman laughed at him. "Don' be scared, pal. It's okay. It's our bonus. Lousy wages they been payin' us, we're entitled to a li'l bonus, huh?"

She advanced on him. The Writer tried to push his emaciated body *through* the concrete wall. Behind the woman's menacing form he could see the other warehouse employees gibbering and gamboling madly. Their insane shouts and laughter were a bedlam. All the robots stood immobile, inert, dead.

"Look, pal, I got a present for ya. . . ." The woman reached into the back pocket of her jeans and tugged out a brand-new paperback book. It had obviously just been taken from its packing crate. The cover glistened pristinely.

"Yer gonna love it," she said, shoving it under the writer's nose.

He tried to bat it away. The pages fell apart and spilled into his lap. A spicy, pungent odor filled the Writer's nostrils. His vision blurred for a moment. He rubbed his eyes, inhaling the wonderful perfume coming from the scattered pages of the book.

When he looked up at the woman again, he saw that she was beautiful. And the music was beautiful. The whole world was just as he had always dreamed it would be, someday.

Smiling, he began to sing the love duet from *Tristan und Isolde* in a better tenor voice than he had ever imagined possessing. She sang back in a breathtaking soprano.

Seventeen

Seven doctors and seven nurses, all in pale green smocks and masks, huddled over the surgical table beneath the shadowless light of powerful overhead lamps. In a corner of the tiny, intense room a row of electronic machines beeped and peeped, while miniature pumps and motors made a soft pocketa-pocketa sound. Otherwise the improvised surgical chamber was silent, except for the terse, whispered commands of the chief surgeon and the responses of the chief nurse:

"Clamp."

"Clamp."

"Retractors ."

"Retractors."

"Inserting left *flexor digitorum longus.*"

"Yes, doctor."

"Microviewer."

The nurse swung the elaborate electro-optical device toward the chief surgeon and deftly adjusted it to his eye level.

"Microstapler."

She put the tiny staple gun in his right hand.

For several moments the only sound from the group crowding around the surgical table was the clicking of the microstapler.

Then the chief surgeon straightened up and wiped his own brow with his own blood-smeared gloved hand.

"That's it," he said. They could all hear the smile behind his mask. "Close him up, Renshaw."

The thirteen men and women clapped their gloved hands in admiration. It sounded something like limp pillows clashing. The chief surgeon bowed, blew them all a kiss, and tottered off to wash up.

Hours later, consciousness returned to the newly rebuilt body of Pandro T. Bunker. He lay on the same table; it had been wheeled into the recovery room (actually a passenger's cabin four decks below the New Amsterdam's waterline, a few yards down the passageway from the movie theater that the plastic surgeons had been using for their operations). A single nurse, young, blond, and nubile, was polishing her fingernails while a bevy of sensors kept tabs on Bunker's recuperation.

The nurse did not notice the first sign of her patient's return to consciousness, a slight trembling of Bunker's fingers. Then his eyelids fluttered.

P.T. Bunker took a deep breath. The sensors arrayed beside his table beeped along merrily. He growled at them. Then he saw the nurse, her back to him.

He felt—strangely powerful. Young. Virile. Horny as hell. Looking from the nurse to the white sheet that covered his body, he saw a large protuberance poking toward the ceiling.

With a malicious grin he slowly pulled himself up to a sitting position. The effort made him grunt slightly. After all, he had spent several hours in surgery.

The noise made the nurse turn toward him in her swivel chair. Her china-blue eyes went wide.

"Mr. Bunker, you're supposed to rest!"

He tried to reply that he did not feel like resting, that he felt strong and fine, but his throat was so dry that all he could utter was a sort of menacing strangled growl.

"No, no!" said the nurse, getting to her feet, never realizing that the sensors were reporting Bunker's condition to be completely healthy.

Bunker swung his legs off the table and stood up. The sheet dropped away. The surgeons had closed his incisions with quick-acting protein glue, so there was not a bandage on his rebuilt naked body.

The nurse's eyes went still wider, focusing on Bunker's aroused musculature. His eyes were focused on the strained front of her starched white blouse. She was panting. He began panting.

With a shriek, the nurse dropped her bottle of nail polish and bolted to the door. She ran down the passageway screaming, "He's alive! He's alive!"

Bunker lumbered after her, staggering slightly as he tried to make his newly muscled body obey the commands of his publisher's brain.

Three decks above the *New Amsterdam*'s waterline, Scarlet Dean was making up her mind—and her face. She stood before the mirror over the sink in her cabin's compact bathroom, wearing only a pink bra and panties, carefully applying as little mascara and lipstick as she dared. The tiny tucks of the plastic surgery had tightened up her face beautifully. And the biochemical toners made her skin glow like a young girl's.

The mirror seemed to be swaying slightly, and she felt a bit of a sinking sensation in the pit of her stomach. Frowning, she tried to concentrate on getting the lipstick on straight. Can't use too much of it, she told herself; can't have its scent masking the pheromone spray.

"Attention, all passengers," said a very male voice from the little speaker grille set into the ceiling. "We are approaching the edge of a small storm system. The sea will be slightly rougher than usual. Please take care walking, especially on the outside decks. Use the handrails, both inside and outside."

Scarlet shot an annoyed glance at the loudspeaker. They could at least wait until I've finished putting on my lipstick!

Satisfied with her work, she stepped through the hatch and opened the clothes closet next to her queen-sized bed. Her clothes swayed slightly on their hangers, like a chorus line in a speeding subway train. As she pondered over what to wear for dinner, she reviewed where her business matters stood.

The negotiation with Murray Swift over Sheldon Stoker's latest horror was successfully concluded. The other editors and most of the sales force were up in arms over the Cyberbooks project. Mrs. Bunker was fretting, and P.T. Bunker was getting his body rebuilt.

Now was the time to bring young Carl Lewis to heel. She had toyed with him for three months. Now she would reel him in and net him, and when she was finished with him she would mount his head on the wall of her trophy room.

She smiled at the thought.

She selected a slim sheath, bright red, of course, and dressed quickly, efficiently. The last thing she did before heading for the dining salon was to dig the tiny phial of pheromone spray out of her locked briefcase and slip it into her glittering red handbag.

Alba Blanca Bunker was also dressing for dinner. Her cabin was very spacious, of course, but it seemed terribly empty without P.T. to share it. She worried about him, alone without her, deep down in the lower decks that had been turned into a hospital. The doctors were using a new type of synthetic steroid mixture to speed his recuperation, but still it would take several days for him to recover from the body-rebuilding surgery.

She studied herself in the full-length mirrors that flanked both sides of the king-sized bed. Here on the ship she need not be a slave to the weekly fashions of New York. She wore a nineteen thirties ball gown of pure white silk that flowed gracefully to the floor and billowed behind her when she danced. She loved it and felt very beautiful and secure in it.

The plastic surgery had erased most of the worry lines in her face, but not in her heart. Ralph Malzone had warned her that the sales force would not like Cyberbooks. Now it looked as if they would openly revolt against the project. She sighed deeply at the prospect of having dinner with Ralph, Woody, and several other disgruntled sales people. But business is business, she told herself firmly. Squaring her bare slim shoulders, she picked up her handbag and went to the stateroom door.

The wind caught at her lovely gown and nearly twirled her around as she stepped out of the cabin. Up here on the topmost deck of the ship she could see in the last rays of the setting sun that the seas were heaving, whitecapped waves arching upward from the deep dark blue. Thick clouds were building up, gloriously crimson and violet in the dying sunset. Alba secretly thrilled to it. The deck slanted and rose beneath her feet, then dropped away. Even up here she could taste the tang of salt spray in the wind. It was exciting!

She made her way on delicate spike heels toward the ladderway that led down to the dining salon's deck. Gripping the handrails, she carefully went down the stairs and stepped through the hatch that opened onto the bar lounge. The ship had been designed so that it was impossible to enter the dining salon without passing through the lounge and bar first. Some of Malzone's salesmen never made it to dinner. Or lunch. The bar did not open before noon, or they might not have gotten any solid nourishment at all.

Ralph was standing in a little knot of people that included Woody, Lori Tashkajian, and Carl Lewis. Alba knew she would have to detach Carl and Lori from the sales people, but she expected that neither of them would mind. They would obviously rather have dinner by themselves than with the sales department.

As she started toward them, a worried-looking gray-haired man fairly dashed across the open space and intercepted her.

"Mrs. Bunker, I'm Dr. Karloff. . . ."

She recognized his immaculately groomed face, the carefully trimmed little gray mustache, the utterly expensive three-piece suit. He seemed unaccustomedly harried, not his usual smiling confident suave self.

"I'm afraid there's been something of a problem. . . ."

"Pandro!" she gasped. "What's happened to Pandro?"

"The surgery went fine, no problems at all, everything went very well." Karloff was visibly upset; perspiration dotted his brow, he was almost babbling.

"What happened?"

"The recuperative chemotherapy. You recall that I specifically explained to you both that the synthetic steroids were new and relatively untried. . . ."

"You assured us they were safe!" Alba felt cold terror clutching her.

"They are! They are. But the dosage . . . we may have given your husband a higher dose than he actually—"

Just then the double doors at the far side of the lounge were ripped off their hinges with a blood-chilling screech, and the naked lumbering figure of Pandro T. Bunker lurched into the area. Women screamed. Men ducked for cover. Dr. Karloff turned whiter than Alba's gown and fainted dead away.

"Alba!" came a strangled cry from deep within P.T. Bunker. Arms outstretched, he staggered across the thickly carpeted lounge toward her.

She stood frozen with shock, her eyes registering that Pandro seemed taller, stronger, more urgently virile than she had seen him in years. He was a naked Greek god, a young Tarzan, an Adonis with a hard-on.

"Alba!" He lurched toward her.

She ran to him. He scooped her up in his mighty arms and staggered off the way he had come, her virginal white gown trailing after them. Alba nestled her head against her husband's new bulging *pectoralis major* and let him carry her back to their private state-room. He seemed rather clumsy, uncoordinated, but she was sure that he would learn to control his rebuilt body properly, given time. Tonight, self-control was the last thing she wanted from him.

Midnight once again.

Everyone aboard seemed to be still in a state of shock over P.T.'s escapade at the start of the evening. In the main salon little four-somes and couples huddled over tiny cocktail tables, largely ignoring the dance music of the robot band, still talking about it.

"You can see why he's the top man." Woody was leering drunk-enly at three of his cohorts, two of them women.

"It's a transplant," said the other man. "Must have been."

One of the women shot back, "And all you got was a tummy tuck, Woody."

Scarlet Dean had suffered through dinner with Maryann Quigly,

Ted Gunn, and the boorish Jack Drain, just so she could keep Carl Lewis in her sight. Maryann had consumed food the way a horde of locusts does, then immediately waddled off to the afterdeck lounge to get ready for the late night snack. Ted had wisecracked that he could hear her body cast creaking from the pressure she was putting against it.

All through dinner, while Maryann stuffed herself and Drain sneered at everything, Scarlet watched for an opportunity to intrude on Carl and Lori. They gazed at one another adoringly and hardly noticed the meal being served to them. Scarlet knew they were not sleeping together, yet they were behaving like a pair of love-smitten teenagers.

Their romance has gone farther than I thought, she realized. The effects of too much salt air and moonlight. Well, I'll put an end to that tonight, she told herself, patting the handbag resting in her lap. One puff of the pheromone spray and he'll never look at another woman again.

The spray had come from the research laboratories of Tarantula Enterprise's biogenetic division in Stuttgart. It was actually an out-growth of their genetic warfare work, an attempt to create a weapon that would selectively incapacitate only the enemy's troops and no one else. Based on an artificial virus that affected certain nerve pathways into the brain, it had been designed to make its victims fall asleep as long as they could smell the subliminal odor of their military uniforms. The Stuttgart scientists fondly hoped that once used on the battlefield, the spray would be so effective that the enemy troops would only wake up after their captors had stripped them down to their skivvies.

Alas, it never worked that well. The virus was *too* specific. In nature, it affected only one individual out of a hundred or more. And instead of putting a man to sleep, it imprinted unbearable sexual longing in the victim. Like a love potion of old, it made the victim fall hopelessly for whomever he or she first smelled after being hit by the spray. The scandal among the volunteer units of the Swabian Rifles led to a dozen resignations, three suicides, and five homosexual marriages.

Scarlet was going to spray Carl and make certain that the first person he smelled was herself. And after that, she knew, she would be the *only* person he would sniff after.

But she had to be very careful to get Carl away from Lori—and everyone else—before she spritzed him.

During dinner, Ralph Malzone had presided over a rowdy table of sales people. Afterward, looking thoroughly wrung out, he had stopped by Lori and Carl's table and the three of them had gone together into the main lounge.

It had been easy enough for Scarlet to insinuate herself into the threesome, and for the past several hours the four of them had been drinking, talking, and dancing. The robot dance band was built and costumed to look like a vague amalgamation of the Beatles, the Beach Boys, and other popular groups of the sixties and seventies. This cruise ship usually catered to retirees who were fixated on the music of their teen years.

Scarlet kept her drinks long and soft, and noticed that Lori did the same. Good old Ralph never drank anything but beer; he seemed to have an infinite capacity for it, although he excused himself every hour or so: "Time to recycle the beer," he would invariably say.

Carl, the innocent one, drank a steady stream of cuba libres. Rum and Coke. He downed them as if there was no rum in them at all, and Scarlet began to suspect that somebody—maybe Lori—had made a deal with the waiter to make his drinks innocuous. While he and Lori were dancing she had stolen a sip. No, the rum was there all right. Young Mr. Edison has a wooden leg, apparently.

Try as she might, though, she could not get Carl off by himself. The handsome young engineer danced with her several times, slipping and tripping as the dance floor sloshed back and form in the storm-tossed sea. But Lori was either on the floor beside them, dancing with Ralph, or sitting at their ringside table watching Carl. And he was always looking around for her.

Maddening.

Scarlet danced with Ralph, too, from time to time. The wiry guy was athletically light on his feet, a good dancer. Despite the worried, preoccupied look on his lank face.

"The sales force giving you hell?" Scarlet asked him as they worked their way uphill on the tilting dance floor.

"Yeah," he said, making it a long flat exasperated syllable. "Worse than I thought it could be."

"Maybe they should drop the Cyberbook project."

Malzone shook his head. "P.T. *never* gives up on anything. You know that. And—dammit! It's a good idea. I think it could work if we'd give it half a chance."

The dance floor shuddered and then started slanting downhill. Ralph held Scarlet firmly in his surprisingly strong arms and guided her past the other dancing couples. The band was playing "Hey Jude" on its synthesized instruments. Carl and Lori were sitting at the table alongside the dance floor, gazing raptly at each other over a forest of tall glasses and empty bottles. Scarlet felt the anger of frustration heating her.

The song ended just as the dance floor gave another lurch. The couple next to Scarlet and Ralph staggered slightly into them. The woman's heel caught in the hem of her floor-length dress and she clutched at Scarlet for support. Scarlet's slim little handbag slid off her shoulder and hit the floor with a thunk as the woman— one of Ralph's sales people—straightened up and murmured an apology.

The couple scurried back to their table as Ralph bent down to pick up Scarlet's purse. She dropped to one knee beside him, anxious to scoop up the things that had spilled out of the bag and onto the polished wood of the dance floor.

Ralph helped her. "Hey, what's this?" he asked, picking up the pheromone spray.

"Ah . . . perfume," Scarlet improvised, making a grab for it. Her hand clutched for the phial just a touch too hard, and a microscopic mist sprayed from it with an almost inaudible hiss.

Malzone blinked as the spray hit his face. "Doesn't smell at all," he muttered, handing the phial back to Scarlet.

Scarlet felt the spray tingle on her face, too. She looked deeply into Ralph Malzone's eyes and knew beyond the trace of any doubt that this was the one man in the world that she absolutely had to have for her very own.

"Ralph," she said, her voice shuddering with the urgency of it all. "Would—would you please take me back to my cabin?"

Nodding absently, as though something had just happened that was beyond his understanding, Ralph straightened up, took Scarlet by the hand, and walked with her right past Lori and Carl without saying a word.

FISHING BOAT EXPLODES, FOUR FEARED KILLED

Brigantine, N.J. A forty-five-foot fishing boat, *Calamara,* was blown to bits last night in a mysterious explosion a few miles off the south Jersey coast, according to a Coast Guard spokesman.

Four men aboard the vessel are missing and feared dead.

"It was like she was hit by a missile," said Lt. (j.g.) Donald Winslow.

Coast Guard radar, on a routine drug surveillance sweep, picked up the *Calamara* while it was heading out to sea. "One instant it was there, the next it was gone," said Lt. Winslow. A Coast Guard helicopter sent to investigate found only floating debris and an oil slick.

"The sea was getting rough, but not dangerously so. There were no other ships within fifty miles of *Calamara* except a cruise liner, the SS *New Amsterdam,*" Lt. Winslow stated.

The missing men are Marco DeAngelo, Guido DeAngelo, and Vincenzio DeAngelo, all of Brooklyn, N.Y., and Salvatore Baccala, of Brigantine, N.J., owner of the boat.

THEFT OF CRUISE MISSILE REPORTED

Staten Island, N.Y. An unnamed Navy official reluctantly admitted that a fully armed cruise missile was stolen from the Staten Island weapons depot three nights ago. She stressed, however, that the missile was armed with a conventional warhead, not a nuclear weapon.

Defense Department and F.B.I. antiterrorist teams are investigating the incident, which may be linked to the mysterious explosion of a New Jersey fishing boat last night.

The Navy spokesperson, who insisted on anonymity, claimed that all cruise missiles in storage are equipped with automatic self-destruct systems, as a protection against terrorist seizure. "If the people who stole the missile tried to launch it, it would blow up in their faces," she averred.

WHITE HOUSE BLAMED

**FOR MISSILE THEFT
AND BOAT EXPLOSION**

Washington, D.C. Sen. Mario Pazzo (D., N.J.) accused the White House today of "culpable guilt" in the explosion last night of a New Jersey fishing boat in which four men were apparently killed.

"The President should realize that all the Navy's cruise missiles are booby-trapped, and thus a danger to those who operate them," said Sen. Pazzo. "And if he doesn't know that, then he isn't doing the job he was elected to do."

Reminded that the only way the four men in question could have obtained a cruise missile was to steal it from the Navy weapons depot in Staten Island, Sen. Pazzo insisted, "The issue here is not crime. It's the safety of human lives."

A Pentagon spokesman, when confronted with the Senator's statement, expressed surprise. "Hell, there's red lettering eight inches high that says 'DO NOT ATTEMPT TO LAUNCH UNTIL SELF-DESTRUCT SYSTEM IS DEACTIVATED.' Maybe the guys who stole the missile couldn't read."

F.B.I. officials theorize that the missile was stolen as part of the gang wars over narcotics smuggling.

"If they're escalating to cruise missiles," said the F.B.I. agent in charge of the investigation, "then we're going to have ask Congress for antimissile weaponry to protect the lives of innocent citizens and the Bureau's agents."

Eighteen

Ralph Malzone struggled up from sleep like a man clawing his way out of an immense, cloying, suffocating ball of cotton candy. He was still half dreaming of childhood guilts and terrors while the rational side of his brain was telling him to open his eyes and wake up.

It was not easy. He was physically exhausted and emotionally spent. But with a supreme effort of will he unglued his gummy eyes and focused blearily on the ceiling panels of off-white acoustical tile.

For long minutes he lay unmoving, almost afraid to look about him. Usually he sprang out of bed full of vigor, ready to start the new day. But he was not home in his bare little studio apartment now, he was aboard the cruise ship.

His heart skipped a beat. He was not in his own cabin, either.

With a mixture of dread and joy he slowly turned his head. Scarlet Dean lay sound asleep beside him, a sweet smile of bliss curving her red lips.

It's true! Ralph gasped to himself. It wasn't a dream. It really happened.

He stared at Scarlet, half-covered by a twisted bedsheet, her blazing red hair flowing across the pillow like molten lava.

It really happened, Ralph repeated to himself, so incredulous that he still could only half believe what he saw and remembered. He squeezed his eyes shut and tried to picture Lori's face. She was the one he truly loved. He had betrayed her. Even though she had no inkling of his unswerving love for her, he had betrayed her. Guilt. Sin. How many Hail Marys would he have to say for this?

But Lori's face would not come into focus for him. He saw her vaguely, but then her features melted and changed into the beautiful, willing, giving face of Scarlet Dean. Ralph popped his eyes open. Yes, it was her. She was really there. This was her cabin, and they had spent the night doing things that Ralph had only fantasized about.

He studied Scarlet's face. Until last night he had thought her to be unfeeling, calculating, a hard-hearted bitch whose only interest was her career. A flame-haired ice princess. Eyes as cold and shrewd as a snake's.

Now he wanted her to open those eyes, so that he could gaze into them while she gazed into his.

Then a horrifying thought caught him. She was drunk. It was all a mistake. Or—worse still—she's trying to use me.

For what? Why would she do that? Ralph sat up and tried to shake the cobwebs from his head. He turned back and stared at the sleeping woman. I love you, Red, he admitted silently. I love you.

As quietly as he could, Ralph got out of the bed and started searching for his clothes. They had been thrown all over the cabin, as if they had exploded off his body.

Scarlet Dean opened her eyes and saw the sinewy form of the man she loved. Without moving she watched him gathering up his

438 *Ben Bova*

clothes. She smiled inwardly at the bite marks on his naked chest and felt a glow deep inside her that she had never known before.

Far, far off in a remote region of her brain a voice—her own—was warning her that this man was nothing more to her than a chemical dependency. Scarlet heard the voice and understood what it was saying. She remembered the pheromone spray and the accident on the dance floor.

So what? she asked herself. This is what I've wanted all my life: a man who loves me and whom I can love, completely, endlessly, forever. The rest of life is meaningless. This wiry redheaded guy is my life.

He had found almost all his clothes and was holding them in a rumpled, tangled mess in one hand as he tiptoed toward the bathroom. There was a puzzled, little-boy expression on his face. He had found only one of his shoes, she realized.

"It's under the bed, I think," Scarlet said in a lazy, happy, sultry voice.

"Oh!" He seemed startled. But then he grinned at her. "Good morning."

"Good evening," she countered.

"I . . . uh . . ."

But Scarlet merely stretched her bare arms out to him and he dropped his clothes in a heap and came back to bed with her.

Lori and Carl, who had spent a chaste and miserable night in their separate cabins, as usual, met for breakfast. As usual, he ordered bacon and eggs, she asked for yogurt and honey.

The dining salon was almost full and buzzing with three stories: P.T.'s dramatic entrance in the bar lounge last evening, Scarlet Dean and Ralph Malzone scurrying away arm in arm at the end of the evening, and the spectacular fireworks display off on the horizon around two in the morning.

"Woody says it looked like something exploding," Lori said to Carl as she dipped a spoon into the honey-covered yogurt.

He shrugged. "Somebody getting an early start on the Fourth of July, I guess."

Looking around the tables of the crowded salon, Lori said, "I don't see Ralph or Scarlet."

"Maybe they jumped ship."

With a smirk, Lori said, "They way they hurried off last night, I think they jumped each other."

Carl felt his face redden.

She smiled at him and patted his hand, which raised his temperature even more. "Ralph is supposed to be at the sales conference this morning . . . I wonder if he's going to make it on time."

"I don't see Mrs. Bee, either," said Carl.

"She usually has breakfast in her stateroom. She'll be at the conference. She never misses a sales meeting."

But when ten o'clock came, neither Mrs. Bunker, Ralph Malzone, nor Scarlet Dean was present. No one knew quite what to do, except that they all knew better than to ring their respective cabins. So the meeting was postponed until two in the afternoon.

Carl went off happily to his workshop, where he spent the morning in conference with the factory in Mexico where the Cyberbook units were being manufactured. Lori took a thick manuscript up to the top deck, ensconced herself on a lounge chair, and spent the morning doing what she was not allowed to do in the office: reading.

Woody Balogna also made use of the "free" morning. He called all the sales representatives together for an informal meeting in the fore-castle lounge. Subject: mutiny.

The forecastle lounge was the smallest of the several lounges aboard the *New Amsterdam*. It was decorated in a "nautical" motif: ropes and nets looped around the portholes, fake buoys hanging from the ceiling low enough for the taller sales people to bump their heads. The lounge was furnished with a few small sofas and deep plush chairs, all in bilious shades of blue-green, plus a built-in bar and a spinet piano—both closed at this time of the morning.

Because it was up forward in the ship, the lounge rose and sank with each bite of the *New Amsterdam*'s bow into the sea's swelling waves. It felt to the assembled sales folk who crowded into the rather small compartment as if they were jammed in an elevator that could not make up its mind; it rose a few floors, then sank a few floors. The motion, the press of bodies in the overcrowded cabin, and the fact that somehow the air-conditioning was not working, quickly turned several of the sales people a sickly shade of green.

Including Woody Balogna. But despite the queasiness of his stomach, he called the meeting to order.

"Okay, quiet down," he said, trying to keep his eyes off the portholes that showed the horizon rising and falling, rising and falling.

"I don't feel so good," said one of the women sales reps.

"You're gonna feel a lot worse if we let the Bunkers put this Cyberbooks deal through," Woody snapped.

"So what do we do?"

"Yeah. What *can* we do—go on strike?"

"Something better than that," said Woody, struggling manfully to hold down his breakfast.

"Such as?"

"What does any red-blooded American do when somebody's tryin' to screw him?"

"Hire a hit man."

"Wait for them to fire you so you can collect your severance pay and pension."

"Relax and enjoy it."

His face growing greener by the millisecond, Woody waved down their asinine cracks. "Nah, you dummies. We sue the bastards."

"Sue?"

"Who?"

"Bunker Books, that's who."

"The Boss?"

"The company?"

"Mr. Bunker?"

"That's right," Woody snarled. "They wanna put in this Cyberbooks thing, right? Get rid of all the distributors, wholesalers, jobbers—all our customers, right? Next thing you know they'll get rid of the bookstores, too. And you know what they'll get rid of after that?"

"What?"

"Us, that's what!"

"But Mrs. Bee said—"

"I don't give a damn what she said! Once they got these friggin' automatic books coming out, they won't need us. Out we'll go, out into the cold on our bare asses."

"She wouldn't do that!"

"The hell she wouldn't. And even if *she* wouldn't, P.T. would. So we sue the bastards."

"About what?"

"About Cyberbooks, of course."

"But how can . . ."

"It can't be done—can it?"

"What do we sue them for?"

Woody could feel the burning remains of breakfast searing up his throat. Still, he managed to say, "Don't worry about that. We can always find some lawyer who'll find some reason for suing."

The sales staff stared at one another, stunned.

"Well?" Woody demanded. "Anybody got a better idea?"

Total silence.

"Then we sue!"

For a moment nobody moved. Then suddenly, like a startled pack of lemmings, they broke for the double doors of the lounge and raced for the ship's railing. Woody stood alone in the empty lounge, satisfied that he had done the right thing. Then he threw up on the bilious blue-green carpeting.

P. Curtis Hawks sat alone in his grandiose office. It had been stripped bare. The electronics console, the conference table, the pool table, even his desk and beautiful leather swivel chair had been removed, sent on their way to (ugh!) Brooklyn. The teak panelling had been torn from the walls. The lighting fixtures had been taken from the ceiling. The carpeting from the floors. There was nothing in this room that he had once loved so dearly except a single cardboard carton, big enough to hold exactly two dozen Webb Press books.

Hawks stood at the window, breathing his final silent farewell to the grand view that once had been his. Now all he had to look forward to was a tiny slit of a window that looked out on a trash-to-energy powerplant. The plastic pacifier in his teeth tasted sour, bitter.

He heard the door behind him open, stealthily, as if a burglar or assassin was trying to slip in unnoticed.

"Come right in, Gunther," he called without turning from his magnificent view. He knew it was Axhelm, worse than any burglar or assassin.

"The movers have finished, except for this single packing case here on the floor," said the Axe in his usual precise, icy tones.

Hawks turned toward him, and made his lips smile. Axhelm was wearing his customary dark turtleneck and slacks, but this time he had a Luftwaffe-blue sports coat over them.

"That package isn't going to Brooklyn. It's a present, from me to you."

"A . . . present?" For the first time since Hawks had met the sonofabitch, Axhelm seemed surprised, unsure of himself.

"A going-away present, you might say." Hawks stepped toward the innocent-looking cardboard box, resting all alone on the vast empty expanse of the bare plywood flooring.

"This is unexpected."

It was laughable, watching the stiff-backed Axhelm trying to figure out how he should behave in the face of a personal gift. Hawks could see a shadow of suspicion in those cold gray Nordic eyes. *He's wondering if I'm trying to bribe him,* Hawks realized, *but he knows there's nothing left for me to bribe him about. He's ruined my life and wrecked my office. His work here is finished. The company will be out of business in another six months; he's seen to that.*

Just before they took away his computer (and the desk on which it rested), Hawks had ran a check on Webb's sales projections. They were down. Shockingly down. Almost to zero. In his zeal to cut costs, Axhelm had decreed that the company stop buying new books and sell only the books it had already published. Like Scribley's and many another publishing house that depended too much on its backlist, Webb Press was on a steep, terminal dive into bankruptcy.

"Open it up," Hawks said as genially as he could manage.

Still somewhat suspicious, Axhelm muttered, "It looks like a carton of our books."

"Very perceptive of you," said Hawks smoothly. "That's exactly what it looks like."

For an awkward moment neither man moved. Then Axhelm slowly bent to one knee and pulled from his back pocket a Swiss army knife. *I might have known he'd have one on him,* thought Hawks. The model with *all* the attachments, even the AM/FM radio and earplug.

Deftly Axhelm sliced the tape holding down the carton's lid. He pulled it open and stared into his "present."

Frowning, he dug into the carton and came up with a handful of loose book pages.

"I don't understand. . . ."

Standing well away from the carton and quickly whipping a triply guaranteed Japanese filter over his face, Hawks replied with a vengeful chortle of glee.

Axhelm looked up at Hawks, his face a portrait of puzzlement. He started to say something, but suddenly his jaw went slack. His entire body sagged, as if every muscle in him had gone limp.

From behind his filter, Hawks crowed, "The goddamned glue you made us buy, you cheap asshole! It turns into a psychedelic gas! Take a *deep* breath, shithead! A *deep* breath!"

Axhelm was indeed breathing deeply, a blissful relaxed smile on his normally cold face. He plunged both hands into the carton and pulled a double handful of loose pages to his face, inhaling them as if they were the most fragrant flowers in the world.

Leaping to his feet, he flung the pages toward the ceiling.

"At last!" he shrieked. "At last I'm free! *Free!*"

Hawks watched with beady eyes as the Axe capered across the bare office, dancing like a Bavarian peasant at a maypole.

"I can sing! I can dance!" the erstwhile management consultant shouted. "All my life I have wanted to be like the immortal Gene Kelly! I'm si-i-ingin' in the rain . . ."

Axhelm was still gibbering and dancing (with a total lack of grace) when Weldon W. Weldon wheeled his power chair into what was left of Hawks's office. Hawks had, of course, arranged for the Old Man to come to his office at precisely this moment. The timing was perfect.

Crunching down viciously on his pacifier, Hawks took the filter from his face and let the astounded CEO of Tarantula watch his vaunted management consultant stumble and lurch up and down the bare office floor boards. The look on the Old Man's face was priceless.

Christ, said Hawks to himself, as happy as the first time he had shot a rabbit, if looks could kill the Axe would be stone cold dead.

Autumn, Book III

The Buyer

The first snow of November was gently sifting past the window of Dee Dee Lowe's office as she held court. It was a gray day in Des Moines, but the chief buyer for Cleaveland Book Stores was dressed in bright oranges and flaming reds. There were even brilliant yellow ribbons in her thick gray hair. Her face was tanned and taut; she looked as if she had just returned from a trip to the Bahamas. Actually, she seldom left her office and had not been on vacation since the entire Cleaveland chain was taken over by Tarantula Enterprises, many years earlier. Her good looks were a combination of cosmetic surgery, makeup, and the tanning parlor in the shopping mall across the road from Cleaveland's offices.

Before her desk, four dozen sales people were seated in neat rows of folding chairs. This was Dee Dee's monthly meeting, where she deigned to allow the sales people into her office and let them show her their companies' wares for the month.

Each sales person, male or female, had a laptop computer open on his or her knees. Each computer was plugged into a complex electronics console that squatted on the floor next to Dee Dee's desk like a square fireplug. The tangle of wires among the folding chairs was so fierce that Dee Dee had put a printed sign on her desk:

CLEAVELAND BOOK STORES INC. IS NOT RESPONSIBLE FOR INJURIES TO VISITING SALES PERSONNEL DUE TO ACCIDENTS OR OTHER NATURAL OR MAN-MADE CAUSES.

Not a word was being spoken. Each sales person was busily tapping on his or her keyboard, relaying glowing information about his or her latest batch of books into the central Cleaveland Stores computer.

In the old days the salesmen—they had all been men when Dee Dee had started in this job—the salesmen would personally show her the information on each and every individual title they were trying to sell. They would show her a color proof of the cover, statistics about the author's previous books, monumental lies about how much money and effort the publisher was going to put into advertising and promotion for this individual title, tremendous whoppers about how wonderful this title was and how it was going to hit the top of the best-seller lists the instant it was released.

"But they can't *all* be best-sellers," Dee Dee would respond, smiling slyly.

The salesmen knew that only one out of a thousand of their titles would be successful. And they knew that if Dee Dee bought a hundred thousand copies or so for the vast chain of Cleaveland Stores, that particular title would be among the precious few. So they wined her and dined her and, when she felt like it, bedded her. Four times salesmen even wedded her. None of them took, although she now wore an impressive array of diamonds on her clawlike fingers.

But those were the good old days, Dee Dee thought with a sigh. Now it's all done by computers. We don't even need to have the sales people come to my office at all, she realized. They could pump their information into my computer system from their own offices, or even from New York.

But if they did it that way, she would not get to see any of the sales people, ever. And she clung to these monthly meetings because, after the computers had completed their intercourse, the sales folk—being sales people—hung around complimenting Dee Dee on her good looks, her great taste in clothes, her incredible business acumen, her deep love for literature.

Actually, Dee Dee had not read a book since she had graduated college, so many years ago that she dreaded even thinking about it.

Every month the sales people seemed to get younger, she said to herself sadly. None of them ever makes a pass at me anymore—except for old lechers like Woody Baloney, and even his leering suggestions were strictly routine these days. I wonder if he can still get it up? A couple of the saleswomen had hinted at availability, but Dee Dee felt she was too old to experiment.

She sighed as she looked out at the office full of bowed heads. All those eager young kids bent over their laptop computers instead of kissing my ass. No, the business isn't what it used to be.

Deep down in the basement of the Cleaveland Stores building, behind electronically locked steel fireproof doors, sat a single Nisei woman in front of a bank of four dozen display screens. The screens cast an eerie flickering light across the young woman's blankly impassive face. They curved around her single swivel chair like the compound eye of some giant insect examining her. But in truth, *she* was examining *them*. Each screen flickered for a bare three seconds with the cover proof and other data on each of the titles the sales people were pumping into the central Cleaveland computer. Then the next title came on. This one lonely woman's task was to select which titles Cleaveland would actually buy.

For the vaunted Cleaveland computer system could not actually decide which titles to buy, out of the thousands presented each month. No automated expert system or decision-tree program could handle the avalanche of incoming data that the sales people unloosed each month. So the entire international chain of bookstores depended on this one solitary young woman to make the selections. Each month she sat on that chair, watched the madly flickering screens, and made selections that determined the fate of most of the books published in North America.

Her right hand gripped a knobbed joystick while the fingers of her left flew madly across a small keyboard. With her left hand she indicated to the computer which screen she was glancing at; if she pushed the joystick *up* that meant the book would be bought by the chain, the amount of upward push indicated the number of copies bought—ten thousand, a hundred thousand, a million. If she pushed the stick *down* the book was bypassed, doomed to oblivion.

Her qualifications for this key position? She had been, as a teenager, the champion video game player of California.

Nineteen

Even with the lawsuit looming over them, and the sales force virtually on strike as far as Cyberbooks was concerned, Bunker Books staggered along, trying to stay solvent.

Lori Tashkajian was in her cubbyhole office that same dreary November morning. The storm that was bringing snow to Iowa was already smothering the New York skyline with gray tendrils of fog and spatterings of drizzle. Mountains of manuscripts still littered Lori's tiny office. But she ignored them as she pondered over the data on her computer display screen.

According to the computer's program, it would be foolhardy to print more than five thousand copies of Capt. Clunker's novel about the Battle of Midway. The title for the book was still under discussion at the editorial meetings. Every one of the editors except Lori thought that *Midway Diary* would not sell, although Ralph Malzone (the only one with sales experience at the conferences) liked the title well enough. Currently its working title was *Forbidden Warrior's Love*, which Lori hated. But at least it was better than *Pacific Lust*, which she had narrowly averted, after several screaming matches.

The computer was saying that, no matter what the book's title, they could expect to sell no more than two or three thousand copies of the hardcover. That meant printing no more than five thousand.

Lori frowned at the glowing screen. Dammit, this novel deserves better than that! But it had been cursed with the strategy of minimal success. The editorial board had decided to take no chances with a first novel by an unknown writer. No money was to be risked on publicity or advertising. No effort made to sell the book to reluctant buyers in bookstore chains or major distribution centers. Minimum success. Spend as little as possible and "let the book find its own level of sales." The level would be on the bottom, Lori knew from bitter experience.

If only she could get to Mrs. Bunker and make a personal pitch for the novel. She *knew* it could sell much better, maybe even make a run at the best-seller lists, if they would give it some support.

But Mrs. Bee was hardly in the office these days. Ever since the cruise—and the lawsuit whipped on them by the sales force—Mrs.

Bunker had spent more time out of the office than in it. Strange, though. Even though the company was in dire trouble, with sales down and morale even lower, with a lawsuit by its own sales force threatening to close down Bunker Books entirely, Mrs. Bee seemed smiling, radiant, even girlishly happy on those increasingly rare occasions when she did make an appearance in the office.

Then Lori's thoughts turned to Carl and his Cyberbooks project. The outlook for him was bleak. Very bleak.

But Carl Lewis was whistling while he worked. Hunched in front of his own computer display screen in the workshop/office he had made out of the apartment the Bunkers were paying for, Carl traced out the circuitry for an improved Cyberbook model that would reduce the costs of the hand-held reader by at least ten percent.

He leaned back in the little typing chair and let out a satisfied sigh. Yep, we can make it cheaper. The cheaper it is, the more poor people will be able to afford Cyberbooks. Carl had tried, during the last few months, to interest Mrs. Bunker in a program of giving away a few hundred thousand Cyberbook readers to the children of urban ghettos. Mrs. Bee had given him a puzzled look and a vague smile instead of a definite answer.

His phone buzzed. Carl rolled in his little chair to the desk and tapped the phone keyboard. Ralph Malzone's long-jawed face appeared on the screen.

"Hey, are we going to lunch or are you on a diet?"

"Lunch! I forgot all about it!"

"Okay. I'm down at Pete's. Meet me at the bar."

"I'll be there in ten minutes."

Carl was damp and chilled by the time he entered Pete's Tavern. The drizzle had not looked serious from his hotel window, but walking three blocks with no umbrella or raincoat had not done his tweed jacket much good.

"Where's the duck?" Ralph asked him, grinning from behind a schooner of beer.

"Duck?" Carl wondered.

"You look like a retriever that's just come out of the water."

Carl laughed, a little self-consciously, and ordered a double sherry to warm himself.

They took their drinks into the crowded dining room beyond the bar and ordered lunch.

"You're still working on the gadget?" Ralph asked, his face more serious now.

"Sure. Why not?"

"The trial starts next week."

"So?"

Ralph leaned forward, bringing his face close to Carl's. "So if Woody and his pals win this suit, the court will enjoin Bunker to stop all work on Cyberbooks."

Despite a slight pang of fear in his gut, Carl replied, "That can't happen."

"Oh no?"

"What judge in his right mind would stop a whole new industry just because some salesmen are afraid it will force them to learn a slightly different way of doing their work?"

Justice Hanson Hapgood Fish was a man of rare perceptions. So rarefied were his perceptions, in fact, that some whispered they actually were hallucinations.

He sat in his chambers, behind the massive mahogany desk that had belonged to Malcolm (Malevolent Mal) F. Fortunata until the unhappy day when the Feds had carted Mal away for seventeen counts of bribery, obstructing justice, and aiding and abetting organized crime. The room was large, panelled in dark wood where it was not lined with glass-enclosed bookcases. The leather chairs and solitary long couch were heavy, massive, uninviting. Thick curtains flanked the windows. A gloomy chamber, dreary even on the sunniest day.

Justice Fish's desk was neurotically bare, except for the inevitable computer display screen, blank and silent. In its empty screen, the judge saw his own face reflected: totally bald, tight-lipped and narrow-eyed, aging pale skin stretched over the skull so tightly that every blue vein could be seen throbbing sluggishly.

He was engaged in his morning ritual. First the mental exercises: reciting the logarithmic tables of his ancient school trigonometry text, then leaning his head back against the padding of his oversized chair and recalling from his memory the looks of every woman in his courtroom the previous day. There had been only two, both of them aging and lumpy. Nothing had happened in his courtroom except the sentencing of a miscreant embezzler. But he enjoyed replaying before his mind's eye the stunned look on the man's face when he sentenced him to ninety-nine years without probation.

The damned superior court will lighten his sentence, he thought grouchily. But still, that look on his face was worth it.

Now he rose slowly from his chair and went to the nearer of the two windows in his office. He moved carefully, with all due deliberation, as much from the desire to appear dramatically dignified as from the arthritis that plagued both his knees. The window was so filthy that he could barely make out the grimy gray City Hall across the way. Standing there, Justice Fish took three deep breaths. Never two, nor four. Never with the window open, either: he knew that fresh air, in Manhattan, could kill.

Now he returned, still with self-conscious dignity, to his desk and lowered himself onto his imposing chair. Reaching out a long lean finger that barely trembled, he touched the computer's keypad to see what his next case would be.

Bunker *vs.* Bunker. A publishing house's sales force was suing its employer over some new contraption that they felt would eliminate their jobs. Hm. Labor relations. Always a thorny issue.

Pressing keypads carefully, Justice Fish called up the secret, coded program that only he could summon from the computer because only he knew the special code word that accessed it: *Polaris.*

It was an astrology program, and the aging judge pecked at the keyboard, asking how he should decide the case he would soon be judging. The computer blinked and hummed, then gave him an answer.

Justice Fish nodded, satisfied. Now he knew what his decision would be. Now he did not have to listen to the evidence that the various lawyers would present over the next long, boring weeks. It was all decided. Sifting evidence and weighing the slick arguments lawyers dished up to him was just a waste of time, he felt. The stars told him what his decision would be, so he could relax and fantasize about the women in his courtroom without the fear of making a wrong decision. Pleased, he shut down the computer and leaned back in his chair for his morning nap.

Murder Six

Detective Lieutenant Jack Moriarty was not merely a good cop, he was a brave man. Brave in two ways: he had physical courage, the ability to stand up to a man with a gun or a gang of street toughs; he also had the courage of his convictions, the strength to play his hunches even when they seemed crazy.

Shortly after the murder of retired detective Miles Archer, several months earlier, Moriarty had come to certain conclusions about the Retiree Murders. The computer records of each victim hinted at the possibility of a motive that seemed so farfetched, so tenuous, that only a man as convinced of himself as Moriarty would dare to act on it. But act he did. He bought stock in a multinational conglomerate corporation called, of all things, Tarantula Enterprises.

It had not been an easy thing to do. Tarantula shares were expensive, more than $1,000 each. And the stockbroker he had contacted told him that not much Tarantula stock was available on the open market.

"Most of it is held by other corporations," the broker had said, sniffling so much that Moriarty began to look for traces of white powder on his fingertips. "The big boys hold it and sell it in enormous blocks. It's not traded in onesy-twoseys very much."

Moriarty had assured him that he only wanted a few shares. He could not afford more; twenty shares cleaned out his savings account.

For months he waited patiently, even buying single shares now and then as they became available. Nothing had happened. His hunch had gone cold. The Retiree Murderer refused to strike at anyone, let alone an active police detective who held a grand total of twenty-four shares of Tarantula Enterprises, Ltd.

On that same foggy, drizzly day in November, Moriarty learned that his hunch was right. At the cost of his life.

He was on a routine call to question a witness to a liquor store holdup in the Village when it happened.

Moriarty stepped out of his vintage Pinto (the auto was his only discernible vice) in front of the liquor store in question. The street was slick from the chilly rain. Only a few people were passing by, and they all were hidden beneath umbrellas. Bunching his tired old trenchcoat around his middle, Moriarty got as far as the liquor store's front entrance.

He felt a sharp jab in his back, then a horrible burning sensation flamed through his whole body. He had stopped breathing before he hit the sidewalk.

The umbrella-toting pedestrians stepped over his prostrate body and continued on their way.

Twenty

That evening, the cold November rain gave way to the season's first snowfall. It was nothing much, as snowstorms go, merely a half inch or less of wet mushy flakes that turned to black slush almost as soon as it hit the streets. But the evening newscasts were agog with the story of the storm: coiffed and pancaked anchorpersons quivered with excitement while reporters at various strategic locations around the city—the airports, the train and bus terminals, the Department of Public Works headquarters, the major highway bottlenecks—stood out in the wet snow and solemnly reported how the city *almost* had been hit by a crisis.

"Although the traffic appears to be flowing smoothly through the Lincoln Tunnel," said the bescarfed young lady on Channel 4, "it wouldn't take much more snow to turn this evening's homeward rush into a commuter's nightmare." Behind her, streams of buses proceeded without a hitch into the tunnel.

Channel 2's stalwart investigative reporter was at the airport offices of the U.S. Weather Service, where he had collared a wimpy-looking meteorologist.

"Why didn't the Weather Bureau provide warnings of this potential disaster?" he demanded.

The wimp's eyebrows rose almost to his receding hairline. "What disaster? You call a half-inch snow a disaster? The Blizzard of '88 this ain't!"

Still, all the channels buzzed with stories about the snow, the most inventive being a satellite report from a ski resort in Vermont, where the slopes were still green with grass.

The news of the storm smothered a human-interest story about a city police detective who had been the apparent victim of a senseless, purposeless murder. Thanks to the miracles of modern medicine, though, the detective had been revived from a state of clinical death and was recuperating in St. Vincent's Hospital, in the Village.

By morning the snow had been obliterated from the city by the ceaseless pounding of millions of buses, trucks, taxicabs, limousines, and pedestrians' feet. The Department of Public Works had not had to call out a single snow plow or digging crew. Still the trains ran two hours late, and the morning backup of traffic at the bridges and tunnels was ferocious.

Ferocious was the mood, also, of P. Curtis Hawks as he rode in his limousine through the crowded city streets to the annual board meeting of Tarantula Enterprises, Ltd. Vinnie DeAngelo, the Beast from the East, slept with the fishes ever since the fiasco of the cruise missile. Weldon W. Weldon, senile and crippled, still ran Tarantula from his infested jungle of an office. Webb Press—what was left of it—was now located in Brooklyn, in a building that had once been a fruit-and-vegetable warehouse. The place still smelled of onions.

This meeting is the shoot-out, Hawks told himself. High noon. There isn't room enough in this corporation for the Old Man and me. One of us has got to go, and it's not going to be me. He shifted the pacifier from one side of his mouth to the other and sucked in his gut. Got to make a good impression on the board of directors, he knew. Got to make them see that the Old Man has run Webb into the ground.

It would not be easy. But Hawks smiled a bitter, cold smile when he thought about his secret weapon. I'll pin the Old Man's balls to the table, or what's left of them. And his own creature, Gunther God-Damned Axhelm, is going to do the job for me.

"All rise."

From the front row of seats in the courtroom, Carl Lewis got to his feet together with everyone else as Justice Hanson H. Fish walked slowly, solemnly, in his black robes to his high chair behind the banc.

Lori stood beside Carl on one side, Ralph and Scarlet Dean were on his other side. Mrs. Bunker was at the table where the defense attorneys—all five of them—sat. Both Mrs. Bee and Scarlet were decked out in the latest fashion: the toothpaste-tube look. Their dresses were tight enough to asphyxiate, and shirred, niched, pleated—wrinkled—so that they looked like the last moments of a toothpaste tube that had been squeezed to death. Skirts were midthigh and so tight that they could barely walk. Alba Bunker wore all white, of course, while Scarlet Dean was completely in red. Between them they wore enough jewelry to ransom a planeload of OPEC oil ministers.

Lori, as usual, ignored the weekly fashion and had dressed in a sensible plaid suit with a light green turtleneck beneath the jacket. Her skirt was knee-length, her jewelry confined to a small pair of earrings and matching copper bracelet and necklace.

Woody Balogna wore his best suit, which still looked ten years old and badly in need of a cleaning. He sat at the table for the plaintiff, with a single odd-looking attorney who represented the sales force.

Woody's lawyer was dressed in a deep blue velvet leisure suit, the kind that had gone out of style with Alan Alda, countless ages ago. A western-type string tie was pulled up against his prominent Adam's apple, cinched by a lump of turquoise big enough to be used in a shot-put contest. The man's wide-brimmed cowboy hat rested on the table before him, next to a battered slim leather case that looked like the saddle bag of an old Pony Express rider. Apparently it contained all the notes and papers he had brought to the courtroom. He had a rugged, seamed, weatherbeaten face and long flowing dark hair with a wild streak of silver in it. He looked as if he had not shaved that morning; his jaw was covered with grayish stubble.

Mrs. Bunker's five defense attorneys all wore traditional gray flannels and Ivy League ties painted on their starched white shirts.

Their faces were shaved clean and scrubbed glowing pink. They looked young, confident, yet serious. Their briefcases were huge and thicker than parachute packs. Mrs. Bee looked nervous, though, and kept glancing over her shoulder toward the door that opened onto the corridor as if the one thought in her mind was to get up and flee from the courtroom.

Carl thought the courtroom was strangely empty, considering the importance of the case. No news reporters, no TV lights, hardly anybody in the visitors' pews at all except for the few Bunker employees and himself. And no jury. Both sides had waived their right to a jury trial; this case would be decided by Justice H. H. Fish alone, in his impartial wisdom. And then appealed, of course, by the loser. The lawyers saw the prospects of many years of high-priced work ahead of them.

While the bailiff read the title of the case and the charges, Carl studied the judge sitting up there above them all. His utterly bald head looked like a death's skull glaring down at them. Carl felt his easy confidence in the unassailable righteousness of the Cyberbooks project begin to melt away under the baleful glower of the judge's implacable eyes.

"Motions?" asked the judge.

One of the defense attorneys popped to his feet. They all looked so much alike that Carl thought they might be clones.

"Move to dismiss," said the attorney in a clear, crisp voice. "This suit is without grounds and totally irrelevant. . . ."

"Motion denied," snapped Justice Fish.

The young lawyer looked surprised. He sat down.

"Opening statements," the judge said. "Plaintiff?"

The westerner gangled to his feet. He was tall and lean as a fence-post.

"What we've got here," he drawled, "is a clear case of a deliberate, intentional—I might even say evil and pernicious—attempt to eliminate the jobs of a whole flock of hardworking, loyal, and faithful employees, and to substitute in their place a heartless, soulless, new-fangled machine whose only purpose is to make money for the greedy employers of these poor and long-suffering working men and women."

The lawyer's words shocked Carl. How could he describe

Cyberbooks that way? It wasn't true. None of what he was saying was true.

But then he saw the expression on the judge's face. A benign smile, such as saint might bestow on a nativity scene.

We're in deep trouble, Carl belatedly realized.

Detective Lieutenant Jack Moriarty opened his eyes and saw a smooth, featureless expanse of pastel blue. I must have made it to heaven, he said to himself.

Then he heard a faint humming sound, and a rhythmic beeping. He tried to turn his head and found that there was no difficulty with it. It's not heaven, he realized as he focused on a bank of electronic monitoring instruments, their screens showing a steady heartbeat and breathing rate. He felt slightly disappointed, immensely relieved. I'm in an intensive care ward. His detective's brain concluded it was St. Vincent's Hospital, in the heart of Greenwich Village.

For an immeasurable length of time he lay in the bed unmoving, reliving in his mind those last few minutes in front of the liquor store. Whoever had attacked him, it was no random act of violence. The perpetrator knew who he was, and had followed him to the liquor store. Of that Moriarty was certain. It was the Retiree Murderer; the method of operation fit, and so did the fact that the victim—himself—owned a few shares of Tarantula Enterprises, Ltd.

"Welcome back to the living!"

Moriarty turned his head toward the heartily cheerful voice and saw a grossly overweight black man in a white doctor's smock with a day's stubble on his fleshy, wattled face. He's got more chins than the Chinatown phone directory, Moriarty said to himself.

"I am Dr. Kildaire," said the medic in a lilting Jamaican accent. "And no jokes, if you please."

For all his unlikely appearance, Kildaire was a first-rate physician. Moriarty learned that he had been clinically dead when the ambulance had brought him in.

"A very rare poison, the kind you only see in the tropics. Distilled from the sap of a jungle flower known in Brazil as the Rita Hayworth orchid, for some obscure reason. Lucky for you I spent my military service in Central America; I bet I'm the only M.D. this side of the Panama Canal who'd recognize the symptoms of Rita Hayworth poisoning."

They had restarted Moriarty's heart and detoxed his bloodstream. Brought him back to life, quite literally. Moriarty mumbled his embarrassed thanks, then asked how the poison was administered.

"The murderer jabbed you with a sharp instrument, right between your shoulder blades. Might have been a needle coated with the toxin. Might even have been a thorn from the plant itself. Did you get a look at him?"

Moriarty closed his eyes briefly and relived the scene. Yes, the sharp pain in his back. He was falling to the sidewalk—no, the entryway of the liquor store. It was all going black. But he had turned his head to glance over his shoulder and he saw a man in a blue trenchcoat, shapeless brimmed hat pulled down low, umbrella in one hand. For the barest instant he had looked into the eyes of his murderer.

"I saw him," Moriarty said. "I'd know him if I see him again. I'd know those eyes of his anywhere."

In all honesty, Weldon W. Weldon had not expected to be stabbed in the back. He sat in his powered wheelchair at the head of the long gleaming conference table and listened with growing incredulity to Curtis Hawks's tirade.

". . . and with all due respect," Hawks was telling the board of directors, the blistering acid of scalding irony dripping from his words, "in this time of crisis we need a CEO who is physically and *mentally* sharp enough to repel the pirates who are trying to take over this corporation."

Hawks was pacing up and down the length of the long polished table, forcing the directors who sat on that side of it to turn in their chairs to follow him. The head of Webb Press was wearing a military-style suit vaguely reminiscent of a World War II general named Patton. Even down to his glossy calf-length cavalry boots and the fake ivory-handled revolvers buckled to his waddling hips.

"Snotty ungrateful sonofabitch," Weldon muttered to himself. I streamline his operation for him, get Webb Press ready to shift over to electronic publishing, and he rewards me with this stab in the back.

". . . and to show you just what kind of senility we're dealing with

here"—Hawks had raised his voice to a near shout—"let me introduce you to the vaunted efficiency expert that was foisted on me, the
superbrain who was given carte blanche by our beloved CEO to wipe
out most of Webb Press's staff and move our base of operations out
of Manhattan altogether!"

He snapped his fingers, and the flunky sitting next to the conference
room's only entrance jumped to his feet and opened the leather-
padded door. There was a slight commotion in the outer room, and
then two burly men in white uniforms led in Gunther Axhelm, who
was securely wrapped in a straitjacket.

Gasps went around the long conference table. Cigars fell out of
hanging mouths. Pouchy eyes widened. They all knew Axhelm, by
reputation if nothing else. They knew of his Prussian precision and
the ruthless thoroughness of his operations. What they now saw was
a wild man, red-rimmed eyes and drooling maniacal grin, straitjacket stained with spittle, baggy gray hospital drawers and bare feet.
Even his crew-cut blond hair seemed askew.

"This is the result of breathing too much of the glue that he himself demanded we use in binding our books, instead of the glue we
normally used. It has cost Webb Press roughly a hundred million
dollars; it's cost Gunther Axhelm his sanity."

Of course, Hawks had made certain that Axhelm had all the glue
he wanted to sniff in the private hospital where he had stashed the
loopy Axe. That, and a steady diet of Gene Kelly videos.

Axhelm suddenly shouldered free of his two handlers and, with a
deranged shriek, ran to the conference table and jumped atop it. Two
directors tumbled backwards in their chairs and fell gracelessly to the
floor. The others backed away in sudden fright.

But Gunther Axhelm meant them no harm. In his bare feet he
capered along the table in a mad parody of tap dancing, the strap
ends of his straitjacket flapping away, singing at the top of his lungs
in a decidedly Teutonic accent, "Be a clown, be a clown, all the world
loves a clown. . . ."

The Writer

In his miserable roach-infested room in the welfare hotel, the Writer pored over the current issue of *Publishers Weekly* that he had stolen from the local branch of the public library.

The State had stepped in and taken charge of his life. When the drugged-out staff of the warehouse had tried to burn the building down (with materials and helpful instructions from the management, incidentally), the apparatus of the State wheeled itself up in the form of (in order of appearance) Fire Department, Police Department, Bureau of Drug Enforcement, the Public Defender's Office, Department of Rehabilitation, Bureau of Unemployment, and the welfare offices of the state of New Jersey and the City of New York, borough of Queens.

Now he lived in a crumbling welfare hotel in Queens, detoxified, unemployed, and seething with an anger that seemed to grow hotter and deeper with every passing useless day.

But now it all focused down to a single point in space and time. For in his trembling hands he saw how and why it would all come together.

BUNKER SALES FORCE SUIT
OPENS IN FEDERAL COURT

The headline in *Publishers Weekly* caught his eye. Bunker Books. They were in a courtroom. All of them. The publisher, the editors.

Out there in a public courtroom, where any member of the public could come in and see them, face to face.

With an immense effort of will, the Writer forced his hands to stop trembling so he could read the entire article and learn exactly where they would be and when.

As he finished reading, he looked up and saw a single ray of light shining through the filth that covered the room's only window. The shaft was blood red. Sunset.

The Writer smiled. Where can I get a gun? he asked himself.

Twenty-One

It was not easy being the son of Pandro T. Bunker. Junior sat in the last row of the half-empty courtroom, listening with only half his attention to the testimony being given up on the witness stand. No one sat near him; he had the entire pew of seats to himself. None of the sales people in the audience wanted to be seen sitting near the son of the publisher. And all of his dad's people, including his mom, were up in the front.

But Junior smiled to himself. They all think I'm just the owner's son, he told himself. They all think I'm a spoiled brat who doesn't know nothing and gets everything handed to him on a silver tray. I'll show them. I'll show them all. Even Mom and Dad.

Junior's work in the office, as a special assistant to the publisher, had not been terribly successful. Most of the editors either distrusted him as a snoop for his parents or belittled his intelligence. After weeks of being alternately ignored and avoided, he transferred to the sales department just in time for Woody's lawsuit to explode in everybody's face. Naturally, the sales people regarded him as a pariah.

But Junior leaned back on the hard wooden bench of the courtroom and grinned openly. I'm smarter than they think. I'm smarter than any of them.

Up on the witness stand, Woody Baloney was being questioned by the cowboy lawyer the sales department had brought in from Colorado.

"And what, in your professional estimation, will be the result of the Cyberbooks program?" asked the cowboy, his weathered, crinkle-eyed face looking serious and concerned.

"The result?" Woody said, glancing at the judge. "We'll all be tossed out on our butts, that's what the result will be!"

"Objection!" shouted three of the five defense clones in unison.

"Overruled," snapped the judge. "The witness will continue."

The lawyer prompted, "So this electronic book gadget, this . . . *thing* they call Cyberbooks, will result in the whole sales force being laid off?"

"That's right," said Woody.

"In your professional opinion," the lawyer amended.

"Uh-huh."

Junior slouched farther on the hard wooden pew. Mom and Dad have pinned everything they've got on this Cyberbooks idea, and the sales force is going to stop it cold. Then what happens? They can't fire Woody or anybody else; they'll be back in court before you could say "prejudice." They won't be able to work with Woody or the rest of the sales force; too much hard feeling.

No, Junior concluded, the company's doomed. Finished. Mom and Dad are going down the tubes.

Which only made him smile more. Because I've been smart enough to take the money I have and invest it wisely. In one of the biggest multinational, diversified corporations in the world. *My* fortune isn't going to depend on some crazy invention, or on a lawsuit by my own employees.

Two days earlier, P.T. Bunker, Jr., had taken every penny in his trust fund and sunk it into Tarantula Enterprises (Ltd.). He had not merely acted on his own, nor did he trust a stockbroker with his money. Junior had first bought the latest computer investment program, and used his own office machine to examine all the various possibilities of the stock market.

Tarantula Enterprises was a great investment, the computer had told him. In order to fight off an unfriendly takeover bid, Tarantula was buying its own stock back at inflated prices. Although this had removed most of the stock from the open market and made the price for Tarantula shares artificially high, the computer program predicted that the price would go even higher as the takeover battle escalated. So Junior instructed his computer to automatically buy whatever Tarantula stock was available, and to keep on buying it until he told it to stop.

Glowing with self-satisfied pride, he told himself that he could even retire right now and just live on the dividends.

Lt. Moriarty, meanwhile, was causing no end of anguish among the staff tending the intensive care unit at St. Vincent's Hospital.

The usual routine was to keep ICU patients calm and quiet, sedated if necessary. Usually such patients were so sick or incapacitated by trauma that there was little trouble with them. Generally the intensive care ward looked somewhat like a morgue, except for the constant beepings and hums of monitoring equipment. Except when there was an emergency, and then a team of frantic doctors and nurses shouted and yelled at one another, dragged in all sorts of heavy equipment, and even pounded on the poor patient as if beating the wretch would force him or her to get better.

No one knew how many times a screaming emergency at bed A had resulted in heart failure at bed B. No one dared even to think about it.

Moriarty was different, though. All the monitors showed that he was in fine fettle, and since he had been in the hospital less than twenty-four hours, the nurses could not even claim that he was too weak to be allowed to get out of bed. But the hospital rules were iron-clad: no one got out of the intensive care ward until their physician had okayed a transfer or release—and his insurance company had initiated payment for the bill.

Moriarty insisted that he was detoxed and feeling fine. They had removed the IV from his arm; the only wires connected to him were sensor probes pasted to various portions of his epidermis. He wanted *out.* But Dr. Kildaire was out for the day; he would not return until the midnight shift started. And the accounting department, its computer merrily tabulating hourly charges, absolutely refused to discharge a patient whose insurance was provided by the city.

Threatening bodily harm and a police investigation produced only partial results. The head ICU nurse, a slim Argentinean with a will of tempered steel, at last agreed to allow Moriarty to sit up and use a laptop computer.

"If you stay quiet and do not disturb the other patients," she added as her final part of the bargain.

Moriarty reluctantly agreed. He had to check out a thousand ideas that were buzzing through his head, and he needed access to the NYPD computer files to do it. The laptop was not as good as his own trusty office machine, but it was better than nothing.

For hours he tapped at its almost silent keys and examined the data flowing across the eerily blood-red plasma discharge screen. Yes, all of the victims had indeed been Tarantula stock owners; most of them had owned shares for years, decades. But he himself had only recently purchased a few shares. So new owners were just as vulnerable to the Retiree Murderer as old ones. The murders had nothing to do with being retired, the victims were owners of Tarantula stock who lived in New York.

Which meant that the murderer was connected in some way to Tarantula. And lived in New York. Or close enough to commute into town to commit the murders.

Pecking away at the keyboard, Moriarty used special police codes to gain access to the New York Stock Exchange files. What happened to the stock of the murder victims? Who was buying the shares?

It was impossible to trace the shares one for one, but there *was* a buyer for the shares of the murder victims. Within weeks after each murder, the victim's shares were sold—and bought immediately. But by whom? Tarantula shares were traded by the thousands every day of the week. Who was buying the shares of the murder victims?

For hours that question stumped Moriarty. Then he got an inspiration. He asked the NYSE computer if any one particular individual person was acquiring shares of Tarantula on a regular basis.

The stock exchange computer regarded corporations as individual persons, and gave Moriarty a long list of buyers that included corporations headquartered in New York, Tokyo, Messina, and elsewhere. It was almost entirely corporations, rather than human beings, who were regularly buying Tarantula stock.

Again Moriarty stared at a blank wall. But slowly it dawned on him that Tarantula Enterprises (Ltd.) was itself one of the largest regular buyers of its own stock. The corporation was buying back its stock wherever and whenever it could. Not an uncommon tactic when a company was trying to fend off an unfriendly takeover, and if Moriarty read the data correctly, Tarantula was fighting savagely to beat off a takeover attempt by a Sicilian outfit.

The Mob? Moriarty asked himself. Could be.

Then could it be the Mob that is knocking off these little stock-holders and buying their shares?

Not likely, he concluded. The Mafia-owned corporations were buying Tarantula stock in big lots, tens of thousands of shares. Not the onesey-twoseys that the Retiree Murder victims had owned. Moreover, there hadn't been much selling to the Mobsters over the past several months. Tarantula was buying back its own stock pretty successfully and preventing the Mafia from gaining a controlling interest.

So who's buying the murder victims' stock? Moriarty asked himself for the hundredth time that afternoon. The computer could not tell him.

It takes two talents to be a good detective: the ability to glean information where others see nothing, and the ability to piece together bits of information in ways that no one else would think of. Perspiration and inspiration, Moriarty called the two.

He had sweated over the computer for practically the entire day. It had told him everything he asked of it; a most cooperative witness. But it had not been enough. Now he had an inspiration.

While the nurses were making their rounds, replacing the IV bottles that fed the comatose patients in the intensive care ward, Moriarty asked the computer for photographs of the members of Tarantula's board of directors. Maybe. Just maybe.

The pictures were slow in coming. The simple laptop computer, with its limited capability, built up each photo a line at a time, rastering back and forth across the screen like the pictures sent by an interplanetary probe from deep space.

The chief nurse herself brought Moriarty a skimpy dinner tray and laid it on the swinging table beside his bed with an expression on her face that said, "Eat everything or we'll stick it into you through an IV tube. Or worse."

Moriarty actually felt hungry enough to reach for the tray and munch on the bland hospital food while the computer screen slowly, slowly painted pictures of Tarantula's board members, one by one, for him to examine.

It wasn't until the very last picture that his blood pressure bounced sky high and his heart rate went into overdrive.

"It's him!" Moriarty shouted. "I'd recognize those eyes anywhere!"

He flung back the bedsheet and started to get to his feet, only to be surrounded instantaneously by a team of nurses and orderlies that included two hefty ex-football players. Despite Moriarty's struggles and protests, they pushed him back in the bed. The chief nurse herself stuck an imperial-sized hypodermic syringe into Moriarty's bare backside and squirted enough tranquilizer into him to calm the entire stock exchange.

"You don't unnerstand," Moriarty mumbled at the faces hovering over his suddenly gummy eyes. "There's a life at stake. Whoever bought Tarantula stock . . . his life's in danger. . . ."

Then he fell fast asleep and the team of nurses and orderlies left, with satisfied smiles on their faces.

Weldon W. Weldon was forced to call a recess to the board of directors meeting after the orderlies had finally cornered the all-singing, all-dancing Gunther Axhelm and carted him away. The conference table was a scuffed-up mess, and several of the older directors needed first aid.

He sat in his powered chair, Angora blanket across his lap, and watched the maintenance robots polish the table and rearrange everyone's papers neatly. The conference room's only door swung open, and a malevolently smiling P. Curtis Hawks stepped in. His red toupee was slightly askew, but Weldon said nothing about it.

"You wanted to see me?" Hawks snapped. He self-consciously planted his fists on his hips, just above the pearl handles of imitation Patton pistols.

"Yes I did," Weldon replied, adding silently, You stupid two-faced idiotic clown.

"Well?"

"Close the door and come down here," said Weldon. "What I have to tell you shouldn't be shouted across the room."

Hawks pushed the leather-padded door shut and slowly walked down the length of the long conference table, avoiding the robots that were industriously polishing its surface back to a mirror-quality sheen.

Pulling up a heavy chair and sitting directly in front of the Old

Man, Hawks slowly took the pacifier from his mouth and said, "You forced me to do this."

"Did I?"

"Yes you did," the younger man said, his voice trembling just a little. Like a little boy, Weldon thought. A little boy who's mad at his daddy but knows in his heart that he's being naughty.

Weldon said carefully, "You thought that I sent Axhelm into your operation to destroy you."

"Didn't you?"

"No. I sent him to Webb Press because the operation had to be cleaned out before we could transfer to electronic publishing. And you wouldn't have the kind of cold-blooded ruthlessness it took to clean house."

"Clean house? He's driven us out of business!"

"Not quite," said Weldon. Then he added with a smirk, "Your losses are going to save Tarantula a walloping tax bite next fiscal year."

"Webb Press shouldn't be run as a tax loss. . . ."

"And it won't be," said Weldon softly, soothingly, "once you've converted to electronic publishing."

"You mean you . . ."

"Haven't you been paying attention to the industry news?" The old man was suddenly impatient. "Haven't you seen what's happening at Bunker Books? Their own sales force is suing Bunker over Cyberbooks."

Hawks gaped at him, uncomprehending.

"I had to clean out Webb Press," Weldon explained, "before you could even hope to start with electronic publishing. One thing I've learned over the years, never expect a staff to change the way it does business. If you're going to go into a new venture, get a new staff. That's an ironclad rule."

"So you were going to get rid of me, too," said Hawks grimly.

Weldon felt exasperation rising inside him like boiling water. "Dammit, Curtis, you can be absolutely obtuse! I *told* you your job was safe! I *told* you I wanted Webb to lead the world into electronic book publishing. What do I have to do, adopt you as my son and heir?"

Hawks thought it over for a long moment, chewing hard on his pacifier.

"It would help," he said at last.

Now it was Weldon's turn to go silent as he thought furiously. This is no time for a split on the board. The Sicilians will take advantage of it and move in for good. Yet—Hawks has already risen to his level of incompetence. If I promote him one more step . . .

The old man smiled at his erstwhile protege, a smile that had neither kindness nor joy in it, the kind of smile a cobra might make just before it strikes, if cobras could smile.

He wheeled his powered chair up to Hawks's seat and reached out to pat the younger man on his epauletted shoulder.

"All right, Curtis," Weldon said softly, almost in a whisper, "I'll do just that. Make you my heir. How would you like to take over the responsibilities of chief executive officer of Tarantula Enterprises?"

The pacifier dropped out of Hawks's mouth. "CEO?"

Nodding, Weldon said, "I'll remain chairman of the board. You will still report to me. But instead of merely running Webb Press, you'll have the entire corporation under your command."

Hawks looked as if he were hyperventilating. It took several gasping tries before he could say, "Under . . . my . . . command!"

"I take it you accept the offer?"

"Yes!"

"Fine. Now let's get the rest of the board in here and finish our business."

Taking a deep breath to calm himself, Hawks agreed, "Right. Let's tell them the good news."

Weldon smiled again. Chief executive officer, he snorted to himself. I'll let you enjoy the office and the perks for a few months, and then out you go, my boy, on your golden parachute. Or maybe without it.

Hawks was grinning ear to ear. Chief executive officer! From that power base I'll be able to get rid of the Old Man in six months and take over the board. You're a gone goose, Weldon W. Weldon, only you don't know it yet.

Telephone Transcript

Harold D. Lapin: Hello, this is Lapin.

Mobile Phone: (Sounds of street traffic in background) Yes, I can hear you.

Lapin: The trial adjourned for the day, just five minutes ago.

Mobile: Justice only works a short day, eh?

Lapin: It will resume tomorrow at ten o'clock.

Mobile: Okay, okay. So how did it go today?

Lapin: The plaintiff scored all the points. Judge Fish seems to be leaning over backwards in their favor. I don't think Bunker has a chance.

Mobile: Good. Good.

Lapin: Bunker himself did not show up. His wife and several of his editorial employees were present. And the inventor, Carl Lewis.

Mobile: He didn't recognize you, did he?

Lapin: No, certainly not. I sat in the last row, while he was all the way up front. I'm wearing a false mustache and an entirely different style of clothing.

Mobile: Good. Good.

Lapin: Bunker Junior was there, too.

Mobile: What did you find out about him?

Lapin: It wasn't easy. I had to bribe three members of the family's personal law firm.

Mobile: But what did you find out? Has he made out a will or hasn't he?

Lapin: He has not.

Mobile: So if he should suddenly die, he dies intestate.

Lapin: That's right.

Mobile: His estate will be tied up in probate court for months, maybe years.

Lapin: Yes.

Mobile: And the Tarantula stock the little fool has been buying will be tied up along with everything else. No one will be able to vote the stock. Not even the Sicilians.

Lapin: I believe that means his proxies will automatically be voted by the corporation, isn't that right?

Mobile: I'm not sure. The lawyers will have to look into it. But at least the Sicilians won't be able to get their hands on it.

Lapin: If young Bunker should suddenly die.

Mobile: When he dies, yes. When he dies.

Twenty-Two

Scarlet Dean ran a lovingly manicured blood-red fingernail along Ralph Malzone's hairless chest and all the way down to his navel.

"Don't stop there," Ralph said, pulling her closer to him.

She giggled girlishly. They were in Scarlet's apartment, where Malzone spent almost every night. It was a spacious room in an old Manhattan building that had once been used as the setting for a horror movie. But although the outside of the building was dark and ornately Gothic, it had been completely modernized inside. The only way to tell it was an old building, from the inside, was to realize that no modern building would have such high ceilings. Nor such elegant moldings where the walls and ceiling met.

Scarlet's bedroom was completely mirrored. All of the walls, including the closet doors (where roughly half of Malzone's haberdashery was stored) and the high ceiling. On the rare occasions when sunshine made it through the polluted air and grime-covered window, the room dazzled and sparkled. It was like being inside a gigantic jewel.

But now the window blinds were drawn tight, and the only light was a dull red flicker from the artificial fireplace.

"Do you still love me?" Scarlet asked him.

Malzone turned his rusty-thatched head to gaze into her emerald eyes. "You bet I do."

"Even though our romance started with chemical warfare?"

It was by now a private joke between them. "I don't care how it started, Red. It started. And I never want it to end."

"Me neither," she said, snuggling closer.

Malzone sighed. "But we'll probably both be out of a job in another few days, the way the trial's going."

"This was just the first day," Scarlet said. "Our side didn't even get a chance to speak, yet."

"You mean management's side."

Propping herself on one elbow, Scarlet replied, "You're on management's side, aren't you?"

"Kinda." Malzone shifted uncomfortably on the bed.

"What do you mean?"

His lean, long face contorting into a miserable frown, Malzone admitted, "I know how Woody and the rest of the sales staff feel. Hell, I was one of them for a lot of years before I got kicked upstairs to sales manager. . . ."

Scarlet's expression softened. "You feel sorry for them."

"I feel sorry for all of us. I don't see this as one side versus the other side. I don't think of us as management versus labor. This is a family fight. It's damned unhappy when members of the same family have to fight. In public, yet."

She plopped back on the mattress and looked at their reflection in the ceiling mirror. Ralph was a coiled bundle of muscle and nervous energy; it excited her to look at his naked body. And she was glad that she kept herself ruthlessly to her diet and exercises; she wanted to keep on looking good to him.

"Maybe there's a way to get both sides together," Ralph was saying, "so we can stop this fighting and be all one happy family again."

Scarlet shook her head. "I don't see how."

"I do," he muttered, so low that she barely heard him.

Without taking her eyes off the ceiling mirror, she asked, "How?"

"We give up on Cyberbooks."

"What?"

"It's the only way. We tell Carl to pack up and leave."

"But you can't do that to him! And P.T. would never—"

"I know P.T. won't back down, so it's all a pipe dream. And I know Carl's a good guy, a friend, somebody I like a lot." Malzone hesitated a moment, then went on, "But the only way to save Bunker Books is to drop the Cyberbooks project. If we don't, the company's going to be torn apart and go down the tubes."

She turned toward him again, her heart suddenly beating faster. "Ralph, I have a confession to make to you."

"Another one? You sure you're not a closet Catholic?"

"Be serious!"

"Okay."

"I was planted at Bunker Books by my boss at Webb Press. I was supposed to be a spy. My assignment was to steal Cyberbooks away from Bunker."

Malzone's face brightened. "Great idea! Let's give it to them! Let *them* tear themselves apart!"

Scarlet stared at him. "Do you think . . . I mean . . ."

Ralph slid a wiry arm around Scarlet's trim bare waist. "Let's do it! And afterward, let's figure out how to get Cyberbooks to Webb Press."

Alba Blanca Bunker was in bed also, but for more than an hour she had nothing to say except moans and howls of passion. The voice-activated computer that ran the bedroom's holographic decor system had run its gamut from deep under the sea to the exhilarating peaks of the Himalayas, from a silent windswept desert in the moonlight to the steaming raucous orchid-drenched depths of the Amazonian jungle.

Ever since his body-restructuring operations, Pandro had been a half-wild animal: a passionate, powerful animal who would sweep Alba up in his strong arms the minute she arrived home from the office and carry her off to bed, like some youthful Tarzan overwhelming a startled but unresisting Jane.

Over the months since his operation, Alba had expected his ardor to cool. It did not. It was as if Pandro were trying to make up for all the years he had allowed business to get in the way of their lovemaking; as if he had stored all this passion inside himself and now, with his newly youthful and energetic body, was sharing his pent-up carnal fury with her.

Now they lay entwined together, tangled in a silk sheet that was thoroughly ripped, soaked with the sweaty musky aura of erotic sexual love. The room's decor had shifted to a warm moonlit meadow. Alba could hear trees rustling in the soft wind, smell fresh-cut grass. Fireflies flickered across the ceiling.

As if struggling up from a deep, deep sleep, P.T. asked in the darkness, "How did things go today?"

"Oh—all right, I suppose. It's only the first day of the trial." She hadn't the heart to tell him her worst fears.

But he sensed them. "All right, you suppose? That doesn't sound too good."

"It wasn't so bad."

Bunker looked into his wife's face. Even in the flickering shadows he could see how troubled she was.

"Maybe I should go to the court with you tomorrow," he muttered.

Her heart fluttered. *He's willing to leave the house, in spite of his fear of people and crowds, just for me. He's willing to face the world, for me!*

Struggling to hold her emotions in check, Alba said, "That's not necessary, darling."

"Are you sure?"

"Yes, of course. It's all right."

"Are you sure?" he repeated.

All day long in that dreadful courtroom Alba had maintained her self-control. She had not cried or screamed when Woody's lawyer accused her of being a heartless money-mad despoiler of the poor. She had not taken after him with one of her spike-heeled shoes, as she had wanted to. She had remained cool and reserved, and had not said a word.

But now, after the evening's wild lovemaking, all her defenses were down. She broke into uncontrollable, inconsolable sobs.

"Oh, Pandro," she wept, "we're going to lose everything. Everything!"

The Writer was astonished at how easy it had been to acquire enough armaments to equal the firepower of a Vietnam War infantry platoon. He had been asweat with nervous fear when he walked into the gun shop. He had nothing bolstering him except the memory of an ancient video of an old Arnold Schwarzenegger flick.

The gun shop owner had been wary at first; a shabby-looking customer coming in just before closing time, dressed in a threadbare gray topcoat and baggy old slacks. But the Writer smiled and explained that he was doing research for a new novel about terrorists, and needed to know the correct names and attributes of the kinds of guns terrorists would use. Within fifteen minutes the owner had locked his front door and pulled down the curtain that said CLOSED. He picked out an array of Uzi, Baretta, Colt, and laser-aimed Sterling guns. With the smile of a man who really cares about his merchandise, the shop owner proceeded to explain the virtues and faults of each weapon.

"And they all use the same ammunition?" the Writer asked naively.

"Oh no! The Baretta takes nine-millimeter . . ." Before long the owner was showing how each gun is loaded.

It was simple, then, for the Writer to pick up the massive Colt automatic and point it at the owner's head.

"Stick 'em up," he said with a slightly crazy grin.

The owner laughed.

The Writer cocked the automatic and repeated, minus the grin, "Stick 'em up."

He walked out of the gun shop burdened by nearly thirty pounds of hardware. He actually clanked as he hurried down the street. The owner lay behind his counter, bound and gagged with electrician's tape that the Writer had bought earlier from a nearby hardware store with his last five dollars.

"I can't believe it," Carl said with a shake of his head.

He and Lori were strolling slowly around Washington Square, still numb with the shock of the first day of the trial. They had gone to a tiny restaurant in the Village for dinner, but neither of them had much of an appetite. They left the food on the table, paid the distraught waiter, and now they walked aimlessly toward the big marble arch at the head of the square.

The November evening was nippy. Carl wore an old tennis sweater under his inevitable tweed jacket; Lori had a black imitation leather midcalf coat over her dress. A chilly breeze drove brittle leaves rattling across the grass and walkways. Only a few diehard musicians and panhandlers sat on the park benches in the gathering darkness, under the watchful optics of squat blue police robots.

"I just can't believe it," Carl repeated. "That lawyer made Cyberbooks sound like something Ebenezer Scrooge would invent just to throw people out of work and make them starve."

"And the judge let him get away with it," Lori said.

"This isn't a trial. It's an inquisition."

With a deep sigh, Lori asked, "What will you do if the Bunkers lose? If the judge actually issues an injunction against Cyberbooks?"

Carl shrugged. "Go find another publishing house, I guess, and sell the idea to them."

"But don't you understand? If the judge issues an injunction against Cyberbooks, it will be a precedent that covers the whole industry!"

Carl looked at her, puzzled.

"If Bunker is enjoined from developing Cyberbooks," Lori explained, "it sets a legal precedent for the entire publishing industry."

"That doesn't mean . . ."

"If any other publishing house decided to develop Cyberbooks with you, what's to stop their sales force—or their editorial department, or anybody else—from doing just what Woody's doing? And they'll have the legal precedent of the Bunker case."

Carl stopped in his tracks, his face awful.

Lori felt just as bad. "No other publishing house will go anywhere near Cyberbooks if we lose this case."

"Cyberbooks will be dead," he muttered.

"That's right. And I'll never get to publish *Mobile, USA.*"

"Huh? What's that?"

"The novel I told you about."

"Oh, that great work of literature." Carl's tone was not sarcastic, merely unbelieving, defeated.

"I'll have to spend the rest of my life working on idiot books and dancing nights to make ends meet."

"You could leave Bunker Books."

"It would be just the same at another publishing house."

"You could leave the publishing business altogether," Carl said.

"And go where? Do what?"

Before he realized what he was saying, Carl answered, "Come back to Boston. I'll take care of you."

And before she knew what *she* was saying, Lori snapped, "On an assistant professor's salary?"

"But I'll have Cyber—" His words choked off in midsentence.

Lori fought back tears. "No, Carl, you won't have Cyberbooks. You'll be back to teaching undergraduate software design and I'll be belly dancing on Ninth Avenue and we'll never see each other again."

His face became grim. He pulled himself to his full height and squared his shoulders. "Then we damned well had better win this trial," he said firmly.

"How?" Lori begged. "Even the judge is against us."

"I don't know how," said Carl. "But we've just got to, that's all."

PW Forecasts

The Terror from Beyond Hell

Sheldon Stoker.
Bunker Books
$37.50. ISBN 9-666-8822-5

Sheldon Stoker's readers are legion, and they will not be disappointed in this latest gory terror by the Master. Terror, devil worship, hideous murders and dismemberments, and—the Stoker trademark—an endangered little child, fill the pages of this page-turner. The plot makes no sense, and the characters are as wooden as usual (except for the child), but Stoker's faithful readers will pop this novel to the top of the best-seller charts the instant it hits the stores. (January 15. Author tour. Major advertising/promotion campaign. First printing of 250,000 copies.)

Passion in the Pacific

Capt. Ron Clanker. USN (Ret.)
Bunker Books.
$24.95. ISBN 6-646-1924-0

A better-than-average first novel by the last living survivor of the epic Battle of Midway (World War II). Tells the tale of a bittersweet romance in the midst of stirring naval action, with the convincing authenticity of a sensitive man capable of great wartime deeds. The characters are alive, and the human drama matches and even surpasses the derring-do of battle. (January 15. No author tour. No advertising/promotion campaign. First printing of 3,500 copies.)

Twenty-Three

As a bullet seeks its target, dozens of men and women from all parts of greater New York converged on the single oak-panelled courtroom in which the Bunker *vs.* Bunker drama was to be played out.

Lori Tashkajian, foreseeing a lifetime of dreary editorial offices and smoky Greek nightclubs ahead of her, rode the Third Avenue bus to the courthouse.

Carl Lewis, after a sleepless night trying to think of some way to turn the tide that was so obviously flowing against Cyberbooks, decided that he could use the exercise and so walked the forty blocks to the courthouse, through the crisp November sunshine.

Scarlet Dean and Ralph Malzone took a taxi together, each of them wrapped in their own gloomy thoughts.

The Writer rode the crowded subway downtown, his heavily laden topcoat clanking loudly every time the train swayed.

P. Curtis Hawks, glowing with his new title of CEO, directed his chauffeur to whisk down the FDR Drive for a firsthand look at the trial that was going to break Bunker Books. Even though his limousine was soon snarled in the usual morning traffic jam (which often lasted until the late afternoon traffic jam overtook it), Hawks smiled happily to himself at the thought of Bunker going down the drain.

P.T. Bunker, Jr., rode with his mother in her white limo the few blocks that separated their Lower East Side mansion from the courthouse. Junior hummed a pop tune to himself, grinning, as he contemplated how the computer in his room at home was busily buying up every spare share of Tarantula stock it could find.

Alba Bunker did not notice her son's self-satisfied delight. She dreaded another day in court and longed to be in the powerful arms of her oversexed husband.

Dozens of curious and idle people with nothing better to do headed for the courtroom, after learning from their TV and newspapers of the fireworks the cowboy attorney had lit off the day before.

Lt. Jack Moriarty had the most difficult course. Upon awakening from the sedatives administered to him the previous evening, he realized with the absolute certainty of the true hunch-player that the Retiree Murderer was going to be in that courtroom. Half an hour with his laptop computer convinced him that P.T. Bunker, Jr., was grabbing Tarantula stock like a drunken sailor reaching for booze, and the murderer was going to strike again that very morning.

Knowing it was hopeless to try to gain release from the hospital through normal channels (which meant waiting for Dr. Kildaire, who had just signed out at the end of his midnight-to-eight shift), Moriarty slowly, carefully detached the sensors monitoring his body functions and, clutching the array of them in his hands so that they would not set off their shrill alarms, he tiptoed to the bed next to his and attached them to the sleeping hemorrhoid case there. The spindly wires stretched almost to the breaking point, but the alarms did not go off.

With barely a satisfied nod, Moriarty raced to the closet and pulled on his clothes. Years of shadowing suspects had taught him how to seem invisible even in plain daylight, so he slithered his way out of the ward, along the corridor, down the elevator, and out the hospital's front entrance in a matter of minutes.

Using his pocket two-way he summoned a patrol car to take him to the courthouse. When the dispatcher asked what authority he had to request the transportation, Moriarty replied quite honestly, "It's a matter of life and death, fuckhead!"

Justice Hanson Hapgood Fish allowed his clerk to help him into his voluminous black robes, then dismissed the young man for his morning pretrial meditation. He sank onto his deep leather desk chair and closed his eyes. The vision of all the lovely women in his courtroom immediately sprang to his mind. Mrs. Bunker, looking so vulnerable and hurt in virginal white. The one in red: stunning. The dark-haired one with the great boobs. This was going to be an enjoyable trial. Justice Fish determined that he would drag it out as long as possible.

Let the goddamnable lawyers talk all they want to, he said to himself. Let them jabber away for weeks. I'll give them all the latitude they want. They'll love it! After all, they bill their clients by the minute. The longer the trial, the more money they squeeze out of their clients. And the longer I can sit up there and gaze at those three beauties. He smiled benignly: a blonde, a redhead, and a brunette. Too bad they're all on the losing side of this case.

One other person was thinking about the Bunker trial, even though he was not heading toward the courtroom.

P.T. Bunker sat alone in his half-unfinished mansion, at the old pine desk he had used since childhood, reviewing the videotape of the previous day's session in court. Thanks to freedom of information laws and instant electronic communications, it was possible for any informed citizen to witness any open trial.

He wore an old *Rambo XXV* T-shirt, from an ancient promotional drive to tie in the novelization with the movie. It was spattered with bloody bullet holes, and showed a crude cartoon of the elderly Rambo shooting up a horde of Haitian zombies from his wheelchair. Below the shirt Bunker was clad only in snug bikini briefs, his legs and feet bare. He no longer needed padding to look impressive.

His handsome face grimaced as he watched the plaintiff's attorney attacking Bunker Book's management—himself! his wife!—in his relentless western invective.

A low animal growl issued from P.T. Bunker's lips as he watched the videotape. After nearly an hour, he glanced once at the Mickey Mouse clock on his desk top, then rose and headed for his clothes closet.

Carl Lewis arrived in the courtroom precisely at one minute before ten. Half a dozen other people were filing in through the double doors and finding seats on the hard wooden pews. Carl saw Lori up in the front row, talking earnestly with Scarlet Dean and Ralph Malzone. As he started toward them, a scruffy man of indeterminate age, wearing a long shapeless gray topcoat and a day's growth of beard, accidentally bumped against him. Carl felt something hard and metallic beneath the man's coat, heard a muffled clank.

But his mind was on Lori and the others. He mumbled a "Pardon me," as he pushed past the man and headed for his friends. He did not even notice Harold D. Lapin sitting on the aisle in the next-to-last row. Lapin sported a dashing little mustache and wore a yachting outfit of white turtleneck, double-breasted navy-blue blazer, and gray flannel slacks. Hidden in plain sight.

P.T. Junior entered the courtroom right behind Carl. He was followed by P. Curtis Hawks, dressed in a fairly conservative business suit. Neither of them recognized the other.

"All rise."

Carl had not yet sat down. The courtroom buzz quieted as Justice Fish made his slow, dramatic, utterly dignified way to his high-backed padded swivel chair. His completely bald skull and malevolently glittering eyes made Carl think once again of a death's head.

There was more of a crowd this morning. The news of the western lawyer's tirade had drawn dozens of onlookers and news reporters, the way a spoor of blood draws hyenas. Just as Judge Fish rapped his gavel to open the morning's proceedings, two more men slipped through the double doors and took seats on opposite sides of the central aisle, in the very last row. One of them was Detective Lieutenant Jack Moriarty, freshly escaped from St. Vincent's Hospital. Just behind him came a rather tall, slim figure in a blue trenchcoat. Neither man paid the slightest notice to the other; their attention was concentrated on the drama at the front of the court-room.

Judge Fish leaned forward slightly in his chair and smiled a vicious smile at the western lawyer.

"Is the plaintiff ready to continue?"

The man was dressed in a tan suede suit cut to suggest an old frontiersman's buckskins. "We are, Your Honor."

"Are you ready to call your first witness?"

"Yes, sir."

"Then proceed."

"I call Mr. Ralph Malzone to the witness stand."

Carl felt a moment of stunned surprise. The courtroom fell absolutely silent for the span of a couple of heartbeats, then buzzed with whispered chatter. The judge banged his gavel and called for silence.

Ralph looked more surprised than anyone as he slowly got to his feet and made his way to the witness box. He ran a nervous hand through his wiry red hair, glanced at Woody Balogna sitting at the plaintiff's table, then at Mrs. Bunker, at the defense table with her five interchangeable lawyers.

The bailiff administered the oath and Ralph sat down. Uneasily.

The western lawyer strolled slowly over to the witness box, asking Ralph to state his name and occupation. Ralph complied.

"Sales manager," drawled the lawyer. "Would y'all mind explaining to us just exactly what that means?"

Slowly, reluctantly, Ralph explained what a sales manager does.

The lawyer asked more questions, and over the next quarter of an hour Ralph laid out the basics of the book distribution system: how books go from printer to wholesalers and jobbers, then from those distributors to the retail stores.

"There's a lot of different steps involved in getting the books from the publisher's warehouse to the ultimate customer, the reader, wouldn't you say?" the lawyer prompted.

Nodding, Ralph replied, "Yes, that's right."

No one noticed P. Curtis Hawks, sitting in the audience, wincing at the word "warehouse."

"A lot of jobs involved in each of those steps?" asked the lawyer.

"Yes."

"Now, if Bunker Books went into this Cyberbooks scheme, how would your distribution system change?"

Ralph hesitated a moment, then replied, "We would market the books electronically. We could send the books by telephone directly from our office to the bookstores."

"Eliminating all those steps you just outlined?"

"All but the final one."

"Isn't it true that you could also sell your books *directly* to the ultimate customer, the reader? Transmit books *directly* to readers over the phone?"

"Yeah, I guess we could, sooner or later."

"Thereby eliminating even the bookstores?"

"I don't think we'd—"

"Thereby eliminating"—the lawyer's voice rose dramatically—"*all* the jobs of *all* the people you deal with today: the printers, the wholesalers, the jobbers, the truck drivers, the store clerks—*and even your own sales force!*"

"We have no plans to eliminate our sales force," Ralph snapped back with some heat.

"Not today."

"Not ever. Books don't sell themselves. You need sales people."

The lawyer strolled away from the witness box a few steps, then whirled back toward Ralph. "But you *admit*, don't you, that all the jobs in the middle—all the jobs involved with book distribution—will be wiped out by this devilish new invention."

"The distribution system will be totally different, that's right,"

With a triumphant gleam in his eye, the lawyer strode to his table and pulled a batch of papers from his slim leather saddle bag.

"Your Honor," he said, approaching the bench, "I have here affidavits from each of the nation's major book distribution companies, and both of the national bookstore chains. They all ask that their interests be considered in this trial. Therefore, I ask you to consider enlarging the venue of this trial. I ask that this trial be considered a class action by the thousands—nay, tens of thousands—of warehouse personnel, truck drivers, bookstore clerks, wholesalers, jobbers, distributors, and their associated office personnel, against Bunker Books!"

The courtroom broke into excited babbling. Judge Fish whacked away with his gavel until everyone quieted down, then said, "I will consider the motion."

The news reporters sitting at the media bench along the side wall of the courtroom tapped frantically at their computer keyboards.

With a satisfied grin, the western lawyer handed his papers to the bailiff, who passed them up to the judge. Then he smirked at the quintet of defense attorneys and made a little bow.

"Your witness," he said.

"No questions," squeaked five mousey voices in unison.

"Court will recess to examine these papers," said Justice Fish. Glancing at the clock on the rear wall of the courtroom, he added, "We might as well break for lunch while we're at it."

The Accountant

Gregory Wo Fat squinted at the printout on his computer screen through old-fashioned eyeglass lenses thick enough to stop bullets.

As chief accountant for Webb Press (and one of the few employees still on Webb's payroll after the company's pruning by the Axe), Wo Fat's duties included supervising the royalty statements sent out to the authors of Webb's books.

The computer screen displayed the new layout for next year's royalty statements, a tangled skein of numbers designed to be as confusing as possible.

Wo Fat's grandfather, the esteemed accountant for the Honolulu branch of the Chinese Mafia, had drilled into his bright young grandson's mind since babyhood one all-important concept: "More money is stolen, my grandson, with a computer than with a gun."

Wo Fat had eschewed a life of crime. Almost. Instead of carrying on in the family tradition in Honolulu, he had come to New York and accepted a position as a lowly accountant with the publishing firm known as Webb Press.

"Your job is a simple one," said his first boss, an elderly gentleman named Kline. "No matter how many books an author sells, we should never have to pay royalties over and above the advance that the dumb editors gave the author in the first place. Got it?"

Wo Fat grasped the concept immediately. Of course, it did not apply to the firm's most prestigious authors. If they did not receive royalty checks every six months they would undoubtedly move to another publishing house. So they were paid—not as much as they actually earned, of course, but enough to keep them and their agents reasonably satisfied.

It was the other authors, the "midlist" authors who made up the great bulk of any publisher's titles and the new writers who had no experience, those were the ones whom Wo Fat slaved over. He regarded it as a personal failure if they received one penny in royalties over and above the advance they got before each book went on sale.

Wo Fat glowered at the computer screen. This new design was seriously lacking! What fool is responsible for this? This column here, if subtracted from the figures in the third column and multiplied by the square root of the figures in the first column, would actually tell the author how many books had been sold during the six months that the statement reported on!

Unacceptable! Someone's head would roll for this. Why, if he let this new design go through, Wo Fat would be besieged by authors demanding to know why they had not been paid for each and every book sold. That would never do.

Twenty-Four

Claude Le Forêt had been born in a logging camp in Manitoba. He had grown up in logging camps, where his father was nothing more than an average cutter of trees and his mother a cook. But Claude had gone far beyond his humble beginnings.

Thanks to two lifetimes of hard work and sacrifice by his parents, Claude had gone to university. He had obtained a degree in management, and when he returned to the logging camp where his parents still slaved away over their tele-operated cutting machines and microwave cookers, he wore a business suit and carried a portable computer rather than a chain saw.

Yet he was still true to his upbringing. Beneath his gray flannel suit jacket he still wore a plaid lumberjack's shirt.

For many years Claude worked his way up the tree trunk of success. He had the brains and the inherited conservative instincts of his parents: he never went out on a limb, never barked at either a superior or an underling, never made a sap of himself. He stayed on the main trunk and rose quietly, unspectacularly, steadily to the very crown of Canada's largest lumber and paper-pulp combine.

Now he sat wedged into a tiny booth in the coffee shop on the ground floor of the courthouse, facing the suede-suited westerner who was representing what seemed to be the entire U.S. book distribution industry. The coffee shop was filled with lunchtime customers. It buzzed with gleaming-eyed lawyers and glumly downcast clients, all of them hunched head to head over tiny tables in cramped little booths, whispering secrets to one another over croissant sandwiches and Perrier.

"Your telegram said the affair was urgent," said Claude with a hint of Quebecois in his accent.

"Shore is urgent," smiled the lawyer.

Claude studied the weather-seamed face of this outlandish-looking lawyer. He himself was a handsome man, his face a bit fleshy from too much rich food, his eyes a bit baggy and bloodshot from the wine he drank with each meal, but otherwise he looked almost dashing with a touch of gray at his temples and a splendid mustache that curled up toward his slightly rouged cheeks. He wore a conservative two-button maroon suit, with his trademark lumberjack's plaid shirt and a tiny little bow tie of forest green. It took no great detective to deduce that he was totally color blind.

"You wish my corporation to join with you in this suit against the book *électronique*, is that it?"

"Yup," said the lawyer in his best Gary Cooper style.

"This would be a serious commitment by my corporation. Not only that, it would create an international incident. Canada would become heavily engaged in this lawsuit. The Canadian government would certainly take an interest. Ottawa and Washington would send observers to the trial, at the very least."

With a nod and a grin, the lawyer said, "Listen, Mr. Le Forêt." He pronounced the final "t," but failed to notice the shudder it sent along Le Forêt's spine. "If we let Bunker bring out Cyberbooks, what do you think it will do to the lumber business in Canada? To the paper and pulp industry?"

Le Forêt shrugged gallicly.

"I'll tell you what it'll do, friend. The more books they publish electronically, the less paper they'll need. Paper mills will shut down. Men will be thrown out of work. Whole cities will become ghost towns. The demand for lumber will be cut in half, then cut in half again. Thousands of lumberjacks will be unemployed. All those fancy tree-cutting machines of yours will be sitting out there in the forest, turning into rust. It'll be a disaster for you. And for Canada."

If there was one thing Le Forêt had learned in a long and successful career, it was to examine carefully the enemy's side of the matter. He sat pensively for a long moment, then steepled his fingers and played devil's advocate.

"If I do as you wish," he said slowly, "do you not think that the movement of environmentalists will come out on the side of Bunker and his Cyberbooks?"

"The environmentalists?"

"*Oui.* After all, they have been scheming for generations to close down the paper mills. They, with their silly nonsense about pollution. How can you make paper without sulfur and smoke? They even demand that we purify the water once we are finished using it!"

The lawyer smiled a thin, superior, knowing, nasty, lawyer's smile. "The environmentalists won't bother us," he said.

"Pah!"

"I have their word on it."

Le Forêt put on his pensive look again. "Their word? How so?"

"It's simple. I pointed out to them that if the paper and pulp industry goes under, the economy of Canada goes down with it."

"That has never bothered them in the past."

"Well, I also pointed out that if the paper mills close down, they lose one of their best targets for raising money. Everybody will think that they've won their battle against you, and stop contributing to the environmental movement. They'll go out of business, too!"

"*Diable!*" Le Forêt broke into a grin that pushed the tips of his mustache almost into his eyes. "And they believed you?"

"Sure they did. They know I'm right. They can't exist without you."

With a thoughtful rub of his chin, Le Forêt murmured, "I must remember this after the trial is finished. It is an interesting new light on a problem that has plagued me all my life."

The lawyer grinned back at him. "Then you'll join our suit?"

Sticking out a huge hand that was made to chop down trees, yet bore nary a callus, Le Forêt said, "I am with you. *Moi,* and the entire Canadian lumber and paper-pulp industries!"

When the trial resumed that afternoon, the lawyer grandly announced that the Canadian lumber and paper-pulp combine had joined in the class action suit against the rapacious forces of evil known as Bunker Books. Woody and the sales personnel attending the trial whooped loudly. Mrs. Bunker went pale, while Carl and the others on that side of the courtroom sagged visibly.

Judge Fish glowered at the cowboy lawyer as he accepted the papers filed by the Canadians.

"Will there be anyone else joining this suit?" he asked in a sharp, almost sneering tone. "Outer Mongolia, perhaps? Or maybe little green men from Mars?"

The lawyer bowed his head slightly, as if embarrassed. "Your Honor, I know this has been a somewhat unusual procedure, but in the interests of justice I beg you to overlook the slightly unorthodox course that this trial has taken so far."

The judge snorted at him.

"I assure you there will be no further enlargement of the plaintiff's co-complainants."

Turning to the clone group of defense attorneys, Justice Fish asked acidly, "Does the defense have any objection to this motion?"

The lawyer closest to Mrs. Bunker got to his feet, looking perplexed. "May we have five minutes to review our position on this, Your Honor? This motion has come as a complete surprise to the defense."

"Yes, I imagine it has," the judge retorted. "Five minutes recess." He banged his gavel and stalked out of the courtroom.

Carl Lewis felt his temperature rising. "This trial is turning into a circus," he whispered to Lori.

"More like a Roman gladiatorial contest," she whispered back. "We're the Christians and they're the lions."

Staring at the defense attorneys, all five of whom were frantically tapping at their briefcase computers, desperately searching for a precedent that would block the entry of the Canadians, Carl pleaded, "Isn't there some group that we could call in to back our side? I mean, how come we're all alone here and they've got so many people to back them up?"

Lori's eyes suddenly sparkled. "You're right! I've got an idea!"

She jumped up from her seat and pushed past Ralph and Scarlet to get to the aisle. Carl came right behind her.

"What is it?" he asked as he followed her to the courtroom doors. "What?"

But Lori said nothing as she half ran to the row of public telephones down the marble corridor.

Picking up the nearest handset, she said to the voice-activated telephone computer, "The Author's League of America."

Carl smiled with sudden understanding.

Raymond Mañana had never been a practical man. The fact that he had now served slightly more than seven years as president of the Author's League of America proved that fact.

Never very tall, Raymond had allowed years of poor eating habits and lack of exercise to round out what had once been a spare body into a globule about the size of a modest weather balloon. His glistening pate was bald, but his chin was covered with a dirty-gray beard of patriarchal length. His once keen vision had fallen victim to endless hours of peering at word processor screens, so he now sported heavy trifocal contact lenses that made his eyes seem slightly bugged out, like a frog's.

But despite these physical failings, Raymond had the heart of a lion. He had practically surrendered a mediocre career writing potboiler novels to accept the onerous and thankless responsibilities of the presidency of the Author's League. He was deeply immersed in reading the latest round of inflammatory letters sent in to the *ALA Bulletin* when the phone unit on his computer chimed out the first few bars of "Brush up Your Shakespeare," the ALA's official song.

Raymond welcomed the call. The letters were boring: two of the most widely read authors in the country reduced to boyish slanders and insults over the issue of whether or not the organization should have an official necktie. He poked the button that consigned the libelous words to the computer's memory bank.

Lori Tashkajian's lovely, worried face took form on the display screen.

"Lori! I thought you'd be in court this morning."

"I am," she answered. "We're on a short recess."

"Oh."

"Ray, we need your help. I need your help. The future of publishing depends on you!"

"On me?"

"On the Author's League."

"I don't understand."

Swiftly, Lori outlined what had been happening at the trial. Raymond nodded his understanding.

"So we need the Author's League to come in here and support us. Otherwise we're going to go down the drain and Cyberbooks will be strangled in its cradle."

"A mixed metaphor," said Raymond.

"We don't have time to argue syntax!" Lori almost shouted. "You've got to get the biggest number of authors you can contact to come into court on our side. Today! This afternoon!"

Raymond sadly shook his bald, bearded head. "What makes you think they'll come out to support Bunker Books? After all, authors and publishers aren't usually the best of friends."

"It's in your own best interest!" Lori insisted. "Cyberbooks will bring down the costs of publishing to the point where thousands of writers who can't get their works published now will have a viable marketplace for their books."

"I know. I understand. And I applaud what you're trying to do. But . . ." His voice trailed off.

"But what?" Lori asked.

Feeling weak and helpless, Raymond explained, "Well, you know this bunch. They're *writers*, Lori. They can't agree on what to have for lunch, for Pete's sake. Half of them think Cyberbooks is the greatest idea since Gutenberg, the other half think it's an invention of Satan."

"Oh, god."

"And they don't like to go into courtrooms. Can't say I blame them. The idea gives me the chills."

"But if the ALA won't support this innovation in publishing, you're dooming all the writers. . . ."

Raymond raised a pudgy finger. "I understand and I agree with you, Lori. I'll do what I can. I'll start calling people right now. But don't expect too much."

"Maybe Sheldon Stoker!" Lori suggested.

"He's in Indonesia, directing the movie they're making from *The Balinese Devil.*"

"Oh."

"I'll do what I can," said Raymond, knowing it sounded feeble.

"Please," Lori begged. "And quickly!"

"I'll do what I can."

Lori nodded and broke the connection. Raymond Mañana sighed a great, heaving sigh and, like a general issuing orders for a hopeless charge against overwhelming odds, he began tapping out phone numbers on his keypad.

"She doesn't understand," he muttered to himself. "Editors just don't understand writers. We're not really organized. It's tough to get us to do *anything* except argue among ourselves. Christ, if we had any real organization, would the tax laws read they way they do?"

The Book Signing

Conrad Velour sat in the middle of the bookstore, ballpoint pen poised, surrounded by stacks and stacks of his latest steamy novel, *Inside Milwaukee*. (After seventy-some "Inside" novels, he was running out of interesting cities.)

Not only was the table at which he sat heaped with copies of *Inside Milwaukee*. All the bookshelves in the front of the store were packed with the novel. Even more were stacked by the cash register, where a discreetly small sign suggested, HAVE YOUR COPY OF *INSIDE MILWAUKEE* SIGNED BY THE AUTHOR.

But the bookstore was strangely, maddeningly, eerily quiet. No customers had come to the table where MR. CONRAD VELOUR, AUTHOR!!! sat under the garish sign proclaiming his presence. Not a single book had been purchased. The ballpoint pen held in his white-knuckled fist had not scrawled out one autograph.

An icy anger was inching along Conrad Velour's blue veins. The store manager was definitely avoiding him. The clerks were tiptoeing across the store's plush carpeting and whispering behind his back.

Someone in the promotion department of S&M books was going to hang by the thumbs for this foul-up, Velour told himself. *Someone* was going to pay for this humiliation. More than an hour sitting on this hard bridge chair at this table heaped high with the best novel anyone's seen in years, and no customers. Not one.

They got the address wrong in the advertisements. Instead of 333 Fourth Avenue, the ads had all read 444 Third Avenue. Velour had discovered the mistake too late to do anything about it. He himself had gone to the address the S&M publicist had given him, only to find that it was not a bookstore at all. It was Ching's Pizza and Chinese Take-Out. He had found the bookstore after some frantic screaming into a street corner telephone's voice-activated computer directory.

Now he sat alone, flanked by piles of unbought books, while the store personnel avoided his furious stare. He had asked the youngsters behind the counter at Ching's to send the thousands of readers who would undoubtedly show up there to the proper address. But they barely understood English and—most crushing of all—not a one of them recognized him or his name.

You'd think that at least *some* of my faithful readers would recognize the mistake and find their way here, he groused to himself. But no, they're probably filling up on pizza and Chinese dumplings, making Ching rich while I sit here like a leper with bad breath and psoriasis.

Oh, they'll pay, he told himself for the millionth time. They'll pay!

A little old lady wandered into the hushed and nearly unpeopled store. Velour straightened up on his chair and gave her his most charming smile. He could be very charming when he wanted to be. He had the slim, elegant, slightly decayed looks of a bankrupt British lord. He wore the uniform of a successful author: white silk turtleneck shirt, informal Angora cardigan of royal blue, crisply creased gray slacks, and butter-soft moccasins of genuine artificial squirrel hide.

The little old lady doddered around the front of the store, casting furtive glances toward the table where Velour and his oversupply of novels were stashed. She hesitated, took a few uncertain steps toward the author, stared up at the sign proclaiming who he was, then made a sour face, shook her head, and turned around and left the store.

Velour's hand clenched so tightly the ballpoint pen snapped in two.

The store manager, a young wisp of a man, approached him as if he were a live bomb.

"Uh, sir . . . there's a telephone call for you, sir."

Velour fixed him with an evil stare. Sweat broke out on the youngster's upper lip.

"Uh . . . I could bring the mobile phone here, I guess."

Velour raised his left eyebrow one centimeter.

"It . . . uh, it doesn't have a picture screen, though. Sir."

"Good," he snapped. "Then whoever is phoning will not see the humiliation I'm being put through."

The store manager scuttled away and returned half a minute later with the portable phone instrument in his trembling hand.

Velour took a deep breath, then made himself smile as he sang, "Velour here!"

"Conrad. Glad I located you. It's Raymond Mañana."

"What can I do for you, Ray?"

"I'm not interrupting important business, am I?"

"For you, Ray, I can set aside business for a few moments. What's so important that you tracked me down here in the middle of a signing session?"

"It's about the Cyberbooks trial, Conrad."

"Oh, yes. I read something about that in *PW* last week, I think."

For the next ten minutes Mañana explained what was happening in the courtroom. "So I thought, you're almost around the corner from the courthouse already, maybe when you've finished your signing you could pop over there and offer them some moral support."

Conrad Velour sighed a patient, long-suffering sigh. It was *so* difficult to deal with fools. "Raymond, it's impossible. I'm not a Bunker author, to begin with, and I don't see why authors should be called upon to pull Bunker's chestnuts out of the fire. If this Cyberbooks deal falls through, so what? It won't affect me or my sales."

"But—"

"No, Raymond. I will not lift a finger to help P.T. Bunker." And he clicked the phone's disconnect button.

It won't affect me or my sales, Velour repeated to himself as he stared out across the empty bookstore. It won't affect me or my sales.

Twenty-Five

Carl was surprised to hear his own name called as the plaintiff's next witness. For a moment he felt the cold pain of fear surging through him. But then he looked the cowboy lawyer squarely in the eyes and rose to his feet. The fear burned away in the rising heat of righteousness. I'll show this hotdog what Cyberbooks is all about. I'll set them *all* straight. He patted his jacket pocket, where he always carried one of the Cyberbooks readers. I'll show them all.

Swearing to a deity he did not believe to exist, Carl took the witness chair and calmly watched the lawyer approach him the way a gunfighter in the Old West might saunter up a dusty town's main street.

"Your name?" the lawyer asked.

"Carl Lewis."

"Your profession?"

"I am an assistant professor at the Massachusetts Institute of Technology."

"That's your position," the lawyer corrected. "What is your profession?"

"Software composer."

"And what does that entail? What do you actually do?"

Glancing up at the judge, who hovered over him like an implacable death's head, Carl said, "I create the software programs that make computers run. Without such programs, a computer is nothing but a box full of electronic or optical switches."

"You make the computers actually perform, is that it?"

"Yes."

"You bring the machines to life."

"Right."

"Sort of like Dr. Frankenstein, huh?"

Carl felt his cheeks heat up. "It's not at all—"

But the lawyer cut him off with more questions. Soon Carl was explaining how Cyberbooks worked, and he even pulled his electro-optical reader from his jacket pocket to show the lawyer and the judge how to operate it. Justice Fish seemed fascinated with the device. The book it showed was Robert Louis Stevenson's *Kidnapped*, complete with dozens of beautiful full-color illustrations.

After nearly fifteen minutes of tinkering with the Cyberbooks reader, while the lawyer and the entire courtroom waited with growing impatience, the judge finally put the device down on his banc next to his silver-plated water pitcher.

"Exhibit A," he instructed the bailiff. Carl began to wonder if he would ever get it back.

"Now, Mr. Lewis," the lawyer said smoothly, running a hand through his long silver-streaked hair, "just what motivated you to invent this here Cyberbook machine?"

"What motivated me?" Carl felt puzzled.

"Why'd you do it? What was going through your mind while you were working to perfect it? The desire for money? Wealth? Fame? A way to get promoted to full professor?"

Shaking his head, Carl said, "None of those."

"Then what?"

Carl smiled slightly. The lawyer had talked himself into a trap. *Now I can tell them the real truth, make them understand why Cyberbooks is so important.*

He took a deep breath, then began, "The main difference between human beings and other animals is our ability to communicate. Speech. Without true speech you can't have a truly intelligent species. The two most important inventions in the history of the human race were writing and printing. Writing allowed us—"

"Mr. Lewis," intoned the judge, "spare us the history lesson and answer the question."

Surprised, Carl said, "But I am, Your Honor."

"The question was about your motivation for creating this invention, not about the history of the human race. Be specific."

There was a slight commotion at the defense table. Carl saw Mrs. Bunker whispering furiously to the lawyer closest to her, who abruptly turned to the one next to him, and so on down the line until the last of the five clones got to his feet and said—rather weakly, Carl thought—"Objection, Your Honor."

"On what grounds?" Judge Fish demanded.

"Plaintiffs' counsel asked the witness about his motivations for inventing Cyberbooks. The question permits the widest allowable interpretation. Restricting the witness to—"

"Denied," snapped the judge. Turning to Carl, he commanded, "Restrict yourself to the time period when you were inventing the device, young man."

Carl's guts churned with boiling hot anger. He glared at the judge, then turned back to the smirking cowboy lawyer.

"My motivations were simple. I wanted to make this world a better place to live in."

Carl had expected a gasp of awe from the audience. Perhaps some scattered applause. Nothing. Dead silence.

He plunged ahead. "Books are the life blood of our society. Our racial memory. Poor people can't afford books. Kids in ghetto schools hardly ever even see a book. Certainly they don't buy any. That's because they can't afford them. Books are too expensive for poor kids. Too expensive for the poor people in Latin America and Africa and Asia. Cyberbooks will bring the cost of buying books down to the point where even the poorest of the poor can afford it."

"But as I understand it," the lawyer said, "the reading device will cost several hundred dollars. How do you expect the poor to buy your fancy machines?"

"The government can buy them and distribute them free, or at nominal cost. The publishing industry could even donate a certain number of them, out of the profits they'll make from Cyberbooks."

"And then all these poor people will have to buy Cyberbooks and nothing else, is that right? You'll have them hooked on your product. Very neat."

"They will be reading books!" Carl countered. "They will be learning. They'll be able to *afford* to learn, to grow, to pick themselves up and make better lives for themselves. Even people who've never learned to read will be able to use Cyberbooks that talk to you. The books themselves will teach them how to read."

"While Bunker Books makes a fortune and corners the entire publishing industry."

Ignoring that, Carl went on. "There's another factor here. Today the publishing industry consumes millions of acres of trees every year. Paper mills pollute the air and water around them. They contribute to the greenhouse effect and alter the world's climate. They contribute to acid rain. When the publishers turn to Cyberbooks we'll be able to stop that awful waste and make the world cleaner and greener."

"Is that so?" The lawyer smiled craftily as he turned back toward the plaintiff's table. He opened his saddle bag and took out a slim sheaf of papers bound in a set of green covers.

"I have here in my hand a report by the Wildlife Foundation, a respected international environmental organization." The lawyer waved the report over his head as he approached the witness box. "It says here that if the existing Canadian logging industry were to cease its operations—which they find environmentally sound, by the way—then the beaver population of the forests would undergo a population explosion that could upset the ecological balance of the entire Canadian forest system!"

Now the audience gasped. One odd-looking fellow in a maroon suit and plaid shirt actually clapped his hands together once.

"Far from making the world cleaner and greener," the lawyer continued, "your invention could lead to an ecological catastrophe!"

Carl sat in stunned silence, unable to summon a word of rebuttal.

The cowboy turned dramatically to the defense table. "Your witness."

The middle one of the five identical mice peeped, "No questions."

"Witness may step down. Call your next witness."

Shakily, Carl walked away from the witness box and headed for his seat. Lori looked sad and sympathetic, waiting for him in the first row of benches. Just before he sat down, Carl heard the western lawyer boom out:

"I call Mrs. Alba Blanca Bunker."

"Mrs. Bunker to the stand."

It was a nightmare. The lawyer badgered and hounded Mrs. Bee, trying to twist every word she said into an admission that Bunker Books was attempting to drive thousands of innocent, hardworking men and women out of their jobs and into miserable lives of perpetual poverty.

Mrs. Bunker, all in white as usual, seemed to shrink on the witness chair like a little girl being scolded by an unforgiving parent. Her face was so pale that Carl thought she was about to faint.

"And isn't it true," the lawyer snarled at Mrs. Bee, "that the *only* reason you became interested in Cyberbooks was your vision of making huge fortunes in profits? That you didn't care if thousands of ordinary men and women were thrown out of work? That sheer, vicious greed was driving you to commit this horrible act of economic mass murder?"

Mrs. Bunker's eyes went wide and her mouth dropped open. She was staring not at the tormenting lawyer but beyond him, at the muscular figure who had barged through the courtroom's double doors, past the startled uniformed guard there, and now strode up the aisle toward the front of the courtroom.

Vaulting over the low rail that divided the audience from the front of the court, Pandro T. Bunker reached the cowboy before Judge Fish could even grasp his gavel. P.T. grabbed the westerner by a padded suede shoulder, whirled him around, and socked him squarely on the jaw. The lawyer sailed four feet off the ground and landed in a crumpled suede heap at the foot of the judge's banc.

Pandemonium broke out. Alba ran to the powerful arms of her protective husband. The judge banged his gavel so hard the head broke off and fell over the edge of the banc, bopping the semiconscious lawyer on the top of his head. The audience was on its feet, pointing, laughing, roaring. The five defense attorneys were running around in circles. The news reporters stared in frozen amazement.

And then a shot rang out.

The Writer, standing on the wooden bench of the rearmost pew, his long topcoat flapping open to reveal a veritable arsenal of small arms, held a smoking automatic pistol over his head.

"Nobody move!" he screamed, his scrawny face red, his eyes wild. "You're all my hostages! First one to make a move gets a bullet!"

The Five O'Clock News

Bobbi Burnheart elbowed her way through a phalanx of carefully coiffed and jacketed news reporters to a spot where she could be seen dramatically posed against the besieged courthouse. Behind her trailed the highly trained team of dedicated specialists who made Ms. Burnheart the most popular TV anchorperson in New York: her hairdresser, her makeup man, her wardrobe manager, and her speech coach.

Behind *them* came the camera crew: two disgruntled guys in greasy coveralls carrying twelve-ounce picocameras with integrated lasers that could light Ms. Burnheart beautifully even in the stygian darkness of a sewer during a power blackout at midnight in the middle of a snowstorm; and her ostensible producer, a young and slimly beautiful black woman recently graduated from the Sorbonne who was the only person at the station naive enough to take on power-house Bobbi.

La Burnheart swept a practiced eye across the facade of the courthouse, its graffiti-covered concrete now glaring with police spotlights. Several battalions of New York police, SWAT teams, FBI agents, and National Guard troops had cordoned off the court-house.

Bobbi Burnheart, though, daintily hiked her miniskirt up over her hips (revealing nothing except support panty hose) and clambered over the blue sawhorses that the NYPD had set up as a barrier.

"Hey, you can't cross . . ."

Bobbi flashed her dazzling shark's smile at the policeman pointing his stun club at her. "It's all right, Officer. Channel 50."

"My orders . . ."

But Bobbi had already turned to her two cameramen. "Get him on tape. Be sure to get his badge and name tag in focus."

They grumbled but rolled twelve seconds worth of tape. The police officer, not certain if this was a chance at fame on TV or a warning not to infringe on the First Amendment, forced a smile for the cameras and then turned and ran to find his sergeant.

"Which windows?" Bobbi asked, now that they were in a clear space. She noted, somewhat smugly, that none of the other TV crews had dared to cross the police barricade even though she had. It confirmed her opinion of her supposed competitors. Of course, none of them had doting fathers who owned a chain of TV stations and a couple of U.S. senators.

The black producer consulted a smudged photocopy of the courthouse's floor plan, then pointed to a row of windows on the fourth floor. "Up there—I think."

"Good enough," said Bobbi. "Nobody will know the difference."

For the next several minutes her team of dresser, hair stylist, and makeup man fussed over her while the two cameramen and the producer talked over the best angles to shoot. Finally Bobbi was ready. She looked splendid in her toothpaste-tube rucked and pleated kelly green dress, her golden hair shining in the glow of the police spotlights like a goddess's helmet. The cameramen knelt at her feet to make a dramatic picture of Bobbi against the courthouse facade.

The producer put one hand to the nearly invisible communicator plugged into her left ear, cocking her head slightly to hear the voices from the control center at the station. She held up three fingers of her other hand, then two, one, and finally pointed straight at Bobbi— who instantly put on her dazzling shark's smile.

"Inside the windows you see behind me, a courtroom drama unlike any courtroom drama you've ever seen is being played out against the lives of dozens of men and women."

Staring earnestly into the nearer of the two picocams, she went on, "At approximately three-thirty this afternoon an unknown gunman seized courtroom number two, up there on the fourth floor, and has been holding several dozen people hostage, including the presiding judge, Justice Hanson H. Fish."

The producer was madly scribbling prompting words on a long roll of what looked like toilet paper and holding them up for Bobbi whenever Ms. Burnheart took a breath between lines.

"The case being tried involved the publishing industry. It was not a criminal case. No one knows who the gunman is, or what his demands are. He has released two hostages, the guard and bailiff on duty in the courtroom, but has issued no statement as to his reasons for taking the hostages or what he intends to do with them."

Breath. New set of prompts.

"Shortly after releasing the two men, a fusillade of shots was heard. But no one knows who has been killed, if anyone. The chances are that human bodies are bleeding inside that courtroom, while the police, the FBI, and the National Guard wait outside, trying to avoid further bloodshed, if possible."

Breath. New set of prompts.

"For now, all we can do is wait. And pray."

Turning toward the courthouse, but making certain that her face was dramatically profiled against the spotlighted courthouse facade, Bobbi Burnheart ad-libbed: "Will justice be done in courtroom two?"

Twenty-Six

Carl Lewis thought of a line from the Statue of Liberty as he gazed around the courtroom. "The wretched refuse of your teeming shores."

The courtroom looked like the steerage class of an old banana boat. Thirty-eight men and women sat, stood, sprawled in various attitudes of fear, frustration, despair, or exasperation, waiting for some unknown fate at the hands of an obvious lunatic.

The gunman had released the two uniformed men, the bailiff and the overweight guard who was supposed to stand duty at the courtroom's entrance door. Then the news reporters, huddled along the wall opposite the empty jury box, demanded that at least one of them be released too. The gunman had lined them against the wall and then used one of his semiautomatic pistols to shoot each and every one of their laptop computers where they rested on the press table. The reporters cringed. Two of them fainted. When the smoke cleared, they gaped at the wreckage of their precious laptops. And stopped making demands.

Shortly after the shooting, the New York Police Department, true to its standard operating procedure for hostage situations, had cut off the building's lights, heat, and water. It was not cold in the courtroom, not this early in the evening. And the police spotlights outside threw slanting beams of glaring bright light that bounced off the high ceiling and scattered an eerie harsh illumination across the courtroom. The problem was water. The women were already complaining about toilet facilities. The only one that the gunman would allow them to use was in the judge's chambers, where there was no exit except through the courtroom. At least a half dozen women were lined up there constantly.

Carl sat on the same stiff bench he had been sitting on when the gunman had seized the courtroom. His back hurt and his buttocks were numb. Lori had stretched out on the bench, looking emotionally drained, and fallen into an exhausted sleep half an hour earlier. Carl had taken off his tweed jacket and bundled it into a rough pillow that now rested under Lori's soft cheek.

He gazed down at her, breathing the slow steady rhythm of deep sleep. She looked so beautiful, so desirable. He knew that he loved her, and he would do anything to keep her from harm, even face death itself if he had to.

The gunman was up at the judge's chair, peering out at the windows that glared with police spotlights. He had taken off his shabby topcoat and spread his arsenal of pistols and submachine guns across the top of the judge's banc. Since he had taken over the courtroom nearly three hours earlier, he had spoken hardly a word.

Ralph Malzone and Scarlet Dean had moved toward the rear of the courtroom, where they sat with their arms wrapped protectively around one another. Mr. and Mrs. Bunker were at the defense table, holding hands and speaking in low, earnest whispers. P.T. Junior had moved from the back of the courtroom to sit with his parents. The five defense attorneys were under the table, cowering.

"Well, son, I don't know how long you intend to hold us here," the cowboy lawyer called to the gunman, "but sooner or later you're gonna need a good defense attorney." He got up from his chair at the plaintiffs table and reached into the breast pocket of his suede jacket.

The gunman jerked as if a spasm had struck him and grabbed the Uzi submachine gun from the collection spread out before him.

"Sit down!" he screeched.

The lawyer took a small white oblong from his pocket and held it above his head. "I just wanna give y'all my card. You're gonna need a lawyer. . . ."

"And you're going to need a mortician if you don't *sit down!*"

The lawyer sat.

"And shut up! Keep your lying goddamned mouth shut!"

Far in the back of the courtroom, Lieutenant Moriarty sat in frustrated silence. He was unarmed, since the hospital personnel had routinely taken his gun, badge, and other possessions from him and stashed them in the hospital's storage center. His unauthorized leavetaking had prevented him from claiming his stuff.

Patience, he told himself. Patience, Jack old boy. This nutcake can't stay awake forever. Sooner or later he'll doze off, and that's when you grab him.

Provided you don't fall asleep yourself, first.

Moriarty studied the lean, lank, scruffy gunman. He can't be the Retiree Murderer. This isn't the same style at all, and therefore not the same man. But the murderer is in this courtroom, I know it. I can feel it. And so is his next intended victim.

He easily identified P.T. Bunker, Jr., up front with his mother and father. But try as he might, he could not find anyone who looked like the man who had tried to kill him. The harsh glow from the reflected searchlights cast strange shadows across faces, making it difficult to see people's eyes.

The murderer sat across the courtroom from Moriarty. He had recognized the police lieutenant shortly after the gunman had taken over, and wondered why Moriarty had not simply shot the maniac between the eyes and gotten this whole ordeal over with. He trusted that his disguise would keep him safe enough; after all, Moriarty hardly got even a moment's glance at him when he had attacked the lieutenant with the poisonous orchid's thorn.

But what was Moriarty doing here, in this courtroom? And why didn't the poison kill him, as it should have? The murderer had taken off his trenchcoat and folded it into a neat little cushion that he now sat on, fairly comfortably. He fingered the slim plastic box in his right jacket pocket. Inside it was another poisonous thorn from the deadly Rita Hayworth orchid.

Should I knock off young Bunker while that police detective is so close? he asked himself. Probably not. Although—if the cops try to break in and grab the idiot up there who's taken us hostage, there's bound to be a lot of shooting. Perhaps I could get to Bunker Junior then and do the job, in all the confusion.

Wait and see, the murderer told himself. Wait and see.

One other man was counseling himself to be patient: Justice Hanson Hapgood Fish. He sat slumped on the witness chair, unwilling to move any farther from his rightful seat of authority. He glowered up at the man who had taken over his chair. The blue veins in his forehead throbbed with unconcealed fury. This mangy bum, this crazed idiot, has taken over my courtroom. My courtroom! He's allowing all sorts of people to use my private toilet. Who knows what kinds of sickies and perverts are pissing in my bowl?

Judge Fish tried to force himself to be calm, without much success. He closed his eyes and imagined himself as the Grand Inquisitor of the good old days in Spain, with this filthy disgusting derelict stretched on the rack. "Boil the oil," Justice Fish muttered to himself. "Heat the branding irons."

He smiled cruelly.

"You people all think I'm crazy, don't you?"

All eyes shifted to the man up at the banc.

"You think I'm just some wild-eyed fruitcake who's gone berserk. I know what you're thinking. I can see it in your faces. Well, I'm not crazy. And even if I am, it's you people who drove me to it." He waved a heavy Colt pistol at the staring audience.

The Writer enjoyed the attention. "You think you're so damned high and mighty. Well, I'm here to tell you that you ain't. I'm here to show you that I'm just as good as you are. Maybe better."

He rambled on for hours, as the night grew colder but not darker, thanks to the spotlights flooding through the windows. People curled up on the hard wooden benches and tried to sleep. Eventually the Writer stopped speaking to them. But he dared not close his eyes.

From time to time the telephone back in Judge Fish's chambers rang, but the Writer would not let anyone answer it.

"I'm not ready to talk to them yet. I still got plenty I want to tell you people."

But he lapsed into a grudging silence, and the thirty-eight hostages drifted into little knots of twos and threes.

"Do you think we'll get out of this alive?" Scarlet Dean asked in a small, frightened voice.

"Sure we will," said Ralph Malzone with a certainty that he did not feel. He put his arm around Scarlet protectively, and felt her trembling. "We'll be okay, Red. We'll be fine, you'll see."

"As long as you're with me," Scarlet said, fighting back tears of terror. "I can stand anything if you're with me, Ralph."

"I'm right beside you, baby. All the way."

Pandro T. Bunker was also comforting his wife as the chill of November began to seep into the unheated courtroom.

"It's all my fault," Alba Bunker was saying softly. "If I hadn't pushed you into this Cyberbooks project . . ."

"No, no," said P.T. "It's *my* fault. I've hidden myself away from the world for too long, left all the burden of running the business on your shoulders."

Junior discreetly got up from his chair beside them and started wandering aimlessly down the central aisle of the courtroom. He knew his mother and father wanted to say things to each other that should be said only when they were alone. Briefly he thought about the five lawyers huddled beneath their table. So they hear Mom and Pop coo at each other; they won't understand a word of it. They're lawyers, not human beings.

"That cruise we took this past summer," P.T. was saying. "I've been thinking . . ."

"It was a wonderful cruise," she murmured.

"Wouldn't it be great if we could cruise the seas all the time? Live on a boat. A sailboat. Just sail to anyplace that strikes our fancy— Tahiti, New Zealand, Copenhagen, Greece, Buffalo."

"Buffalo?"

"I've never been to Buffalo. I've never seen Niagara Falls. I've never been *anyplace*. I've always been too damned busy with the company."

"You've had all the responsibilities of business. . . ."

"*We've* had all the responsibilities. For too long a time, dearest. We're not getting any younger."

Alba smiled up into his handsome face. "Oh, I don't know. That cruise took ten years off your age, or more."

Smiling back at her tenderly, P.T. answered, "What I mean, darling, is that we've worked hard all our lives and now we should start to enjoy what we've made."

"Enjoy?"

He nodded. Glancing up at the mumbling, half-drowsing gunman, P.T. said, "If . . . I mean, when we get out of this, you and I are going to buy a yacht and sail it around the world."

"But the business!"

"Let somebody else worry about the business. Why should we kill ourselves over it? Let's enjoy our lives while we can."

Alba blinked with surprise. Let someone else take over Bunker Books? Leave it all and go sailing around the world? A voice in her head warned against it. But in less than a moment it was drowned out by a surge of joy and wonder and gratitude at the marvelous, wise insight that her loving husband had just shared with her.

"Pandro, you're right," Alba heard herself say. "Leave the business to Woody or whoever wants to slave over it. We *deserve* to enjoy the rest of our lives!"

Carl was half-stupefied with the need to sleep. But he refused to let his eyes close. Sooner or later that lunatic up there was going to nod off, and when he did Carl was determined to race up to the banc and disarm the madman.

Beside him, Lori stirred and pulled herself up to a sitting position. "What time is it?" she asked, rubbing her eyes.

Glancing at the glowing digits on his wristwatch/calculator, Carl replied, "Almost midnight."

"The police haven't done anything?"

"Guess they're afraid of starting a bloodbath."

Lori shivered. "It's cold!"

Carl put his jacket over her shoulders and then wrapped his arm around her. She snuggled so close to him that he could feel her body warmth even through the jacket.

"When will it end?" Lori asked.

Carl shrugged, and kept his bleary eyes on the gunman.

The Writer kept on talking because he knew that once he stopped, the temptation to sleep would overwhelm him. He was babbling about his life, spinning out his autobiography for his captive audience.

". . . and I couldn't afford to go to college. Couldn't get a scholarship, even though I had good marks in high school. I wasn't a member of any recognized minority. I thought about changing my religion, or dyeing my skin, or even a sex-change operation. I wondered how come a group of people who make up fifty-one percent of the population could be classified as a minority. But there wasn't a college in the land that would let me in. Not one. . . ."

I ought to ease on up toward the front of the courtroom, thought Lieutenant Moriarty. This boob can't keep droning on like that forever. He's putting everybody to sleep, and sooner or later he's going to doze off himself.

As he got up slowly from the rearmost bench, a stray thought wafted through his mind, about how blind people seem to compensate for their disability by increasing the sensitivity of their other senses.

Now why would I think of that? he asked himself. Good detective that he was, Moriarty knew from experience that the subconscious mind often comes to realizations and understandings long before they are recognized by the conscious mind. What's my subconscious trying to tell me?

A faint whiff of something strange, a cloying pungent odor, like something from a tropical jungle, some strange hybrid flower that was beautiful but deadly—the Rita Hayworth orchid! The doctor at the hospital had told him that the flower produced a strange, powerful scent. Moriarty turned in the eerily lit courtroom and began to follow his nose, like a true bloodhound.

P. Curtis Hawks sat with the news reporters at their table along the far wall of the courtroom. The shambles of their laptops lay strewn across the long table and scattered on the floor around them. Whenever anyone shifted a foot, it crunched on the remains of silicon chips.

The afternoon and evening had been a revelation to Hawks. He realized, with deep shame, that he was a physical coward. When that psycho had started shooting, Hawks's heart had gone into palpitations and his bowels had let loose. Now, smelly and sticky and thoroughly ashamed of himself, he sat with the reporters. To the others, it looked as if he were doing something brave, deliberately sitting with the group that had come closest to death. Actually, Hawks figured that lightning would not strike twice at the same place. The reporters had been cowed into abject silence. One of them was still comatose, stretched put on the floor with his hands folded funereally over his chest.

All he needs is a goddamned lily, Hawks grumbled to himself.

He had worried, when he had drifted over toward the reporters, that they would object to his awful smell. But they never noticed it. Either that, or they were extending him their professional courtesy.

"You think you're so high and mighty," the Writer was rambling from his perch up at the judge's seat. "Well, I'll tell you something. Without the writers you're *nothing*. Your whole damned industry, all of you—editors, publishers, salesmen, every one of you—you'd be *noplace* without your writers. The writers are your gold mine, your oil field, your natural resource. And how do you treat them? Like a dog, that's how. Like a horse or a mule or worse."

Lori was nodding as she listened to the gunman's increasingly passionate tirade. He must be a writer, she realized. And she found herself agreeing with what he was saying.

"I wrote a book," he went on. "Might not be a very good book, but I wrote it as honest and real as I could. And I sent it to your company. More than a year ago, now. And you never answered me. No letter. Not even a rejection form. You never sent my manuscript back! It was the only copy I had! Now it's lost and it's all your fault and you're going to pay for destroying *Mobile, USA*."

Carl, groggy and sleepy, shook his head. "Did I hear him right? He just accused you of destroying Mobile, Alabama?"

But Lori was suddenly wide-eyed. She gasped. She clutched at Carl's arm. "*Mobile, USA!* That's the novel I want to publish! He's the writer I've been trying to contact!"

She shot to her feet, breathless with excitement. But before she could say a word there was a sudden scuffle off to one side of the courtroom and the writer, screaming with fearful rage, grabbed the Uzi submachine gun from his desk.

((◦)) ((◦)) ((◦))

REJECTION SLIPS

The Usual

Dear Sir or Madam:

Thank you for submitting your manuscript for our consideration. Unfortunately, we find that it does not suit our needs at the present time. Naturally, we cannot give individual comments on each of the many manuscripts we receive.

Sincerely,
The Editors

The Cruel

Dear Sir or Madam:
Who are you trying to fool?

Disgustedly,
The Editors

The Japanese

Most respected author:
We have read your work with inexpressible pleasure. Never in our lives have we seen writing of such sheer genius. We are certain that if we published it, your book would be brought to the attention of the Emperor, who would insist that it serve as a model for all future writings. Since no one could possibly hope to equal your sublime masterpiece, this would put us out of business. Therefore we must return your manuscript to you and lay it at your feet, trembling at the harsh judgment that future generations will have of us.

Most humbly and sincerely,
The Editors

Twenty-Seven

P.T. Bunker, Junior, was standing off to one side of the courtroom, by the empty jury box, wondering if he should get in line for the toilet in the judge's chambers or just whiz out the window. He made his way through the shadowy courtroom to one of the long windows and stood on tiptoes to see outside. Squinting against the powerful glare of the police searchlights, Junior saw that the street below was still jammed with TV news crews, cops, soldiers, and hundreds of onlookers.

No whizzing out the window, Junior said to himself. Not unless you want it shown on *Good Morning, America.*

Junior utterly failed to notice the rather tall, bearded man sidling up behind him with one hand in the side pocket of his suit jacket. The bearded man failed to notice the stocky form of Lieutenant Jack Moriarty stealthily stalking him.

It all happened in a flash. Junior turned away from the window and was suddenly confronted by the bearded man, who whipped his hand from his pocket and started to poke at Junior. But Moriarty grabbed the man's arm and yelled, "Get out of the way, kid! He's a killer!"

A strangled scream came from the judge's banc, where the gunman leaped to his feet and cocked the submachine gun he had grabbed. Then a woman's voice pierced the courtroom:

"Don't shoot! I want to publish *Mobile, USA!*"

Moriarty wrestled the bearded man to the floor and twisted the thorned stalk of the Rita Hayworth orchid from his hand. The false beard slipped off the man's chin. Even in the shadowy light, Moriarty recognized him from the photographs he had studied in his hospital bed.

"Weldon W. Weldon, you're under arrest for five murders and one attempted murder," he said.

Weldon cackled insanely. "You can't arrest me!" he screamed. "I'm the chairman of the board of Tarantula Enterprises! I can buy and sell your whole police force!"

Across the courtroom, P. Curtis Hawks heard the old man's

shrieking voice. "My god!" he gasped. Forgetting the condition of his clothes, he dashed across to where his erstwhile boss was writhing in the grip of the long arm of the law.

"You can walk!" Hawks cried, astonished at the sight of Weldon out of his wheelchair, even though he was stretched on the floor with the solid weight of Lt. Moriarty on his chest.

Weldon glared up at his employee with insane fury flashing in his eyes.

The Writer, meanwhile, stood frozen up at the judge's banc, the Uzi in his hands, cocked and ready to fire.

"You want to publish my novel?" he asked into the midnight air. "Did somebody say they wanted to publish my novel?"

"I do," said Lori, rushing to the foot of me banc. Carl came up beside her, protectively.

"Who're you?" the Writer asked.

"I'm an editor at Bunker Books. I've been trying to contact you for more than six months. I've written half a dozen letters to the address you put on your manuscript, but they were all returned by the post office with a stamp that says you've moved and left no forwarding address."

The Writer put the Uzi down on the desk top. "Uh, yeah, I did move," he mumbled, feeling sheepish.

"I want to publish *Mobile, USA*," Lori said. "I think it's a great work of art."

The Writer sagged back onto the judge's chair, his mouth hanging open, his arms dangling by his sides. He felt suddenly dizzy, weightless. The room swam before his eyes. Slowly his head came forward and clunked on the desk top. He had passed out.

It took nearly a week to straighten out everything. A week of surprise after surprise.

The following Sunday, however, was one of those brilliant Indian summer days that Washington Irving admired so much. The sun was bright and warm, while the air sparkled with the crisp bite of autumn.

Carl, Lori, Ralph Malzone, and Scarlet Dean were having brunch together at the penthouse restaurant atop the recently re-re-renovated Chrysler Building. The restaurant was small and elegantly decorated in art deco style with bold angular motifs that matched the spire's high, slanting windows.

Despite the stylized crystal flutes before each one of them and the silver bucket that bore a heavy magnum of champagne in the middle of the table, Carl stared morosely out the window nearest their table at the skyscrapers that marched row upon row up the long narrow avenues of Manhattan. Like the windmills of Don Quixote, he thought glumly. And like Don Quixote, I've tilted against them and lost.

For this was a farewell party.

Even so, there was laughter. "The crowning blow came the next morning," Scarlet Dean was saying," after we all returned to the office and started to sort things out. Mrs. Bee came running into my office, waving a sheet of paper from the law firm that represented us at the trial. The bastards had charged Bunker Books $45,000 for the nine hours those five twerps had spent as hostages!"

Ralph Malzone wiped at his eyes. "That was the last straw. When P.T. heard that he ran right out of the house and bought the yacht."

"And they've already taken off?" Lori asked.

"Yeah. First stop, Bermuda."

"And P.T. has made you the head of Bunker Books while he and Mrs. Bee sail off around the world," Lori said.

Still looking slightly dazed by it all, Ralph ran a hand through his rust-red thatch of hair and replied, "Yeah. I'm now the chief operating officer of Bunker Books. And Scarlet is taking over Mrs. Bee's role as publisher."

Carl had drunk as much champagne as any of them, but he did not feel drunk. Nor happy. He was numb.

Ralph toyed with his fluted glass, gave a sidelong glance to Scarlet, then turned his attention back to Lori. "And I've got some news for you, kid. You're the new editor-in-chief of Bunker Books."

Lori gasped with surprise. "Me? Editor-in-chief?"

"That's right," said Scarlet. "Ralph and I agreed on that right away."

Forcing a smile that he did not feel, Carl raised his champagne glass. "Here's to your success, Lori," he toasted. "You've earned it." With bitterness burning in his gut, he added, "And to yours, Scarlet. And to yours, Ralph."

They sipped, but then Ralph's face grew somber. "My success isn't going to do you any good, pal."

"I know," said Carl. "I understand."

Scarlet put a hand on Carl's arm. "The only way to keep the company from going down the tubes was to make a deal with Woody and the sales staff. We've agreed to drop Cyberbooks."

Carl's lips pressed into a tight, white line. But at last he said, in a low voice, "Lori's been keeping me informed. I guess it's the only thing you could do."

"I didn't want it to end like this," Ralph said.

"It's not your fault," said Carl. "I understand the fix you're in."

Lori tried to brighten things. "At least I get to publish *Mobile, USA.*"

"Now that's something I don't understand," Carl admitted. "You told me that the novel was a work of art, and if you published it, it wouldn't sell enough copies to pay for the ink used to print it."

"Oh, that was before the author became famous. Taking over the courtroom and holding us hostage has made him a celebrity."

"But he's in jail, isn't he?"

"We got him released into our custody," Scarlet said. "He's doing interviews with all the big news magazines and TV talk shows. We're rushing his novel into print, to take advantage of the publicity."

Carl took a longer swig of his champagne. "You'd be able to get the book out this week if you'd do it as a Cyberbook."

Ralph shook his head. "No can do, pal. We made the deal with Woody and his people and we've got to stick with it. Nobody in the whole publishing industry will touch Cyberbooks."

"It's a damned shame," said Scarlet without much feeling.

Carl took a deep breath. "Yeah. A damned shame."

They finished their brunch in a quiet, subdued mood. Ralph and Scarlet were obviously overjoyed at being handed Bunker Books on a platter, but they could hardly celebrate properly when the price of their good fortune was scuttling Carl's invention.

The four of them took the long elevator ride to the lobby and went out onto the sun-filled street, where Ralph and Scarlet hailed a taxi uptown. Carl and Lori walked toward their apartment building, some twenty short Manhattan blocks downtown.

"What will you do now?" Lori asked him.

Shrugging, "Go back to MIT. My sabbatical is just about over, anyway."

"Carl, I'm so damned sorry about all this. . . ."

"It's not your fault," he said. Then, looking squarely into her dark, limpid eyes, he worked up the courage to ask, "Lori—would you come to Boston with me? Will you marry me?"

Tears welled up in her eyes. "I can't," she said, her voice almost pleading. "I've just gotten the first big break of my career. And with this novel finally coming out, I can't leave now. This is my first real chance. I can't give it up, no matter how much I love you, Carl."

"You do love me?"

"I do. I love you. Didn't you know?"

"I love you!"

They melted into each other's arms and kissed passionately. Thirty-seven pedestrians, including three married couples accompanied by children and fourteen singles walking their dogs, passed them on the sidewalk before they broke their fervent embrace.

"Stay here in New York, Carl," Lori said eagerly.

"No," he said. "This isn't the town for me."

"But . . ."

He shook his head sadly. "It's not like the romantic novels, Lori. This is real life. True love doesn't always win."

"I don't want to lose you!"

"Then leave the publishing business and come up to Massachusetts with me."

"I can't! You can't expect me to throw away my career, my life. . . ."

With a bitter smile, Carl said, "And I can't stay here and let you support me. I've got a career to think about, too."

They walked in dejected silence back to their apartment building. Once in the elevator, going up, Carl said:

"We'd better say good-bye right here and now, Lori. It'll hurt too much to prolong it."

The elevator stopped at Lori's floor with its usual jolt. The doors slid open. Lori leaned a finger against the button that held them open.

"You mean . . . this is it?"

"I'm going to take the next train to Boston. Today. This afternoon."

"But . . ."

"Good-bye, Lori. I love you and it's tearing my guts apart."

They kissed one last time and she pulled away from him and stepped out of the elevator. Carl stood there, frozen with grief and guilt and doubt, staring at Lori's troubled, teary face. Then the elevator doors slid shut and he could no longer see her at all.

Room at the Top

P. Curtis Hawks sat at the broad desk in the spacious office on the next-to-the-top floor of the Synthoil Tower. Chairman of the board of Tarantula Enterprises (Ltd.). At last!

He wore a magnificent military uniform of his own special design, heavy with braid and medals. The emergency meeting of the board of directors the previous week had gone extremely well: he had been elected chairman unanimously. Weldon W. Weldon was safely tucked away in a well-guarded private sanitarium far upstate, pretending to be a cripple once again. The Old Man was hopelessly insane and would spend the rest of his days in his powered chair making imaginary deals with phantom associates and tiptoeing around his funny farm at night to slaughter hallucinatory rivals.

It had taken the better part of two weeks to clear away the jungle that the Old Man had created. Just cleaning the rugs had been a Herculean task. But now the office was back the way it should be: sparkling, grand, imposing, even humbling to the lower-caste visitor.

Hawks inhaled deeply and smelled the new leather and high-gloss aroma of power. He sat in his magnificent elevated chair. It's mine, he congratulated himself. All mine!

The desk phone chirped.

"Answer answer," Hawks said crisply. ,

"Mr. Hawks, sir"—the phone computer's voice was that of a groveling *bhisti*'s singsong—"a certain Mr. MacDonald McDougall requests the honor of your presence in the boardroom of the Synthoil Corporation at eleven o'clock this morning sharply, sir."

Hawks exhaled. The Synthoil board wanted to meet him. The computer was merely reminding him of the appointment in the groveling way it had been programmed.

Hawks took the private elevator up the one flight to the Synthoil offices. While Tarantula was on the next-to-the-top floor of the mighty tower, Synthoil was at the very top.

A slim, dark, curly-haired young man dressed in a jet-black Italian silk suit was waiting for Hawks at the elevator doors. Without a word, he ushered Hawks into the plush and panelled conference room of the Synthoil Corporation.

MacDonald McDougall smiled genially at Hawks. Even though Hawks had never before met the CEO of Synthoil, the Scotsman's bushy red beard and handsome mustache were unmistakable. He wore a bulky tweed business suit, with a plaid sash of the distinctive McDougall tartan slanting beneath his jacket.

"Sit yerself doon, Mr. Hawks," said McDougall, waving his huge hand toward the only empty chair at the long, gleaming conference table.

The chair was at the very foot of the table. All the men on one side of the table were stocky, frozen-faced Orientals, dressed in gray business suits. And every man sitting on the other side was dark of hair, wide of girth, and dressed in jet-black suits of Italian silk. And sunglasses.

Hawks's heart sank as he was introduced to his new masters.

Winter, Book IV

Retired Navy Officer Dies

Chelsea, MA. Capt. Ronald Reginald Clanker, USN (Ret.), died yesterday in the Army/Navy nursing home where he had spent his final ten years.

Capt. Clanker, last remaining veteran of the Battle of Midway in 1942, was 93. He was the author of *Passion in the Pacific*, a novel published three weeks before his death. According to a spokesperson for the nursing home, Capt. Clanker suffered a fatal heart attack shortly after being informed that his book was no longer available for sale, and all unsold copies had been pulped by the publisher.

There are no survivors.

Twenty-Eight

Two things surprised Carl that cold February afternoon.

First had been the telephone call from P.T. Bunker, Junior. Out of the blue, Junior had invited Carl for drinks at the Parker House in downtown Boston.

Second was the snow. The day had dawned frostily clear, and the sky had still been crystalline when Carl had entered his lab building at MIT. He had scooted along the basement tunnels to get to his 2:00 P.M. class, as he usually did. It was quicker and warmer; he didn't need a winter coat. After the class he had returned to his windowless laboratory through the same tunnels.

So when he stepped outside for the first time since early morning, he was surprised that nearly a foot of snow lay on the ground, with more gently sifting down out of a darkened sky.

It took a little longer for the transit train to make the short run from MIT station to Beacon Hill, but Carl reached the cozy bar of the Parker House only a few minutes after four.

Junior was already there, at a little table in the corner, chatting amiably with the cocktail waitress.

They shook hands, Carl took off his snow-wet coat, and settled down onto one of the comfortable easy chairs. He ordered a light beer. Junior was drinking something big and bulbous and frothy, exotic and lethal looking.

Junior looked somehow more mature, more relaxed with himself, than he had a scant few months earlier, the last time Carl had seen him. Maybe it's his clothes, Carl thought. Junior was wearing a conservative beige business suit with an executive's turtleneck shirt of sky blue.

"How've you been?" they asked in unison. Then they laughed.

"You first," Junior insisted.

Carl shrugged. "Doing okay, I guess. Got some bright kids in my classes. Tinkering with some new ideas for electro-optical computers that will link directly to the nerve system. Working with a couple of biologists from Harvard on that one."

Junior nodded. "And the Cyberbooks idea?"

The pang that sliced through him made Carl wince visibly. "That's dead. No publisher wants to touch it."

"Too bad," said Junior.

Carl nodded, thinking more of Lori than his invention.

The waitress brought Carl's beer and smiled prettily at Junior. He grinned back at her. Then, turning to Carl, he said, "I've gotten out of the publishing business, too. With Mom and Dad off sailing around the world and Ralph doing such a good job of running the company, I went out and looked for new worlds to conquer."

"Really?" Carl felt no real curiosity, no interest at all.

"Yup. I'm in the toy business now." Some of the old craftiness seemed to creep back into his expression.

Carl sipped at his beer because he did not know quite what to reply.

Junior went ahead anyway. "Y' know, I've been thinking. The toy industry is a lot different from book publishing. The accent is on innovation, new ideas, new gadgets." He laughed. "You've got to run damned fast to stay ahead of the five-year-olds!"

Carl thought of the nephews and nieces he saw at Christmastime. "Yes," he agreed. "They can be pretty sharp."

Junior licked his lips and leaned closer to Carl. Lowering his voice, he said, "I was wondering if you could make a Cyberbooks kind of thing for kids. You know, something to help them learn to read. And then they could keep it and go on to *real* books as they get older."

The only sound that Carl could get past his utter surprise was, "Huh?"

Junior explained the idea to him again. And then once more.

"But it's the same device, the exact same thing," Carl blurted, once he was certain he understood what Junior was saying. "The only thing that changes is the content of the books we put on the chips. We'd be doing children's books instead of adult books."

Junior's smile widened. "Right, except that there's one other thing that changes."

"What's that?"

"The distribution system. We distribute Cyberbooks through toy stores, not bookstores. We won't have any trouble with guys like Woody Baloney."

"Won't the toy salesmen . . ."

"They already spend most of their time pushing electronic gadgets for the kids. Cyberbooks will be just another toy, as far as they're concerned."

Sinking back in his soft chair under the realization of what Junior was suggesting, Carl said, "You could create a whole new kind of book publishing industry this way."

"That's right," Junior agreed, looking as if he had just swallowed the most delicious canary in the history of the world. "We start in the toy industry, but we end up taking over the entire publishing industry. It'll be Cyberbooks, just the way you wanted it!"

"Through the back door."

"Right."

Carl thought it over. "It could hurt a lot of people. People we know, like Ralph and the others."

"They can come to work for us, when the time comes."

"I don't know. . . ."

Leaning even closer, Junior said, "We'll have to start out on a shoestring. You and I will be equal partners, we'll share everything right down the middle, fifty-fifty. And, of course, you'll have to spend a lot of time in New York. Probably have to come down to the city every week or so."

"Every week?"

A small shrug. "Every week, ten days. Give you a chance to see old friends, huh?"

Lori's phone number flashed through Carl's mind. He thought he had forgotten it, but every digit shone in his thoughts. He stuck his hand out and Junior grabbed it and pumped it hard.

"You've got a deal," Carl said.

Epilogue

Fifty Years Later

New Releases

Washington, D.C. The Library of Congress put on display today the last book to be printed on paper in the United States. Carefully protected in a shatterproof glass airtight casing, the book—the fortieth edition of the classic novel, *Mobile, USA*—will remain on public display until the end of the year.

Carl Lewis, Jr., son of the inventor of Cyberbooks, said at the opening ceremony, "My father would have been proud, I'm sure, to see his invention of the electro-optical publishing system totally replace paper books. He was a dedicated ecologist, and he loved both literature and trees."

Mrs. Lori Tashkajian Lewis, the inventor's widow and managing director of Cyberbooks Inc., added, "Back in the old days, when my late husband first invented Cyberbooks, there were fears that electronic publishing would destroy the book industry. History has shown that those fears were groundless."

With tears in her eyes, Mrs. Lewis continued, "I'm proud to have played a small role in bringing inexpensive literature to the huge masses of poor people all around the world." Cyberbooks' latest publication, she revealed, is *Blood of the Virgin*, by Sheldon Stoker Beta, one of the clones of the late best-selling author.